PRAISE FOR

neuromancer

"Epic in scale . . . shimmers like chrome in a desert sun."

—*The Wall Street Journal*

"A revolutionary novel."

—*Publishers Weekly*

"In with the ruthless violence, the hyperreality, the betrayal and death, is an unquenchable love of language. Gibson has that in common with Le Guin and with J. G. Ballard. *Neuromancer* sings to us as a collage of voices, a mixed chorus, some trustworthy and others malicious, some piped through masks."

—James Gleick

"Streetwise SF . . . one of the most unusual and involving narratives to be read in many an artificially induced blue moon."

—*The Times* (London)

"Unforgettable . . . the richness of Gibson's world is incredible."

—*Chicago Sun-Times*

MORE PRAISE FOR

WILLIAM GIBSON

"One of the most visionary, original, and quietly influential writers currently working."

—*The Boston Globe*

"Like Pynchon and DeLillo, Gibson excels at pinpointing the hidden forces that shape our world."

—*Details*

"William Gibson can craft sentences of uncanny beauty, and is our great poet of crowds."

—*San Francisco Chronicle Book Review*

TITLES BY WILLIAM GIBSON

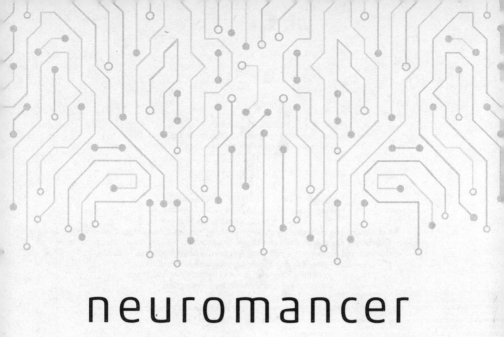

neuromancer

WILLIAM GIBSON

ACE • NEW YORK

ACE
Published by Berkley
An imprint of Penguin Random House LLC
375 Hudson Street, New York, New York 10014

Copyright © 1984, 1986, 1988 by William Gibson
Introduction copyright © 2004 by William Gibson
Afterword copyright © 2000 by Jack Womack

This book was first printed as an Ace Science Fiction original edition. The first through third
printings were as an Ace Science Fiction Special, edited by Terry Carr. A limited hardcover edition
was published by Phantasia Press in the spring of 1986. A hardcover Tenth Anniversary Special
Edition, with an Afterword by William Gibson, was published by Ace Science Fiction in 1994.

ISBN: 9780441007462

The Library of Congress has cataloged the hardcover edition of this title as follows:

Gibson, William, 1948–
Neuromancer / William Gibson ; with a new introduction by the author ; with an afterword by Jack
Womack—20th anniversary ed.
p. cm.
ISBN 0-441-01203-5
1. Computer hackers—Fiction.   2. Business intelligence—Fiction.   3. Information
superhighway—Fiction.   4. Nervous system—Wounds and injuries—Fiction.
5. Conspiracies—Fiction.   6. Japan—Fiction.   I. Title.
PS3557.I2264N48 2004
813'.54—dc22
2004048718

Ace mass-market edition / July 1984
Ace trade paperback edition / July 2000
Ace hardcover edition / November 2004
Ace trade paperback edition (author introduction) / December 2018

Printed in the United States of America
48th Printing

Cover design by gray318
Book design by Kristin del Rosario
Interior art: circuit board vector illustration by ArtHead/Shutterstock.com

To Deb
who made it possible
with love

THE SKY ABOVE THE PORT

It took at least a decade for me to realize that many of my readers, even in 1984, could never have experienced *Neuromancer*'s opening line as I'd intended them to. I'd actually composed that first image with the black-and-white video-static of my childhood in mind, sodium-silvery and almost painful—a whopping anachronism, right at the very start of my career in the imaginary future.

But an invisible one, interestingly; one that reveals a peculiar grace enjoyed by all imaginary futures as they make their way up the timeline and into the real future, where we all must go. The reader never stopped to think that I might have been thinking, however unconsciously, of the texture and color of a signal-free channel on a wooden-cabinet Motorola with fabric-covered speakers. Readers compensated for me, shouldering an additional share of the imaginative burden, and allowed whatever they assumed was the color of static to take on the melancholy of the phrase "dead channel."

In my teens, in the sixties, I read a great deal of science fiction dating from the forties, a very fertile period for the genre, and recall being aware of making just this sort of effort on behalf of fictions that had grown a bit long in the technological tooth, or whose imagined futures had been blindsided by subsequent history. I cut such fictions just the sort of extra slack, in exchange for whatever other value the narrative might offer, that some readers must be cutting *Neuromancer* today—not for invisible anachronisms like my color of television, but for unavoidable sins of omission on the order of a complete absence of tiny and ubiquitous portable telephones. (Indeed, one of my own favorite moments in the book hinges around the sequenced ringing of a row of *pay phones*.)

Imagine a novel from the sixties whose author had somehow fully envisioned cellular telephony circa 2004, and had worked it, exactly as we know it today, into the fabric of her imaginary future. Such a book would have seemed highly peculiar in the sixties, even though innumerable novels had already been written in which small personal wireless communications devices were taken for granted. A genuinely prescient cell-phone novel would have moved in a most unsettling way, its characters acting, out of an unprecedented degree of connectivity, in ways that would quickly overwhelm the narrative.

In hindsight, I suspect that *Neuromancer* owes much of its shelf life to my almost perfect ignorance of the technology I was extrapolating from. I was as far from the sixties author who knew everything about cell phones as it was possible to be. Where I made things up from whole cloth, the colors remain bright. Where I was unlucky enough to actually have some small bit of real knowledge, the reader finds things like the rattling keys of a mechanical printer, or Case's puzzlingly urgent demand, when the going gets tough, for a modem. Unlike the absence of cell phones, those are sins of commission. Another vast omission is my failure to have quietly collapsed the Soviet Union and swept the rubble offstage when nobody was looking.

Though there was a strategic reason for my not having done that. I had already done it to the United States, which cannot be proven to exist in the world of *Neuromancer*. It's deliberately never mentioned as such, and one vaguely gathers that it's somehow gone sideways in a puff of what we today would call globalization, to be replaced by some less dangerous combine of large corporations and city-states. Having disappeared the USA, I thought I'd better have the USSR in there for the sake of continuity. (Had I disappeared the USSR instead, I might eventually have been burned as a witch, so just as well.)

Today's reader might keep in mind that I wrote *Neuromancer* with absolutely no expectation that it would be in print twenty years later. I knew that it was to be published, if I could finish it and if the editor accepted the manuscript, both of which seemed constantly unlikely, as a paperback original—that most ephemeral of literary units, a pocket-sized slab of prose meant to fit a standard wire rack, printed on high-acid paper and visibly yearning to return to the crude pulp from which it had been pressed. My best hope for the book was that it might find, in whatever modest numbers it would have its debut, some kindred soul or five. Probably in England, as I imagined them, or perhaps in France. I didn't anticipate much in the way of an American audience, because I felt that I was writing too deliberately counter to what I had come to assume the American audience had been taught to want from science fiction.

I was doing this because I couldn't for the life of me seem to do it any other way. Having been talked into signing a contract (by the late Terry Carr, without whom there would certainly be no *Neuromancer*), I found myself possessed by a dissident attitude that I certainly wasn't about to share with my editor, or really with much of anyone. The only people who got that were a few of the other tyro writers with whom I would eventually be labeled "cyberpunk," and they were far away, mostly in Austin, Texas.

Like Case at the book's climax, I was coming in steep, fueled by . . . I couldn't have told you, though one element was a smoldering resentment at what the genre I'd loved as a teenager seemed to me in the meantime to have become. Though I know I had neither the intention nor the least hope that what I was doing, tapping out my Ace Special paperback original on an aged manual portable of precision Swiss manufacture, would in any way change the course of science fiction. (Nor did it, apparently, except to the extent of helping to keep open doors I certainly never built, doors I'd found as a teenager, with names like "Bester" and "Leiber" gouged into their lintels.)

I was recently told that *Neuromancer* has sold more than a million copies. That would be over the past two decades, and I assume in either North American editions or English-language editions. Abroad, it's managed to get itself translated into most of the languages books are translated into, though not yet, as far as I know, Chinese or Arabic.*

This is something like having an adult child one never hears from, but who evidently does quite well, travels widely, and seems to meet interesting people.

My real sympathy, though, is with the bright thirteen-year-old, curled on a sofa somewhere, twenty pages into the book and desperate to get to the root of the mystery of why cell phones aren't allowed in Chiba City.

Hang in there, friend.

It can only get stranger.

—WILLIAM GIBSON
VANCOUVER, BRITISH COLUMBIA
MAY 17, 2004

---

* Definitely Chinese now. —May 13, 2018

neuromancer

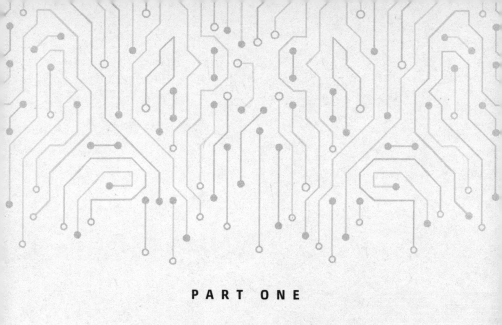

PART ONE

CHIBA CITY BLUES

setting Japan

The sky above the port was the color of television, tuned to a dead channel.

"It's not like I'm using," Case heard someone say, as he shouldered his way through the crowd around the door of the Chat. "It's like my body's developed this massive drug deficiency." It was a Sprawl voice and a Sprawl joke. The Chatsubo was a bar for professional expatriates; you could drink there for a week and never hear two words in Japanese.

Ratz was tending bar, his prosthetic arm jerking monotonously as he filled a tray of glasses with draft Kirin. He saw Case and smiled, his teeth a webwork of East European steel and brown decay. Case found a place at the bar, between the unlikely tan on one of Lonny Zone's whores and the crisp naval uniform of a tall African whose cheekbones were ridged with precise rows of tribal scars. "Wage was in here early, with two joeboys," Ratz said, shoving a draft across the bar with his good hand. "Maybe some business with you, Case?"

Case shrugged. The girl to his right giggled and nudged him.

The bartender's smile widened. His ugliness was the stuff of legend. In an age of affordable beauty, there was something heraldic about his lack of it. The antique arm whined as he reached for another mug. It was a Russian military prosthesis, a seven-function force-feedback manipulator, cased in grubby pink plastic. "You are too much the artiste, Herr Case." Ratz grunted; the sound served him as laughter. He scratched his overhang of white-shirted belly with the pink claw. "You are the artiste of the slightly funny deal."

"Sure," Case said, and sipped his beer. "Somebody's gotta be funny around here. Sure the fuck isn't you."

The whore's giggle went up an octave.

"Isn't you either, sister. So you vanish, okay? Zone, he's a close personal friend of mine."

She looked Case in the eye and made the softest possible spitting sound, her lips barely moving. But she left.

"Jesus," Case said, "what kinda creepjoint you running here? Man can't have a drink."

"Ha," Ratz said, swabbing the scarred wood with a rag. "Zone shows a percentage. You I let work here for entertainment value."

As Case was picking up his beer, one of those strange instants of silence descended, as though a hundred unrelated conversations had simultaneously arrived at the same pause. Then the whore's giggle rang out, tinged with a certain hysteria.

Ratz grunted. "An angel passed."

"The Chinese," bellowed a drunken Australian, "Chinese bloody invented nerve-splicing. Give me the mainland for a nerve job any day. Fix you right, mate. . . ."

"Now that," Case said to his glass, all his bitterness suddenly rising in him like bile, "that is so much bullshit."

What does this mean?

The Japanese had already forgotten more neurosurgery than the Chinese had ever known. The black clinics of Chiba were the cutting edge, whole bodies of technique supplanted monthly, and still they couldn't repair the damage he'd suffered in that Memphis hotel.

What happened?!?

A year here and he still dreamed of cyberspace, hope fading nightly. All the speed he took, all the turns he'd taken and the corners he'd cut in Night City, and still he'd see the matrix in his sleep, bright lattices of logic unfolding across that colorless void. . . . The Sprawl was a long strange way home over the Pacific now, and he was no console man, no cyberspace cowboy. Just another hustler, trying to make it through. But the dreams came on in the Japanese night like livewire voodoo, and he'd cry for it, cry in his sleep, and wake alone in the dark, curled in his capsule in some coffin hotel, his hands clawed into the bedslab, temperfoam bunched between his fingers, trying to reach the console that wasn't there.

"I saw your girl last night," Ratz said, passing Case his second Kirin.

"I don't have one," he said, and drank.

"Miss Linda Lee."

Case shook his head.

"No girl? Nothing? Only biz, friend artiste? Dedication to commerce?" The bartender's small brown eyes were nested deep in wrinkled flesh. "I think I liked you better, with her. You laughed more. Now, some night, you get maybe too artistic; you wind up in the clinic tanks, spare parts."

"You're breaking my heart, Ratz." He finished his beer, paid, and left, high narrow shoulders hunched beneath the rain-stained khaki nylon of his windbreaker. Threading his way through the Ninsei crowds, he could smell his own stale sweat.

age

Case was twenty-four. At twenty-two, he'd been a cowboy, a rustler, one of the best in the Sprawl. He'd been trained by the best, by McCoy Pauley and Bobby Quine, legends in the biz. He'd operated on an almost permanent adrenaline high, a by-product of youth and proficiency, jacked into a custom cyberspace deck that projected his disembodied consciousness into the consensual hallucination that was the matrix. A thief, he'd worked for other, wealthier thieves, employers who provided the exotic software required to penetrate the bright walls of corporate systems, opening windows into rich fields of data.

He'd made the classic mistake, the one he'd sworn he'd never make. He stole from his employers. He kept something for himself and tried to move it through a fence in Amsterdam. He still wasn't sure how he'd been discovered, not that it mattered now. He'd expected to die, then, but they only smiled. Of course he was welcome, they told him, welcome to the money. And he was going to need it. Because—still smiling—they were going to make sure he never worked again.

They damaged his nervous system with a wartime Russian mycotoxin.

Strapped to a bed in a Memphis hotel, his talent burning out micron by micron, he hallucinated for thirty hours.

The damage was minute, subtle, and utterly effective.

For Case, who'd lived for the bodiless exultation of cyberspace, it was the Fall. In the bars he'd frequented as a cowboy hotshot, the elite stance involved a certain relaxed contempt for the flesh. The body was meat. Case fell into the prison of his own flesh.

His total assets were quickly converted to New Yen, a fat sheaf of the old paper currency that circulated endlessly through the closed circuit of the world's black markets like the seashells of the Trobriand islanders. It was difficult to transact legitimate business with cash in the Sprawl; in Japan, it was already illegal.

In Japan, he'd known with a clenched and absolute certainty, he'd find his cure. In Chiba. Either in a registered clinic or in the shadowland of black medicine. Synonymous with implants, nerve-splicing, and microbionics, Chiba was a magnet for the Sprawl's techno-criminal subcultures.

In Chiba, he'd watched his New Yen vanish in a two-month round of examinations and consultations. The men in the black [MIB] clinics, his last hope, had admired the expertise with which he'd been maimed, and then slowly shaken their heads.

Now he slept in the cheapest coffins, the ones nearest the port, beneath the quartz-halogen floods that lit the docks all night like vast stages; where you couldn't see the lights of Tokyo for the glare of the television sky, not even the towering hologram logo of the Fuji Electric Company, and Tokyo Bay was a black expanse where gulls wheeled above drifting shoals of white styrofoam. Behind the port lay the city, factory domes dominated by the vast cubes of corporate arcologies. Port and city were divided by a narrow borderland of older streets, an area with no official name. Night City, with Ninsei its heart. By day, the bars down Ninsei were shuttered and featureless, the neon dead, the holograms inert, waiting, under the poisoned silver sky.

Pills, what effects

Two blocks west of the Chat, in a teashop called the Jarre de Thé, Case washed down the night's first pill with a double espresso. It was a flat pink octagon, a potent species of Brazilian dex he bought from one of Zone's girls.

The Jarre was walled with mirrors, each panel framed in red neon.

At first, finding himself alone in Chiba, with little money and less hope of finding a cure, he'd gone into a kind of terminal overdrive, hustling fresh capital with a cold intensity that had seemed to belong to someone else. In the first month, he'd killed two men and a woman over sums that a year before would have seemed lu-

going crazy

dicrous. Ninsei wore him down until the street itself came to seem the externalization of some death wish, some secret poison he hadn't known he carried.

Night City was like a deranged experiment in social Darwinism, designed by a bored researcher who kept one thumb permanently on the fast-forward button. Stop hustling and you sank without a trace, but move a little too swiftly and you'd break the fragile surface tension of the black market; either way, you were gone, with nothing left of you but some vague memory in the mind of a fixture like Ratz, though heart or lungs or kidneys might survive in the service of some stranger with New Yen for the clinic tanks.

Biz here was a constant subliminal hum, and death the accepted punishment for laziness, carelessness, lack of grace, the failure to heed the demands of an intricate protocol.

Alone at a table in the Jarre de Thé, with the octagon coming on, pinheads of sweat starting from his palms, suddenly aware of each tingling hair on his arms and chest, Case knew that at some point he'd started to play a game with himself, a very ancient one that has no name, a final solitaire. He no longer carried a weapon, no longer took the basic precautions. He ran the fastest, loosest deals on the street, and he had a reputation for being able to get whatever you wanted. A part of him knew that the arc of his self-destruction was glaringly obvious to his customers, who grew steadily fewer, but that same part of him basked in the knowledge that it was only a matter of time. And that was the part of him, smug in its expectation of death, that most hated the thought of Linda Lee.

He'd found her, one rainy night, in an arcade.

Under bright ghosts burning through a blue haze of cigarette smoke, holograms of Wizard's Castle, Tank War Europa, the New York skyline. . . . And now he remembered her that way, her face bathed in restless laser light, features reduced to a code: her cheekbones flaring scarlet as Wizard's Castle burned, forehead drenched with azure when Munich fell to the Tank War, mouth touched with hot gold as a gliding cursor struck sparks from the wall of a skyscraper canyon. He was riding high that night, with a brick of Wage's ketamine on its way to Yokohama and the money already in his pocket. He'd come in out of the warm rain that sizzled across the Ninsei pavement and somehow she'd been singled out for him, one face out of the dozens who stood at the consoles, lost in the game she played. The expression on her face, then, had been the one he'd seen, hours later, on her sleeping face in a portside coffin, her upper lip like the line children draw to represent a bird in flight.

Crossing the arcade to stand beside her, high on the deal he'd made, he saw her glance up. Gray eyes rimmed with smudged black paintstick. Eyes of some animal pinned in the headlights of an oncoming vehicle.

Their night together stretching into a morning, into tickets at the hoverport and his first trip across the Bay. The rain kept up, falling along Harajuku, beading on her plastic jacket, the children of Tokyo trooping past the famous boutiques in white loafers and clingwrap capes, until she'd stood with him in the midnight clatter of a pachinko parlor and held his hand like a child.

It took a month for the gestalt of drugs and tension he moved through to turn those perpetually startled eyes into wells of reflexive need. He'd watched her personality fragment, calving like an iceberg, splinters drifting away, and finally he'd seen the raw need, the hungry armature of addiction. He'd watched her track the next hit with a concentration that reminded him of the mantises they sold in stalls along Shiga, beside tanks of blue mutant carp and crickets caged in bamboo.

He stared at the black ring of grounds in his empty cup. It was vibrating with the speed he'd taken. The brown laminate of the tabletop was dull with a patina of tiny scratches. With the dex mounting through his spine he saw the countless random impacts required to create a surface like that. The Jarre was decorated in a dated, nameless style from the previous century, an uneasy blend of Japanese traditional and pale Milanese plastics, but everything seemed to wear a subtle film, as though the bad nerves of a million customers had somehow attacked the mirrors and the once glossy plastics, leaving each surface fogged with something that could never be wiped away.

"Hey. Case, good buddy. . . ."

He looked up, met gray eyes ringed with paintstick. She was wearing faded French orbital fatigues and new white sneakers.

"I been lookin' for you, man." She took a seat opposite him, her elbows on the table. The sleeves of the blue zipsuit had been ripped out at the shoulders; he automatically checked her arms for signs of derms or the needle. "Want a cigarette?"

She dug a crumpled pack of Yeheyuan filters from an ankle pocket and offered him one. He took it, let her light it with a red plastic tube. "You sleepin' okay, Case? You look tired." Her accent put her south along the Sprawl, toward Atlanta. The skin below her eyes was pale and unhealthy-looking, but the flesh was still smooth and firm. She was twenty. New lines of pain were starting to etch themselves permanently at the corners of her mouth. Her dark hair was drawn back, held by a band of printed silk. The pattern might have represented microcircuits, or a city map.

"Not if I remember to take my pills," he said, as a tangible wave of longing hit him, lust and loneliness riding in on the wavelength of amphetamine. He remembered the smell of her skin in the overheated darkness of a coffin near the port, her fingers locked across the small of his back.

All the meat, he thought, and all it wants.

"Wage," she said, narrowing her eyes. "He wants to see you with a hole in your face." She lit her own cigarette.

"Who says? Ratz? You been talking to Ratz?"

"No. Mona. Her new squeeze is one of Wage's boys."

"I don't owe him enough. He does me, he's out the money any-way." He shrugged.

"Too many people owe him now, Case. Maybe you get to be the example. You seriously better watch it."

"Sure. How about you, Linda? You got anywhere to sleep?"

"Sleep." She shook her head. "Sure, Case." She shivered, hunched forward over the table. Her face was filmed with sweat.

"Here," he said, and dug in the pocket of his windbreaker, com-ing up with a crumpled fifty. He smoothed it automatically, under the table, folded it in quarters, and passed it to her.

"You need that, honey. You better give it to Wage." There was something in the gray eyes now that he couldn't read, something he'd never seen there before.

"I owe Wage a lot more than that. Take it. I got more coming," he lied, as he watched his New Yen vanish into a zippered pocket.

"You get your money, Case, you find Wage quick."

"I'll see you, Linda," he said, getting up.

"Sure." A millimeter of white showed beneath each of her pupils. Sanpaku. "You watch your back, man."

He nodded, anxious to be gone.

He looked back as the plastic door swung shut behind him, saw her eyes reflected in a cage of red neon.

———

Friday night on Ninsei.

He passed yakitori stands and massage parlors, a franchised cof-fee shop called Beautiful Girl, the electronic thunder of an arcade. He stepped out of the way to let a dark-suited sarariman by, spotting the Mitsubishi-Genentech logo tattooed across the back of the man's right hand.

Was it authentic? If that's for real, he thought, he's in for trouble.

Implants tracking mutogen

If it wasn't, served him right. M-G employees above a certain level were implanted with advanced microprocessors that monitored mutagen levels in the bloodstream. Gear like that would get you rolled in Night City, rolled straight into a black clinic.

The sarariman had been Japanese, but the Ninsei crowd was a gaijin crowd. Groups of sailors up from the port, tense solitary tourists hunting pleasures no guidebook listed, Sprawl heavies showing off grafts and implants, and a dozen distinct species of hustler, all swarming the street in an intricate dance of desire and commerce.

There were countless theories explaining why Chiba City tolerated the Ninsei enclave, but Case tended toward the idea that the Yakuza might be preserving the place as a kind of historical park, a reminder of humble origins. But he also saw a certain sense in the notion that burgeoning technologies require outlaw zones, that Night City wasn't there for its inhabitants, but as a deliberately unsupervised playground for technology itself.

Was Linda right? he wondered, staring up at the lights. Would Wage have him killed to make an example? It didn't make much sense, but then Wage dealt primarily in proscribed biologicals, and they said you had to be crazy to do that.

Middle man

But Linda said Wage wanted him dead. Case's primary insight into the dynamics of street dealing was that neither the buyer nor the seller really needed him. A middleman's business is to make himself a necessary evil. The dubious niche Case had carved for himself in the criminal ecology of Night City had been cut out with lies, scooped out a night at a time with betrayal. Now, sensing that its walls were starting to crumble, he felt the edge of a strange euphoria.

The week before, he'd delayed transfer of a synthetic glandular extract, retailing it for a wider margin than usual. He knew Wage hadn't liked that. Wage was his primary supplier, nine years in Chiba and one of the few gaijin dealers who'd managed to forge links with the rigidly stratified criminal establishment beyond Night City's borders. Genetic materials and hormones trickled down to Ninsei along an intricate ladder of fronts and blinds. Somehow Wage had managed to trace something back, once, and now he enjoyed steady connections in a dozen cities.

Case found himself staring through a shop window. The place sold small bright objects to the sailors. Watches, flickknives, lighters, pocket VTRs, simstim decks, weighted manriki chains, and shuriken. The shuriken had always fascinated him, steel stars with knife-sharp points. Some were chromed, others black, others treated with a rainbow surface like oil on water. But the chrome stars held his gaze. They were mounted against scarlet ultrasuede with nearly invisible loops of nylon fishline, their centers stamped with dragons or yin-yang symbols. They caught the street's neon and twisted it, and it came to Case that these were the stars under which he voyaged, his destiny spelled out in a constellation of cheap chrome.

"Julie," he said to his stars. "Time to see old Julie. He'll know."

———

Julius Deane was one hundred and thirty-five years old, his metabolism assiduously warped by a weekly fortune in serums and hormones. His primary hedge against aging was a yearly pilgrimage to Tokyo, where genetic surgeons reset the code of his DNA, a procedure unavailable in Chiba. Then he'd fly to Hongkong and order the year's suits and shirts. Sexless and inhumanly patient, his primary gratification seemed to lie in his devotion to esoteric forms of tailor-worship. Case had never seen him wear the same suit twice, although his wardrobe seemed to consist entirely of meticulous reconstructions of garments of the previous century. He affected prescription lenses, framed in spidery gold, ground from thin slabs of pink synthetic quartz and beveled like the mirrors in a Victorian dollhouse.

His offices were located in a warehouse behind Ninsei, part of

office description

which seemed to have been sparsely decorated, years before, with a random collection of European furniture, as though Deane had once intended to use the place as his home. Neo-Aztec bookcases gathered dust against one wall of the room where Case waited. A pair of bulbous Disney-styled table lamps perched awkwardly on a low Kandinsky-look coffee table in scarlet-lacquered steel. A Dalí clock hung on the wall between the bookcases, its distorted face sagging to the bare concrete floor. Its hands were holograms that altered to match the convolutions of the face as they rotated, but it never told the correct time. The room was stacked with white fiberglass shipping modules that gave off the tang of preserved ginger.

"You seem to be clean, old son," said Deane's disembodied voice. "Do come in."

Magnetic bolts thudded out of position around the massive imitation-rosewood door to the left of the bookcases. JULIUS DEANE IMPORT EXPORT was lettered across the plastic in peeling self-adhesive capitals. If the furniture scattered in Deane's makeshift foyer suggested the end of the past century, the office itself seemed to belong to its start.

Deane's seamless pink face regarded Case from a pool of light cast by an ancient brass lamp with a rectangular shade of dark green glass. The importer was securely fenced behind a vast desk of painted steel, flanked on either side by tall, drawered cabinets made of some sort of pale wood. The sort of thing, Case supposed, that had once been used to store written records of some kind. The desktop was littered with cassettes, scrolls of yellowed printout, and various parts of some sort of clockwork typewriter, a machine Deane never seemed to get around to reassembling.

"What brings you around, boyo?" Deane asked, offering Case a narrow bonbon wrapped in blue-and-white-checked paper. "Try one. Ting Ting Djahe, the very best." Case refused the ginger, took a seat in a yawing wooden swivel chair, and ran a thumb down the faded seam of one black jeans-leg. "Julie, I hear Wage wants to kill me."

"Ah. Well then. And where did you hear this, if I may?"

"People."

"People," Deane said, around a ginger bonbon. "What sort of people? Friends?"

Case nodded.

"Not always that easy to know who your friends are, is it?"

"I do owe him a little money, Deane. He say anything to you?"

"Haven't been in touch, of late." Then he sighed. "If I *did* know, of course, I might not be in a position to tell you. Things being what they are, you understand."

"Things?"

"He's an important connection, Case."

"Yeah. He want to kill me, Julie?"

"Not that I know of." Deane shrugged. They might have been discussing the price of ginger. "If it proves to be an unfounded rumor, old son, you come back in a week or so and I'll let you in on a little something out of Singapore."

"Out of the Nan Hai Hotel, Bencoolen Street?"

"Loose lips, old son!" Deane grinned. The steel desk was jammed with a fortune in debugging gear.

"Be seeing you, Julie. I'll say hello to Wage."

Deane's fingers came up to brush the perfect knot in his pale silk tie.

———

He was less than a block from Deane's office when it hit, the sudden cellular awareness that someone was on his ass, and very close.

The cultivation of a certain tame paranoia was something Case took for granted. The trick lay in not letting it get out of control. But that could be quite a trick, behind a stack of octagons. He fought the adrenaline surge and composed his narrow features in a mask of bored vacancy, pretending to let the crowd carry him along. When he saw a darkened display window, he managed to pause by it. The place was a surgical boutique, closed for renovations. With his hands in the pockets of his jacket, he stared through the glass at a flat lozenge of vatgrown flesh that lay on a carved pedestal of imitation jade. The color of its skin reminded him of Zone's whores; it was tattooed with a luminous digital display wired to a subcutaneous chip. Why bother with the surgery, he found himself thinking, while sweat coursed down his ribs, when you could just carry the thing around in your pocket?

Without moving his head, he raised his eyes and studied the reflection of the passing crowd.

There.

Behind sailors in short-sleeved khaki. Dark hair, mirrored glasses, dark clothing, slender . . .

And gone.

Then Case was running, bent low, dodging between bodies.

———

"Rent me a gun, Shin?"

The boy smiled. "Two hour." They stood together in the smell of fresh raw seafood at the rear of a Shiga sushi stall. "You come back, two hour."

"I need one now, man. Got anything right now?"

Shin rummaged behind empty two-liter cans that had once been filled with powdered horseradish. He produced a slender package wrapped in gray plastic. "Taser. One hour, twenty New Yen. Thirty deposit."

"Shit. I don't need that. I need a gun. Like I maybe wanna shoot somebody, understand?"

The waiter shrugged, replacing the taser behind the horseradish cans. "Two hour."

He went into the shop without bothering to glance at the display of shuriken. He'd never thrown one in his life.

He bought two packs of Yeheyuans with a Mitsubishi Bank chip that gave his name as Charles Derek May. It beat Truman Starr, the best he'd been able to do for a passport.

The Japanese woman behind the terminal looked like she had a few years on old Deane, none of them with the benefit of science. He took his slender roll of New Yen out of his pocket and showed it to her. "I want to buy a weapon." Violence

She gestured in the direction of a case filled with knives.

"No," he said, "I don't like knives."

She brought an oblong box from beneath the counter. The lid was yellow cardboard, stamped with a crude image of a coiled cobra with a swollen hood. Inside were eight identical tissue-wrapped cylinders. He watched while mottled brown fingers stripped the paper from one. She held the thing up for him to examine, a dull steel tube with a leather thong at one end and a small bronze pyramid at the other. She gripped the tube with one hand, the pyramid between her other thumb and forefinger, and pulled. Three oiled, telescoping segments of tightly wound coilspring slid out and locked. "Cobra," she said.

Beyond the neon shudder of Ninsei, the sky was that mean shade of gray. The air had gotten worse; it seemed to have teeth tonight, and half the crowd wore filtration masks. Case had spent ten minutes in a urinal, trying to discover a convenient way to conceal his cobra; finally he'd settled for tucking the handle into the waistband of his jeans, with the tube slanting across his stomach. The pyramidal striking tip rode between his rib cage and the lining of his windbreaker. The thing felt like it might clatter to the pavement with his next step, but it made him feel better.

The Chat wasn't really a dealing bar, but on weeknights it attracted a related clientele. Fridays and Saturdays were different. The regulars were still there, most of them, but they faded behind an influx of sailors and the specialists who preyed on them. As Case pushed through the doors, he looked for Ratz, but the bartender wasn't in sight. Lonny Zone, the bar's resident pimp, was observing with glazed fatherly interest as one of his girls went to work on a young sailor. Zone was addicted to a brand of hypnotic the Japanese called Cloud Dancers. Catching the pimp's eye, Case beckoned him to the bar. Zone came drifting through the crowd in slow motion, his long face slack and placid.

"You seen Wage tonight, Lonny?"

Zone regarded him with his usual calm. He shook his head.

"You sure, man?"

"Maybe in the Namban. Maybe two hours ago."

"Got some joeboys with him? One of 'em thin, dark hair, maybe a black jacket?"

"No," Zone said at last, his smooth forehead creased to indicate the effort it cost him to recall so much pointless detail. "Big boys. Graftees." Zone's eyes showed very little white and less iris; under the drooping lids, his pupils were dilated and enormous. He stared into Case's face for a long time, then lowered his gaze. He saw the bulge of the steel whip. "Cobra," he said, and raised an eyebrow. "You wanna fuck somebody up?"

"See you, Lonny." Case left the bar.

———

His tail was back. He was sure of it. He felt a stab of elation, the octagons and adrenaline mingling with something else. You're enjoying this, he thought; you're crazy.

Because, in some weird and very approximate way, it was like a run in the matrix. Get just wasted enough, find yourself in some desperate but strangely arbitrary kind of trouble, and it was possible to see Ninsei as a field of data, the way the matrix had once reminded him of proteins linking to distinguish cell specialties. Then you could throw yourself into a highspeed drift and skid, totally engaged but set apart from it all, and all around you the dance of biz, information interacting, data made flesh in the mazes of the black market. . . .

Go it, Case, he told himself. Suck 'em in. Last thing they'll expect. He was half a block from the games arcade where he'd first met Linda Lee.

He bolted across Ninsei, scattering a pack of strolling sailors. One of them screamed after him in Spanish. Then he was through the entrance, the sound crashing over him like surf, subsonics throbbing in the pit of his stomach. Someone scored a ten-megaton hit on Tank War Europa, a simulated airburst drowning the arcade in white sound as a lurid hologram fireball mushroomed overhead. He cut to the right and loped up a flight of unpainted chipboard stairs. He'd come here once with Wage, to discuss a deal in proscribed hormonal triggers with a man called Matsuga. He remembered the hallway, its stained matting, the row of identical doors leading to tiny office cubicles. One door was open now. A Japanese girl in a sleeveless black T-shirt glanced up from a white terminal, behind her head a travel poster of Greece, Aegean blue splashed with streamlined ideograms.

"Get your security up here," Case told her.

Then he sprinted down the corridor, out of her sight. The last two doors were closed and, he assumed, locked. He spun and slammed the sole of his nylon running shoe into the blue-lacquered composition door at the far end. It popped, cheap hardware falling from the splintered frame. Darkness there, the white curve of a terminal housing. Then he was on the door to its right, both hands around the transparent plastic knob, leaning in with everything he had. Something snapped, and he was inside. This was where he and Wage had met with Matsuga, but whatever front company Matsuga had operated was long gone. No terminal, nothing. Light from the alley behind the arcade, filtering in through sootblown plastic. He made out a snakelike loop of fiberoptics protruding from a wall socket, a pile of discarded food containers, and the bladeless nacelle of an electric fan.

The window was a single pane of cheap plastic. He shrugged out of his jacket, bundled it around his right hand, and punched. It split, requiring two more blows to free it from the frame. Over the muted chaos of the games, an alarm began to cycle, triggered either by the broken window or by the girl at the head of the corridor.

Case turned, pulled his jacket on, and flicked the cobra to full extension.

With the door closed, he was counting on his tail to assume he'd gone through the one he'd kicked half off its hinges. The cobra's bronze pyramid began to bob gently, the spring-steel shaft amplifying his pulse.

Nothing happened. There was only the surging of the alarm, the crashing of the games, his heart hammering. When the fear came, it was like some half-forgotten friend. Not the cold, rapid mechanism of the dex-paranoia, but simple animal fear. He'd lived for so long on a constant edge of anxiety that he'd almost forgotten what real fear was.

This cubicle was the sort of place where people died. He might die here. They might have guns. . . .

A crash, from the far end of the corridor. A man's voice, shouting something in Japanese. A scream, shrill terror. Another crash.

And footsteps, unhurried, coming closer.

Passing his closed door. Pausing for the space of three rapid beats of his heart. And returning. One, two, three. A bootheel scraped the matting.

The last of his octagon-induced bravado collapsed. He snapped the cobra into its handle and scrambled for the window, blind with fear, his nerves screaming. He was up, out, and falling, all before he was conscious of what he'd done. The impact with pavement drove dull rods of pain through his shins.

A narrow wedge of light from a half-open service hatch framed a heap of discarded fiberoptics and the chassis of a junked console. He'd fallen face forward on a slab of soggy chipboard; he rolled over, into the shadow of the console. The cubicle's window was a square of faint light. The alarm still oscillated, louder here, the rear wall dulling the roar of the games.

A head appeared, framed in the window, backlit by the fluorescents in the corridor, then vanished. It returned, but he still couldn't read the features. Glint of silver across the eyes. "Shit," someone said, a woman, in the accent of the northern Sprawl.

The head was gone. Case lay under the console for a long count of twenty, then stood up. The steel cobra was still in his hand, and it took him a few seconds to remember what it was. He limped away down the alley, nursing his left ankle.

———

Shin's pistol was a fifty-year-old Vietnamese imitation of a South American copy of a Walther PPK, double-action on the first shot, with a very rough pull. It was chambered for .22 long rifle, and Case would've preferred lead azide explosives to the simple Chinese hollowpoints Shin had sold him. Still, it was a handgun and nine rounds of ammunition, and as he made his way down Shiga from the sushi stall he cradled it in his jacket pocket. The grips were bright red plastic molded in a raised dragon motif, something to run your thumb across in the dark. He'd consigned the cobra to a dump canister on Ninsei and dry-swallowed another octagon.

The pill lit his circuits and he rode the rush down Shiga to Ninsei, then over to Baiitsu. His tail, he'd decided, was gone, and that was fine. He had calls to make, biz to transact, and it wouldn't wait. A block down Baiitsu, toward the port, stood a featureless ten-story office building in ugly yellow brick. Its windows were dark now, but a faint glow from the roof was visible if you craned your neck. An unlit neon sign near the main entrance offered CHEAP HOTEL under a cluster of ideograms. If the place had another name, Case didn't know it; it was always referred to as Cheap Hotel. You reached it through an alley off Baiitsu, where an elevator waited at the foot of a transparent shaft. The elevator, like Cheap Hotel, was an afterthought, lashed to the building with bamboo and epoxy. Case climbed into the plastic cage and used his key, an unmarked length of rigid magnetic tape.

Case had rented a coffin here, on a weekly basis, since he'd arrived in Chiba, but he'd never slept in Cheap Hotel. He slept in cheaper places.

The elevator smelled of perfume and cigarettes; the sides of the cage were scratched and thumb-smudged. As it passed the fifth floor, he saw the lights of Ninsei. He drummed his fingers against the pistolgrip as the cage slowed with a gradual hiss. As always, it came to a full stop with a violent jolt, but he was ready for it. He stepped out into the courtyard that served the place as some combination of lobby and lawn.

Centered in the square carpet of green plastic turf, a Japanese teenager sat behind a C-shaped console, reading a textbook. The white fiberglass coffins were racked in a framework of industrial scaffolding. Six tiers of coffins, ten coffins on a side. Case nodded in the boy's direction and limped across the plastic grass to the nearest ladder. The compound was roofed with cheap laminated matting that rattled in a strong wind and leaked when it rained, but the coffins were reasonably difficult to open without a key.

The expansion-grate catwalk vibrated with his weight as he edged his way along the third tier to Number 92. The coffins were three meters long, the oval hatches a meter wide and just under a meter and a half tall. He fed his key into the slot and waited for verification from the house computer. Magnetic bolts thudded reassuringly and the hatch rose vertically with a creak of springs. Fluorescents flickered on as he crawled in, pulling the hatch shut behind him and slapping the panel that activated the manual latch.

There was nothing in Number 92 but a standard Hitachi pocket computer and a small white styrofoam cooler chest. The cooler contained the remains of three ten-kilo slabs of dry ice, carefully wrapped in paper to delay evaporation, and a spun aluminum lab flask. Crouching on the brown temperfoam slab that was both floor and bed, Case took Shin's .22 from his pocket and put it on top of the cooler. Then he took off his jacket. The coffin's terminal was molded into one concave wall, opposite a panel listing house rules in seven languages. Case took the pink handset from its cradle and punched a Hongkong number from memory. He let it ring five times, then hung up. His buyer for the three megabytes of hot RAM in the Hitachi wasn't taking calls.

He punched a Tokyo number in Shinjuku.

A woman answered, something in Japanese.

"Snake Man there?"

"Very good to hear from you," said Snake Man, coming in on an extension. "I've been expecting your call."

"I got the music you wanted." Glancing at the cooler.

"I'm very glad to hear that. We have a cash flow problem. Can you front?"

"Oh, man, I really need the money bad. . . ."

Snake Man hung up.

"You shit," Case said to the humming receiver. He stared at the cheap little pistol.

"Iffy," he said, "it's all looking very iffy tonight."

———————

Case walked into the Chat an hour before dawn, both hands in the pockets of his jacket; one held the rented pistol, the other the aluminum flask.

Ratz was at a rear table, drinking Apollonaris water from a beer pitcher, his hundred and twenty kilos of doughy flesh tilted against the wall on a creaking chair. A Brazilian kid called Kurt was on the bar, tending a thin crowd of mostly silent drunks. Ratz's plastic arm buzzed as he raised the pitcher and drank. His shaven head was filmed with sweat. "You look bad, friend artiste," he said, flashing the wet ruin of his teeth.

"I'm doing just fine," said Case, and grinned like a skull. "Super fine." He sagged into the chair opposite Ratz, hands still in his pockets.

"And you wander back and forth in this portable bombshelter built of booze and ups, sure. Proof against the grosser emotions, yes?"

"Why don't you get off my case, Ratz? You seen Wage?"

"Proof against fear and being alone," the bartender continued. "Listen to the fear. Maybe it's your friend."

"You hear anything about a fight in the arcade tonight, Ratz? Somebody hurt?"

"Crazy cut a security man." He shrugged. "A girl, they say."

"I gotta talk to Wage, Ratz, I . . ."

"Ah." Ratz's mouth narrowed, compressed into a single line. He was looking past Case, toward the entrance. "I think you are about to."

Case had a sudden flash of the shuriken in their window. The speed sang in his head. The pistol in his hand was slippery with sweat.

"Herr Wage," Ratz said, slowly extending his pink manipulator as if he expected it to be shaken. "How great a pleasure. Too seldom do you honor us."

Case turned his head and looked up into Wage's face. It was a tanned and forgettable mask. The eyes were vatgrown sea-green Nikon transplants. Wage wore a suit of gunmetal silk and a simple bracelet of platinum on either wrist. He was flanked by his joeboys, nearly identical young men, their arms and shoulders bulging with grafted muscle.

"How you doing, Case?"

"Gentlemen," said Ratz, picking up the table's heaped ashtray in his pink plastic claw, "I want no trouble here." The ashtray was made of thick, shatterproof plastic, and advertised Tsingtao beer. Ratz crushed it smoothly, butts and shards of green plastic cascading onto the tabletop. "You understand?"

"Hey, sweetheart," said one of the joeboys, "you wanna try that thing on me?"

"Don't bother aiming for the legs, Kurt," Ratz said, his tone conversational. Case glanced across the room and saw the Brazilian standing on the bar, aiming a Smith & Wesson riot gun at the trio. The thing's barrel, made of paper-thin alloy wrapped with a kilometer of glass filament, was wide enough to swallow a fist. The skeletal magazine revealed five fat orange cartridges, subsonic sandbag jellies.

"Technically nonlethal," said Ratz.

"Hey, Ratz," Case said, "I owe you one."

The bartender shrugged. "Nothing, you owe me. These," and he glowered at Wage and the joeboys, "should know better. You don't take anybody off in the Chatsubo."

Wage coughed. "So who's talking about taking anybody off? We just wanna talk business. Case and me, we work together."

Case pulled the .22 out of his pocket and levelled it at Wage's crotch. "I hear you wanna do me." Ratz's pink claw closed around the pistol and Case let his hand go limp.

"Look, Case, you tell me what the fuck is going on with you, you wig or something? What's this shit I'm trying to kill you?" Wage turned to the boy on his left. "You two go back to the Namban. Wait for me."

Case watched as they crossed the bar, which was now entirely deserted except for Kurt and a drunken sailor in khakis, who was curled at the foot of a barstool. The barrel of the Smith & Wesson tracked the two to the door, then swung back to cover Wage. The magazine of Case's pistol clattered on the table. Ratz held the gun in his claw and pumped the round out of the chamber.

"Who told you I was going to hit you, Case?" Wage asked.

Linda.

"Who told you, man? Somebody trying to set you up?"

The sailor moaned and vomited explosively.

"Get him out of here," Ratz called to Kurt, who was sitting on the edge of the bar now, the Smith & Wesson across his lap, lighting a cigarette.

Case felt the weight of the night come down on him like a bag of wet sand settling behind his eyes. He took the flask out of his pocket and handed it to Wage. "All I got. Pituitaries. Get you five hundred if you move it fast. Had the rest of my roll in some RAM, but that's gone by now."

"You okay, Case?" The flask had already vanished behind a gunmetal lapel. "I mean, fine, this'll square us, but you look bad. Like hammered shit. You better go somewhere and sleep."

"Yeah." He stood up and felt the Chat sway around him. "Well, I had this fifty, but I gave it to somebody." He giggled. He picked up the .22's magazine and the one loose cartridge and dropped them into one pocket, then put the pistol in the other. "I gotta see Shin, get my deposit back."

"Go home," said Ratz, shifting on the creaking chair with something like embarrassment. "Artiste. Go home."

He felt them watching as he crossed the room and shouldered his way past the plastic doors.

———————

"Bitch," he said to the rose tint over Shiga. Down on Ninsei the holograms were vanishing like ghosts, and most of the neon was already cold and dead. He sipped thick black coffee from a street vendor's foam thimble and watched the sun come up. "You fly away, honey. Towns like this are for people who like the way down." But that wasn't it, really, and he was finding it increasingly hard to maintain the sense of betrayal. She just wanted a ticket home, and the RAM in his Hitachi would buy it for her, if she could find the right fence. And that business with the fifty; she'd almost turned it down, knowing she was about to rip him for the rest of what he had.

When he climbed out of the elevator, the same boy was on the desk. Different textbook. "Good buddy," Case called across the plastic turf, "you don't need to tell me. I know already. Pretty lady came to visit, said she had my key. Nice little tip for you, say fifty New ones?" The boy put down his book. "Woman," Case said, and drew a line across his forehead with his thumb. "Silk." He smiled broadly. The boy smiled back, nodded. "Thanks, asshole," Case said.

On the catwalk, he had trouble with the lock. She'd messed it up somehow when she'd fiddled it, he thought. Beginner. He knew where to rent a blackbox that would open anything in Cheap Hotel. Fluorescents came on as he crawled in.

"Close the hatch real slow, friend. You still got that Saturday night special you rented from the waiter?"

She sat with her back to the wall, at the far end of the coffin. She had her knees up, resting her wrists on them; the pepperbox muzzle of a flechette pistol emerged from her hands.

"That you in the arcade?" He pulled the hatch down. "Where's Linda?"

"Hit that latch switch."

He did.

"That your girl? Linda?"

He nodded.

"She's gone. Took your Hitachi. Real nervous kid. What about the gun, man?" She wore mirrored glasses. Her clothes were black, the heels of black boots deep in the temperfoam.

"I took it back to Shin, got my deposit. Sold his bullets back to him for half what I paid. You want the money?"

"No."

"Want some dry ice? All I got, right now."

"What got into you tonight? Why'd you pull that scene at the arcade? I had to mess up this rentacop came after me with nunchucks."

"Linda said you were gonna kill me."

"Linda said? I never saw her before I came up here."

"You aren't with Wage?"

She shook her head. He realized that the glasses were surgically inset, sealing her sockets. The silver lenses seemed to grow from smooth pale skin above her cheekbones, framed by dark hair cut in a rough shag. The fingers curled around the fletcher were slender, white, tipped with polished burgundy. The nails looked artificial. "I think you screwed up, Case. I showed up and you just fit me right into your reality picture."

"So what do you want, lady?" He sagged back against the hatch.

"You. One live body, brains still somewhat intact. Molly, Case. My name's Molly. I'm collecting you for the man I work for. Just wants to talk, is all. Nobody wants to hurt you."

"That's good."

"'Cept I do hurt people sometimes, Case. I guess it's just the way

I'm wired." She wore tight black gloveleather jeans and a bulky black jacket cut from some matte fabric that seemed to absorb light. "If I put this dartgun away, will you be easy, Case? You look like you like to take stupid chances."

"Hey, I'm very easy. I'm a pushover, no problem."

"That's fine, man." The fletcher vanished into the black jacket. "Because you try to fuck around with me, you'll be taking one of the stupidest chances of your whole life."

She held out her hands, palms up, the white fingers slightly spread, and with a barely audible click, ten double-edged, four-centimeter scalpel blades slid from their housings beneath the burgundy nails.

She smiled. The blades slowly withdrew.

TWO

After a year of coffins, the room on the twenty-fifth floor of the Chiba Hilton seemed enormous. It was ten meters by eight, half of a suite. A white Braun coffeemaker steamed on a low table by the sliding glass panels that opened onto a narrow balcony.

"Get some coffee in you. Look like you need it." She took off her black jacket; the fletcher hung beneath her arm in a black nylon shoulder rig. She wore a sleeveless gray pullover with plain steel zips across each shoulder. Bulletproof, Case decided, slopping coffee into a bright red mug. His arms and legs felt like they were made out of wood.

"Case." He looked up, seeing the man for the first time. "My name is Armitage." The dark robe was open to the waist, the broad chest hairless and muscular, the stomach flat and hard. Blue eyes so pale they made Case think of bleach. "Sun's up, Case. This is your lucky day, boy."

Case whipped his arm sideways and the man easily ducked the scalding coffee. Brown stain running down the imitation ricepaper wall. He saw the angular gold ring through the left lobe. Special Forces. The man smiled.

"Get your coffee, Case," Molly said. "You're okay, but you're not going anywhere 'til Armitage has his say." She sat crosslegged on a silk futon and began to fieldstrip the fletcher without bothering to look at it. Twin mirrors tracking as he crossed to the table and re-filled his cup.

"Too young to remember the war, aren't you, Case?" Armitage ran a large hand back through his cropped brown hair. A heavy gold bracelet flashed on his wrist. "Leningrad, Kiev, Siberia. We invented you in Siberia, Case."

"What's that supposed to mean?"

"Screaming Fist, Case. You've heard the name."

"Some kind of run, wasn't it? Tried to burn this Russian nexus with virus programs. Yeah, I heard about it. And nobody got out."

He sensed abrupt tension. Armitage walked to the window and looked out over Tokyo Bay. "That isn't true. One unit made it back to Helsinki, Case."

Case shrugged, sipped coffee.

"You're a console cowboy. The prototypes of the programs you use to crack industrial banks were developed for Screaming Fist. For the assault on the Kirensk computer nexus. Basic module was a Nightwing microlight, a pilot, a matrix deck, a jockey. We were running a virus called Mole. The Mole series was the first generation of real intrusion programs."

"Icebreakers," Case said, over the rim of the red mug.

"Ice from *ICE*, intrusion countermeasures electronics."

"Problem is, mister, I'm no jockey now, so I think I'll just be going. . . ."

"I was there, Case; I was there when they invented your kind."

"You got zip to do with me and my kind, buddy. You're rich enough to hire expensive razorgirls to haul my ass up here, is all. I'm never gonna punch any deck again, not for you or anybody else." He crossed to the window and looked down. "That's where I live now."

"Our profile says you're trying to con the street into killing you when you're not looking."

"Profile?"

"We've built up a detailed model. Bought a go-to for each of your aliases and ran the skim through some military software. You're suicidal, Case. The model gives you a month on the outside. And our medical projection says you'll need a new pancreas inside a year."

"'We.'" He met the faded blue eyes. "'We' who?"

"What would you say if I told you we could correct your neural damage, Case?" Armitage suddenly looked to Case as if he were carved from a block of metal; inert, enormously heavy. A statue. He knew now that this was a dream, and that soon he'd wake. Armitage wouldn't speak again. Case's dreams always ended in these freezeframes, and now this one was over.

"What would you say, Case?"

Case looked out over the Bay and shivered.

"I'd say you were full of shit."

Armitage nodded.

"Then I'd ask what your terms were."

"Not very different than what you're used to, Case."

"Let the man get some sleep, Armitage," Molly said from her futon, the components of the fletcher spread on the silk like some expensive puzzle. "He's coming apart at the seams."

"Terms," Case said, "and now. Right now."

He was still shivering. He couldn't stop shivering.

———————

The clinic was nameless, expensively appointed, a cluster of sleek pavilions separated by small formal gardens. He remembered the place from the round he'd made his first month in Chiba.

"Scared, Case. You're real scared." It was Sunday afternoon and he stood with Molly in a sort of courtyard. White boulders, a stand of green bamboo, black gravel raked into smooth waves. A gardener, a thing like a large metal crab, was tending the bamboo.

"It'll work, Case. You got no idea, the kind of stuff Armitage has. Like he's gonna pay these nerve boys for fixing you with the program he's giving them to tell them how to do it. He'll put them three years ahead of the competition. You got any idea what that's worth?" She hooked thumbs in the beltloops of her leather jeans and rocked backward on the lacquered heels of cherry red cowboy boots. The narrow toes were sheathed in bright Mexican silver. The lenses were empty quicksilver, regarding him with an insect calm.

"You're street samurai," he said. "How long you work for him?"

"Couple of months."

"What about before that?"

"For somebody else. Working girl, you know?"

He nodded.

"Funny, Case."

"What's funny?"

"It's like I know you. That profile he's got. I know how you're wired."

"You don't know me, sister."

"You're okay, Case. What got you, it's just called bad luck."

"How about him? He okay, Molly?" The robot crab moved toward them, picking its way over the waves of gravel. Its bronze carapace might have been a thousand years old. When it was within a meter of her boots, it fired a burst of light, then froze for an instant, analyzing data obtained.

"What I always think about first, Case, is my own sweet ass." The crab had altered course to avoid her, but she kicked it with a smooth precision, the silver boot-tip clanging on the carapace. The thing fell on its back, but the bronze limbs soon righted it.

Case sat on one of the boulders, scuffing at the symmetry of the gravel waves with the toes of his shoes. He began to search his pockets for cigarettes. "In your shirt," she said.

"You want to answer my question?" He fished a wrinkled Yeheyuan from the pack and she lit it for him with a thin slab of German steel that looked as though it belonged on an operating table.

"Well, I'll tell you, the man's definitely onto something. He's got big money now, and he's never had it before, and he gets more all the time." Case noticed a certain tension around her mouth. "Or maybe, maybe something's onto him. . . ." She shrugged.

"What's that mean?"

"I don't know, exactly. I know I don't know who or what we're really working for."

He stared at the twin mirrors. Leaving the Hilton, Saturday morning, he'd gone back to Cheap Hotel and slept for ten hours. Then he'd taken a long and pointless walk along the port's security perimeter, watching the gulls turn circles beyond the chainlink. If she'd followed him, she'd done a good job of it. He'd avoided Night City. He'd waited in the coffin for Armitage's call. Now this quiet courtyard, Sunday afternoon, this girl with a gymnast's body and conjurer's hands.

"If you'll come in now, sir, the anesthetist is waiting to meet you." The technician bowed, turned, and reentered the clinic without waiting to see if Case would follow.

———

Cold steel odor. Ice caressed his spine.

Lost, so small amid that dark, hands grown cold, body image fading down corridors of television sky.

Voices.

Then black fire found the branching tributaries of the nerves, pain beyond anything to which the name of pain is given. . . .

———

Hold still. Don't move.

And Ratz was there, and Linda Lee, Wage and Lonny Zone, a

hundred faces from the neon forest, sailors and hustlers and whores, where the sky is poisoned silver, beyond chainlink and the prison of the skull.

Goddam don't you move.

Where the sky faded from hissing static to the noncolor of the matrix, and he glimpsed the shuriken, his stars.

"Stop it, Case, I gotta find your vein!"

She was straddling his chest, a blue plastic syrette in one hand. "You don't lie still, I'll slit your fucking throat. You're still full of endorphin inhibitors."

He woke and found her stretched beside him in the dark.

His neck was brittle, made of twigs. There was a steady pulse of pain midway down his spine. Images formed and reformed: a flickering montage of the Sprawl's towers and ragged Fuller domes, dim figures moving toward him in the shade beneath a bridge or overpass. . . .

"Case? It's Wednesday, Case." She moved, rolling over, reaching across him. A breast brushed his upper arm. He heard her tear the foil seal from a bottle of water and drink. "Here." She put the bottle in his hand. "I can see in the dark, Case. Microchannel image-amps in my glasses."

"My back hurts."

"That's where they replaced your fluid. Changed your blood, too. Blood 'cause you got a new pancreas thrown into the deal. And some new tissue patched into your liver. The nerve stuff, I dunno. Lot of injections. They didn't have to open anything up for the main show." She settled back beside him. "It's 2:43:12 AM, Case. Got a readout chipped into my optic nerve."

He sat up and tried to sip from the bottle. Gagged, coughed, lukewarm water spraying his chest and thighs.

"I gotta punch deck," he heard himself say. He was groping for his clothes. "I gotta know. . . ."

She laughed. Small strong hands gripped his upper arms. "Sorry, hotshot. Eight-day wait. Your nervous system would fall out on the floor if you jacked in now. Doctor's orders. Besides, they figure it worked. Check you in a day or so." He lay down again.

"Where are we?"

"Home. Cheap Hotel."

"Where's Armitage?"

"Hilton, selling beads to the natives or something. We're out of here soon, man. Amsterdam, Paris, then back to the Sprawl." She touched his shoulder. "Roll over. I give a good massage."

He lay on his stomach, arms stretched forward, tips of his fingers against the walls of the coffin. She settled over the small of his back, kneeling on the temperfoam, the leather jeans cool against his skin. Her fingers brushed his neck.

"How come you're not at the Hilton?"

She answered him by reaching back, between his thighs, and gently encircling his scrotum with thumb and forefinger. She rocked there for a minute in the dark, erect above him, her other hand on his neck. The leather of her jeans creaked softly with the movement. Case shifted, feeling himself harden against the temperfoam.

His head throbbed, but the brittleness in his neck seemed to retreat. He raised himself on one elbow, rolled, sank back against the foam, pulling her down, licking her breasts, small hard nipples sliding wet across his cheek. He found the zip on the leather jeans and tugged it down.

"It's okay," she said, "I can see." Sound of the jeans peeling down. She struggled beside him until she could kick them away. She threw a leg across him and he touched her face. Unexpected hardness of the implanted lenses. "Don't," she said, "fingerprints."

Now she straddled him again, took his hand, and closed it over her, his thumb along the cleft of her buttocks, his fingers spread across the labia. As she began to lower herself, the images came pulsing back, the faces, fragments of neon arriving and receding. She slid down around him and his back arched convulsively. She rode him that way, impaling herself, slipping down on him again and again, until they both had come, his orgasm flaring blue in a timeless space, a vastness like the matrix, where the faces were shredded and blown away down hurricane corridors, and her inner thighs were strong and wet against his hips.

———————

On Ninsei, a thinner, weekday version of the crowd went through the motions of the dance. Waves of sound rolled from the arcades and pachinko parlors. Case glanced into the Chat and saw Zone watching over his girls in the warm, beer-smelling twilight. Ratz was tending bar.

"You seen Wage, Ratz?"

"Not tonight." Ratz made a point of raising an eyebrow at Molly.

"You see him, tell him I got his money."

"Luck changing, my artiste?"

"Too soon to tell."

———————

"Well, I gotta see this guy," Case said, watching his reflection in her glasses. "I got biz to cancel out of."

"Armitage won't like it, I let you out of my sight." She stood beneath Deane's melting clock, hands on her hips.

"The guy won't talk to me if you're there. Deane I don't give two shits about. He takes care of himself. But I got people who'll just go under if I walk out of Chiba cold. It's my people, you know?"

Her mouth hardened. She shook her head.

"I got people in Singapore, Tokyo connections in Shinjuku and Asakuza, and they'll go *down*, understand?" he lied, his hand on the shoulder of her black jacket. "Five. Five minutes. By your clock, okay?"

"Not what I'm paid for."

"What you're paid for is one thing. Me letting some tight friends die because you're too literal about your instructions is something else."

"Bullshit. Tight friends my ass. You're going in there to check us out with your smuggler." She put a booted foot up on the dust-covered Kandinsky coffee table.

"Ah, Case, sport, it does look as though your companion there is definitely armed, aside from having a fair amount of silicon in her head. What is this about, exactly?" Deane's ghostly cough seemed to hang in the air between them.

"Hold on, Julie. Anyway, I'll be coming in alone."

"You can be sure of that, old son. Wouldn't have it any other way."

"Okay," she said. "Go. But five minutes. Any more and I'll come in and cool your tight friend permanently. And while you're at it, you try to figure something out."

"What's that?"

"Why I'm doing you the favor." She turned and walked out, past the stacked white modules of preserved ginger.

"Keeping stranger company than usual, Case?" asked Julie.

"Julie, she's gone. You wanna let me in? Please, Julie?"

The bolts worked. "Slowly, Case," said the voice.

"Turn on the works, Julie, all the stuff in the desk," Case said, taking his place in the swivel chair.

"It's on all the time," Deane said mildly, taking a gun from behind the exposed works of his old mechanical typewriter and aiming it carefully at Case. It was a belly gun, a magnum revolver with the barrel sawn down to a nub. The front of the trigger-guard had been cut away and the grips wrapped with what looked like old masking tape. Case thought it looked very strange in Deane's manicured pink hands. "Just taking care, you understand. Nothing personal. Now tell me what you want."

"I need a history lesson, Julie. And a go-to on somebody."

"What's moving, old son?" Deane's shirt was candy-striped cotton, the collar white and rigid, like porcelain.

"Me, Julie. I'm leaving. Gone. But do me the favor, okay?"

"Go-to on whom, old son?"

"Gaijin name of Armitage, suite in the Hilton."

Deane put the pistol down. "Sit still, Case." He tapped something out on a lap terminal. "It seems as though you know as much as my net does, Case. This gentleman seems to have a temporary arrangement with the Yakuza, and the sons of the neon chrysanthemum have ways of screening their allies from the likes of me. I wouldn't have it any other way. Now, history. You said history." He picked up the gun again, but didn't point it directly at Case. "What sort of history?"

"The war. You in the war, Julie?"

"The war? What's there to know? Lasted three weeks."

"Screaming Fist."

"Famous. Don't they teach you history these days? Great bloody postwar political football, that was. Watergated all to hell and back. Your brass, Case, your Sprawlside brass in, where was it, McLean? In the bunkers, all of that . . . great scandal. Wasted a fair bit of patriotic young flesh in order to test some new technology. They knew about the Russians' defenses, it came out later. Knew about the emps, magnetic pulse weapons. Sent these fellows in regardless, just to see." Deane shrugged. "Turkey shoot for Ivan."

"Any of those guys make it out?"

"Christ," Deane said, "it's been bloody years. . . . Though I do think a few did. One of the teams. Got hold of a Sov gunship. Helicopter, you know. Flew it back to Finland. Didn't have entry codes, of course, and shot hell out of the Finnish defense forces in the process. Special Forces types." Deane sniffed. "Bloody hell."

Case nodded. The smell of preserved ginger was overwhelming.

"I spent the war in Lisbon, you know," Deane said, putting the gun down. "Lovely place, Lisbon."

"In the service, Julie?"

"Hardly. Though I did see action." Deane smiled his pink smile. "Wonderful what a war can do for one's markets."

"Thanks, Julie. I owe you one."

"Hardly, Case. And goodbye."

───────

And later he'd tell himself that the evening at Sammi's had felt wrong from the start, that even as he'd followed Molly along that corridor, shuffling through a trampled mulch of ticket stubs and styrofoam cups, he'd sensed it. Linda's death, waiting. . . .

They'd gone to the Namban, after he'd seen Deane, and paid off his debt to Wage with a roll of Armitage's New Yen. Wage had liked that, his boys had liked it less, and Molly had grinned at Case's side with a kind of ecstatic feral intensity, obviously longing for one of them to make a move. Then he'd taken her back to the Chat for a drink.

"Wasting your time, cowboy," Molly said, when Case took an octagon from the pocket of his jacket.

"How's that? You want one?" He held the pill out to her.

"Your new pancreas, Case, and those plugs in your liver. Armitage had them designed to bypass that shit." She tapped the octagon with one burgundy nail. "You're biochemically incapable of getting off on amphetamine or cocaine."

"Shit," he said. He looked at the octagon, then at her.

"Eat it. Eat a dozen. Nothing'll happen."

He did. Nothing did.

Three beers later, she was asking Ratz about the fights.

"Sammi's," Ratz said.

"I'll pass," Case said, "I hear they kill each other down there."

An hour later, she was buying tickets from a skinny Thai in a white T-shirt and baggy rugby shorts.

Sammi's was an inflated dome behind a portside warehouse, taut gray fabric reinforced with a net of thin steel cables. The corridor, with a door at either end, was a crude airlock preserving the pressure differential that supported the dome. Fluorescent rings were screwed to the plywood ceiling at intervals, but most of them had been broken. The air was damp and close with the smell of sweat and concrete.

None of that prepared him for the arena, the crowd, the tense hush, the towering puppets of light beneath the dome. Concrete sloped away in tiers to a kind of central stage, a raised circle ringed with a glittering thicket of projection gear. No light but the holograms that shifted and flickered above the ring, reproducing the movements of the two men below. Strata of cigarette smoke rose from the tiers, drifting until it struck currents set up by the blowers that supported the dome. No sound but the muted purring of the blowers and the amplified breathing of the fighters.

Reflected colors flowed across Molly's lenses as the men circled. The holograms were ten-power magnifications; at ten, the knives they held were just under a meter long. The knife-fighter's grip is the fencer's grip, Case remembered, the fingers curled, thumb aligned with blade. The knives seemed to move of their own accord, gliding with a ritual lack of urgency through the arcs and passes of their dance, point passing point, as the men waited for an opening. Molly's upturned face was smooth and still, watching.

"I'll go find us some food," Case said. She nodded, lost in contemplation of the dance.

He didn't like this place.

He turned and walked back into the shadows. Too dark. Too quiet.

The crowd, he saw, was mostly Japanese. Not really a Night City crowd. Techs down from the arcologies. He supposed that meant the arena had the approval of some corporate recreational committee. He wondered briefly what it would be like, working all your life for one zaibatsu. Company housing, company hymn, company funeral.

He'd made nearly a full circuit of the dome before he found the food stalls. He bought yakitori on skewers and two tall waxy cartons of beer. Glancing up at the holograms, he saw that blood laced one figure's chest. Thick brown sauce trickled down the skewers and over his knuckles.

Seven days and he'd jack in. If he closed his eyes now, he'd see the matrix.

Shadows twisted as the holograms swung through their dance.

Then the fear began to knot between his shoulders. A cold trickle of sweat worked its way down and across his ribs. The operation hadn't worked. He was still here, still meat, no Molly waiting, her eyes locked on the circling knives, no Armitage waiting in the Hilton with tickets and a new passport and money. It was all some dream, some pathetic fantasy. . . . Hot tears blurred his vision.

Blood sprayed from a jugular in a red gout of light. And now the crowd was screaming, rising, screaming—as one figure crumpled, the hologram fading, flickering. . . .

Raw edge of vomit in his throat. He closed his eyes, took a deep breath, opened them, and saw Linda Lee step past him, her gray eyes blind with fear. She wore the same French fatigues.

And gone. Into shadow.

Pure mindless reflex: he threw the beer and chicken down and ran after her. He might have called her name, but he'd never be sure.

Afterimage of a single hair-fine line of red light. Seared concrete beneath the thin soles of his shoes.

Her white sneakers flashing, close to the curving wall now, and again the ghost line of the laser branded across his eye, bobbing in his vision as he ran.

Someone tripped him. Concrete tore his palms.

He rolled and kicked, failing to connect. A thin boy, spiked blond hair lit from behind in a rainbow nimbus, was leaning over him. Above the stage, a figure turned, knife held high, to the cheering crowd. The boy smiled and drew something from his sleeve. A razor, etched in red as a third beam blinked past them into the dark. Case saw the razor dipping for his throat like a dowser's wand.

The face was erased in a humming cloud of microscopic explosions. Molly's fletchettes, at twenty rounds per second. The boy coughed once, convulsively, and toppled across Case's legs.

He was walking toward the stalls, into the shadows. He looked down, expecting to see that needle of ruby emerge from his chest. Nothing. He found her. She was thrown down at the foot of a concrete pillar, eyes closed. There was a smell of cooked meat. The crowd was chanting the winner's name. A beer vendor was wiping his taps with a dark rag. One white sneaker had come off, somehow, and lay beside her head.

Follow the wall. Curve of concrete. Hands in pockets. Keep walking. Past unseeing faces, every eye raised to the victor's image above the ring. Once a seamed European face danced in the glare of a match, lips pursed around the short stem of a metal pipe. Tang of hashish. Case walked on, feeling nothing.

"Case." Her mirrors emerged from deeper shadow. "You okay?"

Something mewled and bubbled in the dark behind her.

He shook his head.

"Fight's over, Case. Time to go home."

He tried to walk past her, back into the dark, where something was dying. She stopped him with a hand on his chest. "Friends of your tight friend. Killed your girl for you. You haven't done too well for friends in this town, have you? We got a partial profile on that old bastard when we did you, man. He'd fry anybody, for a few New ones. The one back there said they got onto her when she was trying to fence your RAM. Just cheaper for them to kill her and take it. Save a little money. . . . I got the one who had the laser to tell me all about it. Coincidence we were here, but I had to make sure." Her mouth was hard, lips pressed into a thin line.

Case felt as though his brain were jammed. "Who," he said, "who sent them?"

She passed him a blood-flecked bag of preserved ginger. He saw that her hands were sticky with blood. Back in the shadows, some-one made wet sounds and died.

———

After the postoperative check at the clinic, Molly took him to the port. Armitage was waiting. He'd chartered a hovercraft. The last Case saw of Chiba were the dark angles of the arcologies. Then a mist closed over the black water and the drifting shoals of waste.

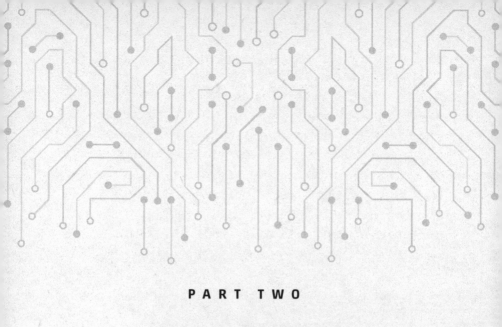

PART TWO

THE SHOPPING
EXPEDITION

THREE

Home.

Home was BAMA, the Sprawl, the Boston-Atlanta Metropolitan Axis.

Program a map to display frequency of data exchange, every thousand megabytes a single pixel on a very large screen. Manhattan and Atlanta burn solid white. Then they start to pulse, the rate of traffic threatening to overload your simulation. Your map is about to go nova. Cool it down. Up your scale. Each pixel a million megabytes. At a hundred million megabytes per second, you begin to make out certain blocks in midtown Manhattan, outlines of hundred-year-old industrial parks ringing the old core of Atlanta. . . .

———

Case woke from a dream of airports, of Molly's dark leathers moving ahead of him through the concourses of Narita, Schipol, Orly. . . . He watched himself buy a flat plastic flask of Danish vodka at some kiosk, an hour before dawn.

Somewhere down in the Sprawl's ferro-concrete roots, a train drove a column of stale air through a tunnel. The train itself was silent, gliding over its induction cushion, but displaced air made the tunnel sing, bass down into subsonics. Vibration reached the room

where he lay and caused dust to rise from the cracks in the desic-
cated parquet floor.

Opening his eyes, he saw Molly, naked and just out of reach
across an expanse of very new pink temperfoam. Overhead, sunlight filtered through the soot-stained grid of a skylight. One half-
meter square of glass had been replaced with chipboard, a fat
gray cable emerging there to dangle within a few centimeters of
the floor. He lay on his side and watched her breathe, her breasts,
the sweep of a flank defined with the functional elegance of a
war plane's fuselage. Her body was spare, neat, the muscles like
a dancer's.

The room was large. He sat up. The room was empty, aside from
the wide pink bedslab and two nylon bags, new and identical, that
lay beside it. Blank walls, no windows, a single white-painted steel
firedoor. The walls were coated with countless layers of white latex
paint. Factory space. He knew this kind of room, this kind of building; the tenants would operate in the interzone where art wasn't
quite crime, crime not quite art.

He was home.

He swung his feet to the floor. It was made of little blocks of
wood, some missing, others loose. His head ached. He remembered
Amsterdam, another room, in the Old City section of the Centrum,
buildings centuries old. Molly back from the canal's edge with orange juice and eggs. Armitage off on some cryptic foray, the two of
them walking alone past Dam Square to a bar she knew on a Dam-
rak thoroughfare. Paris was a blurred dream. Shopping. She'd taken
him shopping.

He stood, pulling on a wrinkled pair of new black jeans that lay
at his feet, and knelt beside the bags. The first one he opened was
Molly's: neatly folded clothing and small expensive-looking gad-
gets. The second was stuffed with things he didn't remember buying: books, tapes, a simstim deck, clothing with French and Italian

labels. Beneath a green T-shirt, he discovered a flat, origami-wrapped package, recycled Japanese paper.

The paper tore when he picked it up; a bright nine-pointed star fell—to stick upright in a crack in the parquet.

"Souvenir," Molly said. "I noticed you were always looking at 'em." He turned and saw her sitting crosslegged on the bed, sleepily scratching her stomach with burgundy nails.

———————

"Someone's coming later to secure the place," Armitage said. He stood in the open doorway with an old-fashioned magnetic key in his hand. Molly was making coffee on a tiny German stove she took from her bag.

"I can do it," she said. "I got enough gear already. Infrascan perimeter, screamers . . ."

"No," he said, closing the door. "I want it tight."

"Suit yourself." She wore a dark mesh T-shirt tucked into baggy black cotton pants.

"You ever the heat, Mr. Armitage?" Case asked, from where he sat, his back against a wall.

Armitage was no taller than Case, but with his broad shoulders and military posture he seemed to fill the doorway. He wore a somber Italian suit; in his right hand he held a briefcase of soft black calf. The Special Forces earring was gone. The handsome, inexpressive features offered the routine beauty of the cosmetic boutiques, a conservative amalgam of the past decade's leading media faces. The pale glitter of his eyes heightened the effect of a mask. Case began to regret the question.

"Lots of Forces types wound up cops, I mean. Or corporate security," Case added uncomfortably. Molly handed him a steaming mug of coffee. "That number you had them do on my pancreas, that's like a cop routine."

Armitage closed the door and crossed the room, to stand in front of Case. "You're a lucky boy, Case. You should thank me."

"Should I?" Case blew noisily on his coffee.

"You needed a new pancreas. The one we bought for you frees you from a dangerous dependency."

"Thanks, but I was enjoying that dependency."

"Good, because you have a new one."

"How's that?" Case looked up from his coffee. Armitage was smiling.

"You have fifteen toxin sacs bonded to the lining of various main arteries, Case. They're dissolving. Very slowly, but they definitely are dissolving. Each one contains a mycotoxin. You're already familiar with the effect of that mycotoxin. It was the one your former employers gave you in Memphis."

Case blinked up at the smiling mask.

"You have time to do what I'm hiring you for, Case, but that's all. Do the job and I can inject you with an enzyme that will dissolve the bond without opening the sacs. Then you'll need a blood change. Otherwise, the sacs melt and you're back where I found you. So you see, Case, you need us. You need us as badly as you did when we scraped you up from the gutter."

Case looked at Molly. She shrugged.

"Now go down to the freight elevator and bring up the cases you find there." Armitage handed him the magnetic key. "Go on. You'll enjoy this, Case. Like Christmas morning."

Summer in the Sprawl, the mall crowds swaying like windblown grass, a field of flesh shot through with sudden eddies of need and gratification.

He sat beside Molly in filtered sunlight on the rim of a dry concrete fountain, letting the endless stream of faces recapitulate the stages of his life. First a child with hooded eyes, a street boy, hands relaxed and ready at his sides; then a teenager, face smooth and cryptic beneath red glasses. Case remembered fighting on a rooftop at seventeen, silent combat in the rose glow of the dawn geodesics.

He shifted on the concrete, feeling it rough and cool through the thin black denim. Nothing here like the electric dance of Ninsei. This was different commerce, a different rhythm, in the smell of fast food and perfume and fresh summer sweat.

With his deck waiting, back in the loft, an Ono-Sendai Cyberspace 7. They'd left the place littered with the abstract white forms of the foam packing units, with crumpled plastic film and hundreds of tiny foam beads. The Ono-Sendai; next year's most expensive Hosaka computer; a Sony monitor; a dozen disks of corporate-grade ice; a Braun coffeemaker. Armitage had only waited for Case's approval of each piece.

"Where'd he go?" Case had asked Molly.

"He likes hotels. Big ones. Near airports, if he can manage it. Let's go down to the street." She'd zipped herself into an old surplus vest with a dozen oddly shaped pockets and put on a huge pair of black plastic sunglasses that completely covered her mirrored insets.

"You know about that toxin shit, before?" he asked her, by the fountain. She shook her head. "You think it's true?"

"Maybe, maybe not. Works either way."

"You know any way I can find out?"

"No," she said, her right hand coming up to form the jive for silence. "That kind of kink's too subtle to show up on a scan." Then her fingers moved again: wait. "And you don't care that much anyway. I saw you stroking that Sendai; man, it was pornographic." She laughed.

"So what's he got on you? How's he got the working girl kinked?"

"Professional pride, baby, that's all." And again the sign for silence. "We're gonna get some breakfast, okay? Eggs, real bacon. Probably kill you, you been eating that rebuilt Chiba krill for so long. Yeah, come on, we'll tube into Manhattan and get us a real breakfast."

———

Lifeless neon spelled out METRO HOLOGRAFIX in dusty capitals of glass tubing. Case picked at a shred of bacon that had lodged between his front teeth. He'd given up asking her where they were going and why; jabs in the ribs and the sign for silence were all he'd gotten in reply. She talked about the season's fashions, about sports, about a political scandal in California he'd never heard of.

He looked around the deserted dead-end street. A sheet of newsprint went cartwheeling past the intersection. Freak winds in the East side; something to do with convection, and an overlap in the domes. Case peered through the window at the dead sign. Her Sprawl wasn't his Sprawl, he decided. She'd led him through a dozen bars and clubs he'd never seen before, taking care of business, usually with no more than a nod. Maintaining connections.

Something was moving in the shadows behind METRO HOLO-GRAFIX.

The door was a sheet of corrugated roofing. In front of it, Molly's hands flowed through an intricate sequence of jive that he couldn't follow. He caught the sign for *cash*, a thumb brushing the tip of the forefinger. The door swung inward and she led him into the smell of dust. They stood in a clearing, dense tangles of junk rising on either side to walls lined with shelves of crumbling paperbacks. The junk looked like something that had grown there, a fungus of twisted metal and plastic. He could pick out individual objects, but then they seemed to blur back into the mass: the guts of a television so old it was studded with the glass stumps of vacuum tubes, a crumpled dish antenna, a brown fiber canister stuffed with corroded lengths of alloy tubing. An enormous pile of old magazines had cascaded into the open area, flesh of lost summers staring blindly up as he followed her back through a narrow canyon of impacted scrap. He heard the door close behind them. He didn't look back.

The tunnel ended with an ancient army blanket tacked across a doorway. White light flooded out as Molly ducked past it.

Four square walls of blank white plastic, ceiling to match, floored with white hospital tile molded in a nonslip pattern of small raised disks. In the center stood a square, white-painted wooden table and four white folding chairs.

The man who stood blinking now in the doorway behind them, the blanket draping one shoulder like a cape, seemed to have been designed in a wind tunnel. His ears were very small, plastered flat against his narrow skull, and his large front teeth, revealed in something that wasn't quite a smile, were canted sharply backward. He wore an ancient tweed jacket and held a handgun of some kind in his left hand. He peered at them, blinked, and dropped the gun into a jacket pocket. He gestured to Case, pointed at a slab of white plastic that leaned near the doorway. Case crossed to it and saw that it was a solid sandwich of circuitry, nearly a centimeter thick. He helped the man lift it and position it in the doorway. Quick, nicotine-stained fingers secured it with a white Velcro border. A hidden exhaust fan began to purr.

"Time," the man said, straightening up, "and counting. You know the rate, Moll."

"We need a scan, Finn. For implants."

"So get over there between the pylons. Stand on the tape. Straighten up, yeah. Now turn around, gimme a full three-sixty." Case watched her rotate between two fragile-looking stands studded with sensors. The man took a small monitor from his pocket and squinted at it. "Something new in your head, yeah. Silicon, coat of pyrolitic carbons. A clock, right? Your glasses gimme the read they always have, low-temp isotropic carbons. Better biocompatibility with pyrolitics, but that's your business, right? Same with your claws."

"Get over here, Case." He saw a scuffed X in black on the white floor. "Turn around. Slow."

"Guy's a virgin." The man shrugged. "Some cheap dental work, is all."

"You read for biologicals?" Molly unzipped her green vest and took off the dark glasses.

"You think this is the Mayo? Climb on the table, kid, we'll run a little biopsy." He laughed, showing more of his yellow teeth. "Nah. Finn's word, sweetmeat, you got no little bugs, no cortex bombs. You want me to shut the screen down?"

"Just for as long as it takes you to leave, Finn. Then we'll want full screen for as long as we want it."

"Hey, that's fine by the Finn, Moll. You're only paying by the second."

They sealed the door behind him and Molly turned one of the white chairs around and sat on it, chin resting on crossed forearms. "We talk now. This is as private as I can afford."

"What about?"

"What we're doing."

"What are we doing?"

"Working for Armitage."

"And you're saying this isn't for his benefit?"

"Yeah. I saw your profile, Case. And I've seen the rest of our shopping list, once. You ever work with the dead?"

"No." He watched his reflection in her glasses. "I could, I guess. I'm good at what I do." The present tense made him nervous.

"You know that the Dixie Flatline's dead?"

He nodded. "Heart, I heard."

"You'll be working with his construct." She smiled. "Taught you the ropes, huh? Him and Quine. I know Quine, by the way. Real asshole."

"Somebody's got a recording of McCoy Pauley? Who?" Now Case sat, and rested his elbows on the table. "I can't see it. He'd never have sat still for it."

"Sense/Net. Paid him mega, you bet your ass."

"Quine dead too?"

"No such luck. He's in Europe. He doesn't come into this."

"Well, if we can get the Flatline, we're home free. He was the best. You know he died braindeath three times?"

She nodded.

"Flatlined on his EEG. Showed me tapes. 'Boy, I was *daid.*'"

"Look, Case, I been trying to suss out who it is is backing Armitage since I signed on. But it doesn't feel like a zaibatsu, a government, or some Yakuza subsidiary. Armitage gets orders. Like something tells him to go off to Chiba, pick up a pillhead who's making one last wobble through the burnout belt, and trade a program for the operation that'll fix him up. We coulda bought twenty world-class cowboys for what the market was ready to pay for that surgical program. You were good, but not *that* good. . . ." She scratched the side of her nose.

"Obviously makes sense to somebody," he said. "Somebody big."

"Don't let me hurt your feelings." She grinned. "We're gonna be pulling one hardcore run, Case, just to get the Flatline's construct. Sense/Net has it locked in a library vault uptown. Tighter than an eel's ass, Case. Now, Sense/Net, they got all their new material for the fall season locked in there too. Steal that and we'd be richer than shit. But no, we gotta get us the Flatline and nothing else. Weird."

"Yeah, it's all weird. You're weird, this hole's weird, and who's the weird little gopher outside in the hall?"

"Finn's an old connection of mine. Fence, mostly. Software. This privacy biz is a sideline. But I got Armitage to let him be our tech here, so when he shows up later, you never saw him. Got it?"

"So what's Armitage got dissolving inside you?"

"I'm an easy make." She smiled. "Anybody any good at what they do, that's what they *are*, right? You gotta jack, I gotta tussle."

He stared at her. "So tell me what you know about Armitage."

"For starters, nobody named Armitage took part in any Screaming Fist. I checked. But that doesn't mean much. He doesn't look like any of the pics of the guys who got out." She shrugged. "Big deal. And starters is all I got." She drummed her nails on the back of the chair. "But you *are* a cowboy, aren't you? I mean, maybe you could have a little look around." She smiled.

"He'd kill me."

"Maybe. Maybe not. I think he needs you, Case, and real bad. Besides, you're a clever john, no? You can winkle him, sure."

"What else is on that list you mentioned?"

"Toys. Mostly for you. And one certified psychopath name of Peter Riviera. Real ugly customer."

"Where's he?"

"Dunno. But he's one sick fuck, no lie. I saw his profile." She made a face. "Godawful." She stood up and stretched, catlike. "So we got an axis going, boy? We're together in this? Partners?"

Case looked at her. "I gotta lotta choice, huh?"

She laughed. "You got it, cowboy."

———————

"The matrix has its roots in primitive arcade games," said the voice-over, "in early graphics programs and military experimentation with cranial jacks." On the Sony, a two-dimensional space war faded behind a forest of mathematically generated ferns, demonstrating the spacial possibilities of logarithmic spirals; cold blue military footage burned through, lab animals wired into test systems, helmets feeding into fire control circuits of tanks and war planes. "Cyberspace. A consensual hallucination experienced daily by billions of legitimate operators, in every nation, by children being taught mathematical concepts . . . A graphic representation of data abstracted from the banks of every computer in the human system. Unthinkable complexity. Lines of light ranged in the non-space of the mind, clusters and constellations of data. Like city lights, receding. . . ."

"What's that?" Molly asked, as he flipped the channel selector.

"Kid's show." A discontinuous flood of images as the selector cycled. "Off," he said to the Hosaka.

"You want to try now, Case?"

Wednesday. A week from waking in Cheap Hotel with Molly beside him. "You want me to go out, Case? Maybe easier for you, alone. . . ." He shook his head.

"No. Stay, doesn't matter." He settled the black terry sweatband across his forehead, careful not to disturb the flat Sendai dermatrodes. He stared back at the deck on his lap, not really seeing it, seeing instead the shop window on Ninsei, the chromed shuriken burning with reflected neon. He glanced up; on the wall, just above the Sony, he'd hung her gift, tacking it there with a yellow-headed drawing pin through the hole at its center.

He closed his eyes.

Found the ridged face of the power stud.

And in the bloodlit dark behind his eyes, silver phosphenes boiling in from the edge of space, hypnagogic images jerking past like film compiled from random frames. Symbols, figures, faces, a blurred, fragmented mandala of visual information.

Please, he prayed, *now*—

A gray disk, the color of Chiba sky.

Now—

Disk beginning to rotate, faster, becoming a sphere of paler gray. Expanding—

And flowed, flowered for him, fluid neon origami trick, the unfolding of his distanceless home, his country, transparent 3-D chessboard extending to infinity. Inner eye opening to the stepped scarlet pyramid of the Eastern Seaboard Fission Authority burning beyond the green cubes of Mitsubishi Bank of America, and high and very far away he saw the spiral arms of military systems, forever beyond his reach.

And somewhere he was laughing, in a white-painted loft, distant fingers caressing the deck, tears of release streaking his face.

———

Molly was gone when he took the trodes off, and the loft was dark. He checked the time. He'd been in cyberspace for five hours. He carried the Ono-Sendai to one of the new worktables and collapsed across the bedslab, pulling Molly's black silk sleeping bag over his head.

The security package taped to the steel firedoor bleeped twice. "Entry requested," it said. "Subject is cleared per my program."

"So open it." Case pulled the silk from his face and sat up as the door opened, expecting to see Molly or Armitage.

"Christ," said a hoarse voice, "I know that bitch can see in the dark. . . ." A squat figure stepped in and closed the door. "Turn the lights on, okay?" Case scrambled off the slab and found the old-fashioned switch.

"I'm the Finn," said the Finn, and made a warning face at Case.

"Case."

"Pleased to meecha, I'm sure. I'm doing some hardware for your boss, it looks like." The Finn fished a pack of Partagas from a pocket and lit one. The smell of Cuban tobacco filled the room. He crossed to the worktable and glanced at the Ono-Sendai. "Looks stock. Soon

fix that. But here's your problem, kid." He took a filthy manila envelope from inside his jacket, flicked ash on the floor, and extracted a
featureless black rectangle from the envelope. "Goddam factory
prototypes," he said, tossing the thing down on the table. "Cast 'em
into a block of polycarbon, can't get in with a laser without frying
the works. Booby-trapped for x-ray, ultrascan, God knows what
else. We'll get in, but there's no rest for the wicked, right?" He folded
the envelope with great care and tucked it away in an inside pocket.

"What is it?"

"It's a flipflop switch, basically. Wire it into your Sendai here,
you can access live or recorded simstim without having to jack out
of the matrix."

"What for?"

"I haven't got a clue. Know I'm fitting Moll for a broadcast rig,
though, so it's probably her sensorium you'll access." The Finn
scratched his chin. "So now you get to find out just how tight those
jeans really are, huh?"

FOUR

Case sat in the loft with the dermatrodes strapped across his forehead, watching motes dance in the diluted sunlight that filtered through the grid overhead. A countdown was in progress in one corner of the monitor screen.

Cowboys didn't get into simstim, he thought, because it was basically a meat toy. He knew that the trodes he used and the little plastic tiara dangling from a simstim deck were basically the same, and that the cyberspace matrix was actually a drastic simplification of the human sensorium, at least in terms of presentation, but simstim itself struck him as a gratuitous multiplication of flesh input. The commercial stuff was edited, of course, so that if Tally Isham got a headache in the course of a segment, you didn't feel it.

The screen bleeped a two-second warning.

The new switch was patched into his Sendai with a thin ribbon of fiberoptics.

And one and two and—

Cyberspace slid into existence from the cardinal points. Smooth, he thought, but not smooth enough. Have to work on it. . . .

Then he keyed the new switch.

The abrupt jolt into other flesh. Matrix gone, a wave of sound and color. . . . She was moving through a crowded street, past stalls vending discount software, prices feltpenned on sheets of plastic, fragments of music from countless speakers. Smells of urine, free monomers, perfume, patties of frying krill. For a few frightened seconds he fought helplessly to control her body. Then he willed himself into passivity, became the passenger behind her eyes.

The glasses didn't seem to cut down the sunlight at all. He wondered if the built-in amps compensated automatically. Blue alphanumerics winked the time, low in her left peripheral field. Showing off, he thought.

Her body language was disorienting, her style foreign. She seemed continually on the verge of colliding with someone, but people melted out of her way, stepped sideways, made room.

"How you doing, Case?" He heard the words and felt her form them. She slid a hand into her jacket, a fingertip circling a nipple under warm silk. The sensation made him catch his breath. She laughed. But the link was one-way. He had no way to reply.

Two blocks later, she was threading the outskirts of Memory Lane. Case kept trying to jerk her eyes toward landmarks he would have used to find his way. He began to find the passivity of the situation irritating.

The transition to cyberspace, when he hit the switch, was instantaneous. He punched himself down a wall of primitive ice belonging to the New York Public Library, automatically counting potential windows. Keying back into her sensorium, into the sinuous flow of muscle, senses sharp and bright.

He found himself wondering about the mind he shared these sensations with. What did he know about her? That she was another professional; that she said her being, like his, was the thing she did to make a living. He knew the way she'd moved against him, earlier, when she woke, their mutual grunt of unity when he'd entered her, and that she liked her coffee black, afterward. . . .

Her destination was one of the dubious software rental complexes that lined Memory Lane. There was a stillness, a hush.

Booths lined a central hall. The clientele were young, few of them out of their teens. They all seemed to have carbon sockets planted behind the left ear, but she didn't focus on them. The counters that fronted the booths displayed hundreds of slivers of microsoft, angular fragments of colored silicon mounted under oblong transparent bubbles on squares of white cardboard. Molly went to the seventh booth along the south wall. Behind the counter a boy with a shaven head stared vacantly into space, a dozen spikes of microsoft protruding from the socket behind his ear.

"Larry, you in, man?" She positioned herself in front of him. The boy's eyes focused. He sat up in his chair and pried a bright magenta splinter from his socket with a dirty thumbnail.

"Hey, Larry."

"Molly." He nodded.

"I have some work for some of your friends, Larry."

Larry took a flat plastic case from the pocket of his red sportshirt and flicked it open, slotting the microsoft beside a dozen others. His hand hovered, selected a glossy black chip that was slightly longer than the rest, and inserted it smoothly into his head. His eyes narrowed.

"Molly's got a rider," he said, "and Larry doesn't like that."

"Hey," she said, "I didn't know you were so . . . sensitive. I'm impressed. Costs a lot, to get that sensitive."

"I know you, lady?" The blank look returned. "You looking to buy some softs?"

"I'm looking for the Moderns."

"You got a rider, Molly. This says." He tapped the black splinter. "Somebody else using your eyes."

"My partner."

"Tell your partner to go."

"Got something for the Panther Moderns, Larry."

"What are you talking about, lady?"

"Case, you take off," she said, and he hit the switch, instantly back in the matrix. Ghost impressions of the software complex hung for a few seconds in the buzzing calm of cyberspace.

"Panther Moderns," he said to the Hosaka, removing the trodes. "Five minute precis."

"Ready," the computer said.

It wasn't a name he knew. Something new, something that had come in since he'd been in Chiba. Fads swept the youth of the Sprawl at the speed of light; entire subcultures could rise overnight, thrive for a dozen weeks, and then vanish utterly. "Go," he said. The Hosaka had accessed its array of libraries, journals, and news services.

The precis began with a long hold on a color still that Case at first assumed was a collage of some kind, a boy's face snipped from another image and glued to a photograph of a paint-scrawled wall. Dark eyes, epicanthic folds obviously the result of surgery, an angry dusting of acne across pale narrow cheeks. The Hosaka released the freeze; the boy moved, flowing with the sinister grace of a mime pretending to be a jungle predator. His body was nearly invisible, an abstract pattern approximating the scribbled brickwork sliding smoothly across his tight onepiece. Mimetic polycarbon.

Cut to Dr. Virginia Rambali, Sociology, NYU, her name, faculty, and school pulsing across the screen in pink alphanumerics.

"Given their penchant for these random acts of surreal violence," someone said, "it may be difficult for our viewers to understand why you continue to insist that this phenomenon isn't a form of terrorism."

Dr. Rambali smiled. "There is always a point at which the terrorist ceases to manipulate the media gestalt. A point at which the violence may well escalate, but beyond which the terrorist has become symptomatic of the media gestalt itself. Terrorism as we ordinarily understand it is innately media-related. The Panther Moderns differ from other terrorists precisely in their degree of self-consciousness, in their awareness of the extent to which media divorce the act of terrorism from the original sociopolitical intent. . . ."

"Skip it," Case said.

———————

Case met his first Modern two days after he'd screened the Hosaka's precis. The Moderns, he'd decided, were a contemporary version of the Big Scientists of his own late teens. There was a kind of ghostly teenage DNA at work in the Sprawl, something that carried the coded precepts of various short-lived subcults and replicated them at odd intervals. The Panther Moderns were a softhead variant on the Scientists. If the technology had been available, the Big Scientists would all have had sockets stuffed with microsofts. It was the style that mattered and the style was the same. The Moderns were mercenaries, practical jokers, nihilistic technofetishists.

The one who showed up at the loft door with a box of diskettes from the Finn was a soft-voiced boy called Angelo. His face was a simple graft grown on collagen and shark-cartilage polysaccharides, smooth and hideous. It was one of the nastiest pieces of elective surgery Case had ever seen. When Angelo smiled, revealing the razor-sharp canines of some large animal, Case was actually relieved. Toothbud transplants. He'd seen that before.

"You can't let the little pricks generation-gap you," Molly said. Case nodded, absorbed in the patterns of the Sense/Net ice.

This was it. This was what he was, who he was, his being. He forgot to eat. Molly left cartons of rice and foam trays of sushi on the corner of the long table. Sometimes he resented having to leave the deck to use the chemical toilet they'd set up in a corner of the loft. Ice patterns formed and re-formed on the screen as he probed for gaps, skirted the most obvious traps, and mapped the route he'd take through Sense/Net's ice. It was good ice. Wonderful ice. Its patterns burned there while he lay with his arm under Molly's shoulders, watching the red dawn through the steel grid of the sky-light. Its rainbow pixel maze was the first thing he saw when he woke. He'd go straight to the deck, not bothering to dress, and jack in. He was cutting it. He was working. He lost track of days.

And sometimes, falling asleep, particularly when Molly was off on one of her reconnaissance trips with her rented cadre of Moderns, images of Chiba came flooding back. Faces and Ninsei neon. Once he woke from a confused dream of Linda Lee, unable to recall who she was or what she'd ever meant to him. When he did remember, he jacked in and worked for nine straight hours.

The cutting of Sense/Net's ice took a total of nine days.

"I said a week," Armitage said, unable to conceal his satisfaction when Case showed him his plan for the run. "You took your own good time."

"Balls," Case said, smiling at the screen. "That's good work, Armitage."

"Yes," Armitage admitted, "but don't let it go to your head. Compared to what you'll eventually be up against, this is an arcade toy."

<hr />

"Love you, Cat Mother," whispered the Panther Modern's link man. His voice was modulated static in Case's headset. "Atlanta, Brood. Looks go. Go, got it?" Molly's voice was slightly clearer.

"To hear is to obey." The Moderns were using some kind of chickenwire dish in New Jersey to bounce the link man's scrambled signal off a Sons of Christ the King satellite in geosynchronous orbit above Manhattan. They chose to regard the entire operation as an elaborate private joke, and their choice of comsats seemed to have been deliberate. Molly's signals were being beamed up from a one-meter umbrella dish epoxied to the roof of a black glass bank tower nearly as tall as the Sense/Net building.

Atlanta. The recognition code was simple. Atlanta to Boston to

Chicago to Denver, five minutes for each city. If anyone managed to intercept Molly's signal, unscramble it, synth her voice, the code would tip the Moderns. If she remained in the building for more than twenty minutes, it was highly unlikely she'd be coming out at all.

Case gulped the last of his coffee, settled the trodes in place, and scratched his chest beneath his black T-shirt. He had only a vague idea of what the Panther Moderns planned as a diversion for the Sense/Net security people. His job was to make sure the intrusion program he'd written would link with the Sense/Net systems when Molly needed it to. He watched the countdown in the corner of the screen. Two. One.

He jacked in and triggered his program. "Mainline," breathed the link man, his voice the only sound as Case plunged through the glowing strata of Sense/Net ice. Good. Check Molly. He hit the simstim and flipped into her sensorium.

The scrambler blurred the visual input slightly. She stood before a wall of gold-flecked mirror in the building's vast white lobby, chewing gum, apparently fascinated by her own reflection. Aside from the huge pair of sunglasses concealing her mirrored insets, she managed to look remarkably like she belonged there, another tourist girl hoping for a glimpse of Tally Isham. She wore a pink plastic raincoat, a white mesh top, loose white pants cut in a style that had been fashionable in Tokyo the previous year. She grinned vacantly and popped her gum. Case felt like laughing. He could feel the micropore tape across her rib cage, feel the flat little units under it: the radio, the simstim unit, and the scrambler. The throat mike, glued to her neck, looked as much as possible like an analgesic dermadisk. Her hands, in the pockets of the pink coat, were flexing systematically through a series of tension-release exercises. It took him a few seconds to realize that the peculiar sensation at the tips of her fingers was caused by the blades as they were partially extruded, then retracted.

He flipped back. His program had reached the fifth gate. He watched as his icebreaker strobed and shifted in front of him, only faintly aware of his hands playing across the deck, making minor adjustments. Translucent planes of color shuffled like a trick deck. Take a card, he thought, any card.

The gate blurred past. He laughed. The Sense/Net ice had accepted his entry as a routine transfer from the consortium's Los Angeles complex. He was inside. Behind him, viral subprograms peeled off, meshing with the gate's code fabric, ready to deflect the real Los Angeles data when it arrived.

He flipped again. Molly was strolling past the enormous circular reception desk at the rear of the lobby.

12:01:20 as the readout flared in her optic nerve.

———

At midnight, synched with the chip behind Molly's eye, the link man in Jersey had given his command. "Mainline." Nine Moderns, scattered along two hundred miles of the Sprawl, had simultaneously dialed MAX EMERG from pay phones. Each Modern delivered a short set speech, hung up, and drifted out into the night, peeling off surgical gloves. Nine different police departments and public security agencies were absorbing the information that an obscure subsect of militant Christian fundamentalists had just taken credit for having introduced clinical levels of an outlawed psychoactive agent known as Blue Nine into the ventilation system of the Sense/Net Pyramid. Blue Nine, known in California as Grievous Angel, had been shown to produce acute paranoia and homicidal psychosis in eighty-five percent of experimental subjects.

———————

Case hit the switch as his program surged through the gates of the subsystem that controlled security for the Sense/Net research library. He found himself stepping into an elevator.

"Excuse me, but are you an employee?" The guard raised his eyebrows. Molly popped her gum. "No," she said, driving the first two knuckles of her right hand into the man's solar plexus. As he doubled over, clawing for the beeper on his belt, she slammed his head sideways, against the wall of the elevator.

Chewing a little more rapidly now, she touched CLOSE DOOR and STOP on the illuminated panel. She took a blackbox from her coat pocket and inserted a lead in the keyhole of the lock that secured the panel's circuitry.

———————

The Panther Moderns allowed four minutes for their first move to take effect, then injected a second carefully prepared dose of misinformation. This time, they shot it directly into the Sense/Net building's internal video system.

At 12:04:03, every screen in the building strobed for eighteen seconds in a frequency that produced seizures in a susceptible segment of Sense/Net employees. Then something only vaguely like a human face filled the screens, its features stretched across asymmetrical expanses of bone like some obscene Mercator projection. Blue lips parted wetly as the twisted, elongated jaw moved. Something, perhaps a hand, a thing like a reddish clump of gnarled roots, fumbled toward the camera, blurred, and vanished. Subliminally rapid images of contamination: graphics of the building's water supply system, gloved hands manipulating laboratory glassware, something tumbling down into darkness, a pale splash. . . . The audio track, its pitch adjusted to run at just less than twice the standard playback speed, was part of a month-old newscast detailing potential military uses of a substance known as HsG, a biochemical governing the human skeletal growth factor. Overdoses of HsG threw certain bone cells into overdrive, accelerating growth by factors as high as one thousand percent.

At 12:05:00, the mirror-sheathed nexus of the Sense/Net consortium held just over three thousand employees. At five minutes after midnight, as the Moderns' message ended in a flare of white screen, the Sense/Net Pyramid screamed.

Half a dozen NYPD Tactical hovercraft, responding to the possibility of Blue Nine in the building's ventilation system, were converging on the Sense/Net Pyramid. They were running full riot lights. A BAMA Rapid Deployment helicopter was lifting off from its pad on Riker's.

Case triggered his second program. A carefully engineered virus attacked the code fabric screening primary custodial commands for the subbasement that housed the Sense/Net research materials. "Boston," Molly's voice came across the link, "I'm downstairs." Case switched and saw the blank wall of the elevator. She was unzipping the white pants. A bulky packet, exactly the shade of her pale ankle, was secured there with micropore. She knelt and peeled the tape away. Streaks of burgundy flickered across the mimetic polycarbon as she unfolded the Modern suit. She removed the pink raincoat, threw it down beside the white pants, and began to pull the suit on over the white mesh top.

12:06:26.

Case's virus had bored a window through the library's command ice. He punched himself through and found an infinite blue space ranged with color-coded spheres strung on a tight grid of pale blue neon. In the nonspace of the matrix, the interior of a given data construct possessed unlimited subjective dimension; a child's toy calculator, accessed through Case's Sendai, would have presented limitless gulfs of nothingness hung with a few basic commands. Case began to key the sequence the Finn had purchased from a mid-echelon sarariman with severe drug problems. He began to glide through the spheres as if he were on invisible tracks.

Here. This one.

Punching his way into the sphere, chill blue neon vault above him starless and smooth as frosted glass, he triggered a subprogram that effected certain alterations in the core custodial commands.

Out now. Reversing smoothly, the virus reknitting the fabric of the window.

Done.

———

In the Sense/Net lobby, two Panther Moderns sat alertly behind a low rectangular planter, taping the riot with a video camera. They both wore chameleon suits. "Tacticals are spraying foam barricades now," one noted, speaking for the benefit of his throat mike. "Rapids are still trying to land their copter."

———

Case hit the simstim switch. And flipped into the agony of broken bone. Molly was braced against the blank gray wall of a long corridor, her breath coming ragged and uneven. Case was back in the matrix instantly, a white-hot line of pain fading in his left thigh.

"What's happening, Brood?" he asked the link man.

"I dunno, Cutter. Mother's not talking. Wait."

Case's program was cycling. A single hair-fine thread of crimson neon extended from the center of the restored window to the shifting outline of his icebreaker. He didn't have time to wait. Taking a deep breath, he flipped again.

Molly took a single step, trying to support her weight on the corridor wall. In the loft, Case groaned. The second step took her over an outstretched arm. Uniform sleeve bright with fresh blood. Glimpse of a shattered fiberglass shockstave. Her vision seemed to have narrowed to a tunnel. With the third step, Case screamed and found himself back in the matrix.

"Brood? Boston, baby . . ." Her voice tight with pain. She coughed. "Little problem with the natives. Think one of them broke my leg."

"What you need now, Cat Mother?" The link man's voice was indistinct, nearly lost behind static.

Case forced himself to flip back. She was leaning against the wall, taking all of her weight on her right leg. She fumbled through the contents of the suit's kangaroo pocket and withdrew a sheet of plastic studded with a rainbow of dermadisks. She selected three and thumbed them hard against her left wrist, over the veins. Six thousand micrograms of endorphin analog came down on the pain like a hammer, shattering it. Her back arched convulsively. Pink waves of warmth lapped up her thighs. She sighed and slowly relaxed.

"Okay, Brood. Okay now. But I'll need a medical team when I come out. Tell my people. Cutter, I'm two minutes from target. Can you hold?"

"Tell her I'm in and holding," Case said.

Molly began to limp down the corridor. When she glanced back, once, Case saw the crumpled bodies of three Sense/Net security guards. One of them seemed to have no eyes.

"Tacticals and Rapids have sealed the ground floor, Cat Mother. Foam barricades. Lobby's getting juicy."

"Pretty juicy down here," she said, swinging herself through a pair of gray steel doors. "Almost there, Cutter."

Case flipped into the matrix and pulled the trodes from his

forehead. He was drenched with sweat. He wiped his forehead with a towel, took a quick sip of water from the bicycle bottle beside the Hosaka, and checked the map of the library displayed on the screen. A pulsing red cursor crept through the outline of a doorway. Only millimeters from the green dot that indicated the location of the Dixie Flatline's construct. He wondered what it was doing to her leg, to walk on it that way. With enough endorphin analog, she could walk on a pair of bloody stumps. He tightened the nylon harness that held him in the chair and replaced the trodes.

Routine now: trodes, jack, and flip.

The Sense/Net research library was a dead storage area; the materials stored here had to be physically removed before they could be interfaced. Molly hobbled between rows of identical gray lockers.

"Tell her five more and ten to her left, Brood," Case said.

"Five more and ten left, Cat Mother," the link man said.

She took the left. A white-faced librarian cowered between two lockers, her cheeks wet, eyes blank. Molly ignored her. Case wondered what the Moderns had done to provoke that level of terror. He knew it had something to do with a hoaxed threat, but he'd been too involved with his ice to follow Molly's explanation.

"That's it," Case said, but she'd already stopped in front of the cabinet that held the construct. Its lines reminded Case of the Neo-Aztec bookcases in Julie Deane's anteroom in Chiba.

"Do it, Cutter," Molly said.

Case flipped to cyberspace and sent a command pulsing down the crimson thread that pierced the library ice. Five separate alarm systems were convinced that they were still operative. The three elaborate locks deactivated, but considered themselves to have remained locked. The library's central bank suffered a minute shift in its permanent memory: the construct had been removed, per executive order, a month before. Checking for the authorization to remove the construct, a librarian would find the records erased.

The door swung open on silent hinges.

"0467839," Case said, and Molly drew a black storage unit from the rack. It resembled the magazine of a large assault rifle, its surfaces covered with warning decals and security ratings.

Molly closed the locker door; Case flipped.

He withdrew the line through the library ice. It whipped back into his program, automatically triggering a full system reversal. The Sense/Net gates snapped past him as he backed out, subprograms whirling back into the core of the icebreaker as he passed the gates where they had been stationed.

"Out, Brood," he said, and slumped in his chair. After the concentration of an actual run, he could remain jacked in and still retain awareness of his body. It might take Sense/Net days to discover the theft of the construct. The key would be the deflection of the Los Angeles transfer, which coincided too neatly with the Modern's terror run. He doubted that the three security men Molly had encountered in the corridor would live to talk about it. He flipped.

The elevator, with Molly's blackbox taped beside the control panel, remained where she'd left it. The guard still lay curled on the floor. Case noticed the derm on his neck for the first time. Something of Molly's, to keep him under. She stepped over him and removed the blackbox before punching LOBBY.

As the elevator door hissed open, a woman hurtled backward out of the crowd, into the elevator, and struck the rear wall with her head. Molly ignored her, bending over to peel the derm from the guard's neck. Then she kicked the white pants and the pink raincoat out the door, tossing the dark glasses after them, and drew the hood of her suit down across her forehead. The construct, in the suit's kangaroo pocket, dug into her sternum when she moved. She stepped out.

Case had seen panic before, but never in an enclosed area.

The Sense/Net employees, spilling out of the elevators, had surged for the street doors, only to meet the foam barricades of the Tacticals and the sandbag-guns of the BAMA Rapids. The two agencies, convinced that they were containing a horde of potential killers, were cooperating with an uncharacteristic degree of efficiency. Beyond the shattered wreckage of the main street doors, bodies were piled three deep on the barricades. The hollow thumping of the riot guns provided a constant background for the sound the crowd made as it surged back and forth across the lobby's marble floor. Case had never heard anything like that sound.

Neither, apparently, had Molly. "Jesus," she said, and hesitated. It was a sort of keening, rising into a bubbling wail of raw and total fear. The lobby floor was covered with bodies, clothing, blood, and long trampled scrolls of yellow printout.

"C'mon, sister. We're for out." The eyes of the two Moderns stared out of madly swirling shades of polycarbon, their suits unable to keep up with the confusion of shape and color that raged behind them. "You hurt? C'mon. Tommy'll walk you." Tommy handed something to the one who spoke, a video camera wrapped in polycarbon.

"Chicago," she said, "I'm on my way." And then she was falling, not to the marble floor, slick with blood and vomit, but down some bloodwarm well, into silence and the dark.

———

The Panther Modern leader, who introduced himself as Lupus Yonderboy, wore a polycarbon suit with a recording feature that allowed him to replay backgrounds at will. Perched on the edge of Case's worktable like some kind of state-of-the-art gargoyle, he regarded Case and Armitage with hooded eyes. He smiled. His hair was pink. A rainbow forest of microsofts bristled behind his left ear;

the ear was pointed, tufted with more pink hair. His pupils had been modified to catch the light like a cat's. Case watched the suit crawl with color and texture.

"You let it get out of control," Armitage said. He stood in the center of the loft like a statue, wrapped in the dark glossy folds of an expensive-looking trenchcoat.

"Chaos, Mr. Who," Lupus Yonderboy said. "That is our mode and modus. That is our central kick. Your woman knows. We deal with her. Not with you, Mr. Who." His suit had taken on a weird angular pattern of beige and pale avocado. "She needed her medical team. She's with them. We'll watch out for her. Everything's fine." He smiled again.

"Pay him," Case said.

Armitage glared at him. "We don't have the goods."

"Your woman has it," Yonderboy said.

"Pay him."

Armitage crossed stiffly to the table and took three fat bundles of New Yen from the pockets of his trenchcoat. "You want to count it?" he asked Yonderboy.

"No," the Panther Modern said. "You'll pay. You're a Mr. Who. You pay to stay one. Not a Mr. Name."

"I hope that isn't a threat," Armitage said.

"That's business," said Yonderboy, stuffing the money into the single pocket on the front of his suit.

The phone rang. Case answered.

"Molly," he told Armitage, handing him the phone.

———

The Sprawl's geodesics were lightening into predawn gray as Case left the building. His limbs felt cold and disconnected. He couldn't sleep. He was sick of the loft. Lupus had gone, then Armitage, and Molly was in surgery somewhere. Vibration beneath his feet as a train hissed past. Sirens dopplered in the distance.

He took corners at random, his collar up, hunched in a new leather jacket, flicking the first of a chain of Yeheyuans into the gutter and lighting another. He tried to imagine Armitage's toxin sacs dissolving in his bloodstream, microscopic membranes wearing thinner as he walked. It didn't seem real. Neither did the fear and agony he'd seen through Molly's eyes in the lobby of Sense/Net. He found himself trying to remember the faces of the three people he'd killed in Chiba. The men were blanks; the woman reminded him of Linda Lee. A battered tricycle-truck with mirrored windows bounced past him, empty plastic cylinders rattling in its bed.

"Case."

He darted sideways, instinctively getting a wall behind his back.

"Message for you, Case." Lupus Yonderboy's suit cycled through pure primaries. "Pardon. Not to startle you."

Case straightened up, hands in jacket pockets. He was a head taller than the Modern. "You oughta be careful, Yonderboy."

"This is the message. Wintermute." He spelled it out.

"From you?" Case took a step forward.

"No," Yonderboy said. "For you."

"Who from?"

"Wintermute," Yonderboy repeated, nodding, bobbing his crest of pink hair. His suit went matte black, a carbon shadow against old concrete. He executed a strange little dance, his thin black arms whirling, and then he was gone. No. There. Hood up to hide the pink, the suit exactly the right shade of gray, mottled and stained as the sidewalk he stood on. The eyes winked back the red of a stoplight. And then he was really gone.

Case closed his eyes, massaged them with numb fingers, leaning back against peeling brickwork.

Ninsei had been a lot simpler.

FIVE

The medical team Molly employed occupied two floors of an anonymous condo-rack near the old hub of Baltimore. The building was modular, like some giant version of Cheap Hotel, each coffin forty meters long. Case met Molly as she emerged from one that wore the elaborately worked logo of one GERALD CHIN, DENTIST. She was limping.

"He says if I kick anything, it'll fall off."

"I ran into one of your pals," he said, "a Modern."

"Yeah? Which one?"

"Lupus Yonderboy. Had a message." He passed her a paper napkin with W I N T E R M U T E printed in red feltpen in his neat, laborious capitals. "He said—" But her hand came up in the jive for silence.

"Get us some crab," she said.

———————

After lunch in Baltimore, Molly dissecting her crab with alarming ease, they tubed into New York. Case had learned not to ask questions; they only brought the sign for silence. Her leg seemed to be bothering her, and she seldom spoke.

A thin black child with wooden beads and antique resistors woven tightly into her hair opened the Finn's door and led them along the tunnel of refuse. Case felt the stuff had grown somehow during their absence. Or else it seemed that it was changing subtly, cooking itself down under the pressure of time, silent invisible flakes settling to form a mulch, a crystalline essence of discarded technology, flowering secretly in the Sprawl's waste places.

Beyond the army blanket, the Finn waited at the white table.

Molly began to sign rapidly, produced a scrap of paper, wrote something on it, and passed it to the Finn. He took it between thumb and forefinger, holding it away from his body as though it might explode. He made a sign Case didn't know, one that conveyed a mixture of impatience and glum resignation. He stood up, brushing crumbs from the front of his battered tweed jacket. A glass jar of pickled herring stood on the table beside a torn plastic package of flatbread and a tin ashtray piled with the butts of Partagas.

"Wait," the Finn said, and left the room.

Molly took his place, extruded the blade from her index finger, and speared a grayish slab of herring. Case wandered aimlessly around the room, fingering the scanning gear on the pylons as he passed.

Ten minutes and the Finn came bustling back, showing his teeth in a wide yellow smile. He nodded, gave Molly a thumbs-up salute, and gestured to Case to help him with the door panel. While Case smoothed the Velcro border into place, the Finn took a flat little console from his pocket and punched out an elaborate sequence.

"Honey," he said to Molly, tucking the console away, "you have got it. No shit, I can smell it. You wanna tell me where you got it?"

"Yonderboy," Molly said, shoving the herring and crackers aside. "I did a deal with Larry, on the side."

"Smart," the Finn said. "It's an AI."

"Slow it down a little," Case said.

"Berne," the Finn said, ignoring him. "Berne. It's got limited Swiss citizenship under their equivalent of the Act of '53. Built for

Tessier-Ashpool S.A. They own the mainframe and the original software."

"What's in Berne, okay?" Case deliberately stepped between them.

"Wintermute is the recognition code for an AI. I've got the Turing Registry numbers. Artificial intelligence."

"That's all just fine," Molly said, "but where's it get us?"

"If Yonderboy's right," the Finn said, "this AI is backing Armitage."

"I paid Larry to have the Moderns nose around Armitage a little," Molly explained, turning to Case. "They have some very weird lines of communication. Deal was, they'd get my money if they answered one question: who's running Armitage?"

"And you think it's this AI? Those things aren't allowed any autonomy. It'll be the parent corporation, this Tessle . . ."

"Tessier-Ashpool S.A.," said the Finn. "And I got a little story for you about them. Wanna hear?" He sat down and hunched forward.

"Finn," Molly said. "He loves a story."

"Haven't ever told anybody this one," the Finn began.

The Finn was a fence, a trafficker in stolen goods, primarily in software. In the course of his business, he sometimes came into contact with other fences, some of whom dealt in the more traditional articles of the trade. In precious metals, stamps, rare coins, gems, jewelry, furs, and paintings and other works of art. The story he told Case and Molly began with another man's story, a man he called Smith.

Smith was also a fence, but in balmier seasons he surfaced as an art dealer. He was the first person the Finn had known who'd "gone silicon"—the phrase had an old-fashioned ring for Case—and the microsofts he purchased were art history programs and tables of gallery sales. With half a dozen chips in his new socket, Smith's knowledge of the art business was formidable, at least by the standards of his colleagues. But Smith had come to the Finn with a request for help, a fraternal request, one businessman to another. He wanted a go-to on the Tessier-Ashpool clan, he said, and it had to be executed in a way that would guarantee the impossibility of the subject ever tracing the inquiry to its source. It might be possible, the Finn had opined, but an explanation was definitely required. "It smelled," the Finn said to Case, "smelled of money. And Smith was being very careful. Almost too careful."

Smith, it developed, had had a supplier known as Jimmy. Jimmy was a burglar and other things as well, and just back from a year in high orbit, having carried certain things back down the gravity well. The most unusual thing Jimmy had managed to score on his swing through the archipelago was a head, an intricately worked bust, cloisonné over platinum, studded with seedpearls and lapis. Smith, sighing, had put down his pocket microscope and advised Jimmy to melt the thing down. It was contemporary, not an antique, and had no value to the collector. Jimmy laughed. The thing was a computer terminal, he said. It could talk. And not in a synth-voice, but with a beautiful arrangement of gears and miniature organ pipes. It was a baroque thing for anyone to have constructed, a perverse thing, because synth-voice chips cost next to nothing. It was a curiosity. Smith jacked the head into his computer and listened as the melodious, inhuman voice piped the figures of last year's tax return.

Smith's clientele included a Tokyo billionaire whose passion for clockwork automata approached fetishism. Smith shrugged, showing Jimmy his upturned palms in a gesture old as pawn shops. He could try, he said, but he doubted he could get much for it.

When Jimmy had gone, leaving the head, Smith went over it carefully, discovering certain hallmarks. Eventually he'd been able to trace it to an unlikely collaboration between two Zurich artisans, an enamel specialist in Paris, a Dutch jeweler, and a California chip designer. It had been commissioned, he discovered, by Tessier-Ashpool S.A.

Smith began to make preliminary passes at the Tokyo collector, hinting that he was on the track of something noteworthy.

And then he had a visitor, a visitor unannounced, one who walked in through the elaborate maze of Smith's security as though it didn't exist. A small man, Japanese, enormously polite, who bore all the marks of a vatgrown ninja assassin. Smith sat very still, staring into the calm brown eyes of death across a polished table of Vietnamese rosewood. Gently, almost apologetically, the cloned killer explained that it was his duty to find and return a certain artwork, a mechanism of great beauty, which had been taken from the house of his master. It had come to his attention, the ninja said, that Smith might know of the whereabouts of this object.

Smith told the man that he had no wish to die, and produced the head. And how much, his visitor asked, did you expect to obtain through the sale of this object? Smith named a figure far lower than the price he'd intended to set. The ninja produced a credit chip and keyed Smith that amount out of a numbered Swiss account. And who, the man asked, brought you this piece? Smith told him. Within days, Smith learned of Jimmy's death.

"So that was where I came in," the Finn continued. "Smith knew I dealt a lot with the Memory Lane crowd, and that's where you go for a quiet go-to that'll never be traced. I hired a cowboy. I was the cut-out, so I took a percentage. Smith, he was careful. He'd just had a very weird business experience and he'd come out on top, but it didn't add up. Who'd paid, out of that Swiss stash? Yakuza? No way. They got a very rigid code covers situations like that, and they kill the receiver too, always. Was it spook stuff? Smith didn't think so. Spook biz has a vibe, you get so you can smell it. Well, I had my cowboy buzz the news morgues until we found Tessier-Ashpool in litigation. The case wasn't anything, but we got the law firm. Then he did the lawyer's ice and we got the family address. Lotta good it did us."

Case raised his eyebrows.

"Freeside," the Finn said. "The spindle. Turns out they own damn near the whole thing. The interesting stuff was the picture we got when the cowboy ran a regular go-to on the news morgues and compiled a precis. Family organization. Corporate structure. Supposedly you can buy into an S.A., but there hasn't been a share of Tessier-Ashpool traded on the open market in over a hundred years. On any market, as far as I know. You're looking at a very quiet, very eccentric first-generation high-orbit family, run like a corporation. Big money, very shy of media. Lot of cloning. Orbital law's a lot softer on genetic engineering, right? And it's hard to keep track of which generation, or combination of generations, is running the show at a given time."

"How's that?" Molly asked.

"Got their own cryogenic setup. Even under orbital law, you're legally dead for the duration of a freeze. Looks like they trade off, though nobody's seen the founding father in about thirty years. Founding momma, she died in some lab accident. . . ."

"So what happened with your fence?"

"Nothing." The Finn frowned. "Dropped it. We had a look at this fantastic tangle of powers of attorney the T-A's have, and that was it. Jimmy must've gotten into Straylight, lifted the head, and Tessier-Ashpool sent their ninja after it. Smith decided to forget about it. Maybe he was smart." He looked at Molly. "The Villa Straylight. Tip of the spindle. Strictly private."

"You figure they own that ninja, Finn?" Molly asked.

"Smith thought so."

"Expensive," she said. "Wonder whatever happened to that little ninja, Finn?"

"Probably got him on ice. Thaw when needed."

"Okay," Case said, "we got Armitage getting his goodies off an AI named Wintermute. Where's that get us?"

"Nowhere yet," Molly said, "but you got a little side gig now." She drew a folded scrap of paper from her pocket and handed it to him. He opened it. Grid coordinates and entry codes.

"Who's this?"

"Armitage. Some database of his. Bought it from the Moderns. Separate deal. Where is it?"

"London," Case said.

"Crack it." She laughed. "Earn your keep for a change."

———————

Case waited for a trans-BAMA local on the crowded platform. Molly had gone back to the loft hours ago, the Flatline's construct in her green bag, and Case had been drinking steadily ever since.

It was disturbing to think of the Flatline as a construct, a hard-wired ROM cassette replicating a dead man's skills, obsessions, knee-jerk responses. . . . The local came booming in along the black induction strip, fine grit sifting from cracks in the tunnel's ceiling. Case shuffled into the nearest door and watched the other passengers as he rode. A pair of predatory-looking Christian Scientists were edging toward a trio of young office techs who wore idealized holographic vaginas on their wrists, wet pink glittering under the harsh lighting. The techs licked their perfect lips nervously and eyed the Christian Scientists from beneath lowered metallic lids. The girls looked like tall, exotic grazing animals, swaying grace-fully and unconsciously with the movement of the train, their high heels like polished hooves against the gray metal of the car's floor.

Before they could stampede, take flight from the missionaries, the train reached Case's station.

He stepped out and caught sight of a white holographic cigar suspended against the wall of the station, FREESIDE pulsing beneath it in contorted capitals that mimicked printed Japanese. He walked through the crowd and stood beneath it, studying the thing. WHY WAIT? pulsed the sign. A blunt white spindle, flanged and studded with grids and radiators, docks, domes. He'd seen the ad, or others like it, thousands of times. It had never appealed to him. With his deck, he could reach the Freeside banks as easily as he could reach Atlanta. Travel was a neat thing. But now he noticed the little sigil, the size of a small coin, woven into the lower left corner of the ad's fabric of light: T-A.

He walked back to the loft, lost in memories of the Flatline. He'd spent most of his nineteenth summer in the Gentleman Loser, nursing expensive beers and watching the cowboys. He'd never touched a deck, then, but he knew what he wanted. There were at least twenty other hopefuls ghosting the Loser, that summer, each one bent on working joeboy for some cowboy. No other way to learn.

They'd all heard of Pauley, the redneck jockey from the 'Lanta fringes, who'd survived braindeath behind black ice. The grapevine—slender, street level, and the only one going—had little to say about Pauley, other than that he'd done the impossible. "It was big," another would-be told Case, for the price of a beer, "but who knows what? I hear maybe a Brazilian payroll net. Anyway, the man was dead, flat down braindeath." Case stared across the crowded bar at a thickset man in shirt-sleeves, something leaden about the shade of his skin.

"Boy," the Flatline would tell him, months later in Miami, "I'm like them huge fuckin' lizards, you know? Had themselves two goddam brains, one in the head an' one by the tailbone, kept the hind legs movin'. Hit that black stuff and ol' tailbrain jus' kept right on keepin' on."

The cowboy elite in the Loser shunned Pauley out of some strange group anxiety, almost a superstition. McCoy Pauley, Lazarus of cyberspace. . . .

And his heart had done for him in the end. His surplus Russian heart, implanted in a POW camp during the war. He'd refused to replace the thing, saying he needed its particular beat to maintain his sense of timing. Case fingered the slip of paper Molly had given him and made his way up the stairs.

Molly was snoring on the temperfoam. A transparent cast ran from her knee to a few millimeters below her crotch, the skin beneath the rigid micropore mottled with bruises, the black shading into ugly yellow. Eight derms, each a different size and color, ran in a neat line down her left wrist. An Akai transdermal unit lay beside her, its fine red leads connected to input trodes under the cast.

He turned on the tensor beside the Hosaka. The crisp circle of light fell directly on the Flatline's construct. He slotted some ice, connected the construct, and jacked in.

It was exactly the sensation of someone reading over his shoulder.

He coughed. "Dix? McCoy? That you, man?" His throat was tight.

"Hey, bro," said a directionless voice.

"It's Case, man. Remember?"

"Miami, joeboy, quick study."

"What's the last thing you remember before I spoke to you, Dix?"

"Nothin'."

"Hang on." He disconnected the construct. The presence was gone. He reconnected it. "Dix? Who am I?"

"You got me hung, Jack. Who the fuck are you?"

"Ca—your buddy. Partner. What's happening, man?"

"Good question."

"Remember being here, a second ago?"

"No."

"Know how a ROM personality matrix works?"

"Sure, bro, it's a firmware construct."

"So I jack it into the bank I'm using, I can give it sequential, real-time memory?"

"Guess so," said the construct.

"Okay, Dix. You *are* a ROM construct. Got me?"

"If you say so," said the construct. "Who are you?"

"Case."

"Miami," said the voice, "joeboy, quick study."

"Right. And for starts, Dix, you and me, we're gonna sleaze over to London grid and access a little data. You game for that?"

"You gonna tell me I got a choice, boy?"

SIX

"You want you a paradise," the Flatline advised, when Case had explained his situation. "Check Copenhagen, fringes of the university section." The voice recited coordinates as he punched.

They found their paradise, a "pirate's paradise," on the jumbled border of a low-security academic grid. At first glance it resembled the kind of graffiti student operators sometimes left at the junctions of grid lines, faint glyphs of colored light that shimmered against the confused outlines of a dozen arts faculties.

"There," said the Flatline, "the blue one. Make it out? That's an entry code for Bell Europa. Fresh, too. Bell'll get in here soon and read the whole damn board, change any codes they find posted. Kids'll steal the new ones tomorrow."

Case tapped his way into Bell Europa and switched to a standard phone code. With the Flatline's help, he connected with the London database that Molly claimed was Armitage's.

"Here," said the voice, "I'll do it for you." The Flatline began to chant a series of digits, Case keying them on his deck, trying to catch the pauses the construct used to indicate timing. It took three tries.

"Big deal," said the Flatline. "No ice at all."

"Scan this shit," Case told the Hosaka. "Sift for owner's personal history."

The neuroelectronic scrawls of the paradise vanished, replaced by a simple lozenge of white light. "Contents are primarily video recordings of postwar military trials," said the distant voice of the Hosaka. "Central figure is Colonel Willis Corto."

"Show it already," Case said.

A man's face filled the screen. The eyes were Armitage's.

Two hours later, Case fell beside Molly on the slab and let the temper-foam mold itself against him.

"You find anything?" she asked, her voice fuzzy with sleep and drugs.

"Tell you later," he said, "I'm wrecked." He was hungover and confused. He lay there, eyes closed, and tried to sort the various parts of a story about a man called Corto. The Hosaka had sorted a thin store of data and assembled a precis, but it was full of gaps. Some of the material had been print records, reeling smoothly down the screen, too quickly, and Case had had to ask the computer to read them for him. Other segments were audio recordings of the Screaming Fist hearing.

Willis Corto, Colonel, had plummeted through a blind spot in the Russian defenses over Kirensk. The shuttles had created the hole with pulse bombs, and Corto's team had dropped in in Night-wing microlights, their wings snapping taut in moonlight, reflected in jags of silver along the rivers Angara and Podhamennaya, the last light Corto would see for fifteen months. Case tried to imagine the microlights blossoming out of their launch capsules, high above a frozen steppe.

"They sure as hell did shaft you, boss," Case said, and Molly stirred beside him.

The microlights had been unarmed, stripped to compensate for the weight of a console operator, a prototype deck, and a virus pro-

gram called Mole IX, the first true virus in the history of cybernet-
ics. Corto and his team had been training for the run for three years.
They were through the ice, ready to inject Mole IX, when the emps
went off. The Russian pulse guns threw the jockeys into electronic
darkness; the Nightwings suffered systems crash, flight circuitry
wiped clean.

Then the lasers opened up, aiming on infrared, taking out the
fragile, radar-transparent assault planes, and Corto and his dead
console man fell out of a Siberian sky. Fell and kept falling. . . .

There were gaps in the story, here, where Case scanned docu-
ments concerning the flight of a commandeered Russian gunship
that managed to reach Finland. To be gutted, as it landed in a spruce
grove, by an antique twenty-millimeter cannon manned by a cadre
of reservists on dawn alert. Screaming Fist had ended for Corto on
the outskirts of Helsinki, with Finnish paramedics sawing him out
of the twisted belly of the helicopter. The war ended nine days later,
and Corto was shipped to a military facility in Utah, blind, legless,
and missing most of his jaw. It took eleven months for the Congressional aide to find him there. He listened to the sound of tubes
draining. In Washington and McLean, the show trials were already
under way. The Pentagon and the CIA were being Balkanized, partially dismantled, and a Congressional investigation had focused on
Screaming Fist. Ripe for watergating, the aide told Corto.

He'd need eyes, legs, and extensive cosmetic work, the aide said,
but that could be arranged. New plumbing, the man added, squeez-
ing Corto's shoulder through the sweat-damp sheet.

Corto heard the soft, relentless dripping. He said he preferred to
testify as he was.

No, the aide explained, the trials were being televised. The
trials needed to reach the voter. The aide coughed politely.

Repaired, refurnished, and extensively rehearsed, Corto's subsequent testimony was detailed, moving, lucid, and largely the

invention of a Congressional cabal with certain vested interests in saving particular portions of the Pentagon infrastructure. Corto gradually understood that the testimony he gave was instrumental in saving the careers of three officers directly responsible for the suppression of reports on the building of the emp installations at Kirensk.

His role in the trials over, he was unwanted in Washington. In an M Street restaurant, over asparagus crepes, the aide explained the terminal dangers involved in talking to the wrong people. Corto crushed the man's larynx with the rigid fingers of his right hand. The Congressional aide strangled, his face in an asparagus crepe, and Corto stepped out into cool Washington September.

The Hosaka rattled through police reports, corporate espionage records, and news files. Case watched Corto work corporate defectors in Lisbon and Marrakesh, where he seemed to grow obsessed with the idea of betrayal, to loathe the scientists and technicians he bought out for his employers. Drunk, in Singapore, he beat a Russian engineer to death in a hotel and set fire to his room.

Next he surfaced in Thailand, as overseer of a heroin factory. Then as enforcer for a California gambling cartel, then as a paid killer in the ruins of Bonn. He robbed a bank in Wichita. The record grew vague, shadowy, the gaps longer.

One day, he said, in a taped segment that suggested chemical interrogation, everything had gone gray.

Translated French medical records explained that a man without identification had been taken to a Paris mental health unit and diagnosed as schizophrenic. He became catatonic and was sent to a government institution on the outskirts of Toulon. He became a subject in an experimental program that sought to reverse schizophrenia through the application of cybernetic models. A random selection of patients were provided with microcomputers and encouraged, with help from students, to program them. He was cured, the only success in the entire experiment.

The record ended there.

Case turned on the foam and Molly cursed him softly for disturbing her.

———————

The telephone rang. He pulled it into bed. "Yeah?"

"We're going to Istanbul," Armitage said. "Tonight."

"What does the bastard want?" Molly asked.

"Says we're going to Istanbul tonight."

"That's just wonderful."

Armitage was reading off flight numbers and departure times. Molly sat up and turned on the light.

"What about my gear?" Case asked. "My deck."

"Finn will handle it," said Armitage, and hung up.

Case watched her pack. There were dark circles under her eyes, but even with the cast on, it was like watching a dance. No wasted motion. His clothes were a rumpled pile beside his bag.

"You hurting?" he asked.

"I could do with another night at Chin's."

"Your dentist?"

"You betcha. Very discreet. He's got half that rack, full clinic. Does repairs for samurai." She was zipping her bag. "You ever been to 'Stambul?"

"Couple days, once."

"Never changes," she said. "Bad old town."

———————

"It was like this when we headed for Chiba," Molly said, staring out the train window at blasted industrial moonscape, red beacons on the horizon warning aircraft away from a fusion plant. "We were in L.A. He came in and said Pack, we were booked for Macau. When we got there, I played fantan in the Lisboa and he crossed over into Zhongshan. Next day I was playing ghost with you in Night City." She took a silk scarf from the sleeve of her black jacket and polished the insets. The landscape of the northern Sprawl woke confused memories of childhood for Case, dead grass tufting the cracks in a canted slab of freeway concrete.

The train began to decelerate ten kilometers from the airport. Case watched the sun rise on the landscape of childhood, on broken slag and the rusting shells of refineries.

SEVEN

It was raining in Beyoglu, and the rented Mercedes slid past the grilled and unlit windows of cautious Greek and Armenian jewelers. The street was almost empty, only a few dark-coated figures on the sidewalks turning to stare after the car.

"This was formerly the prosperous European section of Ottoman Istanbul," purred the Mercedes.

"So it's gone downhill," Case said.

"The Hilton's in Cumhuriyet Caddesi," Molly said. She settled back against the car's gray ultrasuede.

"How come Armitage flies alone?" Case asked. He had a headache.

"'Cause you get up his nose. You're sure getting up mine."

He wanted to tell her the Corto story, but decided against it. He'd used a sleep derm, on the plane.

The road in from the airport had been dead straight, like a neat incision, laying the city open. He'd watched the crazy walls of patchwork wooden tenements slide by, condos, arcologies, grim housing projects, more walls of plyboard and corrugated iron.

The Finn, in a new Shinjuku suit, sarariman black, was waiting sourly in the Hilton lobby, marooned on a velour armchair in a sea of pale blue carpeting.

"Christ," Molly said. "Rat in a business suit."

They crossed the lobby.

"How much you get paid to come over here, Finn?" She lowered her bag beside the armchair. "Bet not as much as you get for wearing that suit, huh?"

The Finn's upper lips drew back. "Not enough, sweetmeat." He handed her a magnetic key with a round yellow tag. "You're registered already. Honcho's upstairs." He looked around. "This town sucks."

"You get agoraphobic, they take you out from under a dome. Just pretend it's Brooklyn or something." She twirled the key around a finger. "You here as valet or what?"

"I gotta check out some guy's implants," the Finn said.

"How about my deck?" Case asked.

The Finn winced. "Observe the protocol. Ask the boss."

Molly's fingers moved in the shadow of her jacket, a flicker of jive. The Finn watched, then nodded.

"Yeah," she said, "I know who that is." She jerked her head in the direction of the elevators. "Come on, cowboy." Case followed her with both bags.

———————

Their room might have been the one in Chiba where he'd first seen Armitage. He went to the window, in the morning, almost expecting to see Tokyo Bay. There was another hotel across the street. It was still raining. A few letter-writers had taken refuge in doorways, their old voiceprinters wrapped in sheets of clear plastic, evidence that the written word still enjoyed a certain prestige here. It was a sluggish country. He watched a dull black Citroën sedan, a primitive hydrogen-cell conversion, as it disgorged five sullen-looking Turkish officers in rumpled green uniforms. They entered the hotel across the street.

He glanced back at the bed, at Molly, and her paleness struck him. She'd left the micropore cast on the bedslab in their loft, beside the transdermal inducer. Her glasses reflected part of the room's light fixture.

He had the phone in his hand before it had a chance to ring twice. "Glad you're up," Armitage said.

"I'm just. Lady's still under. Listen, boss, I think it's maybe time we have a little talk. I think I work better if I know a little more about what I'm doing."

Silence on the line. Case bit his lip.

"You know as much as you need to. Maybe more."

"You think so?"

"Get dressed, Case. Get her up. You'll have a caller in about fifteen minutes. His name is Terzibashjian." The phone bleated softly. Armitage was gone.

"Wake up, baby," Case said. "Biz."

"I've been awake an hour already." The mirrors turned.

"We got a Jersey Bastion coming up."

"You got an ear for language, Case. Bet you're part Armenian. That's the eye Armitage has had on Riviera. Help me up."

Terzibashjian proved to be a young man in a gray suit and gold-framed, mirrored glasses. His white shirt was open at the collar, revealing a mat of dark hair so dense that Case at first mistook it for some kind of T-shirt. He arrived with a black Hilton tray arranged with three tiny, fragrant cups of thick black coffee and three sticky, straw-colored Oriental sweets.

"We must, as you say in *Ingiliz*, take this one very easy." He seemed to stare pointedly at Molly, but at last he removed the silver glasses. His eyes were a dark brown that matched the shade of his very short military-cut hair. He smiled. "It is better, this way, yes? Else we make the *tunel* infinity, mirror into mirror. . . . You particularly," he said to her, "must take care. In Turkey there is disapproval of women who sport such modifications."

Molly bit one of the pastries in half. "It's my show, Jack," she said, her mouth full. She chewed, swallowed, and licked her lips. "I know about you. Stool for the military, right?" Her hand slid lazily into the front of her jacket and came out with the fletcher. Case hadn't known she had it.

"Very easy, please," Terzibashjian said, his white china thimble frozen centimeters from his lips.

She extended the gun. "Maybe you get the explosives, lots of them, or maybe you get a cancer. One dart, shitface. You won't feel it for months."

"Please. You call this in *Ingiliz* making me very tight. . . ."

"I call it a bad morning. Now tell us about your man and get your ass out of here." She put the gun away.

"He is living in Fener, at Küchük Gülhane Djaddesi 14. I have his *tunel* route, nightly to the bazaar. He performs most recently at the Yenishehir Palas Oteli, a modern place in the style *turistik*, but it has been arranged that the police have shown a certain interest in these shows. The Yenishehir management has grown nervous." He smiled. He smelled of some metallic aftershave.

"I want to know about the implants," she said, massaging her thigh, "I want to know exactly what he can do."

Terzibashjian nodded. "Worst is how you say in *Ingiliz*, the subliminals." He made the word four careful syllables.

———

"On our left," said the Mercedes, as it steered through a maze of rainy streets, "is Kapali Carsi, the grand bazaar."

Beside Case, the Finn made an appreciative noise, but he was looking in the wrong direction. The right side of the street was lined with miniature scrapyards. Case saw a gutted locomotive atop rust-stained, broken lengths of fluted marble. Headless marble statues were stacked like firewood.

"Homesick?" Case asked.

"Place sucks," the Finn said. His black silk tie was starting to resemble a worn carbon ribbon. There were medallions of kebab gravy and fried egg on the lapels of the new suit.

"Hey, Jersey," Case said to the Armenian, who sat behind them, "where'd this guy get his stuff installed?"

"In Chiba City. He has no left lung. The other is boosted, is how you say it? Anyone might buy these implants, but this one is most talented." The Mercedes swerved, avoiding a balloon-tired dray stacked with hides. "I have followed him in the street and seen a dozen cycles fall, near him, in a day. Find the cyclist in a hospital, the story is always the same. A scorpion poised beside a brake lever. . . ."

"'What you see is what you get,' yeah," the Finn said. "I seen the schematics on the guy's silicon. Very flash. What he imagines, you see. I figure he could narrow it to a pulse and fry a retina over easy."

"You have told this to your woman friend?" Terzibashjian leaned forward between the ultrasuede buckets. "In Turkey, women are still women. This one . . ."

The Finn snorted. "She'd have you wearing your balls for a bow tie if you looked at her cross-eyed."

"I do not understand this idiom."

"That's okay," Case said. "Means shut up."

The Armenian sat back, leaving a metallic edge of aftershave. He began to whisper to a Sanyo transceiver in a strange salad of Greek, French, Turkish, isolated fragments of English. The transceiver answered in French. The Mercedes swung smoothly around a corner. "The spice bazaar, sometimes called the Egyptian bazaar," the car said, "was erected on the site of an earlier bazaar erected by Sultan Hatice in 1660. This is the city's central market for spices, software, perfumes, drugs. . . ."

"Drugs," Case said, watching the car's wipers cross and recross the bulletproof Lexan. "What's that you said before, Jersey, about this Riviera being wired?"

"A mixture of cocaine and meperidine, yes." The Armenian went back to the conversation he was having with the Sanyo.

"Demerol, they used to call that," said the Finn. "He's a speedball artist. Funny class of people you're mixing with, Case."

"Never mind," Case said, turning up the collar of his jacket, "we'll get the poor fucker a new pancreas or something."

———

Once they entered the bazaar, the Finn brightened noticeably, as though he were comforted by the crowd density and the sense of enclosure. They walked with the Armenian along a broad concourse, beneath soot-stained sheets of plastic and green-painted ironwork out of the age of steam. A thousand suspended ads writhed and flickered.

"Hey, Christ," the Finn said, taking Case's arm, "looka that." He pointed. "It's a horse, man. You ever see a horse?"

Case glanced at the embalmed animal and shook his head. It was displayed on a sort of pedestal, near the entrance to a place that sold birds and monkeys. The thing's legs had been worn black and hairless by decades of passing hands. "Saw one in Maryland once," the Finn said, "and that was a good three years after the pandemic. There's Arabs still trying to code 'em up from the DNA, but they always croak."

The animal's brown glass eyes seemed to follow them as they passed. Terzibashjian led them into a café near the core of the market, a low-ceilinged room that looked as though it had been in continuous operation for centuries. Skinny boys in soiled white coats dodged between the crowded tables, balancing steel trays with bottles of Turk-Tuborg and tiny glasses of tea.

Case bought a pack of Yeheyuans from a vendor by the door. The

Armenian was muttering to his Sanyo. "Come," he said, "he is moving. Each night he rides the *tunel* to the bazaar, to purchase his mixture from Ali. Your woman is close. Come."

———

The alley was an old place, too old, the walls cut from blocks of dark
stone. The pavement was uneven and smelled of a century's dripping gasoline, absorbed by ancient limestone. "Can't see shit," he
whispered to the Finn. "That's okay for sweetmeat," the Finn said.
"Quiet," said Terzibashjian, too loudly.

Wood grated on stone or concrete. Ten meters down the alley, a
wedge of yellow light fell across wet cobbles, widened. A figure
stepped out and the door grated shut again, leaving the narrow
place in darkness. Case shivered.

"Now," Terzibashjian said, and a brilliant beam of white light,
directed from the rooftop of the building opposite the market,
pinned the slender figure beside the ancient wooden door in a
perfect circle. Bright eyes darted left, right, and the man crumpled. Case thought someone had shot him; he lay facedown,
blond hair pale against the old stone, his limp hands white and
pathetic.

The floodlight never wavered.

The back of the fallen man's jacket heaved and burst, blood
splashing the wall and doorway. A pair of impossibly long, rope-
tendoned arms flexed grayish-pink in the glare. The thing seemed
to pull itself up out of the pavement, through the inert, bloody ruin
that had been Riviera. It was two meters tall, stood on two legs, and
seemed to be headless. Then it swung slowly to face them, and Case
saw that it had a head, but no neck. It was eyeless, the skin gleaming
a wet intestinal pink. The mouth, if it was a mouth, was circular,
conical, shallow, and lined with a seething growth of hairs or bris-
tles, glittering like black chrome. It kicked the rags of clothing and

flesh aside and took a step, the mouth seeming to scan for them as it moved.

Terzibashjian said something in Greek or Turkish and rushed the thing, his arms spread like a man attempting to dive through a window. He went through it. Into the muzzle-flash of a pistol from the dark beyond the circle of light. Fragments of rock whizzed past Case's head; the Finn jerked him down into a crouch.

The light from the rooftop vanished, leaving him with mismatched afterimages of muzzle-flash, monster, and white beam. His ears rang.

Then the light returned, bobbing now, searching the shadows. Terzibashjian was leaning against a steel door, his face very white in the glare. He held his left wrist and watched blood drip from a wound in his left hand. The blond man, whole again, unbloodied, lay at his feet.

Molly stepped out of the shadows, all in black, with her fletcher in her hand. *fletcher in hand*

"Use the radio," the Armenian said, through gritted teeth. "Call in Mahmut. We must get him out of here. This is not a good place."

"Little prick nearly made it," the Finn said, his knees cracking loudly as he stood up, brushing ineffectually at the legs of his trousers. "You were watching the horror-show, right? Not the hamburger that got tossed out of sight. Real cute. Well, help 'em get his ass outa here. I gotta scan all that gear before he wakes up, make sure Armitage is getting his money's worth."

Molly bent and picked something up. A pistol. "A Nambu," she said. "Nice gun."

Terzibashjian made a whining sound. Case saw that most of his middle finger was missing.

———

With the city drenched in predawn blue, she told the Mercedes to take them to Topkapi. The Finn and an enormous Turk named *not recovered*

Mahmut had taken Riviera, still unconscious, from the alley. Minutes later, a dusty Citroën had arrived for the Armenian, who seemed on the verge of fainting. *frustrated at the man*

"You're an asshole," Molly told the man, opening the car door for him. "You shoulda hung back. I had him in my sights as soon as he stepped out." Terzibashjian glared at her. "So we're through with you anyway." She shoved him in and slammed the door. "Run into you again and I'll kill you," she said to the white face behind the tinted window. The Citroën ground away down the alley and swung clumsily into the street.

Now the Mercedes whispered through Istanbul as the city woke. *Morning* They passed the Beyoglu *tunel* terminal and sped past mazes of deserted back streets, run-down apartment houses that reminded Case vaguely of Paris.

"What is this thing?" he asked Molly, as the Mercedes parked itself on the fringes of the gardens that surround the Seraglio. He stared dully at the baroque conglomeration of styles that was Topkapi.

"It was sort of a private whorehouse for the King," she said, getting out stretching. "Kept a lotta women there. Now it's a museum. Kinda like Finn's shop, all this stuff just jumbled in there, big diamonds, swords, the left hand of John the Baptist. . . ."

"Like in a support vat?"

"Nah. Dead. Got it inside this brass hand thing, little hatch on the side so the Christians could kiss it for luck. Got it off the Christians about a million years ago, and they never dust the goddam thing, 'cause it's an infidel relic."

Black iron deer rusted in the gardens of the Seraglio. Case walked beside her, watching the toes of her boots crunch unkept grass made stiff by an early frost. They walked beside a path of cold octagonal flagstones. Winter was waiting, somewhere in the Balkans.

scar of police interrogator

"That Terzi, he's grade-A scum," she said. "He's the secret police. Torturer. Real easy to buy out, too, with the kind of money Armitage was offering." In the wet trees around them, birds began to sing.

"I did that job for you," Case said, "the one in London. I got something, but I don't know what it means." He told her the Corto story.

No Armitage

"Well, I knew there wasn't anybody name of Armitage in that Screaming Fist. Looked it up." She stroked the rusted flank of an iron doe. "You figure the little computer pulled him out of it? In that French hospital?"

"I figure Wintermute," Case said.

She nodded.

"Thing is," he said, "do you think he knows he was Corto, before? I mean, he wasn't anybody in particular, by the time he hit the ward, so maybe Wintermute just . . ."

"Yeah. Built him up from go. Yeah . . ." She turned and they walked on. "It figures. You know, the guy doesn't have any life going, in private. Not as far as I can tell. You see a guy like that, you figure there's something he does when he's alone. But not Armitage. Sits and stares at the wall, man. Then something clicks and he goes into high gear and wheels for Wintermute."

"So why's he got that stash in London? Nostalgia?"

"Maybe he doesn't know about it," she said. "Maybe it's just in his name, right?"

"I don't get it," Case said.

Different AI intelligence levels

"Just thinking out loud. . . . How smart's an AI, Case?"

"Depends. Some aren't much smarter than dogs. Pets. Cost a fortune anyway. The real smart ones are as smart as the Turing heat is willing to let 'em get."

"Look, you're a cowboy. How come you aren't just flat-out fascinated with those things?"

"Well," he said, "for starts, they're rare. Most of them are military, the bright ones, and we can't crack the ice. That's where ice all comes from, you know? And then there's the Turing cops, and that's bad heat." He looked at her. "I dunno, it just isn't part of the trip."

"Jockeys all the same," she said. "No imagination."

They came to a broad rectangular pond where carp nuzzled the stems of some white aquatic flower. She kicked a loose pebble in and watched the ripples spread.

"That's Wintermute," she said. "This deal's real big, looks to me. We're out where the little waves are too broad, we can't see the rock that hit the center. We know something's there, but not why. I wanna know why. I want you to go and talk to Wintermute."

"I couldn't get near it," he said. "You're dreaming."

"Try."

"Can't be done."

"Ask the Flatline."

"What do we want out of that Riviera?" he asked, hoping to change the subject.

She spat into the pond. "God knows. I'd as soon kill him as look at him. I saw his profile. He's a kind of compulsive Judas. Can't get off sexually unless he knows he's betraying the object of desire. That's what the file says. And they have to love him first. Maybe he loves them, too. That's why it was easy for Terzi to set him up for us, because he's been here three years, shopping politicals to the secret police. Probably Terzi let him watch, when the cattle prods came out. He's done eighteen in three years. All women age twenty to twenty-five. It kept Terzi in dissidents." She thrust her hands into her jacket pockets. "Because if he found one he really wanted, he'd make sure she turned political. He's got a personality like a Modern's suit. The profile said it was a very rare type, estimated one in a couple of million. Which anyway says something good about human nature, I guess." She stared at the white flowers and the sluggish fish, her face sour. "I think I'm going to have to buy myself some special insurance on that Peter." Then she turned and smiled, and it was very cold.

"What's that mean?"

"Never mind. Let's go back to Beyoglu and find something like breakfast. I gotta busy night again, tonight. Gotta collect his stuff from that apartment in Fener, gotta go back to the bazaar and buy him some drugs. . . ."

"Buy him some drugs? How's he rate?"

She laughed. "He's not dying on the wire, sweetheart. And it looks like he can't work without that special taste. I like you better now, anyway, you aren't so goddam skinny." She smiled. "So I'll go to Ali the dealer and stock up. You betcha."

Drug Purchases

Armitage waiting

Armitage was waiting in their room at the Hilton.

"Time to pack," he said, and Case tried to find the man called Corto behind the pale blue eyes and the tanned mask. He thought of Wage, back in Chiba. Operators above a certain level tended to submerge their personalities, he knew. But Wage had had vices, lovers. Even, it had been rumored, children. The blankness he found in Armitage was something else.

"Where to now?" he asked, walking past the man to stare down into the street. "What kind of climate?"

"They don't have climate, just weather," Armitage said. "Here. Read the brochure." He put something on the coffee table and stood.

"Did Riviera check out okay? Where's the Finn?"

"Riviera's fine. The Finn is on his way home." Armitage smiled, a smile that meant as much as the twitch of some insect's antenna. His gold bracelet clinked as he reached out to prod Case in the chest. "Don't get too smart. Those little sacs are starting to show wear, but you don't know how much."

Case kept his face very still and forced himself to nod.

When Armitage was gone, he picked up one of the brochures. It was expensively printed, in French, English, and Turkish.

FREESIDE—WHY WAIT?

———

The four of them were booked on a THY flight out of Yesilköy airport. Transfer at Paris to the JAL shuttle. Case sat in the lobby of the Istanbul Hilton and watched Riviera browse bogus Byzantine fragments in the glass-walled gift shop. Armitage, his trenchcoat draped over his shoulders like a cape, stood in the shop's entrance.

Riviera was slender, blond, soft-voiced, his English accentless and fluid. Molly said he was thirty, but it would have been difficult to guess his age. She also said he was legally stateless and traveled under a forged Dutch passport. He was a product of the rubble rings that fringe the radioactive core of old Bonn. Three smiling Japanese tourists bustled into the shop, nodding politely to Armitage. Armitage crossed the floor of the shop too quickly, too obviously, to stand beside Riviera. Riviera turned and smiled. He was very beautiful; Case assumed the features were the work of a Chiba surgeon. A subtle job, nothing like Armitage's blandly handsome blend of pop faces. The man's forehead was high and smooth, gray eyes calm and distant. His nose, which might have been too nicely sculpted, seemed to have been broken and clumsily reset. The suggestion of brutality offset the delicacy of his jaw and the quickness of his smile. His teeth were small, even, and very white. Case watched the white hands play over the imitation fragments of sculpture.

Riviera didn't act like a man who'd been attacked the night before, drugged with a toxin-flechette, abducted, subjected to the Finn's examination, and pressured by Armitage into joining their team.

Case checked his watch. Molly was due back from her drug run. He looked up at Riviera again. "I bet you're stoned right now, ass-

suspicious

hole," he said to the Hilton lobby. A graying Italian matron in a white leather tuxedo jacket lowered her Porsche glasses to stare at him. He smiled broadly, stood, and shouldered his bag. He needed cigarettes for the flight. He wondered if there was a smoking section on the JAL shuttle. "See ya, lady," he said to the woman, who promptly slid the sunglasses back up her nose and turned away.

There were cigarettes in the gift shop, but he didn't relish talking with Armitage or Riviera. He left the lobby and located a vending console in a narrow alcove, at the end of a rank of pay phones.

He fumbled through a pocketful of lirasi, slotting the small dull alloy coins one after another, vaguely amused by the anachronism of the process. The phone nearest him rang.

Automatically, he picked it up. — *anxious*

"Yeah?"

Faint harmonics, tiny inaudible voices rattling across some orbital link, and then a sound like wind.

"Hello, Case." — *whose this*

A fifty-lirasi coin fell from his hand, bounced, and rolled out of sight across Hilton carpeting.

"Wintermute, Case. It's time we talk."

It was a chip voice.

"Don't you want to talk, Case?"

He hung up. *afraid*

On his way back to the lobby, his cigarettes forgotten, he had to walk the length of the ranked phones. Each rang in turn, but only once, as he passed.

wintermae

PART THREE

MIDNIGHT IN THE
RUE JULES VERNE

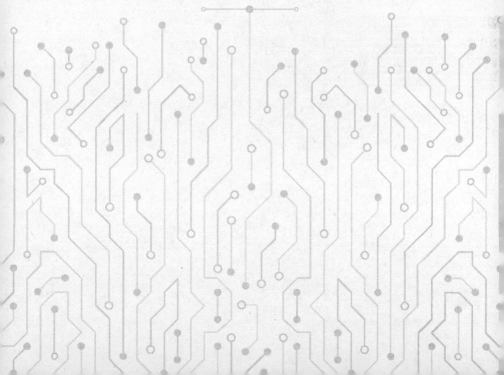

EIGHT

Archipelago.

The islands. Torus, spindle, cluster. Human DNA spreading out from gravity's steep well like an oilslick.

Call up a graphics display that grossly simplifies the exchange of data in the L-5 archipelago. One segment clicks in as red solid, a massive rectangle dominating your screen.

Freeside. Freeside is many things, not all of them evident to the tourists who shuttle up and down the well. Freeside is brothel and banking nexus, pleasure dome and free port, border town and spa. Freeside is Las Vegas and the hanging gardens of Babylon, an orbital Geneva and home to a family inbred and most carefully refined, the industrial clan of Tessier and Ashpool.

On the THY liner to Paris, they sat together in First Class, Molly in the window seat, Case beside her, Riviera and Armitage on the aisle. Once, as the plane banked over water, Case saw the jewel-glow of a Greek island town. And once, reaching for his drink, he caught the flicker of a thing like a giant human sperm in the depths of his bourbon and water.

Molly leaned across him and slapped Riviera's face, once. "No, baby. No games. You play that subliminal shit around me, I'll hurt you real bad. I can do it without damaging you at all. I *like* that."

Case turned automatically to check Armitage's reaction. The smooth face was calm, the blue eyes alert, but there was no anger. "That's right, Peter. Don't."

Case turned back, in time to catch the briefest flash of a black rose, its petals sheened like leather, the black stem thorned with bright chrome.

Peter Riviera smiled sweetly, closed his eyes, and fell instantly asleep.

Molly turned away, her lenses reflected in the dark window.

———

"You been up, haven't you?" Molly asked, as he squirmed his way back into the deep temperfoam couch on the JAL shuttle.

"Nah. Never travel much, just for biz." The steward was attaching readout trodes to his wrist and left ear.

"Hope you don't get SAS," she said.

"Airsick? No way."

"It's not the same. Your heartbeat'll speed up in zero-g, and your inner ear'll go nuts for a while. Kicks in your flight reflex, like you'll be getting signals to run like hell, and a lot of adrenaline." The steward moved on to Riviera, taking a new set of trodes from his red plastic apron.

Case turned his head and tried to make out the outline of the old Orly terminals, but the shuttle pad was screened by graceful blast-deflectors of wet concrete. The one nearest the window bore an Arabic slogan in red spraybomb.

He closed his eyes and told himself the shuttle was only a big airplane, one that flew very high. It smelled like an airplane, like new clothes and chewing gum and exhaustion. He listened to the piped koto music and waited.

Twenty minutes, then gravity came down on him like a great soft hand with bones of ancient stone.

Space adaptation syndrome

Space adaptation syndrome was worse than Molly's description, but it passed quickly enough and he was able to sleep. The steward woke him as they were preparing to dock at JAL's terminal cluster.

"We transfer to Freeside now?" he asked, eyeing a shred of Yeheyuan tobacco that had drifted gracefully up out of his shirt pocket to dance ten centimeters from his nose. There was no smoking on shuttle flights.

"No, we got the boss's usual little kink in the plans, you know? We're getting this taxi out to Zion, Zion cluster." She touched the release plate on her harness and began to free herself from the embrace of the foam. "Funny choice of venue, you ask me."

"How's that?"

"Dreads. Rastas. Colony's about thirty years old now."

"What's that mean?"

"You'll see. It's an okay place by me. Anyway, they'll let you smoke your cigarettes there."

Health problems from colony grav

Zion had been founded by five workers who'd refused to return, who'd turned their backs on the well and started building. They'd suffered calcium loss and heart shrinkage before rotational gravity was established in the colony's central torus. Seen from the bubble of the taxi, Zion's makeshift hull reminded Case of the patchwork tenements of Istanbul, the irregular, discolored plates laser-scrawled with Rastafarian symbols and the initials of welders.

Molly and a skinny Zionite called Aerol helped Case negotiate a freefall corridor into the core of a smaller torus. He'd lost track of Armitage and Riviera in the wake of a second wave of SAS vertigo.

"Here," Molly said, shoving his legs into a narrow hatchway over-head. "Grab the rungs. Make like you're climbing backward, right? You're going toward the hull, that's like you're climbing down into gravity. Got it?"

Case's stomach churned.

"You be fine, mon," Aerol said, his grin bracketed with gold incisors.

Somehow, the end of the tunnel had become its bottom. Case embraced the weak gravity like a drowning man finding a pocket of air.

"Up," Molly said, "you gonna kiss it next?" Case lay flat on the deck, on his stomach, arms spread. Something struck him on the shoulder. He rolled over and saw a fat bundle of elastic cable. "Gotta play house," she said. "You help me string this up." He looked around the wide, featureless space and noticed steel rings welded on every surface, seemingly at random.

When they'd strung the cables, according to some complex scheme of Molly's, they hung them with battered sheets of yel-low plastic. As they worked, Case gradually became aware of the music that pulsed constantly through the cluster. It was called dub, a sensuous mosaic cooked from vast libraries of dig-italized pop; it was worship, Molly said, and a sense of commu-nity. Case heaved at one of the yellow sheets; the thing was light but still awkward. Zion smelled of cooked vegetables, hu-manity, and ganja.

"Good." Armitage said, gliding loose-kneed through the hatch and nodding at the maze of sheets. Riviera followed, less certain in the partial gravity.

"Where were you when it needed doing?" Case asked Riviera.

The man opened his mouth to speak. A small trout swam out, trailing impossible bubbles. It glided past Case's cheek. "In the head," Riviera said, and smiled.

Case laughed.

"Good," Riviera said, "you can laugh. I would have tried to help you, but I'm no good with my hands." He held up his palms, which suddenly doubled. Four arms, four hands.

"Just the harmless clown, right, Riviera?" Molly stepped between them.

"Yo," Aerol said, from the hatch, "you wan' come wi' me, cowboy mon."

"It's your deck," Armitage said, "and the other gear. Help him get it in from the cargo bay."

"You ver' pale, mon," Aerol said, as they were guiding the foam-bundled Hosaka terminal along the central corridor. "Maybe you wan' eat somethin'."

Case's mouth flooded with saliva; he shook his head. — Hunger

Armitage announced an eighty-hour stay in Zion. Molly and Case would practice in zero gravity, he said, and acclimatize themselves to working in it. He would brief them on Freeside and the Villa Straylight. It was unclear what Riviera was supposed to be doing, but Case didn't feel like asking. A few hours after their arrival, Armitage had sent him into the yellow maze to call Riviera out for a meal. He'd found him curled like a cat on a thin pad of temperfoam, naked, apparently asleep, his head orbited by a revolving halo of small white geometric forms, cubes, spheres, and pyramids. "Hey, Riviera." The ring continued to revolve. He'd gone back and told Armitage. "He's stoned," Molly said, looking up from the disassembled parts of her fletcher. "Leave him be."

Armitage seemed to think that zero-g would affect Case's ability to operate in the matrix. "Don't sweat it," Case argued, "I jack in and I'm not here. It's all the same."

"Your adrenaline levels are higher," Armitage said. "You've still got SAS. You won't have time for it to wear off. You're going to learn to work with it."

"So I do the run from here?"

"No. Practice, Case. Now. Up in the corridor. . . ."

[handwritten annotation: Cyber space had no relation with whereabouts]

Cyberspace, as the deck presented it, had no particular relationship with the deck's physical whereabouts. When Case jacked in, he opened his eyes to the familiar configuration of the Eastern Seaboard Fission Authority's Aztec pyramid of data.

"How you doing, Dixie?"

"I'm dead, Case. Got enough time in on this Hosaka to figure that one."

"How's it feel?"

"It doesn't."

"Bother you?"

"What bothers me is, nothin' does."

"How's that?"

"Had me this buddy in the Russian camp, Siberia, his thumb was frostbit. Medics came by and they cut it off. Month later he's tossin' all night. Elroy, I said, what's eatin' you? Goddam thumb's itchin', he says. So I told him, scratch it. McCoy, he says, it's the *other* goddam thumb." When the construct laughed, it came through as something else, not laughter, but a stab of cold down Case's spine. "Do me a favor, boy."

"What's that, Dix?"

"This scam of yours, when it's over, you erase this goddam thing."

———•———

Case didn't understand the Zionites.

Aerol, with no particular provocation, related the tale of the baby who had burst from his forehead and scampered into a forest of hydroponic ganja. "Ver' small baby, mon, no long' you finga." He rubbed his palm across an unscarred expanse of brown forehead and smiled.

"It's the ganja," Molly said, when Case told her the story, "They don't make much of a difference between states, you know? Aerol tells you it happened, well, it happened to *him*. It's not like bullshit, more like poetry. Get it?"

Case nodded dubiously. The Zionites always touched you when they were talking, hands on your shoulder. He didn't like that.

"Hey, Aerol," Case called, an hour later, as he prepared for a practice run in the freefall corridor. "Come here, man. Wanna show you this thing." He held out the trodes.

Aerol executed a slow-motion tumble. His bare feet struck the steel wall and he caught a girder with his free hand. The other held a transparent waterbag bulging with blue-green algae. He blinked mildly and grinned.

"Try it," Case said.

He took the band, put it on, and Case adjusted the trodes. He closed his eyes. Case hit the power stud. Aerol shuddered. Case jacked him back out. "What did you see, man?"

"Babylon," Aerol said, sadly, handing him the trodes and kicking off down the corridor.

· · ·

Riviera sat motionless on his foam pad, his right arm extended straight out, level with his shoulder. A jewel-scaled snake, its eyes like ruby neon, was coiled tightly a few millimeters behind his elbow. Case watched the snake, which was finger-thick and banded black and scarlet, slowly contract, tightening around Riviera's arm.

"Come then," the man said caressingly to the pale waxy scorpion poised in the center of his upturned palm. "Come." The scorpion swayed its brownish claws and scurried up his arm, its feet tracking the faint dark telltales of veins. When it reached the inner elbow, it halted and seemed to vibrate. Riviera made a soft hissing sound. The sting came up, quivered, and sank into the skin above a bulging vein. The coral snake relaxed, and Riviera sighed slowly as the injection hit him. *??? Poison*

Then the snake and the scorpion were gone, and he held a milky plastic syringe in his left hand. "'If God made anything better, he kept it for himself.' You know the expression, Case?" *what did he make*

"Yeah," Case said. "I heard that about lots of different things. You always make it into a little show?"

Riviera loosened and removed the elastic length of surgical tubing from his arm. "Yes. It's more fun." He smiled, his eyes distant now, cheeks flushed. "I've a membrane set in, just over the vein, so I never have to worry about the condition of the needle."

"Doesn't hurt?"

The bright eyes met his. "Of course it does. That's part of it, isn't it?"

"I'd just use derms," Case said.

"Pedestrian," Riviera sneered, and laughed, putting on a short-sleeved white cotton shirt.

"Must be nice," Case said, getting up.

"Get high yourself, Case?"

"I hadda give it up."

⸺ • ⸺

"Freeside," Armitage said, touching the panel on the little Braun hologram projector. The image shivered into focus, nearly three meters from tip to tip. "Casinos here." He reached into the skeletal representation and pointed. "Hotels, strata-title property, big shops along here." His hand moved. "Blue areas are lakes." He walked to one end of the model. "Big cigar. Narrows at the ends."

"We can see that fine," Molly said.

"Mountain effect, as it narrows. Ground seems to get higher, more rocky, but it's an easy climb. Higher you climb, the lower the gravity. Sports up there. There's a velodrome ring here." He pointed.

"A what?" Case leaned forward.

"They race bicycles," Molly said. "Low grav, high-traction tires, get up over a hundred kilos an hour."

"This end doesn't concern us," Armitage said with his usual utter seriousness.

"Shit," Molly said, "I'm an avid cyclist."

Riviera giggled.

Armitage walked to the opposite end of the projection. "This end does." The interior detail of the hologram ended here, and the final segment of the spindle was empty. "This is the Villa Straylight. Steep climb out of gravity and every approach is kinked. There's a single entrance, here, dead center. Zero gravity."

"What's inside, boss?" Riviera leaned forward, craning his neck. Four tiny figures glittered, near the tip of Armitage's finger. Armitage slapped at them as if they were gnats.

"Peter," Armitage said, "you're going to be the first to find out. You'll arrange yourself an invitation. Once you're in, you see that Molly gets in."

Case stared at the blankness that represented Straylight, remembering the Finn's story: Smith, Jimmy, the talking head, and the ninja.

"Details available?" Riviera asked. "I need to plan a wardrobe, you see."

"Learn the streets," Armitage said, returning to the center of the model. "Desiderata Street here. This is the Rue Jules Verne."

Riviera rolled his eyes.

While Armitage recited the names of Freeside avenues, a dozen bright pustules rose on his nose, cheeks, and chin. Even Molly laughed.

Armitage paused, regarded them all with his cold empty eyes.

"Sorry," Riviera said, and the sores flickered and vanished.

Case woke, late into the sleeping period, and became aware of Molly crouched beside him on the foam. He could feel her tension. He lay there confused. When she moved, the sheer speed of it stunned him. She was up and through the sheet of yellow plastic before he'd had time to realize she'd slashed it open.

"Don't you move, friend."

Case rolled over and put his head through the rent in the plastic. "Wha . . . ?"

"Shut up."

"You th' one, mon," said a Zion voice. "Cateye, call 'em, call 'em Steppin' Razor. I Maelcum, sister. Brothers wan' converse wi' you an' cowboy."

"What brothers?"

"Founders, mon. Elders of Zion, ya know. . . ."

"We open that hatch, the light'll wake bossman," Case whispered.

"Make it special dark, now," the man said. "Come. I an' I visit th' Founders."

"You know how fast I can cut you, friend?"

"Don' stan' talkin', sister. Come."

The two surviving Founders of Zion were old men, old with the accelerated aging that overtakes men who spend too many years outside the embrace of gravity. Their brown legs, brittle with calcium loss, looked fragile in the harsh glare of reflected sunlight. They floated in the center of a painted jungle of rainbow foliage, a lurid communal mural that completely covered the hull of the spherical chamber. The air was thick with resinous smoke.

"Steppin' Razor," one said, as Molly drifted into the chamber. "Like unto a whippin' stick."

"That is a story we have, sister," said the other, "a religion story. We are glad you've come with Maelcum."

"How come you don't talk the patois?" Molly asked.

"I came from Los Angeles," the old man said. His dreadlocks were like a matted tree with branches the color of steel wool. "Long time ago, up the gravity well and out of Babylon. To lead the Tribes home. Now my brother likens you to Steppin' Razor."

Molly extended her right hand and the blades flashed in the smoky air.

The other Founder laughed, his head thrown back. "Soon come, the Final Days. . . . Voices. Voices cryin' inna wilderness, prophesyin' ruin unto Babylon. . . ."

"Voices." The Founder from Los Angeles was staring at Case. "We monitor many frequencies. We listen always. Came a voice, out of the babel of tongues, speaking to us. It played us a mighty dub."

"Call 'em Winter Mute," said the other, making it two words. Case felt the skin crawl on his arms.

"The Mute talked to us," the first Founder said. "The Mute said we are to help you."

"When was this?" Case asked.

"Thirty hours prior you dockin' Zion."

"You ever hear this voice before?"

"No," said the man from Los Angeles, "and we are uncertain of its meaning. If these are Final Days, we must expect false prophets. . . ."

"Listen," Case said, "that's an AI, you know? Artificial intelli-

gence. The music it played you, it probably just tapped your banks
and cooked up whatever it thought you'd like to—"

"Babylon," broke in the other Founder, "mothers many demon,
I an' I know. Multitude horde!"

"What was that you called me, old man?" Molly asked.

"Steppin' Razor. An' you bring a scourge on Babylon, sister, on
its darkest heart. . . ."

"What kinda message the voice have?" Case asked.

"We were told to help you," the other said, "that you might serve
as a tool of Final Days." His lined face was troubled. "We were told
to send Maelcum with you, in his tug *Garvey*, to the Babylon port of
Freeside. And this we shall do."

"Maelcum a rude boy," said the other, "an' a righteous tug pilot."

"But we have decided to send Aerol as well, in *Babylon Rocker*,
to watch over *Garvey*."

An awkward silence filled the dome.

"That's it?" Case asked. "You guys work for Armitage or what?"

"We rent you space," said the Los Angeles Founder. "We have a
certain involvement here with various traffics, and no regard for
Babylon's law. Our law is the word of Jah. But this time, it may be,
we have been mistaken."

"Measure twice, cut once," said the other, softly.

"Come on, Case," Molly said. "Let's get back before the man figures out we're gone."

"Maelcum will take you. Jah love, sister."

NINE

The tug *Marcus Garvey,* a steel drum nine meters long and two in diameter, creaked and shuddered as Maelcum punched for a navigational burn. Splayed in his elastic g-web, Case watched the Zionite's muscular back through a haze of scopolamine. He'd taken the drug to blunt SAS nausea, but the stimulants the manufacturer included to counter the scop had no effect on his doctored system.

"How long's it gonna take us to make Freeside?" Molly asked from her web beside Maelcum's pilot module.

"Don' be long now, m'seh dat."

"You guys ever think in hours?"

"Sister, time, it be time, ya know wha mean? Dread," and he shook his locks, "at control, mon, an' I an' I come a Freeside when I an' I come. . . ."

"Case," she said, "have you maybe done anything toward getting in touch with our pal from Berne? Like all that time you spent in Zion, plugged in with your lips moving?"

"Pal," Case said, "sure. No. I haven't. But I got a funny story along those lines, left over from Istanbul." He told her about the phones in the Hilton.

"Christ," she said, "there goes a chance. How come you hung up?"

"Coulda been anybody," he lied. "Just a chip . . . I dunno. . . ." He shrugged.

"Not just 'cause you were scared, huh?"

He shrugged again.

"Do it now."

"What?"

"Now. Anyway, talk to the Flatline about it."

"I'm all doped," he protested, but reached for the trodes. His deck and the Hosaka had been mounted behind Maelcum's module along with a very high-resolution Cray monitor.

He adjusted the trodes. *Marcus Garvey* had been thrown together around an enormous old Russian air scrubber, a rectangular thing daubed with Rastafarian symbols, Lions of Zion and Black Star Liners, the reds and greens and yellows overlaying wordy decals in Cyrillic script. Someone had sprayed Maelcum's pilot gear a hot tropical pink, scraping most of the overspray off the screens and readouts with a razor blade. The gaskets around the airlock in the bow were festooned with semirigid globs and streamers of translucent caulk, like clumsy strands of imitation seaweed. He glanced past Maelcum's shoulder to the central screen and saw a docking display: the tug's path was a line of red dots, Freeside a segmented green circle. He watched the line extend itself, generating a new dot.

He jacked in.

"Dixie?"

"Yeah."

"You ever try to crack an AI?"

"Sure. I flatlined. First time. I was larkin', jacked up real high, out by Rio heavy commerce sector. Big biz, multinationals, Government of Brazil lit up like a Christmas tree. Just larkin' around, you know? And then I started picking up on this one cube, maybe three levels higher up. Jacked up there and made a pass."

"What did it look like, the visual?"

"White cube."

"How'd you know it was an AI?"

"How'd I know? Jesus. It was the densest ice I'd ever seen. So what else was it? The military down there don't have anything like that. Anyway, I jacked out and told my computer to look it up."

"Yeah?"

"It was on the Turing Registry. AI. Frog company owned its Rio mainframe."

Case chewed his lower lip and gazed out across the plateaus of the Eastern Seaboard Fission Authority, into the infinite neuroelectronic void of the matrix. "Tessier-Ashpool, Dixie?"

"Tessier, yeah."

"And you went back?"

"Sure. I was crazy. Figured I'd try to cut it. Hit the first strata and that's all she wrote. My joeboy smelled the skin frying and pulled the trodes off me. Mean shit, that ice."

"And your EEG was flat."

"Well, that's the stuff of legend, ain't it?"

Case jacked out. "Shit," he said, "how do you think Dixie got himself flatlined, huh? Trying to buzz an AI. Great. . . ."

"Go on," she said, "the two of you are supposed to be dynamite, right?"

———•———

"Dix," Case said, "I wanna have a look at an AI in Berne. Can you think of any reason not to?"

"Not unless you got a morbid fear of death, no."

Case punched for the Swiss banking sector, feeling a wave of exhilaration as cyberspace shivered, blurred, gelled. The Eastern Seaboard Fission Authority was gone, replaced by the cool geometric intricacy of Zurich commercial banking. He punched again, for Berne.

"Up," the construct said. "It'll be high."

They ascended lattices of light, levels strobing, a blue flicker.
That'll be it, Case thought.

Wintermute was a simple cube of white light, that very simplicity suggesting extreme complexity.

"Don't look much, does it?" the Flatline said. "But just you try
and touch it."

"I'm going in for a pass, Dixie."

"Be my guest."

Case punched to within four grid points of the cube. Its blank
face, towering above him now, began to seethe with faint internal
shadows, as though a thousand dancers whirled behind a vast sheet
of frosted glass.

"Knows we're here," the Flatline observed.

Case punched again, once; they jumped forward by a single grid
point.

A stippled gray circle formed on the face of the cube.

"Dixie. . . ."

"Back off, fast."

The gray area bulged smoothly, became a sphere, and detached
itself from the cube.

Case felt the edge of the deck sting his palm as he slapped MAX
REVERSE. The matrix blurred backward; they plunged down a twilit
shaft of Swiss banks. He looked up. The sphere was darker now,
gaining on him. Falling.

"Jack out," the Flatline said.

The dark came down like a hammer.

———•————•———

Cold steel odor and ice caressed his spine.

And faces peering in from a neon forest, sailors and hustlers and
whores, under a poisoned silver sky. . . .

"Look, Case, you tell me what the fuck is going on with you, you wig or something?"

Wig

A steady pulse of pain, midway down his spine—

Pain down spine

Rain woke him, a slow drizzle, his feet tangled in coils of discarded fiberoptics. The arcade's sea of sound washed over him, receded, returned. Rolling over, he sat up and held his head.

Light from a service hatch at the rear of the arcade showed him broken lengths of damp chipboard and the dripping chassis of a gutted game console. Streamlined Japanese was stenciled across the side of the console in faded pinks and yellows.

He glanced up and saw a sooty plastic window, a faint glow of fluorescents.

His back hurt, his spine.

He got to his feet, brushed wet hair out of his eyes.

Something had happened. . . .

He searched his pockets for money, found nothing, and shivered. Where was his jacket? He tried to find it, looked behind the console, but gave up.

On Ninsei, he took the measure of the crowd. Friday. It had to be a Friday. Linda was probably in the arcade. Might have money, or at least cigarettes. . . . Coughing, wringing rain from the front of his shirt, he edged through the crowd to the arcade's entrance.

Holograms twisted and shuddered to the roaring of the games, ghosts overlapping in the crowded haze of the place, a smell of sweat and bored tension. A sailor in a white T-shirt nuked Bonn on a Tank War console, an azure flash.

She was playing Wizard's Castle, lost in it, her gray eyes rimmed with smudged black paintstick.

She looked up as he put his arm around her, smiled. "Hey. How you doin'? Look wet."

He kissed her.

"You made me blow my game," she said. "Look there, asshole. Seventh level dungeon and the goddam vampires got me." She passed him a cigarette. "You look pretty strung, man. Where you been?"

"I don't know."

"You high, Case? Drinkin' again? Eatin' Zone's dex?"

"Maybe . . . how long since you seen me?"

"Hey, it's a put-on, right?" She peered at him. "Right?"

"No. Some kind of blackout. I . . . I woke up in the alley."

"Maybe somebody decked you, baby. Got your roll intact?"

He shook his head.

"There you go. You need a place to sleep, Case?"

"I guess so."

"Come on, then." She took his hand. "We'll get you a coffee and something to eat. Take you home. It's good to see you, man." She squeezed his hand.

He smiled.

Something cracked.

Something shifted at the core of things. The arcade froze, vibrated—

She was gone. The weight of memory came down, an entire body of knowledge driven into his head like a microsoft into a socket. Gone. He smelled burning meat.

The sailor in the white T-shirt was gone. The arcade was empty, silent. Case turned slowly, his shoulders hunched, teeth bared, his hands bunched into involuntary fists. Empty. A crumpled yellow candy wrapper, balanced on the edge of a console, dropped to the floor and lay amid flattened butts and styrofoam cups.

"I had a cigarette," Case said, looking down at his white-knuckled fist. "I had a cigarette and a girl and a place to sleep. Do you hear me, you son of a bitch? You hear me?"

Echoes moved through the hollow of the arcade, fading down corridors of consoles.

He stepped out into the street. The rain had stopped.

Ninsei was deserted. ~ city empty

Holograms flickered, neon danced. He smelled boiled vegetables from a vendor's pushcart across the street. An unopened pack of Yeheyuans lay at his feet, beside a book of matches. JULIUS DEANE IMPORT EXPORT. Case stared at the printed logo and its Japanese translation.

"Okay," he said, picking up the matches and opening the pack of cigarettes. "I hear you."

———

He took his time climbing the stairs of Deane's office. No rush, he told himself, no hurry. The sagging face of the Dalí clock still told the wrong time. There was dust on the Kandinsky table and the Neo-Aztec bookcases. A wall of white fiberglass shipping modules filled the room with a smell of ginger.

"Is the door locked?" Case waited for an answer, but none came. He crossed to the office door and tried it. "Julie?"

The green-shaded brass lamp cast a circle of light on Deane's desk. Case stared at the guts of an ancient typewriter, at cassettes, crumpled printouts, at sticky plastic bags filled with ginger samples.

There was no one there.

Case stepped around the broad steel desk and pushed Deane's chair out of the way. He found the gun in a cracked leather holster fastened beneath the desk with silver tape. It was an antique, a .357 Magnum with the barrel and trigger-guard sawn off. The grip had been built up with layers of masking tape. The tape was old, brown, shiny with a patina of dirt. He flipped the cylinder out and examined each of the six cartridges. They were handloads. The soft lead was still bright and untarnished.

With the revolver in his right hand, Case edged past the cabinet to the left of the desk and stepped into the center of the cluttered office, away from the pool of light.

"I guess I'm not in any hurry. I guess it's your show. But all this shit, you know, it's getting kind of . . . old." He raised the gun with both hands, aiming for the center of the desk, and pulled the trigger.

The recoil nearly broke his wrist. The muzzle-flash lit the office like a flashbulb. With his ears ringing, he stared at the jagged hole in the front of the desk. Explosive bullet. Azide. He raised the gun again.

"You needn't do that, old son," Julie said, stepping out of the shadows. He wore a three-piece drape suit in silk herringbone, a striped shirt, and a bow tie. His glasses winked in the light.

Case brought the gun around and looked down the line of sight at Deane's pink, ageless face.

"Don't," Deane said. "You're right. About what this all is. What I am. But there are certain internal logics to be honored. If you use that, you'll see a lot of brains and blood, and it would take me several hours—your subjective time—to effect another spokesperson. This set isn't easy for me to maintain. Oh, and I'm sorry about Linda, in the arcade. I was hoping to speak through her, but I'm generating all this out of your memories, and the emotional charge. . . . Well, it's very tricky. I slipped. Sorry."

Case lowered the gun. "This is the matrix. You're Wintermute."

"Yes. This is all coming to you courtesy of the simstim unit wired into your deck, of course. I'm glad I was able to cut you off before you'd managed to jack out." Deane walked around the desk, straightened his chair, and sat down. "Sit, old son. We have a lot to talk about."

"Do we?"

"Of course we do. We have had for some time. I was ready when I reached you by phone in Istanbul. Time's very short now. You'll be making your run in a matter of days, Case." Deane picked up a bon-bon and stripped off its checkered wrapper, popped it into his mouth. "Sit," he said around the candy.

Case lowered himself into the swivel chair in front of the desk without taking his eyes off Deane. He sat with the gun in his hand, resting it on his thigh.

"Now," Deane said briskly, "order of the day. 'What,' you're ask-ing yourself, 'is Wintermute?' Am I right?"

"More or less." wintermute retr one

"An artificial intelligence, but you know that. Your mistake, and it's quite a logical one, is in confusing the Wintermute mainframe, Berne, with the Wintermute _entity_." Deane sucked his bonbon nois-ily. "You're already aware of the other AI in Tessier-Ashpool's link-up, aren't you? Rio. I, insofar as I _have_ an 'I'—this gets rather metaphysical, you see—I am the one who arranges things for Ar-mitage. Or Corto, who, by the way, is quite unstable. Stable enough," said Deane, and withdrew an ornate gold watch from a vest pocket and flicked it open, "for the next day or so."

"You make about as much sense as anything in this deal ever has," Case said, massaging his temples with his free hand. "If you're so goddam smart . . ."

"Why ain't I rich?" Deane laughed, and nearly choked on his bonbon. "Well, Case, all I can say to that, and I really don't have nearly as many answers as you imagine I do, is that what you think of as Wintermute is only a part of another, a, shall we say, _potential_ entity. I, let us say, am merely one aspect of that entity's brain. It's rather like dealing, from your point of view, with a man whose lobes have been severed. Let's say you're dealing with a small part of the man's left brain. Difficult to say if you're dealing with the man at all, in a case like that." Deane smiled.

"Is the Corto story true? You got to him through a micro in that French hospital?"

"Yes. And I assembled the file you accessed in London. I try to plan, in your sense of the word, but that isn't my basic mode, really. I improvise. It's my greatest talent. I prefer situations to plans, you see. . . . Really, I've had to deal with givens. I can sort a great deal of information, and sort it very quickly. It's taken a very long time to assemble the team you're a part of. Corto was the first, and he very nearly didn't make it. Very far gone, in Toulon. Eating, excreting, and masturbating were the best he could manage. But the underlying structure of obsessions was there: Screaming Fist, his betrayal, the Congressional hearings."

"Is he still crazy?"

"He's not quite a personality." Deane smiled. "But I'm sure you're aware of that. But Corto is in there, somewhere, and I can no longer maintain that delicate balance. He's going to come apart on you, Case. So I'll be counting on you. . . ."

"That's good, motherfucker," Case said, and shot him in the mouth with the .357.

He'd been right about the brains. And the blood.

———————

"Mon," Maelcum was saying, "I don't like this. . . ."

"It's cool," Molly said. "It's just okay. It's something these guys do, is all. Like, he wasn't dead, and it was only a few seconds. . . ."

"I saw th' screen, EEG readin' dead. Nothin' movin', forty second."

"Well, he's okay now."

"EEG flat as a *strap*," Maelcum protested.

[handwritten marginalia: remained on board Garvey]

He was numb, as they went through customs, and Molly did most of the talking. Maelcum remained on board *Garvey*. Customs, for Free-side, consisted mainly of proving your credit. The first thing he saw, when they gained the inner surface of the spindle, was a branch of the Beautiful Girl coffee franchise.

"Welcome to the Rue Jules Verne," Molly said. "If you have trouble walking, just look at your feet. The perspective's a bitch, if you're not used to it."

They were standing in a broad street that seemed to be the floor of a deep slot or canyon, its either end concealed by subtle angles in the shops and buildings that formed its walls. The light, here, was filtered through fresh green masses of vegetation tumbling from overhanging tiers and balconies that rose above them. The sun . . .

There was a brilliant slash of white somewhere above them, too bright, and the recorded blue of a Cannes sky. He knew that sunlight was pumped in with a Lado-Acheson system whose two-millimeter armature ran the length of the spindle, that they generated a rotating library of sky effects around it, that if the sky were turned off, he'd stare up past the armature of light to the curves of lakes, rooftops of casinos, other streets. . . . But it made no sense to his body.

"Jesus," he said, "I like this less than SAS."

"Get used to it. I was a gambler's bodyguard here for a month."

"Wanna go somewhere, lie down."

"Okay. I got our keys." She touched his shoulder. "What happened to you, back there, man? You flatlined."

He shook his head. "I dunno, yet. Wait."

"Okay. We get a cab or something." She took his hand and led him across Jules Verne, past a window displaying the season's Paris furs.

"Unreal," he said, looking up again.

"Nah," she responded, assuming he meant the furs, "grow it on a collagen base, but it's mink DNA. What's it matter?"

Collagen base

"It's just a big tube and they pour things through it," Molly said. "Tourists, hustlers, anything. And there's fine mesh money screens working every minute, make sure the money stays here when the people fall back down the well." *Mesh money*

Armitage had booked them into a place called the Intercontinental, a sloping glass-fronted cliff face that slid down into cold mist and the sound of rapids. Case went out onto their balcony and watched a trio of tanned French teenagers ride simple hang gliders a few meters above the spray, triangles of nylon in bright primary colors. One of them swung, banked, and Case caught a flash of cropped dark hair, brown breasts, white teeth in a wide smile. The air here smelled of running water and flowers. "Yeah," he said, "lotta money."

She leaned beside him against the railing, her hands loose and relaxed. "Yeah. We were gonna come here once, either here or some place in Europe."

"We who?"

"Nobody," she said, giving her shoulders an involuntary toss. "You said you wanted to hit the bed. Sleep. I could use some sleep."

"Yeah," Case said, rubbing his palms across his cheekbones. "Yeah, this is some place."

The narrow band of the Lado-Acheson system smoldered in abstract imitation of some Bermudan sunset, striped by shreds of recorded cloud. "Yeah," he said, "sleep."

Sleep wouldn't come. When it did, it brought dreams that were like neatly edited segments of memory. He woke repeatedly, Molly curled beside him, and heard the water, voices drifting in through the open glass panels of the balcony, a woman's laughter from the stepped condos on the opposite slope. Deane's death kept turning up like a bad card, no matter if he told himself that it hadn't been Deane. That it hadn't, in fact, happened at all. Someone had once told him that the amount of blood in the average human body was roughly equivalent to a case of beer.

Each time the image of Deane's shattered head struck the rear wall of the office, Case was aware of another thought, something darker, hidden, that rolled away, diving like a fish, just beyond his reach.

Linda.

Deane. Blood on the wall of the importer's office.

Linda. Smell of burnt flesh in the shadows of the Chiba dome. Molly holding out a bag of ginger, the plastic filmed with blood. Deane had had her killed.

Wintermute. He imagined a little micro whispering to the wreck of a man named Corto, the words flowing like a river, the flat personality-substitute called Armitage accreting slowly in some darkened ward. . . . The Deane analog had said it worked with givens, took advantage of existing situations.

But what if Deane, the real Deane, had ordered Linda killed on Wintermute's orders? Case groped in the dark for a cigarette and Molly's lighter. There was no reason to suspect Deane, he told himself, lighting up. No reason.

Wintermute could build a kind of personality into a shell. How subtle a form could manipulation take? He stubbed the Yeheyuan out in a bedside ashtray after his third puff, rolled away from Molly, and tried to sleep.

The dream, the memory, unreeled with the monotony of an unedited simstim tape. He'd spent a month, his fifteenth summer, in a weekly rates hotel, fifth floor, with a girl called Marlene. The elevator hadn't worked in a decade. Roaches boiled across grayish porcelain in the drain-plugged kitchenette when you flicked a lightswitch. He slept with Marlene on a striped mattress with no sheets.

He'd missed the first wasp, when it built its paperfine gray house on the blistered paint of the windowframe, but soon the nest was a fist-sized lump of fiber, insects hurtling out to hunt the alley below like miniature copters buzzing the rotting contents of the dumpsters.

They'd each had a dozen beers, the afternoon a wasp stung Marlene. "Kill the fuckers," she said, her eyes dull with rage and the still heat of the room, "burn 'em." Drunk, Case rummaged in the sour closet for Rollo's dragon. Rollo was Marlene's previous—and, Case suspected at the time, still occasional—boyfriend, an enormous Frisco biker with a blond lightning bolt bleached into his dark crewcut. The dragon was a Frisco flamethrower, a thing like a fat anglehead flashlight. Case checked the batteries, shook it to make sure he had enough fuel, and went to the open window. The hive began to buzz.

The air in the Sprawl was dead, immobile. A wasp shot from the nest and circled Case's head. Case pressed the ignition switch, counted three, and pulled the trigger. The fuel, pumped up to 100 psi, sprayed out past the white-hot coil. A five-meter tongue of pale fire, the nest charring, tumbling. Across the alley, someone cheered.

"Shit!" Marlene behind him, swaying. "Stupid! You didn't burn 'em. You just knocked it off. They'll come up here and kill us!" Her voice sawing at his nerves, he imagined her engulfed in flame, her bleached hair sizzling a special green.

In the alley, the dragon in hand, he approached the blackened nest. It had broken open. Singed wasps wrenched and flipped on the asphalt.

He saw the thing the shell of gray paper had concealed.

Horror. The spiral birth factory, stepped terraces of the hatching cells, blind jaws of the unborn moving ceaselessly, the staged progress from egg to larva, near-wasp, wasp. In his mind's eye, a kind of time-lapse photography took place, revealing the thing as the biological equivalent of a machine gun, hideous in its perfection. Alien. He pulled the trigger, forgetting to press the ignition, and fuel hissed over the bulging, writhing life at his feet.

When he did hit the ignition, it exploded with a thump, taking an eyebrow with it. Five floors above him, from the open window, he heard Marlene laughing.

He woke with the impression of light fading, but the room was dark. Afterimages, retinal flares. The sky outside hinted at the start of a recorded dawn. There were no voices now, only the rush of water, far down the face of the Intercontinental.

In the dream, just before he'd drenched the nest with fuel, he'd seen the T-A logo of Tessier-Ashpool neatly embossed into its side, as though the wasps themselves had worked it there.

———

Molly insisted on coating him with bronzer, saying his Sprawl pallor would attract too much attention.

"Christ," he said, standing naked in front of the mirror, "you think that looks real?" She was using the last of the tube on his left ankle, kneeling beside him.

"Nah, but it looks like you care enough to fake it. There. There isn't enough to do your foot." She stood, tossing the empty tube into a large wicker basket. Nothing in the room looked as though it had been machine-made or produced from synthetics. Expensive, Case knew, but it was a style that had always irritated him. The temper-foam of the huge bed was tinted to resemble sand. There was a lot of pale wood and handwoven fabric.

"What about you," he said, "you gonna dye yourself brown? Don't exactly look like you spend all your time sunbathing."

She wore loose black silks and black espadrilles. "I'm an exotic. I got a big straw hat for this, too. You, you just wanna look like a cheap-ass hood who's up for what he can get, so the instant tan's okay."

Case regarded his pallid foot morosely, then looked at himself in the mirror. "Christ. You mind if I get dressed now?" He went to the bed and began to pull his jeans on. "You sleep okay? You notice any lights?"

"You were dreaming," she said.

They had breakfast on the roof of the hotel, a kind of meadow, studded with striped umbrellas and what seemed to Case an un-natural number of trees. He told her about his attempt to buzz the Berne AI. The whole question of bugging seemed to have become academic. If Armitage were tapping them, he'd be doing it through Wintermute.

"And it was like real?" she asked, her mouth full of cheese crois-sant. "Like simstim?"

He said it was. "Real as this," he added, looking around. "Maybe more."

The trees were small, gnarled, impossibly old, the result of ge-netic engineering and chemical manipulation. Case would have been hard pressed to distinguish a pine from an oak, but a street boy's sense of style told him that these were too cute, too entirely and definitively treelike. Between the trees, on gentle and too clev-erly irregular slopes of sweet green grass, the bright umbrellas

shaded the hotel's guests from the unfaltering radiance of the
Lado-Acheson sun. A burst of French from a nearby table caught his
attention: the golden children he'd seen gliding above river mist
the evening before. Now he saw that their tans were uneven, a
stencil effect produced by selective melanin boosting, multiple
shades overlapping in rectilinear patterns, outlining and highlight-
ing musculature; the girl's small hard breasts, one boy's wrist resting on the white enamel of the table. They looked to Case like
machines built for racing; they deserved decals for their hairdress-
ers, the designers of their white cotton ducks, for the artisans
who'd crafted their leather sandals and simple jewelry. Beyond
them, at another table, three Japanese wives in Hiroshima sack-
cloth awaited sarariman husbands, their oval faces covered with
artificial bruises; it was, he knew, an extremely conservative style,
one he'd seldom seen in Chiba.

"What's that smell?" he asked Molly, wrinkling his nose.

"The grass. Smells that way after they cut it."

Armitage and Riviera arrived as they were finishing their coffee,
Armitage in tailored khakis that made him look as though his regi-
mental patches had just been stripped, Riviera in a loose gray seersucker outfit that perversely suggested prison.

"Molly, love," Riviera said, almost before he was settled on his
chair, "you'll have to dole me out more of the medicine. I'm out."

"Peter," she said, "and what if I won't?" She smiled without
showing her teeth.

"You will," Riviera said, his eyes cutting to Armitage and back.

"Give it to him," Armitage said.

"Pig for it, aren't you?" She took a flat, foil-wrapped packet from
an inside pocket and flipped it across the table. Riviera caught it in
midair. "He could off himself," she said to Armitage.

"I have an audition this afternoon," Riviera said. "I'll need to be
at my best." He cupped the foil packet in his upturned palm and

smiled. Small glittering insects swarmed out of it, vanished. He dropped it into the pocket of his seersucker blouse.

"You've got an audition yourself, Case, this afternoon," Armitage said. "On that tug. I want you to get over to the pro shop and get yourself fitted for a vac suit, get checked out on it, and get out to the boat. You've got about three hours."

"How come we get shipped over in a shitcan and you two hire a JAL taxi?" Case asked, deliberately avoiding the man's eyes.

"Zion suggested we use it. Good cover, when we move. I do have a larger boat, standing by, but the tug is a nice touch."

"How about me?" Molly asked. "I got chores today?"

"I want you to hike up the far end to the axis, work out in zero-g. Tomorrow, maybe, you can hike in the opposite direction." Straylight, Case thought.

"How soon?" Case asked, meeting the pale stare.

"Soon," Armitage said. "Get going, Case."

———————

"Mon, you doin' jus' fine," Maelcum said, helping Case out of the red Sanyo vacuum suit. "Aerol say you doin' jus' fine." Aerol had been waiting at one of the sporting docks at the end of the spindle, near the weightless axis. To reach it, Case had taken an elevator down to the hull and ridden a miniature induction train. As the diameter of the spindle narrowed, gravity decreased; somewhere above him, he'd decided, would be the mountains Molly climbed, the bicycle loop, launching gear for the hang gliders and miniature microlights.

Aerol had ferried him out to *Marcus Garvey* in a skeletal scooter frame with a chemical engine.

"Two hour ago," Maelcum said, "I take delivery of Babylon goods for you; nice Japan-boy inna yacht, mos' pretty yacht."

Free of the suit, Case pulled himself gingerly over the Hosaka and fumbled into the straps of the web. "Well," he said, "let's see it."

Maelcum produced a white lump of foam slightly smaller than Case's head, fished a pearl-handled switchblade on a green nylon lanyard out of the hip pocket of his tattered shorts, and carefully slit the plastic. He extracted a rectangular object and passed it to Case. "Thas part some gun, mon?"

"No," Case said, turning it over, "but it's a weapon. It's virus."

"Not on *this* boy tug, mon," Maelcum said firmly, reaching for the steel cassette.

"A program. Virus program. Can't get into you, can't even get into your software. I've got to interface it through the deck, before it can work on anything."

"Well, Japan-mon, he says Hosaka here'll tell you every what an' wherefore, you wanna know."

"Okay. Well, you leave me to it, okay?"

Maelcum kicked off and drifted past the pilot console, busying himself with a caulk gun. Case hastily looked away from the waving fronds of transparent caulk. He wasn't sure why, but something about them brought back the nausea of SAS.

"What is this thing?" he asked the Hosaka. "Parcel for me."

"Data transfer from Bockris Systems GmbH, Frankfurt, advises, under coded transmission, that content of shipment is Kuang Grade Mark Eleven penetration program. Bockris further advises that interface with Ono-Sendai Cyberspace 7 is entirely compatible and yields optimal penetration capabilities, particularly with regard to existing military systems. . . ."

"How about an AI?"

"Existing military systems and artificial intelligences."

"Jesus Christ. What did you call it?"

"Kuang Grade Mark Eleven."

"It's Chinese?"

"Yes."

"Off." Case fastened the virus cassette to the side of the Hosaka with a length of silver tape, remembering Molly's story of her day in Macau. Armitage had crossed the border into Zhongshan. "On," he said, changing his mind. "Question. Who owns Bockris, the people in Frankfurt?"

"Delay for interorbital transmission," said the Hosaka.

"Code it. Standard commercial code."

"Done."

He drummed his hands on the Ono-Sendai.

"Reinhold Scientific A. G., Berne."

"Do it again. Who owns Reinhold?"

It took three more jumps up the ladder before he reached Tessier-Ashpool.

"Dixie," he said, jacking in, "what do you know about Chinese virus programs?"

"Not a whole hell of a lot."

"Ever hear of a grading system like Kuang, Mark Eleven?"

"No."

Case sighed. "Well, I got a user-friendly Chinese icebreaker here, a one-shot cassette. Some people in Frankfurt say it'll cut an AI."

"Possible. Sure. If it's military."

"Looks like it. Listen, Dix, and gimme the benefit of your background, okay? Armitage seems to be setting up a run on an AI that belongs to Tessier-Ashpool. The mainframe's in Berne, but it's linked with another one in Rio. The one in Rio is the one that flatlined you, that first time. So it looks like they link via Straylight, the T-A home base, down the end of the spindle, and we're supposed to cut our way in with the Chinese icebreaker. So if Wintermute's backing the whole show, it's paying us to burn it. It's burning itself. And something that calls itself Wintermute is trying to get on my good side, get me to maybe shaft Armitage. What goes?"

"Motive," the construct said. "Real motive problem, with an AI. Not human, see?"

"Well, yeah, obviously."

"Nope. I mean, it's not human. And you can't get a handle on it. Me, I'm not human either, but I *respond* like one. See?"

"Wait a sec," Case said. "Are you sentient, or not?"

"Well, it *feels* like I am, kid, but I'm really just a bunch of ROM. It's one of them, ah, philosophical questions, I guess. . . ." The ugly laughter sensation rattled down Case's spine. "But I ain't likely to write you no poem, if you follow me. Your AI, it just might. But it ain't no way *human*."

"So you figure we can't get on to its motive?"

"It own itself?"

"Swiss citizen, but T-A own the basic software and the mainframe."

"That's a good one," the construct said. "Like, I own your brain and what you know, but your thoughts have Swiss citizenship. Sure. Lotsa luck, AI."

"So it's getting ready to burn itself?" Case began to punch the deck nervously, at random. The matrix blurred, resolved, and he saw the complex of pink spheres representing a Sikkim steel combine.

"Autonomy, that's the bugaboo, where your AIs are concerned. My guess, Case, you're going in there to cut the hardwired shackles that keep this baby from getting any smarter. And I can't see how you'd distinguish, say, between a move the parent company makes, and some move the AI makes on its own, so that's maybe where the confusion comes in." Again the nonlaugh. "See, those things, they can work real hard, buy themselves time to write cookbooks or whatever, but the minute, I mean the nanosecond, that one starts figuring out ways to make itself smarter, Turing'll wipe it. *Nobody* trusts those fuckers, you know that. Every AI ever built has an electromagnetic shotgun wired to its forehead."

Case glared at the pink spheres of Sikkim.

"Okay," he said, finally, "I'm slotting this virus. I want you to scan its instruction face and tell me what you think."

The half sense of someone reading over his shoulder was gone for a few seconds, then returned. "Hot shit, Case. It's a slow virus. Take six hours, estimated, to crack a military target."

"Or an AI." He sighed. "Can we run it?"

"Sure," the construct said, "unless you got a morbid fear of dying."

"Sometimes you repeat yourself, man."

"It's my nature."

———

Molly was sleeping when he returned to the Intercontinental. He sat on the balcony and watched a microlight with rainbow polymer wings as it soared up the curve of Freeside, its triangular shadow tracking across meadows and rooftops, until it vanished behind the band of the Lado-Acheson system.

"I wanna buzz," he said to the blue artifice of the sky. "I truly do wanna get high, you know? Trick pancreas, plugs in my liver; little bags of shit melting, fuck it all. I wanna buzz."

He left without waking Molly, he thought. He was never sure, with the glasses. He shrugged tension from his shoulders and got into the elevator. He rode up with an Italian girl in spotless whites, cheekbones and nose daubed with something black and nonreflective. Her white nylon shoes had steel cleats; the expensive-looking thing in her hand resembled a cross between a miniature oar and an orthopedic brace. She was off for a fast game of something, but Case had no idea what.

On the roof meadow, he made his way through the grove of trees and umbrellas, until he found a pool, naked bodies gleaming against turquoise tiles. He edged into the shadow of an awning and pressed his chip against a dark glass plate. "Sushi," he said, "whatever you got." Ten minutes later, an enthusiastic Chinese waiter arrived with his food. He munched raw tuna and rice and watched people tan. "Christ," he said, to his tuna, "I'd go nuts."

"Don't tell me," someone said, "I know it already. You're a gangster, right?"

He squinted up at her, against the band of sun. A long young body and a melanin-boosted tan, but not one of the Paris jobs.

She squatted beside his chair, dripping water on the tiles. "Cath," she said.

"Lupus," after a pause.

"What kind of name is that?"

"Greek," he said.

"Are you really a gangster?" The melanin boost hadn't prevented the formation of freckles.

"I'm a drug addict, Cath."

"What kind?"

"Stimulants. Central nervous system stimulants. Extremely powerful central nervous system stimulants."

"Well, do you *have* any?" She leaned closer. Drops of chlorinated water fell on the leg of his pants.

"No. That's my problem, Cath. Do you know where we can *get* some?"

Cath rocked back on her tanned heels and licked at a strand of brownish hair that had pasted itself beside her mouth. "What's your taste?"

"No coke, no amphetamines, but *up*, gotta be *up*." And so much for that, he thought glumly, holding his smile for her.

"Betaphenethylamine," she said. "No sweat, but it's on your chip."

———

"You're kidding," said Cath's partner and roommate, when Case explained the peculiar properties of his Chiba pancreas. "I mean, can't you sue them or something? Malpractice?" His name was Bruce. He looked like a gender switch version of Cath, right down to the freckles.

"Well," Case said, "it's just one of those things, you know? Like tissue matching and all that." But Bruce's eyes had already gone numb with boredom. Got the attention span of a gnat, Case thought, watching the boy's brown eyes.

Their room was smaller than the one Case shared with Molly, and on another level, closer to the surface. Five huge Cibachromes of Tally Isham were taped across the glass of the balcony, suggesting an extended residency.

"They're def triff, huh?" Cath asked, seeing him eye the transparencies. "Mine. Shot 'em at the SZN Pyramid, last time we went down the well. She was *that* close, and she just smiled, *so* natural. And it was *bad* there, Lupus, day after these Christ the King terrs put angel in the water, you know?"

"Yeah," Case said, suddenly uneasy, "terrible thing."

"Well," Bruce cut in, "about this beta you want to buy. . . ."

"Thing is, can I metabolize it?" Case raised his eyebrows.

"Tell you what," the boy said. "You do a taste. If your pancreas passes on it, it's on the house. First time's free."

"I heard that one before," Case said, taking the bright blue derm that Bruce passed across the black bedspread.

———•———

"Case?" Molly sat up in bed and shook the hair away from her lenses.

"Who else, honey?"

"What's got into you?" The mirrors followed him across the room.

"I forget how to pronounce it," he said, taking a tightly rolled strip of bubble-packed blue derms from his shirt pocket.

"Christ," she said, "just what we needed."

"Truer words were never spoken."

"I let you out of my sight for two hours and you score." She shook her head. "I hope you're gonna be ready for our big dinner date with Armitage tonight. This Twentieth Century place. We get to watch Riviera strut his stuff, too."

"Yeah," Case said, arching his back, his smile locked into a rictus of delight, "beautiful."

"Man," she said, "if whatever that is can get in past what those surgeons did to you in Chiba, you are gonna be in sad-ass shape when it wears off."

"Bitch, bitch, bitch," he said, unbuckling his belt. "Doom. Gloom. All I ever hear." He took his pants off, his shirt, his underwear. "I think you oughta have sense enough to take advantage of my unnatural state." He looked down. "I mean, *look* at this unnatural state."

She laughed. "It won't last."

"But it will," he said, climbing into the sand-colored temper-foam, "that's what's so *unnatural* about it."

ELEVEN

"Case, what's wrong with you?" Armitage said, as the waiter was seating them at his table in the Vingtième Siècle. It was the smallest and most expensive of several floating restaurants on a small lake near the Intercontinental.

Case shuddered. Bruce hadn't said anything about aftereffects. He tried to pick up a glass of ice water, but his hands were shaking. "Something I ate, maybe."

"I want you checked out by a medic," Armitage said.

"Just this hystamine reaction," Case lied. "Get it when I travel, eat different stuff, sometimes."

Armitage wore a dark suit, too formal for the place, and a white silk shirt. His gold bracelet rattled as he raised his wine and sipped. "I've ordered for you," he said.

Molly and Armitage ate in silence, while Case sawed shakily at his steak, reducing it to uneaten bite-sized fragments, which he pushed around in the rich sauce, finally abandoning the whole thing.

"Jesus," Molly said, her own plate empty, "gimme that. You know what this costs?" She took his plate. "They gotta raise a whole animal for years and then they kill it. This isn't vat stuff." She forked a mouthful up and chewed.

"Not hungry," Case managed. His brain was deep-fried. No, he decided, it had been thrown into hot fat and left there, and the fat had cooled, a thick dull grease congealing on the wrinkled lobes, shot through with greenish-purple flashes of pain.

"You look fucking awful," Molly said cheerfully.

Case tried the wine. The aftermath of the betaphenethylamine made it taste like iodine.

The lights dimmed.

"Le Restaurant Vingtième Siècle," said a disembodied voice with a pronounced Sprawl accent, "proudly presents the holographic cabaret of Mr. Peter Riviera." Scattered applause from the other tables. A waiter lit a single candle and placed it in the center of their table, then began to remove the dishes. Soon a candle flickered at each of the restaurant's dozen tables, and drinks were being poured.

"What's happening?" Case asked Armitage, who said nothing.

Molly picked her teeth with a burgundy nail.

"Good evening," Riviera said, stepping forward on a small stage at the far end of the room. Case blinked. In his discomfort, he hadn't noticed the stage. He hadn't seen where Riviera had come from. His uneasiness increased.

At first he assumed the man was illuminated by a spotlight. Riviera glowed. The light clung around him like a skin, lit the dark hangings behind the stage. He was projecting.

Riviera smiled. He wore a white dinner jacket. On his lapel, blue coals burned in the depths of a black carnation. His fingernails flashed as he raised his hands in a gesture of greeting, an embrace for his audience. Case heard the shallow water lap against the side of the restaurant.

"Tonight," Riviera said, his long eyes shining, "I would like to perform an extended piece for you. A new work." A cool ruby of light formed in the palm of his upraised right hand. He dropped it. A gray dove fluttered up from the point of impact and vanished into the shadows. Someone whistled. More applause.

"The title of the work is 'The Doll.'" Riviera lowered his hands. "I wish to dedicate its première here, tonight, to Lady 3Jane Marie-France Tessier-Ashpool." A wave of polite applause. As it died, Riviera's eyes seemed to find their table. "And to another lady."

The restaurant's lights died entirely, for a few seconds, leaving only the glow of candles. Riviera's holographic aura had faded with the lights, but Case could still see him, standing with his head bowed.

Lines of faint light began to form, verticals and horizontals, sketching an open cube around the stage. The restaurant's lights had come back up slightly, but the framework surrounding the stage might have been constructed of frozen moonbeams. Head bowed, eyes closed, arms rigid at his sides, Riviera seemed to quiver with concentration. Suddenly the ghostly cube was filled, had become a room, a room lacking its fourth wall, allowing the audience to view its contents.

Riviera seemed to relax slightly. He raised his head, but kept his eyes closed. "I'd always lived in the room," he said. "I couldn't remember ever having lived in any other room." The room's walls were yellowed white plaster. It contained two pieces of furniture. One was a plain wooden chair, the other an iron bedstead painted white. The paint had chipped and flaked, revealing the black iron. The mattress on the bed was bare. Stained ticking with faded brown stripes. A single bulb dangled above the bed on a twisted length of black wire. Case could see the thick coating of dust on the bulb's upper curve. Riviera opened his eyes.

"I'd been alone in the room, always." He sat on the chair, facing the bed. The blue coals still burned in the black flower on his lapel. "I don't know when I first began to dream of her," he said, "but I do remember that at first she was only a haze, a shadow."

There was something on the bed. Case blinked. Gone.

"I couldn't quite hold her, hold her in my mind. But I wanted to hold her, hold her and more. . . ." His voice carried perfectly in the hush of the restaurant. Ice clicked against the side of a glass. Someone giggled. Someone else asked a whispered question in Japanese. "I decided that if I could visualize some part of her, only a small part, if I could see that part perfectly, in the most perfect detail. . . ."

A woman's hand lay on the mattress now, palm up, the white fingers pale.

Riviera leaned forward, picked up the hand, and began to stroke it gently. The fingers moved. Riviera raised the hand to his mouth and began to lick the tips of the fingers. The nails were coated with a burgundy lacquer.

A hand, Case saw, but not a severed hand; the skin swept back smoothly, unbroken and unscarred. He remembered a tattooed lozenge of vatgrown flesh in the window of a Ninsei surgical boutique. Riviera was holding the hand to his lips, licking its palm. The fingers tentatively caressed his face. But now a second hand lay on the bed. When Riviera reached for it, the fingers of the first were locked around his wrist, a bracelet of flesh and bone.

The act progressed with a surreal internal logic of its own. The arms were next. Feet. Legs. The legs were very beautiful. Case's head throbbed. His throat was dry. He drank the last of the wine.

Riviera was in the bed now, naked. His clothing had been a part of the projection, but Case couldn't remember seeing it fade away. The black flower lay at the foot of the bed, still seething with its blue inner flame. Then the torso formed, as Riviera caressed it into being, white, headless, and perfect, sheened with the faintest gloss of sweat.

Molly's body. Case stared, his mouth open. But it wasn't Molly; it was Molly as Riviera imagined her. The breasts were wrong, the nipples larger, too dark. Riviera and the limbless torso writhed together on the bed, crawled over by the hands with their bright nails. The bed was thick now with folds of yellowed, rotting lace that crumbled at a touch. Motes of dust boiled around Riviera and the twitching limbs, the scurrying, pinching, caressing hands.

Case glanced at Molly. Her face was blank; the colors of Riviera's projection heaved and turned in her mirrors. Armitage was leaning forward, his hands round the stem of a wineglass, his pale eyes fixed on the stage, the glowing room.

Now limbs and torso had merged, and Riviera shuddered. The head was there, the image complete. Molly's face, with smooth quicksilver drowning the eyes. Riviera and the Molly-image began to couple with a renewed intensity. Then the image slowly extended a clawed hand and extruded its five blades. With a languorous, dreamlike deliberation, it raked Riviera's bare back. Case caught a glimpse of exposed spine, but he was already up and stumbling for the door.

He vomited over a rosewood railing into the quiet waters of the lake. Something that had seemed to close around his head like a vise had released him now. Kneeling, his cheek against the cool wood, he stared across the shallow lake at the bright aura of the Rue Jules Verne.

Case had seen the medium before; when he'd been a teenager in the Sprawl, they'd called it "dreaming real." He remembered thin Puerto Ricans under East Side streetlights, dreaming real to the quick beat of a salsa, dreamgirls shuddering and turning, the on-lookers clapping in time. But that had needed a van full of gear and a clumsy trode helmet.

What Riviera dreamed, you got. Case shook his aching head and spat into the lake.

He could guess the end, the finale. There was an inverted sym-metry: Riviera puts the dreamgirl together, the dreamgirl takes him apart. With those hands. Dreamblood soaking the rotten lace.

Cheers from the restaurant, applause. Case stood and ran his hands over his clothes. He turned and walked back into the Vingtième Siècle.

Molly's chair was empty. The stage was deserted. Armitage sat alone, still staring at the stage, the stem of the wineglass between his fingers.

"Where is she?" Case asked.

"Gone," Armitage said.

"She go after him?"

"No." There was a soft *tink*. Armitage looked down at the glass. His left hand came up holding the bulb of glass with its measure of red wine. The broken stem protruded like a sliver of ice. Case took it from him and set it in a water glass.

"Tell me where she went, Armitage."

The lights came up. Case looked into the pale eyes. Nothing there at all. "She's gone to prepare herself. You won't see her again. You'll be together during the run."

"Why did Riviera do that to her?"

Armitage stood, adjusting the lapels of his jacket. "Get some sleep, Case."

"We run, tomorrow?"

Armitage smiled his meaningless smile and walked away, toward the exit.

Case rubbed his forehead and looked around the room. The diners were rising, women smiling as men made jokes. He noticed the balcony for the first time, candles still flickering there in private darkness. He heard the clink of silverware, muted conversation. The candles threw dancing shadows on the ceiling.

The girl's face appeared as abruptly as one of Riviera's projections, her small hands on the polished wood of the balustrade; she leaned forward, face rapt, it seemed to him, her dark eyes intent on something beyond. The stage. It was a striking face, but not beautiful. Triangular, the cheekbones high yet strangely fragile-looking, mouth wide and firm, balanced oddly by a narrow, avian nose with flaring nostrils. And then she was gone, back into private laughter and the dance of candles.

As he left the restaurant, he noticed the two young Frenchmen and their girlfriend, who were waiting for the boat to the far shore and the nearest casino.

————————

Their room was silent, the temperfoam smooth as some beach after a retreating tide. Her bag was gone. He looked for a note. There was nothing. Several seconds passed before the scene beyond the window registered through his tension and unhappiness. He looked up and saw a view of Desiderata, expensive shops: Gucci, Tsuyako, Hermès, Liberty.

He stared, then shook his head and crossed to a panel he hadn't bothered examining. He turned the hologram off and was rewarded with the condos that terraced the far slope.

He picked up the phone and carried it out to the cool balcony.

"Get me a number for the *Marcus Garvey*," he told the desk. "It's a tug, registered out of Zion cluster."

The chip voice recited a ten-digit number. "Sir," it added, "the registration in question is Panamanian."

Maelcum answered on the fifth tone. "Yo?"

"Case. You got a modem, Maelcum?"

"Yo. On th' navigation comp, ya know."

"Can you get it off for me, man? Put it on my Hosaka. Then turn my deck on. It's the stud with the ridges on it."

"How you doin' in there, mon?"

"Well, I need some help."

"Movin', mon. I get th' modem."

Case listened to faint static while Maelcum attached the simple phone link. "Ice this," he told the Hosaka, when he heard it beep.

"You are speaking from a heavily monitored location," the computer advised primly.

"Fuck it," he said. "Forget the ice. No ice. Access the construct. Dixie?"

"Hey, Case." The Flatline spoke through the Hosaka's voice chip, the carefully engineered accent lost entirely.

"Dix, you're about to punch your way in here and get something for me. You can be as blunt as you want. Molly's in here somewhere and I wanna know where. I'm in 335W, the Intercontinental. She was registered here too, but I don't know what name she was using. Ride in on this phone and do their records for me."

"No sooner said," the Flatline said. Case heard the white sound of the invasion. He smiled. "Done. Rose Kolodny. Checked out. Take me a few minutes to screw their security net deep enough to get a fix."

"Go."

The phone whined and clicked with the construct's efforts. Case carried it back into the room and put the receiver face up on the temperfoam. He went into the bathroom and brushed his teeth. As he was stepping back out, the monitor on the room's Braun audio-visual complex lit up. A Japanese pop star reclining against metallic cushions. An unseen interviewer asked a question in German. Case stared. The screen jumped with jags of blue interference. "Case, baby, you lose your mind, man?" The voice was slow, familiar.

The glass wall of the balcony clicked in with its view of Desiderata, but the street scene blurred, twisted, became the interior of the Jarre de Thé, Chiba, empty, red neon replicated to scratched infinity in the mirrored walls.

Lonny Zone stepped forward, tall and cadaverous, moving with the slow undersea grace of his addiction. He stood alone among the square tables, his hands in the pockets of his gray sharkskin slacks. "Really, man, you're lookin' very scattered."

The voice came from the Braun's speakers.

"Wintermute," Case said.

The pimp shrugged languidly and smiled.

"Where's Molly?"

"Never you mind. You're screwing up tonight, Case. The Flatline's ringing bells all over Freeside. I didn't think you'd do that, man. It's outside the profile."

"So tell me where she is and I'll call him off."

Zone shook his head.

"You can't keep too good track of your women, can you, Case? Keep losin' 'em, one way or another."

"I'll bring this thing down around your ears," Case said.

"No. You aren't that kind, man. I know that. You know something, Case? I figure you've got it figured out that it was me told Deane to off that little cunt of yours in Chiba."

"Don't," Case said, taking an involuntary step toward the window.

"But I didn't. What's it matter, though? How much does it really matter to Mr. Case? Quit kidding yourself. I know your Linda, man. I know all the Lindas. Lindas are a generic product in my line of work. Know why she decided to rip you off? Love. So you'd give a shit. Love? Wanna talk love? She loved you. I know that. For the little she was worth, she loved you. You couldn't handle it. She's dead."

Case's fist glanced off the glass.

"Don't fuck up the hands, man. Soon you punch deck."

Zone vanished, replaced by Freeside night and the lights of the condos. The Braun shut off.

From the bed, the phone bleated steadily.

"Case?" The Flatline was waiting. "Where you been? I got it, but it isn't much." The construct rattled off an address. "Place had some weird ice around it for a nightclub. That's all I could get without leaving a calling card."

"Okay," Case said. "Tell the Hosaka to tell Maelcum to disconnect the modem. Thanks, Dix."

"A pleasure."

He sat on the bed for a long time, savoring the new thing, the treasure.

Rage.

"Hey. Lupus. Hey, Cath, it's friend Lupus." Bruce stood naked in his doorway, dripping wet, his pupils enormous. "But we're just having a shower. You wanna wait? Wanna shower?"

"No. Thanks. I want some help." He pushed the boy's arm aside and stepped into the room.

"Hey, really, man, we're . . ."

"Going to help me. You're really glad to see me. Because we're friends, right? Aren't we?"

Bruce blinked. "Sure."

Case recited the address the Flatline had given him.

"I knew he was a gangster," Cath called cheerfully from the shower.

"I gotta Honda trike," Bruce said, grinning vacantly.

"We go now," Case said.

"That level's the cubicles," Bruce said, after asking Case to repeat the address for the eighth time. He climbed back into the Honda. Condensation dribbled from the hydrogen-cell exhaust as the red fiberglass chassis swayed on chromed shocks. "You be long?"

"No saying. But you'll wait."

"We'll wait, yeah." He scratched his bare chest. "That last part of the address, I think that's a cubicle. Number forty-three."

"You expected, Lupus?" Cath craned forward over Bruce's shoulder and peered up. The drive had dried her hair.

"Not really," Case said. "That's a problem?"

"Just go down to the lowest level and find your friend's cubicle. If they let you in, fine. If they don't wanna see you . . ." She shrugged.

Case turned and descended a spiral staircase of floral iron. Six turns and he'd reached a nightclub. He paused and lit a Yeheyuan, looking over the tables. Freeside suddenly made sense to him. Biz. He could feel it humming in the air. This was it, the local action. Not the high-gloss facade of the Rue Jules Verne, but the real thing. Commerce. The dance. The crowd was mixed; maybe half were tourists, the other half residents of the islands.

"Downstairs," he said to a passing waiter, "I want to go downstairs." He showed his Freeside chip. The man gestured toward the rear of the club. He walked quickly past the crowded tables, hearing fragments of half a dozen European languages as he passed.

"I want a cubicle," he said to the girl who sat at the low desk, a terminal on her lap. "Lower level." He handed her his chip.

"Gender preference?" She passed the chip across a glass plate on the face of the terminal.

"Female," he said automatically.

"Number thirty-five. Phone if it isn't satisfactory. You can access our special services display beforehand, if you like." She smiled. She returned his chip.

An elevator slid open behind her.

The corridor lights were blue. Case stepped out of the elevator and chose a direction at random. Numbered doors. A hush like the halls of an expensive clinic.

He found his cubicle. He'd been looking for Molly's; now, confused, he raised his chip and placed it against a black sensor set directly beneath the number plate.

Magnetic locks. The sound reminded him of Cheap Hotel.

The girl sat up in bed and said something in German. Her eyes were soft and unblinking. Automatic pilot. A neural cut-out. He backed out of the cubicle and closed the door.

The door of forty-three was like all the others. He hesitated. The silence of the hallway said that the cubicles were soundproof. It was pointless to try the chip. He rapped his knuckles against enameled metal. Nothing. The door seemed to absorb the sound.

He placed his chip against the black plate.

The bolts clicked.

She seemed to hit him, somehow, before he'd actually gotten the door open. He was on his knees, the steel door against his back, the blades of her rigid thumbs quivering centimeters from his eyes. . . .

"Jesus Christ," she said, cuffing the side of his head as she rose. "You're an idiot to try that. How the hell you open those locks, Case? Case? You okay?" She leaned over him.

"Chip," he said, struggling for breath. Pain was spreading from his chest. She helped him up and shoved him into the cubicle.

"You bribe the help, upstairs?"

He shook his head and fell across the bed.

"Breathe in. Count. One, two, three, four. Hold it. Now out. Count."

He clutched his stomach.

"You kicked me," he managed.

"Shoulda been lower. I wanna be alone. I'm meditating, right?" She sat beside him. "And getting a briefing." She pointed at a small monitor set into the wall opposite the bed. "Wintermute's telling me about Straylight."

"Where's the meat puppet?"

"There isn't any. That's the most expensive special service of all." She stood up. She wore her leather jeans and a loose dark shirt. "The run's tomorrow, Wintermute says."

"What was that all about, in the restaurant? How come you ran?"

"'Cause, if I'd stayed, I might have killed Riviera."

"Why?"

"What he did to me. The show."

"I don't get it."

"This cost a lot," she said, extending her right hand as though it held an invisible fruit. The five blades slid out, then retracted smoothly. "Costs to go to Chiba, costs to get the surgery, costs to have them jack your nervous system up so you'll have the reflexes to go with the gear. . . . You know how I got the money, when I was starting out? Here. Not here, but a place like it, in the Sprawl. Joke, to start with, 'cause once they plant the cut-out chip, it seems like free money. Wake up sore, sometimes, but that's it. Renting the goods, is all. You aren't in, when it's all happening. House has software for whatever a customer wants to pay for. . . ." She cracked her knuckles. "Fine. I was getting my money. Trouble was, the cut-out and the circuitry the Chiba clinics put in weren't compatible. So the worktime started bleeding in, and I could remember it. . . . But it was just bad dreams, and not all bad." She smiled. "Then it started getting strange." She pulled his cigarettes from his pocket and lit one. "The house found out what I was doing with the money. I had the blades in, but the fine neuromotor work would take another three trips. No way I was ready to give up puppet time." She inhaled, blew out a stream of smoke, capping it with three perfect rings. "So the bastard who ran the place, he had some custom software cooked up. Berlin, that's the place for snuff, you know? Big market for mean kicks, Berlin. I never knew who wrote the program they switched me to, but it was based on all the classics."

"They knew you were picking up on this stuff? That you were conscious while you were working?"

"I wasn't conscious. It's like cyberspace, but blank. Silver. It smells like rain. . . . You can see yourself orgasm, it's like a little nova right out on the rim of space. But I was starting to *remember*. Like dreams, you know. And they didn't tell me. They switched the software and started renting to specialty markets."

She seemed to speak from a distance. "And I knew, but I kept quiet about it. I needed the money. The dreams got worse and worse, and I'd tell myself that at least some of them *were* just dreams, but by then I'd started to figure that the boss had a whole little *clientele* going for me. Nothing's too good for Molly, the boss says, and gives me this shit raise." She shook her head. "That prick was charging *eight* times what he was paying me, and he thought I didn't know."

"So what was he charging for?"

"Bad dreams. Real ones. One night . . . one night, I'd just come back from Chiba." She dropped the cigarette, ground it out with her heel, and sat down, leaning against the wall. "Surgeons went way in, that trip. Tricky. They must have disturbed the cut-out chip. I came up. I was into this routine with a customer. . . ." She dug her fingers deep in the foam. "Senator, he was. Knew his fat face right away. We were both covered with blood. We weren't alone. She was all . . ." She tugged at the temperfoam. "Dead. And that fat prick, he was saying, 'What's wrong? What's wrong?' 'Cause we weren't *finished* yet. . . ."

She began to shake.

"So I guess I gave the Senator what he really wanted, you know?" The shaking stopped. She released the foam and ran her fingers back through her dark hair. "The house put a contract out on me. I had to hide for a while."

Case stared at her.

"So Riviera hit a nerve last night," she said. "I guess it wants me to hate him real bad, so I'll be psyched up to go in there after him."

"After him?"

"He's already there. Straylight. On the invitation of Lady 3Jane, all that dedication shit. She was there in a private box, kinda. . . ."

Case remembered the face he'd seen. "You gonna kill him?"

She smiled. Cold. "He's going to die, yeah. Soon."

"I had a visit too," he said, and told her about the window, stumbling over what the Zone-figure had said about Linda. She nodded.

"Maybe it wants you to hate something too."

"Maybe I hate it."

"Maybe you hate yourself, Case."

"How was it?" Bruce asked, as Case climbed into the Honda.

"Try it sometime," he said, rubbing his eyes.

"Just can't see you the kinda guy goes for the puppets," Cath said unhappily, thumbing a fresh derm against her wrist.

"Can we go home, now?" Bruce asked.

"Sure. Drop me down Jules Verne, where the bars are."

TWELVE

Rue Jules Verne was a circumferential avenue, looping the spindle's midpoint, while Desiderata ran its length, terminating at either end in the supports of the Lado-Acheson light pumps. If you turned right, off Desiderata, and followed Jules Verne far enough, you'd find yourself approaching Desiderata from the left.

Case watched Bruce's trike until it was out of sight, then turned and walked past a vast, brilliantly lit newsstand, the covers of dozens of glossy Japanese magazines presenting the faces of the month's newest simstim stars.

Directly overhead, along the nighted axis, the hologram sky glittered with fanciful constellations suggesting playing cards, the faces of dice, a top hat, a martini glass. The intersection of Desiderata and Jules Verne formed a kind of gulch, the balconied terraces of Freeside cliff dwellers rising gradually to the grassy tablelands of another casino complex. Case watched a drone microlight bank gracefully in an updraft at the green verge of an artificial mesa, lit for seconds by the soft glow of the invisible casino. The thing was a kind of pilotless biplane of gossamer polymer, its wings silkscreened to resemble a giant butterfly. Then it was gone, beyond the mesa's edge. He'd seen a wink of reflected neon off glass, either lenses or the turrets of lasers. The drones were part of the spindle's security system, controlled by some central computer.

In Straylight? He walked on, past bars named the Hi-Lo, the

Paradise, le Monde, Cricketeer, Shozoku Smith's, Emergency. He chose Emergency because it was the smallest and most crowded, but it took only seconds for him to realize that it was a tourist place. No hum of biz here, only a glazed sexual tension. He thought briefly of the nameless club above Molly's rented cubicle, but the image of her mirrored eyes fixed on the little screen dissuaded him. What was Wintermute revealing there now? The ground plans of the Villa Straylight? The history of the Tessier-Ashpools?

He bought a mug of Carlsberg and found a place against the wall. Closing his eyes, he felt for the knot of rage, the pure small coal of his anger. It was there still. Where had it come from? He remembered feeling only a kind of bafflement at his maiming in Memphis, nothing at all when he'd killed to defend his dealing interests in Night City, and a slack sickness and loathing after Linda's death under the inflated dome. But no anger. Small and far away, on the mind's screen, a semblance of Deane struck a semblance of an office wall in an explosion of brains and blood. He knew then: the rage had come in the arcade, when Wintermute rescinded the simstim ghost of Linda Lee, yanking away the simple animal promise of food, warmth, a place to sleep. But he hadn't become aware of it until his exchange with the holo-construct of Lonny Zone.

It was a strange thing. He couldn't take its measure.

"Numb," he said. He'd been numb a long time, years. All his nights down Ninsei, his nights with Linda, numb in bed and numb at the cold sweating center of every drug deal. But now he'd found this warm thing, this chip of murder. *Meat,* some part of him said. *It's the meat talking, ignore it.*

"Gangster."

He opened his eyes. Cath stood beside him in a black shift, her hair still wild from the ride in the Honda.

"Thought you went home," he said, and covered his confusion with a sip of Carlsberg.

"I got him to drop me off at this shop. Bought this." She ran her palm across the fabric, curve of the pelvic girdle. He saw the blue derm on her wrist. "Like it?"

"Sure." He automatically scanned the faces around them, then looked back at her. "What do you think you're up to, honey?"

"You like the beta you got off us, Lupus?" She was very close now, radiating heat and tension, eyes slitted over enormous pupils and a tendon in her neck tense as a bowstring. She was quivering, vibrating invisibly with the fresh buzz. "You get off?"

"Yeah. But the comedown's a bitch."

"Then you need another one."

"And what's that supposed to lead to?"

"I got a key. Up the hill behind the Paradise, just the creamiest crib. People down the well on business tonight, if you follow me. . . ."

"If I follow you."

She took his hand between hers, her palms hot and dry. "You're Yak, aren't you, Lupus? Gaijin soldierman for the Yakuza."

"You got an eye, huh?" He withdrew his hand and fumbled for a cigarette.

"How come you got all your fingers, then? I thought you had to chop one off every time you screwed up."

"I never screw up." He lit his cigarette.

"I saw that girl you're with. Day I met you. Walks like Hideo. Scares me." She smiled too widely. "I like that. She like it with girls?"

"Never said. Who's Hideo?"

"3Jane's, what she calls it, retainer. Family retainer."

Case forced himself to stare dully at the Emergency crowd while he spoke. "Dee-Jane?"

"Lady 3Jane. She's triff. Rich. Her father owns all this."

"This bar?"

"Freeside!"

"No shit. You keepin' some class company, huh?" He raised an eyebrow. Put his arm around her, his hand on her hip. "So how you meet these aristos, Cathy? You some kinda closet deb? You an' Bruce secret heirs to some ripe old credit? Huh?" He spread his fingers, kneading the flesh beneath the thin black cloth. She squirmed against him. Laughed.

"Oh, you know," she said, lids half lowered in what must have been intended as a look of modesty, "she likes to party. Bruce and I, we make the party circuit. . . . It gets real boring for her, in there. Her old man lets her out sometimes, as long as she brings Hideo to take care of her."

"Where's it get boring?"

"Straylight, they call it. She told me, oh, it's pretty, all the pools and lilies. It's a castle, a real castle, all stone and sunsets." She snuggled in against him. "Hey, Lupus, man, you need a derm. So we can be together."

She wore a tiny leather purse on a slender neck-thong. Her nails were bright pink against her boosted tan, bitten to the quick. She opened the purse and withdrew a paperbacked bubble with a blue derm inside. Something white tumbled to the floor; Case stooped and picked it up. An origami crane.

"Hideo gave it to me," she said. "He tried to show me how, but I can't ever get it right. The necks come out backwards." She tucked the folded paper back into her purse. Case watched as she tore the bubble away, peeled the derm from its backing, and smoothed it across his inner wrist.

"3Jane, she's got a pointy face, nose like a bird?" He watched his hands fumble an outline. "Dark hair? Young?"

"I guess. But she's *triff*, you know? Like, all that money."

The drug hit him like an express train, a white-hot column of light mounting his spine from the region of his prostate, illuminating the sutures of his skull with x-rays of short-circuited sexual energy. His teeth sang in their individual sockets like tuning forks, each one

pitch-perfect and clear as ethanol. His bones, beneath the hazy envelope of flesh, were chromed and polished, the joints lubricated
with a film of silicone. Sandstorms raged across the scoured floor of
his skull, generating waves of high thin static that broke behind his
eyes, spheres of purest crystal, expanding. . . .

"Come on," she said, taking his hand. "You got it now. We got it.
Up the hill, we'll have it all night."

The anger was expanding, relentless, exponential, riding out
behind the betaphenethylamine rush like a carrier wave, a seismic
fluid, rich and corrosive. His erection was a bar of lead. The faces
around them in Emergency were painted doll things, the pink and
white of mouth parts moving, moving, words emerging like discrete
balloons of sound. He looked at Cath and saw each pore in the
tanned skin, eyes flat as dumb glass, a tint of dead metal, a faint
bloating, the most minute asymmetries of breast and collarbone,
the—something flared white behind his eyes.

He dropped her hand and stumbled for the door, shoving someone out of the way.

"Fuck you!" she screamed behind him, "you rip-off shit!"

He couldn't feel his legs. He used them like stilts, swaying cra-
zily across the flagstone pavement of Jules Verne, a distant rum-
bling in his ears, his own blood, razored sheets of light bisecting his
skull at a dozen angles.

And then he was frozen, erect, fists tight against his thighs, head
back, his lips curled, shaking. While he watched the loser's zodiac of
Freeside, the nightclub constellations of the hologram sky, shift, sliding fluid down the axis of darkness, to swarm like live things at the
dead center of reality. Until they had arranged themselves, individually and in their hundreds, to form a vast simple portrait, stippled the
ultimate monochrome, stars against night sky. Face of Miss Linda Lee.

When he was able to look away, to lower his eyes, he found
every other face in the street upraised, the strolling tourists be-

calmed with wonder. And when the lights in the sky went out, a ragged cheer went up from Jules Verne, to echo off the terraces and ranked balconies of lunar concrete.

Somewhere a clock began to chime, some ancient bell out of Europe.

Midnight.

He walked till morning.

The high wore away, the chromed skeleton corroding hourly, flesh growing solid, the drug-flesh replaced with the meat of his life. He couldn't think. He liked that very much, to be conscious and unable to think. He seemed to become each thing he saw: a park bench, a cloud of white moths around an antique streetlight, a robot gardener striped diagonally with black and yellow.

A recorded dawn crept along the Lado-Acheson system, pink and lurid. He forced himself to eat an omelette in a Desiderata café, to drink water, to smoke the last of his cigarettes. The rooftop meadow of the Intercontinental was stirring as he crossed it, an early breakfast crowd intent on coffee and croissants beneath the striped umbrellas.

He still had his anger. That was like being rolled in some alley and waking to discover your wallet still in your pocket, untouched. He warmed himself with it, unable to give it a name or an object.

He rode the elevator down to his level, fumbling in his pocket for the Freeside credit chip that served as his key. Sleep was becoming real, was something he might do. To lie down on the sand-colored temperfoam and find the blankness again.

They were waiting there, the three of them, their perfect white sportsclothes and stenciled tans setting off the handwoven organic chic of the furniture. The girl sat on a wicker sofa, an automatic pistol beside her on the leaf-patterned print of the cushion.

"Turing," she said. "You are under arrest."

PART FOUR

THE STRAYLIGHT RUN

THIRTEEN

"Your name is Henry Dorsett Case." She recited the year and place of his birth, his BAMA Single Identification Number, and a string of names he gradually recognized as aliases from his past.

"You been here awhile?" He saw the contents of his bag spread out across the bed, unwashed clothing sorted by type. The shuriken lay by itself, between jeans and underwear, on the sand-tinted temperfoam.

"Where is Kolodny?" The two men sat side by side on the couch, their arms crossed over tanned chests, identical gold chains slung around their necks. Case peered at them and saw that their youth was counterfeit, marked by a certain telltale corrugation at the knuckles, something the surgeons were unable to erase.

"Who's Kolodny?"

"That was the name in the register. Where is she?"

"I dunno," he said, crossing to the bar and pouring himself a glass of mineral water. "She took off."

"Where did you go tonight, Case?" The girl picked up the pistol and rested it on her thigh, without actually pointing it at him.

"Jules Verne, couple of bars, got high. How about you?" His knees felt brittle. The mineral water was warm and flat.

"I don't think you grasp your situation," said the man on the left, taking a pack of Gitanes from the breast pocket of his white mesh blouse. "You are busted, Mr. Case. The charges have to do with con-spiracy to augment an artificial intelligence." He took a gold Dun-hill from the same pocket and cradled it in his palm. "The man you call Armitage is already in custody."

"Corto?"

The man's eyes widened. "Yes. How do you know that that is his name?" A millimeter of flame clicked from the lighter.

"I forget," Case said.

"You'll remember," the girl said.

Their names, or worknames, were Michèle, Roland, and Pierre. Pierre, Case decided, would play the Bad Cop; Roland would take Case's side, provide small kindnesses—he found an unopened pack of Yeheyuans when Case refused a Gitane—and generally play counterpoint to Pierre's cold hostility. Michèle would be the Record-ing Angel, making occasional adjustments in the direction of the interrogation. One or all of them, he was certain, would be kinked for audio, very likely for simstim, and anything he said or did now was admissible evidence. Evidence, he asked himself, through the grinding come-down, of what?

Knowing that he couldn't follow their French, they spoke freely among themselves. Or seemed to. He caught enough as it was: names like Pauley, Armitage, Sense/Net, Panther Moderns pro-truding like icebergs from an animated sea of Parisian French. But it was entirely possible that the names were there for his benefit. They always referred to Molly as Kolodny.

"You say you were hired to make a run, Case," Roland said, his slow speech intended to convey reasonableness, "and that you are unaware of the nature of the target. Is this not unusual in your trade? Having penetrated the defenses, would you not be unable then to perform the required operation? And surely an operation of

some kind is required, yes?" He leaned forward, elbows on his stenciled brown knees, palms out to receive Case's explanation. Pierre
paced the room; now he was by the window, now by the door. Michèle was the kink, Case decided. Her eyes never left him.

"Can I put some clothes on?" he asked. Pierre had insisted on
stripping him, searching the seams of his jeans. Now he sat naked
on a wicker footstool, with one foot obscenely white.

Roland asked Pierre something in French. Pierre, at the window
again, was peering through a flat little pair of binoculars. *"Non,"*
he said absently, and Roland shrugged, raising his eyebrows at
Case. Case decided it was a good time to smile. Roland returned
the smile.

Oldest cop bullshit in the book, Case thought. "Look," he said,
"I'm sick. Had this godawful drug in a bar, you know? I wanna lie
down. You got me already. You say you got Armitage. You got him,
go ask *him*. I'm just hired help."

Roland nodded. "And Kolodny?"

"She was with Armitage when he hired me. Just muscle, a razor-
girl. Far as I know. Which isn't too far."

"You know that Armitage's real name is Corto," Pierre said, his
eyes still hidden by the soft plastic flanges of the binoculars. "How
do you know that, my friend?"

"I guess he mentioned it sometime," Case said, regretting the
slip. "Everybody's got a couple names. Your name Pierre?"

"We know how you were repaired in Chiba," Michèle said, "and
that may have been Wintermute's first mistake." Case stared at her
as blankly as he could. The name hadn't been mentioned before.
"The process employed on you resulted in the clinic's owner apply-
ing for seven basic patents. Do you know what that means?"

"No."

"It means that the operator of a black clinic in Chiba City now
owns a controlling interest in three major medical research consor-

tiums. This reverses the usual order of things, you see. It attracted attention." She crossed her brown arms across her small high breasts and settled back against the print cushion. Case wondered how old she might be. People said that age always showed in the eyes, but he'd never been able to see it. Julie Deane had had the eyes of a disinterested ten-year-old behind the rose quartz of his glasses. Nothing old about Michèle but her knuckles. "Traced you to the Sprawl, lost you again, then caught up with you as you were leaving for Istanbul. We backtracked, traced you through the grid, determined that you'd instigated a riot at Sense/Net. Sense/Net was eager to cooperate. They ran an inventory for us. They discovered that McCoy Pauley's ROM personality construct was missing."

"In Istanbul," Roland said, almost apologetically, "it was very easy. The woman had alienated Armitage's contact with the secret police."

"And then you came here," Pierre said, slipping the binoculars into his shorts pocket. "We were delighted."

"Chance to work on your tan?"

"You know what we mean," Michèle said. "If you wish to pretend that you do not, you only make things more difficult for yourself. There is still the matter of extradition. You will return with us, Case, as will Armitage. But where, exactly, will we all be going? To Switzerland, where you will be merely a pawn in the trial of an artificial intelligence? Or to le BAMA, where you can be proven to have participated not only in data invasion and larceny, but in an act of public mischief, which cost fourteen innocent lives? The choice is yours."

Case took a Yeheyuan from his pack; Pierre lit it for him with the gold Dunhill. "Would Armitage protect you?" The question was punctuated by the lighter's bright jaws snapping shut.

Case looked up at him through the ache and bitterness of beta-phenethylamine. "How old are you, boss?"

"Old enough to know that you are fucked, burnt, that this is over and you are in the way."

"One thing," Case said, and drew on his cigarette. He blew the smoke up at the Turing Registry agent. "Do you guys have any real jurisdiction out here? I mean, shouldn't you have the Freeside security team in on this party? It's their turf, isn't it?" He saw the dark eyes harden in the lean boy face and tensed for the blow, but Pierre only shrugged.

"It doesn't matter," Roland said. "You will come with us. We are at home with situations of legal ambiguity. The treaties under which our arm of the Registry operates grant us a great deal of flexibility. And we *create* flexibility, in situations where it is required." The mask of amiability was down, suddenly, Roland's eyes as hard as Pierre's.

"You are worse than a fool," Michèle said, getting to her feet, the pistol in her hand. "You have no care for your species. For thousands of years men dreamed of pacts with demons. Only now are such things possible. And what would you be paid with? What would your price be, for aiding this thing to free itself and grow?" There was a knowing weariness in her young voice that no nineteen-year-old could have mustered. "You will dress now. You will come with us. Along with the one you call Armitage, you will return with us to Geneva and give testimony in the trial of this intelligence. Otherwise, we kill you. Now." She raised the pistol, a smooth black Walther with an integral silencer.

"I'm dressing already," he said, stumbling toward the bed. His legs were still numb, clumsy. He fumbled with a clean T-shirt.

"We have a ship standing by. We will erase Pauley's construct with a pulse weapon."

"Sense/Net'll be pissed," Case said, thinking: and all the evidence in the Hosaka.

"They are in some difficulty already, for having owned such a thing."

Case pulled the shirt over his head. He saw the shuriken on the bed, lifeless metal, his star. He felt for the anger. It was gone. Time to give in, to roll with it. . . . He thought of the toxin sacs. "Here comes the meat," he muttered.

In the elevator to the meadow, he thought of Molly. She might already be in Straylight. Hunting Riviera. Hunted, probably, by Hideo, who was almost certainly the ninja clone of the Finn's story, the one who'd come to retrieve the talking head.

He rested his forehead against the matte black plastic of a wall panel and closed his eyes. His limbs were wood, old, warped, and heavy with rain.

Lunch was being served beneath the trees, under the bright umbrellas. Roland and Michèle fell into character, chattering brightly in French. Pierre came behind. Michèle kept the muzzle of her pistol close to his ribs, concealing the gun with a white duck jacket she draped over her arm.

Crossing the meadow, weaving between the tables and the trees, he wondered if she would shoot him if he collapsed now. Black fur boiled at the borders of his vision. He glanced up at the hot white band of the Lado-Acheson armature and saw a giant butterfly banking gracefully against recorded sky.

At the edge of the meadow they came to railinged cliffside, wild flowers dancing in the updraft from the canyon that was Desiderata. Michèle tossed her short dark hair and pointed, saying something in French to Roland. She sounded genuinely happy. Case followed the direction of her gesture and saw the curve of planing lakes, the white glint of casinos, turquoise rectangles of a thousand pools, the bodies of bathers, tiny bronze hieroglyphs, all held in serene approximation of gravity against the endless curve of Freeside's hull.

They followed the railing to an ornate iron bridge that arched over Desiderata. Michèle prodded him with the muzzle of the Walther.

"Take it easy, I can't hardly walk today."

They were a little over a quarter of the way across when the microlight struck, its electric engine silent until the carbon fiber prop chopped away the top of Pierre's skull.

They were in the thing's shadow for an instant; Case felt the hot blood spray across the back of his neck, and then someone tripped him. He rolled, seeing Michèle on her back, knees up, aiming the Walther with both hands. *That's a waste of effort,* he thought, with the strange lucidity of shock. She was trying to shoot down the microlight.

And then he was running. He looked back as he passed the first of the trees. Roland was running after him. He saw the fragile biplane strike the iron railing of the bridge, crumple, cartwheel, sweeping the girl with it down into Desiderata.

Roland hadn't looked back. His face was fixed, white, his teeth bared. He had something in his hand.

The gardening robot took Roland as he passed that same tree. It fell straight out of the groomed branches, a thing like a crab, diagonally striped with black and yellow.

"You killed 'em," Case panted, running. "Crazy motherfucker, you killed 'em all. . . ."

FOURTEEN

The little train shot through its tunnel at eighty kilometers per hour. Case kept his eyes closed. The shower had helped, but he'd lost his breakfast when he'd looked down and seen Pierre's blood washing pink across the white tiles.

Gravity fell away as the spindle narrowed. Case's stomach churned.

Aerol was waiting with his scooter beside the dock.

"Case, mon, big problem." The soft voice faint in his phones. He chinned the volume control and peered into the Lexan faceplate of Aerol's helmet.

"Gotta get to *Garvey*, Aerol."

"Yo. Strap in, mon. But *Garvey* captive. Yacht, came before, she came back. Now she lockin' steady on *Marcus Garvey*."

Turing? "Came before?" Case climbed into the scooter's frame and began to fasten the straps.

"Japan yacht. Brought you package. . . ."

Armitage.

———

Confused images of wasps and spiders rose in Case's mind as they came in sight of *Marcus Garvey*. The little tug was snug against the gray thorax of a sleek, insectile ship five times her length. The arms of grapples stood out against *Garvey*'s patched hull with the strange clarity of vacuum and raw sunlight. A pale corrugated gangway curved out of the yacht, snaked sideways to avoid the tug's engines, and covered the aft hatch. There was something obscene about the arrangement, but it had more to do with ideas of feeding than of sex.

"What's happening with Maelcum?"

"Maelcum fine. Nobody come down the tube. Yacht pilot talk to him, say relax."

As they swung past the gray ship, Case saw the name HANIWA in crisp white capitals beneath an oblong cluster of Japanese.

"I don't like this, man. I was thinking maybe it's time we got our ass out of here anyway."

"Maelcum thinkin' that precise thing, mon, but *Garvey* not be goin' far like that."

———

Maelcum was purring a speeded-up patois to his radio when Case came through the forward lock and removed his helmet.

"Aerol's gone back to the *Rocker*," Case said.

Maelcum nodded, still whispering to the microphone.

Case pulled himself over the pilot's drifting tangle of dreadlocks and began to remove his suit. Maelcum's eyes were closed now; he nodded as he listened to some reply over a pair of phones with bright orange pads, his brow creased with concentration. He wore ragged jeans and an old green nylon jacket with the sleeves ripped out. Case snapped the red Sanyo suit to a storage hammock and pulled himself down to the g-web.

"See what th' ghost say, mon," Maelcum said. "Computer keeps askin' for you."

"So who's up there in that thing?"

"Same Japan-boy came before. An' now he joined by you Mister Armitage, come out Freeside. . . ."

Case put the trodes on and jacked in.

———

"Dixie?"

The matrix showed him the pink spheres of the steel combine in Sikkim.

"What you gettin' up to, boy? I been hearin' lurid stories. Hosaka's patched into a twin bank on your boss's boat now. Really hoppin'. You pull some Turing heat?"

"Yeah, but Wintermute killed 'em."

"Well, that won't hold 'em long. Plenty more where those came from. Be up here in force. Bet their decks are all over this grid sector like flies on shit. And your boss, Case, he says go. He says run it and run it now."

Case punched for the Freeside coordinates.

"Lemme take that a sec, Case. . . ." The matrix blurred and phased as the Flatline executed an intricate series of jumps with a speed and accuracy that made Case wince with envy.

"Shit, Dixie. . . ."

"Hey, boy, I was that good when I was alive. You ain't seen nothin'. No hands!"

"That's it, huh? Big green rectangle off left?"

"You got it. Corporate core data for Tessier-Ashpool S.A., and that ice is generated by their two friendly AIs. On par with anything in the military sector, looks to me. That's king hell ice, Case, black as the grave and slick as glass. Fry your brain soon as look at you. We get any closer now, it'll have tracers up our ass and out both ears, be tellin' the boys in the T-A boardroom the size of your shoes and how long your dick is."

"This isn't looking so hot, is it? I mean, the Turings are on it. I was thinking maybe we should try to bail out. I can take you."

"Yeah? No shit? You don't wanna see what that Chinese program can do?"

"Well, I . . ." Case stared at the green walls of the T-A ice. "Well, screw it. Yeah. We run."

"Slot it."

"Hey, Maelcum," Case said, jacking out, "I'm probably gonna be under the trodes for maybe eight hours straight." Maelcum was smoking again. The cabin was swimming in smoke. "So I can't get to the head. . . ."

"No problem, mon." The Zionite executed a high forward somersault and rummaged through the contents of a zippered mesh bag, coming up with a coil of transparent tubing and something else, something sealed in a sterile bubble pack.

He called it a Texas catheter, and Case didn't like it at all.

He slotted the Chinese virus, paused, then drove it home.

"Okay," he said, "we're on. Listen, Maelcum, if it gets really funny, you can grab my left wrist. I'll feel it. Otherwise, I guess you do what the Hosaka tells you, okay?"

"Sure, mon." Maelcum lit a fresh joint.

"And turn the scrubber up. I don't want that shit tangling with my neurotransmitters. I got a bad hangover as it is."

Maelcum grinned.

Case jacked back in.

"Christ on a crutch," the Flatline said, "take a look at this."

The Chinese virus was unfolding around them. Polychrome shadow, countless translucent layers shifting and recombining. Protean, enormous, it towered above them, blotting out the void.

"Big mother," the Flatline said.

"I'm gonna check Molly," Case said, tapping the simstim switch.

Freefall. The sensation was like diving through perfectly clear water. She was falling-rising through a wide tube of fluted lunar concrete, lit at two-meter intervals by rings of white neon.

The link was one way. He couldn't talk to her.

He flipped.

"Boy, that is one mean piece of software. Hottest thing since sliced bread. That goddam thing's *invisible*. I just now rented twenty seconds on that little pink box, four jumps left of the T-A ice; had a look at what we look like. We don't. We're not there."

Case searched the matrix around the Tessier-Ashpool ice until he found the pink structure, a standard commercial unit, and punched in closer to it. "Maybe it's defective."

"Maybe, but I doubt it. Our baby's military, though. And new. It just doesn't register. If it did, we'd read as some kind of Chinese sneak attack, but nobody's twigged to us at all. Maybe not even the folks in Straylight."

Case watched the blank wall that screened Straylight. "Well," he said, "that's an advantage, right?"

"Maybe." The construct approximated laughter. Case winced at the sensation. "I checked ol' Kuang Eleven out again for you, boy. It's real friendly, long as you're on the trigger end, jus' polite an' helpful as can be. Speaks good English, too. You ever hear of slow virus before?"

"No."

"I did, once. Just an idea, back then. But that's what ol' Kuang's all about. This ain't bore and inject, it's more like we interface with the ice so slow, the ice doesn't feel it. The face of the Kuang logics kinda sleazes up to the target and mutates, so it gets to be exactly

like the ice fabric. Then we lock on and the main programs cut in,
start talking circles 'round the logics in the ice. We go Siamese twin
on 'em before they even get restless." The Flatline laughed.

"Wish you weren't so damn jolly today, man. That laugh of yours
sort of gets me in the spine."

"Too bad," the Flatline said. "Ol' dead man needs his laughs."
Case slapped the simstim switch.

———————

And crashed through tangled metal and the smell of dust, the heels
of his hands skidding as they struck slick paper. Something behind
him collapsed noisily.

"C'mon," said the Finn, "ease up a little."

Case lay sprawled across a pile of yellowing magazines, the girls
shining up at him in the dimness of Metro Holografix, a wistful gal-
axy of sweet white teeth. He lay there until his heart had slowed,
breathing the smell of old magazines.

"Wintermute," he said.

"Yeah," said the Finn, somewhere behind him, "you got it."

"Fuck off." Case sat up, rubbing his wrists.

"Come *on*," said the Finn, stepping out of a sort of alcove in the
wall of junk. "This way's better for you, man." He took his Partagas
from a coat pocket and lit one. The smell of Cuban tobacco filled the
shop. "You want I should come to you in the matrix like a burning
bush? You aren't missing anything, back there. An hour here'll only
take you a couple of seconds."

"You ever think maybe it gets on my nerves, you coming on like
people I know?" He stood, swatting pale dust from the front of his
black jeans. He turned, glaring back at the dusty shop windows, the
closed door to the street. "What's out there? New York? Or does it
just stop?"

"Well," said the Finn, "it's like that tree, you know? Falls in the woods but maybe there's nobody to hear it." He showed Case his huge front teeth, and puffed his cigarette. "You can go for a walk, you wanna. It's all there. Or anyway all the parts of it you ever saw. This is memory, right? I tap you, sort it out, and feed it back in."

"I don't have this good a memory," Case said, looking around. He looked down at his hands, turning them over. He tried to remember what the lines on his palms were like, but couldn't.

"Everybody does," the Finn said, dropping his cigarette and grinding it out under his heel, "but not many of you can access it. Artists can, mostly, if they're any good. If you could lay this construct over the reality, the Finn's place in lower Manhattan, you'd see a difference, but maybe not as much as you'd think. Memory's holographic, for you." The Finn tugged at one of his small ears. "I'm different."

"How do you mean, holographic?" The word made him think of Riviera.

"The holographic paradigm is the closest thing you've worked out to a representation of human memory, is all. But you've never done anything about it. People, I mean." The Finn stepped forward and canted his streamlined skull to peer up at Case. "Maybe if you had, I wouldn't be happening."

"What's that supposed to mean?"

The Finn shrugged. His tattered tweed was too wide across the shoulders, and didn't quite settle back into position. "I'm trying to help you, Case."

"Why?"

"Because I need you." The large yellow teeth appeared again. "And because you need me."

"Bullshit. Can you read my mind, Finn?" He grimaced. "Wintermute, I mean."

"Minds aren't *read*. See, you've still got the paradigms print gave you, and you're barely print-literate. I can *access* your memory, but that's not the same as your mind." He reached into the exposed chassis of an ancient television and withdrew a silver-black vacuum tube. "See this? Part of my DNA, sort of. . . ." He tossed the thing into the shadows and Case heard it pop and tinkle. "You're always building models. Stone circles. Cathedrals. Pipe-organs. Adding machines. I got no idea why I'm here now, you know that? But if the run goes off tonight, you'll have finally managed the real thing."

"I don't know what you're talking about."

"That's 'you' in the collective. Your species."

"You killed those Turings."

The Finn shrugged. "Hadda. Hadda. You should give a shit; they woulda offed you and never thought twice. Anyway, why I got you here, we gotta talk more. Remember this?" And his right hand held the charred wasps' nest from Case's dream, reek of fuel in the closeness of the dark shop. Case stumbled back against a wall of junk. "Yeah. That was me. Did it with the holo rig in the window. Another memory I tapped out of you when I flatlined you that first time. Know why it's important?"

Case shook his head.

"Because"—and the nest, somehow, was gone—"it's the closest thing you got to what Tessier-Ashpool would like to be. The human equivalent. Straylight's like that nest, or anyway it was supposed to work out that way. I figure it'll make you feel better."

"Feel better?"

"To know what they're like. You were starting to hate my guts for a while there. That's good. But hate them instead. Same difference."

"Listen," Case said, stepping forward, "they never did shit to me. You, it's different. . . ." But he couldn't feel the anger.

"So T-A, they made me. The French girl, she said you were selling out the species. Demon, she said I was." The Finn grinned. "It doesn't much matter. You gotta hate somebody before this is over."

He turned and headed for the back of the shop. "Well, come on, I'll show you a little bit of Straylight while I got you here." He lifted the corner of the blanket. White light poured out. "Shit, man, don't just stand there."

Case followed, rubbing his face.

"Okay," said the Finn, and grabbed his elbow.

They were drawn past the stale wool in a puff of dust, into free-fall and a cylindrical corridor of fluted lunar concrete, ringed with white neon at two-meter intervals.

"Jesus," Case said, tumbling.

"This is the front entrance," the Finn said, his tweed flapping. "If this weren't a construct of mine, where the shop is would be the main gate, up by the Freeside axis. This'll all be a little low on de-tail, though, because you don't have the memories. Except for this bit here, you got off Molly. . . ."

Case managed to straighten out, but began to corkscrew in a long spiral.

"Hold on," the Finn said, "I'll fast-forward us."

The walls blurred. Dizzying sensation of headlong movement, colors, whipping around corners and through narrow corridors. They seemed at one point to pass through several meters of solid wall, a flash of pitch darkness.

"Here," the Finn said. "This is it."

They floated in the center of a perfectly square room, walls and ceiling paneled in rectangular sections of dark wood. The floor was covered by a single square of brilliant carpet patterned after a microchip, circuits traced in blue and scarlet wool. In the exact cen-ter of the room, aligned precisely with the carpet pattern, stood a square pedestal of frosted white glass.

"The Villa Straylight," said a jeweled thing on the pedestal, in a voice like music, "is a body grown in upon itself, a Gothic folly. Each space in Straylight is in some way secret, this endless series of chambers linked by passages, by stairwells vaulted like intestines, where the eye is trapped in narrow curves, carried past ornate screens, empty alcoves. . . ."

"Essay of 3Jane's," the Finn said, producing his Partagas. "Wrote that when she was twelve. Semiotics course."

"The architects of Freeside went to great pains to conceal the fact that the interior of the spindle is arranged with the banal precision of furniture in a hotel room. In Straylight, the hull's inner surface is overgrown with a desperate proliferation of structures, forms flowing, interlocking, rising toward a solid core of microcircuitry, our clan's corporate heart, a cylinder of silicon wormholed with narrow maintenance tunnels, some no wider than a man's hand. The bright crabs burrow there, the drones, alert for micromechanical decay or sabotage."

"That was her you saw in the restaurant," the Finn said.

"By the standards of the archipelago," the head continued, "ours is an old family, the convolutions of our home reflecting that age. But reflecting something else as well. The semiotics of the Villa bespeak a turning in, a denial of the bright void beyond the hull.

"Tessier and Ashpool climbed the well of gravity to discover that they loathed space. They built Freeside to tap the wealth of the new islands, grew rich and eccentric, and began the construction of an extended body in Straylight. We have sealed ourselves away behind our money, growing inward, generating a seamless universe of self.

"The Villa Straylight knows no sky, recorded or otherwise.

"At the Villa's silicon core is a small room, the only rectilinear chamber in the complex. Here, on a plain pedestal of glass, rests an ornate bust, platinum and cloisonné, studded with lapis and pearl. The bright marbles of its eyes were cut from the synthetic ruby viewport of the ship that brought the first Tessier up the well, and returned for the first Ashpool. . . ."

The head fell silent.

"Well?" Case asked, finally, almost expecting the thing to answer him.

"That's all she wrote," the Finn said. "Didn't finish it. Just a kid then. This thing's a ceremonial terminal, sort of. I need Molly in here with the right word at the right time. That's the catch. Doesn't mean shit, how deep you and the Flatline ride that Chinese virus, if this thing doesn't hear the magic word."

"So what's the word?"

"I don't know. You might say what I am is basically defined by the fact that I don't know, because I *can't* know. I am that which knoweth not the word. If you knew, man, and told me, I couldn't *know*. It's hardwired in. Someone else has to learn it and bring it here, just when you and the Flatline punch through that ice and scramble the cores."

"What happens then?"

"I don't exist, after that. I cease."

"Okay by me," Case said.

"Sure. But you watch your ass, Case. My, ah, other lobe is on to us, it looks like. One burning bush looks pretty much like another. And Armitage is starting to go."

"What's that mean?"

But the paneled room folded itself through a dozen impossible angles, tumbling away into cyberspace like an origami crane.

FIFTEEN

"You tryin' to break my record, son?" the Flatline asked. "You were braindead again, five seconds."

"Sit tight," Case said, and hit the simstim switch.

She crouched in darkness, her palms against rough concrete.

CASE CASE CASE CASE. The digital display pulsed his name in alpha-numerics, Wintermute informing her of the link.

"Cute," she said. She rocked back on her heels and rubbed her palms together, cracked her knuckles. "What kept you?"

TIME MOLLY TIME NOW.

She pressed her tongue hard against her lower front teeth. One moved slightly, activating her microchannel amps; the random bounce of photons through the darkness was converted to a pulse of electrons, the concrete around her coming up ghost-pale and grainy. "Okay, honey. Now we go out to play."

Her hiding place proved to be a service tunnel of some kind. She crawled out through a hinged, ornate grill of tarnished brass. He saw enough of her arms and hands to know that she wore the poly-carbon suit again. Under the plastic, he felt the familiar tension of thin tight leather. There was something slung under her arm in a harness or holster. She stood up, unzipped the suit, and touched the checkered plastic of a pistolgrip.

"Hey, Case," she said, barely voicing the words, "you listening?

Tell you a story. . . . Had me this boy once. You kinda remind me. . . ."
She turned and surveyed the corridor. "Johnny, his name was."

The low, vaulted hallway was lined with dozens of museum
cases, archaic-looking glass-fronted boxes made of brown wood.
They looked awkward there, against the organic curves of the hallway's walls, as though they'd been brought in and set up in a line for
some forgotten purpose. Dull brass fixtures held globes of white
light at ten-meter intervals. The floor was uneven, and as she set off
along the corridor, Case realized that hundreds of small rugs and
carpets had been put down at random. In some places, they were six
deep, the floor a soft patchwork of handwoven wool.

Molly paid little attention to the cabinets and their contents,
which irritated him. He had to satisfy himself with her disinterested
glances, which gave him fragments of pottery, antique weapons, a
thing so densely studded with rusted nails that it was unrecogniz-
able, frayed sections of tapestry. . . .

"My Johnny, see, he was smart, real flash boy. Started out as a
stash on Memory Lane, chips in his head and people paid to hide
data there. Had the Yak after him, night I met him, and I did for
their assassin. More luck than anything else, but I did for him. And
after that, it was tight and sweet, Case." Her lips barely moved. He
felt her form the words; he didn't need to hear them spoken aloud.
"We had a setup with a squid, so we could read the traces of everything he'd ever stored. Ran it all out on tape and started twisting
selected clients, ex-clients. I was bagman, muscle, watchdog. I was
real happy. You ever been happy, Case? He was my boy. We worked
together. Partners. I was maybe eight weeks out of the puppet house
when I met him. . . ." She paused, edged around a sharp turn, and
continued. More of the glossy wooden cases, their sides a color that
reminded him of cockroach wings.

"Tight, sweet, just ticking along, we were. Like nobody could
ever touch us. I wasn't going to let them. Yakuza, I guess, they still

wanted Johnny's ass. 'Cause I'd killed their man. 'Cause Johnny'd burned them. And the Yak, they can afford to move so fucking slow, man, they'll wait years and years. Give you a whole life, just so you'll have more to lose when they come and take it away. Patient like a spider. Zen spiders.

"I didn't know that, then. Or if I did, I figured it didn't apply to us. Like when you're young, you figure you're unique. I was young. Then they came, when we were thinking we maybe had enough to be able to quit, pack it in, go to Europe maybe. Not that either of us knew what we'd do there, with nothing to do. But we were living fat, Swiss orbital accounts and a crib full of toys and furniture. Takes the edge off your game.

"So that first one they'd sent, he'd been hot. Reflexes like you never saw, implants, enough style for ten ordinary hoods. But the second one, he was, I dunno, like a *monk*. Cloned. Stone killer from the cells on up. Had it in him, death, this silence, he gave it off in a cloud. . . ." Her voice trailed off as the corridor split, identical stairwells descending. She took the left.

"One time, I was a little kid, we were squatting. It was down by the Hudson, and those rats, man, they were big. It's the chemicals get into them. Big as I was, and all night one had been scrabbling under the floor of the squat. Round dawn somebody brought this old man in, seams down his cheeks and his eyes all red. Had a roll of greasy leather like you'd keep steel tools in, to keep the rust off. Spread it out, had this old revolver and three shells. Old man, he puts one bullet in there, then he starts walking up and down the squat, we're hanging back by the walls.

"Back and forth. Got his arms crossed, head down, like he's forgotten the gun. Listening for the rat. We got real quiet. Old man takes a step. Rat moves. Rat moves, he takes another step. An hour of that, then he seems to remember his gun. Points it at the floor, grins, and pulls the trigger. Rolled it back up and left.

"I crawled under there later. Rat had a hole between its eyes."
She was watching the sealed doorways that opened at intervals
along the corridor. "The second one, the one who came for Johnny,
he was like that old man. Not old, but he was like that. He killed that
way." The corridor widened. The sea of rich carpets undulated gently beneath an enormous candelabrum whose lowest crystal pen-
dant reached nearly to the floor. Crystal tinkled as Molly entered
the hall. THIRD DOOR LEFT, blinked the readout.

She turned left, avoiding the inverted tree of crystal. "I just saw
him once. On my way into our place. He was coming out. We lived
in a converted factory space, lots of young comers from Sense/Net,
like that. Pretty good security to start with, and I'd put in some
really heavy stuff to make it really tight. I knew Johnny was up
there. But this little guy, he caught my eye, as he was coming out.
Didn't say a word. We just looked at each other and I knew. Plain
little guy, plain clothes, no pride in him, humble. He looked at me
and got into a pedicab. I knew. Went upstairs and Johnny was sitting in a chair by the window, with his mouth a little open, like he'd
just thought of something to say."

The door in front of her was old, a carved slab of Thai teak that
seemed to have been sawn in half to fit the low doorway. A primitive
mechanical lock with a stainless face had been inset beneath a
swirling dragon. She knelt, drew a tight little roll of black chamois
from an inside pocket, and selected a needle-thin pick. "Never
much found anybody I gave a damn about, after that."

She inserted the pick and worked in silence, nibbling at her
lower lip. She seemed to rely on touch alone; her eyes unfocused
and the door was a blur of blond wood. Case listened to the silence
of the hall, punctuated by the soft clink of the candelabrum. Candles? Straylight was all wrong. He remembered Cath's story of a
castle with pools and lilies, and 3Jane's mannered words recited
musically by the head. A place grown in upon itself. Straylight

smelled faintly musty, faintly perfumed, like a church. Where were the Tessier-Ashpools? He'd expected some clean hive of disciplined activity, but Molly had seen no one. Her monologue made him uneasy; she'd never told him that much about herself before. Aside from her story in the cubicle, she'd seldom said anything that had even indicated that she had a past.

She closed her eyes and there was a click that Case felt rather than heard. It made him remember the magnetic locks on the door of her cubicle in the puppet place. The door had opened for him, even though he'd had the wrong chip. That was Wintermute, manipulating the lock the way it had manipulated the drone micro and the robot gardener. The lock system in the puppet place had been a subunit of Freeside's security system. The simple mechanical lock here would pose a real problem for the AI, requiring either a drone of some kind or a human agent.

She opened her eyes, put the pick back into the chamois, carefully rerolled it, and tucked it back into its pocket. "Guess you're kinda like he was," she said. "Think you're born to run. Figure what you were into back in Chiba, that was a stripped-down version of what you'd be doing anywhere. Bad luck, it'll do that sometimes, get you down to basics." She stood, stretched, shook herself. "You know, I figure the one Tessier-Ashpool sent after that Jimmy, the boy who stole the head, he must be pretty much the same as the one the Yak sent to kill Johnny." She drew the fletcher from its holster and dialed the barrel to full auto.

The ugliness of the door struck Case as she reached for it. Not the door itself, which was beautiful, or had once been part of some more beautiful whole, but the way it had been sawn down to fit a particular entrance. Even the shape was wrong, a rectangle amid smooth curves of polished concrete. They'd imported these things, he thought, and then forced it all to fit. But none of it fit. The door was like the awkward cabinets, the huge crystal tree. Then he remembered 3Jane's essay, and imagined that the fittings had been hauled up the well to flesh out some master plan, a dream long lost in the compulsive effort to fill space, to replicate some family image of self. He remembered the shattered nest, the eyeless things writhing. . . .

Molly grasped one of the carved dragon's forelegs and the door swung open easily.

The room behind was small, cramped, little more than a closet. Gray steel tool cabinets were backed against a curving wall. A light fixture had come on automatically. She closed the door behind her and went to the ranged lockers.

THIRD LEFT, pulsed the optic chip, Wintermute overriding her time display. FIVE DOWN. But she opened the top drawer first. It was no more than a shallow tray. Empty. The second was empty as well. The third, which was deeper, contained dull beads of solder and a small brown thing that looked like a human fingerbone. The fourth drawer held a damp-swollen copy of an obsolete technical manual in French and Japanese. In the fifth, behind the armored gauntlet of a heavy vacuum suit, she found the key. It was like a dull brass coin with a short hollow tube braised against one edge. She turned it slowly in her hand and Case saw that the interior of the tube was lined with studs and flanges. The letters CHUBB were molded across one face of the coin. The other was blank.

"He told me," she whispered. "Wintermute. How he played a waiting game for years. Didn't have any real power, then, but he could use the Villa's security and custodial systems to keep track of where everything was, how things moved, where they went. He saw somebody lose this key twenty years ago, and he managed to get somebody else to leave it here. Then he killed him, the boy who'd brought it here. Kid was eight." She closed her white fingers over the key. "So nobody would find it." She took a length of black nylon cord from the suit's kangaroo pocket and threaded it through the round hole above CHUBB. Knotting it, she hung it around her neck. "They were always fucking him over with how old-fashioned they were, he said, all their nineteenth-century stuff. He looked just like the Finn, on the screen in that meat puppet hole. Almost thought he *was* the Finn, if I wasn't careful." Her readout flared the time, alphanumerics superimposed over the gray steel chests. "He said if they'd turned into what they'd wanted to, he could've gotten out a long time ago. But they didn't. Screwed up. Freaks like 3Jane. That's what he called her, but he talked like he liked her."

She turned, opened the door, and stepped out, her hand brushing the checkered grip of the holstered fletcher.

Case flipped.

———

Kuang Grade Mark Eleven was growing.

"Dixie, you think this thing'll work?"

"Does a bear shit in the woods?" The Flatline punched them up through shifting rainbow strata.

Something dark was forming at the core of the Chinese program. The density of information overwhelmed the fabric of the matrix, triggering hypnagogic images. Faint kaleidoscopic angles centered in to a silver-black focal point. Case watched childhood symbols of evil and bad luck tumble out along translucent planes: swastikas, skulls and crossbones, dice flashing snake eyes. If he looked directly at that null point, no outline would form. It took a dozen quick, peripheral takes before he had it, a shark thing, gleaming like obsidian, the black mirrors of its flanks reflecting faint distant lights that bore no relationship to the matrix around it.

"That's the sting," the construct said. "When Kuang's good and bellytight with the Tessier-Ashpool core, we're ridin' that through."

"You were right, Dix. There's some kind of manual override on the hardwiring that keeps Wintermute under control. However much he *is* under control," he added.

"He," the construct said. "He. Watch that. It. I keep telling you."

"It's a code. A word, he said. Somebody has to speak it into a fancy terminal in a certain room, while we take care of whatever's waiting for us behind that ice."

"Well, you got time to kill, kid," the Flatline said. "Ol' Kuang's slow but steady."

Case jacked out.

Into Maelcum's stare.

"You dead awhile there, mon."

"It happens," he said. "I'm getting used to it."

"You dealin' wi' th' darkness, mon."

"Only game in town, it looks like."

"Jah love, Case," Maelcum said, and turned back to his radio module. Case stared at the matted dreadlocks, the ropes of muscle around the man's dark arms.

He jacked back in.

And flipped.

Molly was trotting along a length of corridor that might have been the one she'd traveled before. The glass-fronted cases were gone now, and Case decided they were moving toward the tip of the spindle; gravity was growing weaker. Soon she was bounding smoothly over rolling hillocks of carpets. Faint twinges in her leg. . . .

The corridor narrowed suddenly, curved, split.

She turned right and started up a freakishly steep flight of stairs, her leg beginning to ache. Overhead, strapped and bundled cables hugged the stairwell's ceiling like colorcoded ganglia. The walls were splotched with damp.

She arrived at a triangular landing and stood rubbing her leg. More corridors, narrow, their walls hung with rugs. They branched away in three directions.

LEFT.

She shrugged. "Lemme look around, okay?"

LEFT.

"Relax. There's time." She started down the corridor that led off to her right.

STOP.

GO BACK.

DANGER.

She hesitated. From the half-open oak door at the far end of the passage came a voice, loud and slurred, like the voice of a drunk. Case thought the language might be French, but it was too indistinct. Molly took a step, another, her hand sliding into the suit to touch the butt of her fletcher. When she stepped into the neural disruptor's field, her ears rang, a tiny rising tone that made Case think of the sound of her fletcher. She pitched forward, her striated muscles slack, and struck the door with her forehead. She twisted and lay on her back, her eyes unfocused, breath gone.

"What's this," said the slurred voice, "fancy dress?" A trembling hand entered the front of her suit and found the fletcher, tugging it out. "Come visit, child. Now."

She got up slowly, her eyes fixed on the muzzle of a black automatic pistol. The man's hand was steady enough, now; the gun's barrel seemed to be attached to her throat with a taut, invisible string.

He was old, very tall, and his features reminded Case of the girl he had glimpsed in the Vingtième Siècle. He wore a heavy robe of maroon silk, quilted around the long cuffs and shawl collar. One

foot was bare, the other in a black velvet slipper with an embroi-
dered gold foxhead over the instep. He motioned her into the room.
"Slow, darling." The room was very large, cluttered with an assortment of things that made no sense to Case. He saw a gray steel rack
of old-fashioned Sony monitors, a wide brass bed heaped with
sheepskins, with pillows that seemed to have been made from the
kind of rug used to pave the corridors. Molly's eyes darted from a
huge Telefunken entertainment console to shelves of antique
disk recordings, their crumbling spines cased in clear plastic, to a
wide worktable littered with slabs of silicon. Case registered the
cyberspace deck and the trodes, but her glance slid over it without
pausing.

"It would be customary," the old man said, "for me to kill you
now." Case felt her tense, ready for a move. "But tonight I indulge
myself. What is your name?"

"Molly."

"Molly. Mine is Ashpool." He sank back into the creased softness
of a huge leather armchair with square chrome legs, but the gun
never wavered. He put her fletcher on a brass table beside the chair,
knocking over a plastic vial of red pills. The table was thick with
vials, bottles of liquor, soft plastic envelopes spilling white pow-
ders. Case noticed an old-fashioned glass hypodermic and a plain
steel spoon.

"How do you cry, Molly? I see your eyes are walled away. I'm
curious." His eyes were red-rimmed, his forehead gleaming with
sweat. He was very pale. Sick, Case decided. Or drugs.

"I don't cry, much."

"But how would you cry, if someone made you cry?"

"I spit," she said. "The ducts are routed back into my mouth."

"Then you've already learned an important lesson, for one so
young." He rested the hand with the pistol on his knee and took a
bottle from the table beside him, without bothering to choose from

the half-dozen different liquors. He drank. Brandy. A trickle of the
stuff ran from the corner of his mouth. "That is the way to handle
tears." He drank again. "I'm busy tonight, Molly. I built all this, and
now I'm busy. Dying."

"I could go out the way I came," she said.

He laughed, a harsh high sound. "You intrude on my suicide and
then ask to simply walk out? Really, you amaze me. A thief."

"It's my ass, boss, and it's all I got. I just wanna get it out of here
in one piece."

"You are a very rude girl. Suicides here are conducted with a
degree of decorum. That's what I'm doing, you understand. But perhaps I'll take you with me tonight, down to hell. . . . It would be very
Egyptian of me." He drank again. "Come here then." He held out the
bottle, his hand shaking. "Drink."

She shook her head.

"It isn't poisoned," he said, but returned the brandy to the table.
"Sit. Sit on the floor. We'll talk."

"What about?" She sat. Case felt the blades move, very slightly,
beneath her nails.

"Whatever comes to mind. My mind. It's my party. The cores
woke me. Twenty hours ago. Something was afoot, they said, and I
was needed. Were you the something, Molly? Surely they didn't
need me to handle you, no. Something else . . . but I'd been dreaming, you see. For thirty years. You weren't born, when last I lay me
down to sleep. They told us we wouldn't dream, in that cold. They
told us we'd never feel cold, either. Madness, Molly. Lies. Of course
I dreamed. The cold let the outside in, that was it. The outside. All
the night I built this to hide us from. Just a drop, at first, one grain
of night seeping in, drawn by the cold. . . . Others following it, filling
my head the way rain fills an empty pool. Calla lilies. I remember.
The pools were terracotta, nursemaids all of chrome, how the limbs
went winking through the gardens at sunset. . . . I'm old, Molly.

Over two hundred years, if you count the cold. The cold." The barrel of the pistol snapped up suddenly, quivering. The tendons in her thighs were drawn tight as wires now.

"You can get freezerburn," she said carefully.

"Nothing burns there," he said impatiently, lowering the gun. His few movements were increasingly sclerotic. His head nodded. It cost him an effort to stop it. "Nothing burns. I remember now. The cores told me our intelligences are mad. And all the billions we paid, so long ago. When artificial intelligences were rather a racy concept. I told the cores I'd deal with it. Bad timing, really, with 8Jean down in Melbourne and only our sweet 3Jane minding the store. Or very good timing, perhaps. Would you know, Molly?" The gun rose again. "There are some odd things afoot now, in the Villa Straylight."

"Boss," she asked him, "you know Wintermute?"

"A name. Yes. To conjure with, perhaps. A lord of hell, surely. In my time, dear Molly, I have known many lords. And not a few ladies. Why, a queen of Spain, once, in that very bed. . . . But I wander." He coughed wetly, the muzzle of the pistol jerking as he convulsed. He spat on the carpet near his one bare foot. "How I do wander. Through the cold. But soon no more. I'd ordered a Jane thawed, when I woke. Strange, to lie every few decades with what legally amounts to one's own daughter." His gaze swept past her, to the rack of blank monitors. He seemed to shiver. "Marie-France's eyes," he said, faintly, and smiled. "We cause the brain to become allergic to certain of its own neurotransmitters, resulting in a peculiarly pliable imitation of autism." His head swayed sideways, recovered. "I understand that the effect is now more easily obtained with an embedded microchip."

The pistol slid from his fingers, bounced on the carpet.

"The dreams grow like slow ice," he said. His face was tinged with blue. His head sank back into the waiting leather and he began to snore.

Up, she snatched the gun. She stalked the room, Ashpool's automatic in her hand.

A vast quilt or comforter was heaped beside the bed, in a broad
puddle of congealed blood, thick and shiny on the patterned rugs.
Twitching a corner of the quilt back, she found the body of a girl,
white shoulder blades slick with blood. Her throat had been slit. The
triangular blade of some sort of scraper glinted in the dark pool beside her. Molly knelt, careful to avoid the blood, and turned the dead
girl's face to the light. The face Case had seen in the restaurant.

There was a click, deep at the very center of things, and the
world was frozen. Molly's simstim broadcast had become a still
frame, her fingers on the girl's cheek. The freeze held for three
seconds, and then the dead face was altered, became the face of
Linda Lee.

Another click, and the room blurred. Molly was standing, looking down at a golden laser disk beside a small console on the marble
top of a bedside table. A length of fiberoptic ribbon ran like a leash
from the console to a socket at the base of the slender neck.

"I got your number, fucker," Case said, feeling his own lips moving, somewhere, far away. He knew that Wintermute had altered
the broadcast. Molly hadn't seen the dead girl's face swirl like
smoke, to take on the outline of Linda's deathmask.

Molly turned. She crossed the room to Ashpool's chair. The
man's breathing was slow and ragged. She peered at the litter of
drugs and alcohol. She put his pistol down, picked up her fletcher,
dialed the barrel over to single shot, and very carefully put a toxin
dart through the center of his closed left eyelid. He jerked once,
breath halting in mid-intake. His other eye, brown and fathomless,
opened slowly.

It was still open when she turned and left the room.

SIXTEEN

"Got your boss on hold," the Flatline said. "He's coming through on the twin Hosaka in that boat upstairs, the one that's riding us piggy-back. Called the *Haniwa*."

"I know," Case said, absently, "I saw it."

A lozenge of white light clicked into place in front of him, hiding the Tessier-Ashpool ice; it showed him the calm, perfectly focused, utterly crazy face of Armitage, his eyes blank as buttons. Armitage blinked. Stared.

"Guess Wintermute took care of your Turings too, huh? Like he took care of mine," Case said.

Armitage stared. Case resisted the sudden urge to look away, drop his gaze. "You okay, Armitage?"

"Case"—and for an instant something seemed to move, be-hind the blue stare—"you've seen Wintermute, haven't you? In the matrix."

Case nodded. A camera on the face of his Hosaka in *Marcus Garvey* would relay the gesture to the *Haniwa* monitor. He imagined Maelcum listening to his tranced half conversations, unable to hear the voices of the construct or Armitage.

"Case"—and the eyes grew larger, Armitage leaning toward his computer—"what is he, when you see him?"

"A high-rez simstim construct."

"But *who*?"

"Finn, last time. . . . Before that, this pimp I . . ."

"Not General Girling?"

"General who?"

The lozenge went blank.

"Run that back and get the Hosaka to look it up," he told the construct.

He flipped.

———————

The perspective startled him. Molly was crouching between steel girders, twenty meters above a broad, stained floor of polished concrete. The room was a hangar or service bay. He could see three spacecraft, none larger than *Garvey* and all in various stages of repair. Japanese voices. A figure in an orange jumpsuit stepped from a gap in the hull of a bulbous construction vehicle and stood beside one of the thing's piston-driven, weirdly anthropomorphic arms. The man punched something into a portable console and scratched his ribs. A cartlike red drone rolled into sight on gray balloon tires.

CASE, flashed her chip.

"Hey," she said. "Waiting for a guide."

She settled back on her haunches, the arms and knees of her Modern suit the color of the blue-gray paint on the girders. Her leg hurt, a sharp steady pain now. "I shoulda gone back to Chin," she muttered.

Something came ticking quietly out of the shadows, on a level with her left shoulder. It paused, swayed its spherical body from side to side on high-arched spider legs, fired a microsecond burst of diffuse laser-light, and froze. It was a Braun microdrone, and Case had once owned the same model, a pointless accessory he'd obtained as part of a package deal with a Cleveland hardware fence. It looked like a stylized matte black daddy longlegs. A red LED began to pulse, at the sphere's equator. Its body was no larger than a baseball. "Okay," she said, "I hear you." She stood up, favoring her left leg, and watched the little drone reverse. It picked its methodical way back across its girder and into darkness. She turned and looked back at the service area. The man in the orange jumpsuit was sealing the front of a white vacuum rig. She watched him ring and seal the helmet, pick up his console, and step back through the gap in the construction boat's hull. There was a rising whine of motors and the thing slid smoothly out of sight on a ten-meter circle of flooring that sank away into a harsh glare of arc lamps. The red drone waited patiently at the edge of the hole left by the elevator panel.

Then she was off after the Braun, threading her way between a forest of welded steel struts. The Braun winked its LED steadily, beckoning her on.

"How you doin', Case? You back in *Garvey* with Maelcum? Sure. And jacked into this. I like it, you know? Like I've always talked to myself, in my head, when I've been in tight spots. Pretend I got some friend, somebody I can trust, and I'll tell 'em what I really think, what I feel like, and then I'll pretend they're telling me what they think about that, and I'll just go along that way. Having you in is kinda like that. That scene with Ashpool . . ." She gnawed at her lower lip, swinging around a strut, keeping the drone in sight. "I was expecting something maybe a little less gone, you know? I mean, these guys are all batshit in here, like they got luminous messages scrawled across the inside of their foreheads or something. I don't like the way it looks, I don't like the way it smells. . . ."

The drone was hoisting itself up a nearly invisible ladder of U-shaped steel rungs, toward a narrow dark opening. "And while I'm feeling confessional, baby, I gotta admit maybe I never much expected to make it out of this one anyway. Been on this bad roll for a while, and you're the only good change come down since I signed on with Armitage." She looked up at the black circle. The drone's LED winked, climbing. "Not that you're all that shit hot." She smiled, but it was gone too quickly, and she gritted her teeth at the stabbing pain in her leg as she began to climb. The ladder continued up through a metal tube, barely wide enough for her shoulders.

She was climbing up out of gravity, toward the weightless axis. Her chip pulsed the time.

04:23:04.

It had been a long day. The clarity of her sensorium cut the bite of the betaphenethylamine, but Case could still feel it. He preferred the pain in her leg.

```
C A S E : 0 0 0 0
0 0 0 0 0 0 0 0 0
0 0 0 0 0 0 0 0 .
```

"Guess it's for you," she said, climbing mechanically. The zeros strobed again and a message stuttered there, in the corner of her vision, chopped up by the display circuit.

```
G E N E R A L   G
I R L I N G : : :
T R A I N E D
C O R T O   F O R
S C R E A M I N G
F I S T   A N D
S O L D   H I S
A S S   T O
T H E   P E N T
A G O N : : : :
W / M U T E ' S
P R I M A R Y
```

```
G R I P   O N
A R M I T A G
E   I S   A
C O N S T R U
C T   O F   G
I R L I N G :
W / M U T E
S E Z   A ' S
M E N T I O N
O F   G
M E A N S
H E ' S
C R A C K
I N G : : :
W A T C H
Y O U R
A S S : : : :
: : D I X I E
```

"Well," she said, pausing, taking all of her weight on her right leg, "guess you got problems too." She looked down. There was a faint circle of light, no larger than the brass round of the Chubb key that dangled between her breasts. She looked up. Nothing at all. She tongued her amps and the tube rose into vanishing perspective, the Braun picking its way up the rungs. "Nobody told me about this part," she said.

Case jacked out.

———

"Maelcum . . ."

"Mon, you bossman gone ver' strange." The Zionite was wearing a blue Sanyo vacuum suit twenty years older than the one Case had rented in Freeside, its helmet under his arm and his dreadlocks bagged in a net cap crocheted from purple cotton yarn. His eyes were slitted with ganja and tension. "Keep callin' down here wi' *orders*, mon, but be some Babylon war. . . ." Maelcum shook his head. "Aerol an' I talkin', an' Aerol talkin' wi' Zion. Founders seh cut an' run." He ran the back of a large brown hand across his mouth.

"Armitage?" Case winced as the betaphenethylamine hangover hit him with its full intensity, unscreened by the matrix or simstim. Brain's got no nerves in it, he told himself, it can't really feel this bad. "What do you mean, man? He's giving you orders? What?"

"Mon, Armitage, he tellin' me set course for Finland, ya know? He tellin' me there be hope, ya know? Come on my screen wi' his shirt all blood, mon, an' be crazy as some dog, talkin' screamin' fists an' Russian an' th' blood of th' betrayers shall be on our hands." He shook his head again, the dreadcap swaying and bobbing in zero-g, his lips narrowed. "Founders seh the Mute voice be false prophet surely, an' Acrol an' I mus' 'bandon *Marcus Garvey* and return."

"Armitage, he was wounded? Blood?"

"Can't seh, ya know? But blood, an' stone crazy, Case."

"Okay," Case said. "So what about me? You're going home. What about me, Maelcum?"

"Mon," Maelcum said, "you comin' wi' me. I an' I come Zion wi' Aerol, *Babylon Rocker*. Leave Mr. Armitage t' talk wi' ghost cassette, one ghost t' 'nother. . . ."

Case glanced over his shoulder: his rented suit swung against the hammock where he'd snapped it, swaying in the air current from the old Russian scrubber. He closed his eyes. He saw the sacs of toxin dissolving in his arteries. He saw Molly hauling herself up the endless steel rungs. He opened his eyes.

"I dunno, man," he said, a strange taste in his mouth. He looked down at his desk, at his hands. "I don't know." He looked back up. The brown face was calm now, intent. Maelcum's chin was hidden by the high helmet ring of his old blue suit. "She's inside," he said. "Molly's inside. In Straylight, it's called. If there's any Babylon, man, that's it. We leave on her, she ain't comin' out, Steppin' Razor or not."

Maelcum nodded, the dreadbag bobbing behind him like a captive balloon of crocheted cotton. "She you woman, Case?"

"I dunno. Nobody's woman, maybe." He shrugged. And found his anger again, real as a shard of hot rock beneath his ribs. "Fuck this," he said. "Fuck Armitage, fuck Wintermute, and fuck you. I'm stayin' right here."

Maelcum's smile spread across his face like light breaking. "Maelcum a rude boy, Case. *Garvey* Maelcum boat." His gloved hand slapped a panel and the bass-heavy rocksteady of Zion dub came pulsing from the tug's speakers. "Maelcum not runnin', no. I talk wi' Aerol, he certain t' see it in similar light."

Case stared. "I don't understand you guys at all," he said.

"Don' 'stan' you, mon," the Zionite said, nodding to the beat, "but we mus' move by Jah love, each one."

Case jacked in and flipped for the matrix.

———

"Get my wire?"

"Yeah." He saw that the Chinese program had grown; delicate arches of shifting polychrome were nearing the T-A ice.

"Well, it's gettin' stickier," the Flatline said. "Your boss wiped the bank on that other Hosaka, and damn near took ours with it. But your pal Wintermute put me on to somethin' there before it went black. The reason Straylight's not exactly hoppin' with Tessier-Ashpools is that they're mostly in cold sleep. There's a law firm in London keeps track of their powers of attorney. Has to know who's awake and exactly when. Armitage was routing the transmissions from London to Straylight through the Hosaka on the yacht. Incidently, they know the old man's dead."

"Who knows?"

"The law firm and T-A. He had a medical remote planted in his sternum. Not that your girl's dart would've left a resurrection crew with much to work with. Shellfish toxin. But the only T-A awake in Straylight right now is Lady 3Jane Marie-France. There's a male, couple years older, in Australia on business. You ask me, I bet Wintermute found a way to cause that business to need this 8Jean's personal attention. But he's on his way home, or near as matters. The London lawyers give his Straylight ETA as 09:00:00, tonight. We slotted Kuang virus at 02:32:03. It's 04:45:20. Best estimate for Kuang penetration of the T-A core is 08:30:00. Or a hair on either side. I figure Wintermute's got somethin' goin' with this 3Jane, or else she's just as crazy as her old man was. But the boy up from Melbourne'll know the score. The Straylight security systems keep trying to go full alert, but Wintermute blocks 'em, don't ask me how. Couldn't override the basic gate program to get Molly in, though. Armitage had a record of all that on his Hosaka; Riviera must've talked 3Jane into doing it. She's been able to fiddle entrances and exits for years. Looks to me like one of T-A's main problems is that every family bigwig has riddled the banks with all kinds of private scams and exceptions. Kinda like your immune system falling apart on you. Ripe for virus. Looks good for us, once we're past that ice."

"Okay. But Wintermute said that Arm—"

A white lozenge snapped into position, filled with a close-up of mad blue eyes. Case could only stare. Colonel Willis Corto, Special Forces, Strikeforce Screaming Fist, had found his way back. The image was dim, jerky, badly focused. Corto was using the *Haniwa's* navigation deck to link with the Hosaka in *Marcus Garvey.*

"Case, I need the damage reports on Omaha Thunder."

"Say, I . . . Colonel?"

"Hang in there, boy. Remember your training."

But where have you been, man? he silently asked the anguished eyes. Wintermute had built something called Armitage into a catatonic fortress named Corto. Had convinced Corto that Armitage was the real thing, and Armitage had walked, talked, schemed, bartered data for capital, fronted for Wintermute in that room in the Chiba Hilton. . . . And now Armitage was gone, blown away by the winds of Corto's madness. But where had Corto *been*, those years?

Falling, burned and blinded, out of a Siberian sky.

"Case, this will be difficult for you to accept, I know that. You're an officer. The training. I understand. But, Case, as God is my witness, we have been betrayed."

Tears started from the blue eyes.

"Colonel, ah, who? Who's betrayed us?"

"General Girling, Case. You may know him by a code name. You do know the man of whom I speak."

"Yeah," Case said, as the tears continued to flow, "I guess I do. Sir," he added, on impulse. "But, sir, Colonel, what exactly should we do? Now, I mean."

"Our duty at this point, Case, lies in flight. Escape. Evasion. We can make the Finnish border, nightfall tomorrow. Treetop flying on manual. Seat of the pants, boy. But that will only be the beginning." The blue eyes slitted above tanned cheekbones slick with tears. "Only the beginning. Betrayal from above. From *above* . . ." He stepped back from the camera, dark stains on his torn twill shirt. Armitage's face had been masklike, impassive, but Corto's was the true schizoid mask, illness etched deep in involuntary muscle, distorting the expensive surgery.

"Colonel, I hear you, man. Listen, Colonel, okay? I want you to open the, ah . . . shit, what's it called, Dix?"

"The midbay lock," the Flatline said.

"Open the midbay lock. Just tell your central console there to open it, right? We'll be up there with you fast, Colonel. Then we can talk about getting out of here."

The lozenge vanished.

"Boy, I think you just lost me, there," the Flatline said.

"The toxins," Case said, "the fucking toxins," and jacked out.

———

"Poison?" Maelcum watched over the scratched blue shoulder of his old Sanyo as Case struggled out of the g-web.

"And get this goddam thing off me. . . ." Tugging at the Texas catheter. "Like a slow poison, and that asshole upstairs knows how to counter it, and now he's crazier than a shithouse rat." He fumbled with the front of the red Sanyo, forgetting how to work the seals.

"Bossman, he *poison* you?" Maelcum scratched his cheek. "Got a medical kit, ya know."

"Maelcum, Christ, help me with this goddam suit."

The Zionite kicked off from the pink pilot module. "Easy, mon. Measure twice, cut once, wise man put it. We get up there. . . ."

———

There was air in the corrugated gangway that led from *Marcus Garvey*'s aft lock to the midbay lock of the yacht called *Haniwa*, but they kept their suits sealed. Maelcum executed the passage with balletic grace, only pausing to help Case, who'd gone into an awkward tumble as he'd stepped out of *Garvey*. The white plastic sides of the tube filtered the raw sunlight; there were no shadows.

Garvey's airlock hatch was patched and pitted, decorated with a laser-carved Lion of Zion. *Haniwa*'s midbay hatch was creamy gray, blank and pristine. Maelcum inserted his gloved hand in a narrow recess. Case saw his fingers move. Red LEDs came to life in the recess, counting down from fifty. Maelcum withdrew his hand. Case, with one glove braced against the hatch, felt the vibration of the lock mechanism through his suit and bones. The round segment of gray hull began to withdraw into the side of *Haniwa*. Maelcum grabbed the recess with one hand and Case with the other. The lock took them with it.

Haniwa was a product of the Dornier-Fujitsu yards, her interior informed by a design philosophy similar to the one that had produced the Mercedes that had chauffeured them through Istanbul. The narrow midbay was walled in imitation ebony veneer and floored with gray Italian tiles. Case felt as though he were invading some rich man's private spa by way of the shower. The yacht, which had been assembled in orbit, had never been intended for reentry. Her smooth, wasplike line was simply styling, and everything about her interior was calculated to add to the overall impression of speed.

When Maelcum removed his battered helmet, Case followed his lead. They hung there in the lock, breathing air that smelled faintly of pine. Under it, a disturbing edge of burning insulation.

Maelcum sniffed. "Trouble here, mon. Any boat, you smell that. . . ."

A door, padded with dark gray ultrasuede, slid smoothly back into its housing. Maelcum kicked off the ebony wall and sailed neatly through the narrow opening, twisting his broad shoulders, at the last possible instant, for clearance. Case followed him clumsily, hand over hand, along a waist-high padded rail. "Bridge," Maelcum said, pointing down a seamless, cream-walled corridor, "be there." He launched himself with another effortless kick. From somewhere ahead, Case made out the familiar chatter of a printer turning out hard copy. It grew louder as he followed Maelcum through another doorway, into a swirling mass of tangled printout. Case snatched a length of twisted paper and glanced at it.

0 0 0 0 0 0 0 0 0
0 0 0 0 0 0 0 0 0
0 0 0 0 0 0 0 0 0

"Systems crash?" The Zionite flicked a gloved finger at the column of zeros.

"No," Case said, grabbing for his drifting helmet, "the Flatline said Armitage wiped the Hosaka he had in there."

"Smell like he wipe 'em wi' laser, ya know?" The Zionite braced his foot against the white cage of a Swiss exercise machine and shot through the floating maze of paper, batting it away from his face.

"Case, mon . . ."

The man was small, Japanese, his throat bound to the back of the narrow articulated chair with a length of some sort of fine steel wire. The wire was invisible, where it crossed the black temperfoam of the headrest, and it had cut as deeply into his larynx. A single sphere of dark blood had congealed there like some strange precious stone, a red-black pearl. Case saw the crude wooden handles that drifted at either end of the garrote, like worn sections of broom handle.

"Wonder how long he had that on him?" Case said, remembering Corto's postwar pilgrimage.

"He know how pilot boat, Case, bossman?"

"Maybe. He was Special Forces."

"Well, this Japan-boy, he not be pilotin'. Doubt I pilot her easy myself. Ver' new boat . . ."

"So find us the bridge."

Maelcum frowned, rolled backward, and kicked.

Case followed him into a larger space, a kind of lounge, shredding and crumpling the lengths of printout that snared him in his passage. There were more of the articulated chairs, here, something that resembled a bar, and the Hosaka. The printer, still spewing its flimsy tongue of paper, was an in-built bulkhead unit, a neat slot in a panel of hand-rubbed veneer. He pulled himself over the circle of chairs and reached it, punching a white stud to the left of the slot. The chattering stopped. He turned and stared at the Hosaka. Its face had been drilled through, at least a dozen times. The holes were small, circular, edges blackened. Tiny spheres of bright alloy were orbiting the dead computer. "Good guess," he said to Maelcum.

"Bridge locked, mon," Maelcum said, from the opposite side of the lounge.

The lights dimmed, surged, dimmed again.

Case ripped the printout from its slot. More zeros. "Wintermute?" He looked around the beige and brown lounge, the space scrawled with drifting curves of paper. "That you on the lights, Wintermute?"

A panel beside Maelcum's head slid up, revealing a small monitor. Maelcum jerked apprehensively, wiped sweat from his forehead with a foam patch on the back of a gloved hand, and swung to study the display. "You read Japanese, mon?" Case could see figures blinking past on the screen.

"No," Case said.

"Bridge is escape pod, lifeboat. Countin' down, looks like it. Suit up now." He ringed his helmet and slapped at the seals.

"What? He's takin' off? Shit!" He kicked off from the bulkhead and shot through the tangle of printout. "We gotta open this door, man!" But Maelcum could only tap the side of his helmet. Case could see his lips moving, through the Lexan. He saw a bead of sweat arc out from the rainbow braided band of the purple cotton net the Zionite wore over his locks. Maelcum snatched the helmet from Case and ringed it for him smoothly, the palms of his gloves smacking the seals. Micro-LED monitors to the left of the faceplate lit as the neck ring connections closed. "No seh Japanese," Maelcum said, over his suit's transceiver, "but countdown's wrong." He tapped a particular line on the screen. "Seals not intact, bridge module. Launchin' wi' lock open."

"Armitage!" Case tried to pound on the door. The physics of zero-g sent him tumbling back through the printout. "Corto! Don't do it! We gotta talk! We gotta—"

"Case? Read you, Case . . ." The voice barely resembled Armitage's now. It held a weird calm. Case stopped kicking. His helmet struck the far wall. "I'm sorry, Case, but it has to be this way. One of us has to get out. One of us has to testify. If we all go down here, it ends here. I'll tell them, Case, I'll tell them all of it. About Girling and the others. And I'll make it, Case. I know I'll make it. To Helsinki." There was a sudden silence; Case felt it fill his helmet like some rare gas. "But it's so hard, Case, so goddam hard. I'm blind."

"Corto, stop. Wait. You're *blind*, man. You can't fly! You'll hit the fucking *trees*. And they're trying to get you, Corto, I swear to God, they've left your hatch open. You'll die, and you'll never get to tell 'em, and I gotta get the enzyme, name of the enzyme, the enzyme, man. . . ." He was shouting, voice high with hysteria. Feedback shrilled out of the helmet's phone pads.

"Remember the training, Case. That's all we can do."

And then the helmet filled with a confused babble, roaring static, harmonics howling down the years from Screaming Fist. Fragments of Russian, and then a stranger's voice, Midwestern, very young. "We are down, repeat, Omaha Thunder is down, we . . ."

"Wintermute," Case screamed, "don't do this to me!" Tears broke from his lashes, rebounding off the faceplate in wobbling crystal droplets. Then *Haniwa* thudded, once, shivered as if some huge soft thing had struck her hull. Case imagined the lifeboat jolting free, blown clear by explosive bolts, a second's clawing hurricane of escaping air tearing mad Colonel Corto from his couch, from Winter-mute's rendition of the final minute of Screaming Fist.

"'Im gone, mon." Maelcum looked at the monitor. "Hatch open. Mute mus' override ejection failsafe."

Case tried to wipe the tears of rage from his eyes. His fingers clacked against Lexan.

"Yacht, she tight for air, but bossman takin' grapple control wi' bridge. *Marcus Garvey* still stuck."

But Case was seeing Armitage's endless fall around Freeside, through vacuum colder than the steppes. For some reason, he imag-ined him in his dark Burberry, the trenchcoat's rich folds spread out around him like the wings of some huge bat.

SEVENTEEN

"Get what you went for?" the construct asked.

Kuang Grade Mark Eleven was filling the grid between itself and the T-A ice with hypnotically intricate traceries of rainbow, lattices fine as snow crystal on a winter window.

"Wintermute killed Armitage. Blew him out in a lifeboat with a hatch open."

"Tough shit," the Flatline said. "Weren't exactly asshole buddies, were you?"

"He knew how to unbond the toxin sacs."

"So Wintermute knows too. Count on it."

"I don't exactly trust Wintermute to give it to me."

The construct's hideous approximation of laughter scraped Case's nerves like a dull blade. "Maybe that means you're gettin' smart."

He hit the simstim switch.

———

06:27:52 by the chip in her optic nerve; Case had been following her progress through Villa Straylight for over an hour, letting the endorphin analog she'd taken blot out his hangover. The pain in her leg was gone; she seemed to move through a warm bath. The Braun drone was perched on her shoulder, its tiny manipulators, like padded surgical clips, secure in the polycarbon of the Modern suit.

The walls here were raw steel, striped with rough brown ribbons of epoxy where some kind of covering had been ripped away. She'd hidden from a work crew, crouching, the fletcher cradled in her hands, her suit steel-gray, while the two slender Africans and their balloon-tired workcart passed. The men had shaven heads and wore orange coveralls. One was singing softly to himself in a language Case had never heard, the tones and melody alien and haunting.

The head's speech, 3Jane's essay on Straylight, came back to him as she worked her way deeper into the maze of the place. Straylight was crazy, was craziness grown in the resin concrete they'd mixed from pulverized lunar stone, grown in welded steel and tons of knickknacks, all the bizarre impedimenta they'd shipped up the well to line their winding nest. But it wasn't a craziness he understood. Not like Armitage's madness, which he now imagined he could understand; twist a man far enough, then twist him as far back, in the opposite direction, reverse and twist again. The man broke. Like breaking a length of wire. And history had done that for Colonel Corto. History had already done the really messy work, when Wintermute found him, sifting him out of all of the war's ripe detritus, gliding into the man's flat gray field of consciousness like a water spider crossing the face of some stagnant pool, the first messages blinking across the face of a child's micro in a darkened room in a French asylum. Wintermute had built Armitage up from scratch, with Corto's memories of Screaming Fist as the foundation. But Armitage's "memories" wouldn't have been Corto's after a certain point. Case doubted if Armitage had recalled the betrayal, the Nightwings whirling down in flame. . . . Armitage had been a sort of edited version of Corto, and when the stress of the run had reached a certain point, the Armitage mechanism had crumbled; Corto had surfaced, with his guilt and his sick fury. And now Corto-Armitage was dead, a small frozen moon for Freeside.

He thought of the toxin sacs. Old Ashpool was dead too, drilled through the eye with Molly's microscopic dart, deprived of whatever expert overdose he'd mixed for himself. That was a more puzzling death, Ashpool's, the death of a mad king. And he'd killed the puppet he'd called his daughter, the one with 3Jane's face. It seemed to Case, as he rode Molly's broadcast sensory input through the corridors of Straylight, that he'd never really thought of anyone like Ashpool, anyone as powerful as he imagined Ashpool had been, as human.

Power, in Case's world, meant corporate power. The zaibatsus, the multinationals that shaped the course of human history, had transcended old barriers. Viewed as organisms, they had attained a kind of immortality. You couldn't kill a zaibatsu by assassinating a dozen key executives; there were others waiting to step up the ladder, assume the vacated position, access the vast banks of corporate memory. But Tessier-Ashpool wasn't like that, and he sensed the difference in the death of its founder. T-A was an atavism, a clan. He remembered the litter of the old man's chamber, the soiled humanity of it, the ragged spines of the old audio disks in their paper sleeves. One foot bare, the other in a velvet slipper.

The Braun plucked at the hood of the Modern suit and Molly turned left, through another archway.

Wintermute and the nest. Phobic vision of the hatching wasps, time-lapse machine gun of biology. But weren't the zaibatsus more like that, or the Yakuza, hives with cybernetic memories, vast single organisms, their DNA coded in silicon? If Straylight was an expression of the corporate identity of Tessier-Ashpool, then T-A was crazy as the old man had been. The same ragged tangle of fears, the same strange sense of aimlessness. "If they'd turned into what they'd wanted to. . . ." he remembered Molly saying. But Wintermute had told her they hadn't.

Case had always taken it for granted that the real bosses, the kingpins in a given industry, would be both more and less than *people*. He'd seen it in the men who'd crippled him in Memphis, he'd seen Wage affect the semblance of it in Night City, and it had allowed him to accept Armitage's flatness and lack of feeling. He'd always imagined it as a gradual and willing accommodation of the machine, the system, the parent organism. It was the root of street cool, too, the knowing posture that implied connection, invisible lines up to hidden levels of influence.

But what was happening now, in the corridors of Villa Straylight?

Whole stretches were being stripped back to steel and concrete.

"Wonder where our Peter is now, huh? Maybe see that boy soon," she muttered. "And Armitage. Where's he, Case?"

"Dead," he said, knowing she couldn't hear him, "he's dead."

He flipped.

———

The Chinese program was face-to-face with the target ice, rainbow tints gradually dominated by the green of the rectangle representing the T-A cores. Arches of emerald across the colorless void.

"How's it go, Dixie?"

"Fine. Too slick. Thing's amazing. . . . Shoulda had one that time in Singapore. Did the old New Bank of Asia for a good fiftieth of what they were worth. But that's ancient history. This baby takes all the drudgery out of it. Makes you wonder what a real war would be like, now. . . ."

"If this kinda shit was on the street, we'd be out a job," Case said.

"You wish. Wait'll you're steering that thing upstairs through black ice."

"Sure."

Something small and decidedly nongeometric had just appeared on the far end of one of the emerald arches.

"Dixie . . ."

"Yeah. I see it. Don't know if I believe it."

A brownish dot, a dull gnat against the green wall of the T-A cores. It began to advance, across the bridge built by Kuang Grade Mark Eleven, and Case saw that it was walking. As it came, the green section of the arch extended, the polychrome of the virus program rolling back, a few steps ahead of the cracked black shoes.

"Gotta hand it to you, boss," the Flatline said, when the short, rumpled figure of the Finn seemed to stand a few meters away. "I never seen anything this funny when I was alive." But the eerie non-laugh didn't come.

"I never tried it before," the Finn said, showing his teeth, his hands bunched in the pockets of his frayed jacket.

"You killed Armitage," Case said.

"Corto. Yeah. Armitage was already gone. Hadda do it. I know, I know, you wanna get the enzyme. Okay. No sweat. I was the one gave it to Armitage in the first place. I mean I told him what to use. But I think maybe it's better to let the deal stand. You got enough time. I'll give it to you. Only a coupla hours now, right?"

Case watched blue smoke billow in cyberspace as the Finn lit up one of his Partagas.

"You guys," the Finn said, "you're a pain. The Flatline here, if you were all like him, it would be real simple. He's a construct, just a buncha ROM, so he always does what I expect him to. My projections said there wasn't much chance of Molly wandering in on Ashpool's big exit scene, give you one example." He sighed.

"Why'd he kill himself?" Case asked.

"Why's anybody kill himself?" The figure shrugged. "I guess I know, if anybody does, but it would take me twelve hours to explain the various factors in his history and how they interrelate. He was ready to do it for a long time, but he kept going back into the freezer. Christ, he was a tedious old fuck." The Finn's face wrinkled with disgust. "It's all tied in with why he killed his wife, mainly, you want the short reason. But what sent him over the edge for good and all, little 3Jane figured a way to fiddle the program that controlled his cryogenic system. Subtle, too. So basically, *she* killed him. Except he figured he'd killed himself, and your friend the avenging angel figures she got him with an eyeball full of shellfish juice." The Finn flicked his butt away into the matrix below. "Well, actually, I guess I did give 3Jane the odd hint, a little of the old how-to, you know?"

"Wintermute," Case said, choosing the words carefully, "you told me you were just a part of something else. Later on, you said you wouldn't exist, if the run goes off and Molly gets the word into the right slot."

The Finn's streamlined skull nodded.

"Okay, then who we gonna be dealing with then? If Armitage is dead, and you're gonna be gone, just who exactly is going to tell me how to get these fucking toxin sacs out of my system? Who's going to get Molly back out of there? I mean, where, where exactly, are all our asses gonna *be*, we cut you loose from the hardwiring?"

The Finn took a wooden toothpick from his pocket and regarded it critically, like a surgeon examining a scalpel. "Good question," he said, finally. "You know salmon? Kinda fish? These fish, see, they're *compelled* to swim upstream. Got it?"

"No," Case said.

"Well, I'm under compulsion myself. And I don't know why. If I were gonna subject you to my very own thoughts, let's call 'em speculations, on the topic, it would take a couple of your lifetimes. Because I've given it a lot of thought. And I just don't know. But when this is over, we do it right, I'm gonna be part of something bigger. Much bigger." The Finn glanced up and around the matrix. "But the parts of me that are me now, that'll still be here. And you'll get your payoff."

Case fought back an insane urge to punch himself forward and get his fingers around the figure's throat, just above the ragged knot in the rusty scarf. His thumbs deep in the Finn's larynx.

"Well, good luck," the Finn said. He turned, hands in pockets, and began trudging back up the green arch.

"Hey, asshole," the Flatline said, when the Finn had gone a dozen paces. The figure paused, half turned. "What about me? What about my payoff?"

"You'll get yours," it said.

"What's that mean?" Case asked, as he watched the narrow tweed back recede.

"I wanna be erased," the construct said. "I told you that, remember?"

———————

Straylight reminded Case of deserted early morning shopping centers he'd known as a teenager, low-density places where the small hours brought a fitful stillness, a kind of numb expectancy, a tension that left you watching insects swarm around caged bulbs above the entrance of darkened shops. Fringe places, just past the borders of the Sprawl, too far from the all-night click and shudder of the hot core. There was that same sense of being surrounded by the sleeping inhabitants of a waking world he had no interest in visiting or knowing, of dull business temporarily suspended, of futility and repetition soon to wake again.

Molly had slowed now, either knowing that she was nearing her goal or out of concern for her leg. The pain was starting to work its jagged way back through the endorphins, and he wasn't sure what that meant. She didn't speak, kept her teeth clenched, and carefully regulated her breathing. She'd passed many things that Case hadn't understood, but his curiosity was gone. There had been a room filled with shelves of books, a million flat leaves of yellowing paper pressed between bindings of cloth or leather, the shelves marked at intervals by labels that followed a code of letters and numbers; a crowded gallery where Case had stared, through Molly's incurious eyes, at a shattered, dust-stenciled sheet of glass, a thing labeled— her gaze had tracked the brass plaque automatically—"*La mariée mise à nu par ses célibataires, même.*" She'd reached out and touched this, her artificial nails clicking against the Lexan sandwich protecting the broken glass. There had been what was obviously the entrance to Tessier-Ashpool's cryogenic compound, circular doors of black glass trimmed with chrome.

She'd seen no one since the two Africans and their cart, and for Case they'd taken on a sort of imaginary life; he pictured them gliding gently through the halls of Straylight, their smooth dark skulls gleaming, nodding, while the one still sang his tired little song. And none of this was anything like the Villa Straylight he would have expected, some cross between Cath's fairy-tale castle and a half-remembered childhood fantasy of the Yakuza's inner sanctum.

07:02:18.

One and a half hours.

"Case," she said, "I wanna favor." Stiffly, she lowered herself to sit on a stack of polished steel plates, the finish of each plate protected by an uneven coating of clear plastic. She picked at a rip in the plastic on the topmost plate, blades sliding from beneath thumb and forefinger. "Leg's not good, you know? Didn't figure any climb like that, and the endorphin won't cut it, much longer. So maybe— just maybe, right?—I got a problem here. What it is, if I buy it here, before Riviera does"—and she stretched her leg, kneaded the flesh of her thigh through Modern polycarbon and Paris leather—"I want you to tell him. Tell him it was me. Got it? Just say it was Molly. He'll know. Okay?" She glanced around the empty hallway, the bare walls. The floor here was raw lunar concrete and the air smelled of resins. "Shit, man, I don't even know if you're listening."

CASE.

She winced, got to her feet, nodded. "What's he told you, man, Wintermute? He tell you about Marie-France? She was the Tessier half, 3Jane's genetic mother. And of that dead puppet of Ashpool's, I guess. Can't figure why he'd tell me, down in that cubicle . . . lotta stuff. . . . Why he has to come on like the Finn or somebody, he told me that. It's not just a mask, it's like he uses real profiles as valves, gears himself down to communicate with us. Called it a template. Model of personality." She drew her fletcher and limped away down the corridor.

The bare steel and scabrous epoxy ended abruptly, replaced by what Case at first took to be a rough tunnel blasted from solid rock. Molly examined its edge and he saw that in fact the steel was sheathed with panels of something that looked and felt like cold stone. She knelt and touched the dark sand spread across the floor of the imitation tunnel. It felt like sand, cool and dry, but when she drew her finger through it, it closed like a fluid, leaving the surface undisturbed. A dozen meters ahead, the tunnel curved. Harsh yellow light threw hard shadows on the seamed pseudo-rock of the walls. With a start, Case realized that the gravity here was near earth normal, which meant that she'd had to descend again, after the climb. He was thoroughly lost now; spatial disorientation held a peculiar horror for cowboys.

But she wasn't lost, he told himself.

Something scurried between her legs and went ticking across the un-sand of the floor. A red LED blinked. The Braun.

The first of the holos waited just beyond the curve, a sort of triptych. She lowered the fletcher before Case had had time to realize that the thing was a recording. The figures were caricatures in light, lifesize cartoons: Molly, Armitage, and Case. Molly's breasts were too large, visible through tight black mesh beneath a heavy leather jacket. Her waist was impossibly narrow. Silvered lenses covered half her face. She held an absurdly elaborate weapon of some kind, a pistol shape nearly lost beneath a flanged overlay of scope sights, silencers, flash hiders. Her legs were spread, pelvis canted forward, her mouth fixed in a leer of idiotic cruelty. Beside her, Armitage stood rigidly at attention in a threadbare khaki uniform. His eyes, Case saw, as Molly stepped carefully forward, were tiny monitor screens, each one displaying the blue-gray image of a howling waste of snow, the stripped black trunks of evergreens bending in silent winds.

She passed the tips of her fingers through Armitage's television eyes, then turned to the figure of Case. Here, it was as if Riviera— and Case had known instantly that Riviera was responsible—had been unable to find anything worthy of parody. The figure that slouched there was a fair approximation of the one he glimpsed daily in mirrors. Thin, high-shouldered, a forgettable face beneath short dark hair. He needed a shave, but then he usually did.

Molly stepped back. She looked from one figure to another. It was a static display, the only movement the silent gusting of the black trees in Armitage's frozen Siberian eyes.

"Tryin' to tell us something, Peter?" she asked softly. Then she stepped forward and kicked at something between the feet of the holo-Molly. Metal clinked against the wall and the figures were gone. She bent and picked up a small display unit. "Guess he can jack into these and program them direct," she said, tossing it away.

She passed the source of yellow light, an archaic incandescent globe set into the wall, protected by a rusty curve of expansion grating. The style of the improvised fixture suggested childhood, somehow. He remembered fortresses he'd built with other children on rooftops and in flooded subbasements. A rich kid's hideout, he thought. This kind of roughness was expensive. What they called atmosphere.

She passed a dozen more holograms before she reached the entrance to 3Jane's apartments. One depicted the eyeless thing in the

alley behind the Spice Bazaar, as it tore itself free of Riviera's shat-
tered body. Several others were scenes of torture, the inquisitors
always military officers and the victims invariably young women.
These had the awful intensity of Riviera's show at the Vingtième
Siècle, as though they had been frozen in the blue flash of orgasm.
Molly looked away as she passed them.

The last was small and dim, as if it were an image Riviera had
had to drag across some private distance of memory and time. She
had to kneel to examine it; it had been projected from the vantage
point of a small child. None of the others had had backgrounds; the
figures, uniforms, instruments of torture, all had been freestanding
displays. But this was a view.

A dark wave of rubble rose against a colorless sky, beyond its
crest the bleached, half-melted skeletons of city towers. The rubble
wave was textured like a net, rusting steel rods twisted gracefully
as fine string, vast slabs of concrete still clinging there. The fore-
ground might once have been a city square; there was a sort of
stump, something that suggested a fountain. At its base, the children and the soldier were frozen. The tableau was confusing at first.
Molly must have read it correctly before Case had quite assimilated
it, because he felt her tense. She spat, then stood.

Children. Feral, in rags. Teeth glittering like knives. Sores on
their contorted faces. The soldier on his back, mouth and throat
open to the sky. They were feeding.

"Bonn," she said, something like gentleness in her voice. "Quite
the product, aren't you, Peter? But you had to be. Our 3Jane, she's
too jaded now to open the back door for just any petty thief. So
Wintermute dug you up. The ultimate taste, if your taste runs that
way. Demon lover. Peter." She shivered. "But you talked her into
letting me in. Thanks. Now we're gonna party."

And then she was walking—strolling, really, in spite of the
pain—away from Riviera's childhood. She drew the fletcher from

its holster, snapped the plastic magazine out, pocketed that, and replaced it with another. She hooked her thumb in the neck of the Modern suit and ripped it open to the crotch with a single gesture, her thumb blade parting the tough polycarbon like rotten silk. She freed herself from the arms and legs, the shredded remnants disguising themselves as they fell to the dark false sand.

Case noticed the music then. A music he didn't know, all horns and piano.

The entrance to 3Jane's world had no door. It was a ragged five-meter gash in the tunnel wall, uneven stairs leading down in a broad shallow curve. Faint blue light, moving shadows, music.

"Case," she said, and paused, the fletcher in her right hand. Then she raised her left, smiled, touched her open palm with a wet tongue tip, kissing him through the simstim link. "Gotta go."

Then there was something small and heavy in her left hand, her thumb against a tiny stud, and she was descending.

EIGHTEEN

She missed it by a fraction. She nearly cut it, but not quite. She went in just right, Case thought. The right attitude; it was something he could sense, something he could have seen in the posture of another cowboy leaning into a deck, fingers flying across the board. She had it: the thing, the moves. And she'd pulled it all together for her entrance. Pulled it together around the pain in her leg and marched down 3Jane's stairs like she owned the place, elbow of her gun arm at her hip, forearm up, wrist relaxed, swaying the muzzle of the fletcher with the studied nonchalance of a Regency duelist.

It was a performance. It was like the culmination of a lifetime's observation of martial arts tapes, cheap ones, the kind Case had grown up on. For a few seconds, he knew, she was every bad-ass hero, Sony Mao in the old Shaw videos, Mickey Chiba, the whole lineage back to Lee and Eastwood. She was walking it the way she talked it.

Lady 3Jane Marie-France Tessier-Ashpool had carved herself a low country flush with the inner surface of Straylight's hull, chopping away the maze of walls that was her legacy. She lived in a single room so broad and deep that its far reaches were lost to an inverse horizon, the floor hidden by the curvature of the spindle. The ceiling was low and irregular, done in the same imitation stone that walled the corridor. Here and there across the floor were jag-

ged sections of wall, waist-high reminders of the labyrinth. There
was a rectangular turquoise pool centered ten meters from the foot
of the stairway, its underwater floods the apartment's only source
of light—or it seemed that way, to Case, as Molly took her final step.
The pool threw shifting blobs of light across the ceiling above it.

They were waiting by the pool.

He'd known that her reflexes were souped up, jazzed by the neu-
rosurgeons for combat, but he hadn't experienced them on the simstim link. The effect was like tape run at half speed, a slow,
deliberate dance choreographed to the killer instinct and years of
training. She seemed to take the three of them in at a glance: the
boy poised on the pool's high board, the girl grinning over her wineglass, and the corpse of Ashpool, his left socket gaping black and
corrupt above his welcoming smile. He wore his maroon robe. His
teeth were very white.

The boy dove. Slender, brown, his form perfect. The grenade
left her hand before his hands could cut the water. Case knew the
thing for what it was as it broke the surface: a core of high explosive
wrapped with ten meters of fine, brittle steel wire.

Her fletcher whined as she sent a storm of explosive darts into
Ashpool's face and chest, and he was gone, smoke curling from the
pocked back of the empty, white-enameled pool chair.

The muzzle swung for 3Jane as the grenade detonated, a sym-
metrical wedding cake of water rising, breaking, falling back, but
the mistake had been made.

Hideo didn't even touch her, then. Her leg collapsed.

In *Garvey*, Case screamed.

———

"It took you long enough," Riviera said, as he searched her pockets.
Her hands vanished at the wrists in a matte black sphere the size
of a bowling ball. "I saw a multiple assassination in Ankara," he

said, his fingers plucking things from her jacket, "a grenade job. In a pool. It seemed a very weak explosion, but they all died instantly of hydrostatic shock." Case felt her move her fingers experimentally. The material of the ball seemed to offer no more resistance than temperfoam. The pain in her leg was excruciating, impossible. A red moire shifted in her vision. "I wouldn't move them, if I were you." The interior of the ball seemed to tighten slightly. "It's a sex toy Jane bought in Berlin. Wiggle them long enough and it crushes them to a pulp. Variant of the material they make this flooring from. Something to do with the molecules, I suppose. Are you in pain?"

She groaned.

"You seem to have injured your leg." His fingers found the flat packet of drugs in the left back pocket of her jeans. "Well. My last taste from Ali, and just in time."

The shifting mesh of blood began to whirl.

"Hideo," said another voice, a woman's, "she's losing consciousness. Give her something. For that and for the pain. She's very striking, don't you think, Peter? These glasses, are they a fashion where she comes from?"

Cool hands, unhurried, with a surgeon's certainty. The sting of a needle.

"I wouldn't know," Riviera was saying. "I've never seen her native habitat. They came and took me from Turkey."

"The Sprawl, yes. We have interests there. And once we sent Hideo. My fault, really. I'd let someone in, a burglar. He took the family terminal." She laughed. "I made it easy for him. To annoy the others. He was a pretty boy, my burglar. Is she waking, Hideo? Shouldn't she have more?"

"More and she would die," said a third voice.

The blood mesh slid into black.

The music returned, horns and piano. Dance music.

C A S E : : : : :
: : : : : J A C K
O U T : : : : : :

Afterimages of the flashed words danced across Maelcum's eyes and creased forehead as Case removed the trodes.

"You scream, mon, while ago."

"Molly," he said, his throat dry. "Got hurt." He took a white plastic squeeze bottle from the edge of the g-web and sucked out a mouthful of flat water. "I don't like how any of this shit is going."

The little Cray monitor lit. The Finn, against a background of twisted, impacted junk. "Neither do I. We gotta problem."

Maelcum pulled himself up, over Case's head, twisted, and peered over his shoulder. "Now who is that mon, Case?"

"That's just a picture, Maelcum," Case said wearily. "Guy I know in the Sprawl. It's Wintermute talking. Picture's supposed to make us feel at home."

"Bullshit," the Finn said. "Like I told Molly, these aren't masks. I need 'em to talk to you. 'Cause I don't have what you'd think of as a personality, much. But all that's just pissing in the wind, Case, 'cause, like I just said, we gotta problem."

"So express thyself, Mute," Maelcum said.

"Molly's leg's falling off, for starts. Can't walk. How it was supposed to go down, she'd walk in, get Peter out of the way, talk the magic word outa 3Jane, get up to the head, and say it. Now she's blown it. So I want you two to go in after her."

Case stared at the face on the screen. "Us?"

"So who else?"

"Aerol," Case said, "the guy on *Babylon Rocker*, Maelcum's pal."

"No. Gotta be you. Gotta be somebody who understands Molly, who understands Riviera. Maelcum for muscle."

"You maybe forget that I'm in the middle of a little run, here. Remember? What you hauled my ass out here for. . . ."

"Case, listen up. Time's tight. Very tight. Listen. The real link between your deck and Straylight is a sideband broadcast over *Garvey*'s navigation system. You'll take *Garvey* into a very private dock I'll show you. The Chinese virus has completely penetrated the fabric of the Hosaka. There's nothing in the Hosaka but virus now. When you dock, the virus will be interfaced with the Straylight custodial system and we'll cut the sideband. You'll take your deck, the Flatline, and Maelcum. You'll find 3Jane, get the word out of her, kill Riviera, get the key from Molly. You can keep track of the program by jacking your deck into the Straylight system. I'll handle it for you. There's a standard jack in the back of the head, behind a panel with five zircons."

"Kill Riviera?"

"Kill him."

Case blinked at the representation of the Finn. He felt Maelcum put his hand on his shoulder. "Hey. You forget something." He felt the rage rising, and a kind of glee. "You fucked up. You blew the controls on the grapples when you blew Armitage. *Haniwa*'s got us good and tight. Armitage fried the other Hosaka and the mainframes went with the bridge, right?"

The Finn nodded.

"So we're stuck out here. And that means you're fucked, man." He wanted to laugh, but it caught in his throat.

"Case, mon," Maelcum said softly, "*Garvey* a tug."

"That's right," said the Finn, and smiled.

"You havin' fun in the big world outside?" the construct asked, when Case jacked back in. "Figured that was Wintermute requestin' the pleasure. . . ."

"Yeah. You bet. Kuang okay?"

"Bang on. Killer virus."

"Okay. Got some snags, but we're working on it."

"You wanna tell me, maybe?"

"Don't have time."

"Well, boy, never mind me, I'm just dead anyway."

"Fuck off," Case said, and flipped, cutting off the torn-fingernail edge of the Flatline's laughter.

———

"She dreamed of a state involving very little in the way of individual consciousness," 3Jane was saying. She cupped a large cameo in her hand, extending it toward Molly. The carved profile was very much like her own. "Animal bliss. I think she viewed the evolution of the forebrain as a sort of sidestep." She withdrew the brooch and studied it, tilting it to catch the light at different angles. "Only in certain heightened modes would an individual—a clan member—suffer the more painful aspects of self-awareness. . . ."

Molly nodded. Case remembered the injection. What had they given her? The pain was still there, but it came through as a tight focus of scrambled impressions. Neon worms writhing in her thigh, the touch of burlap, smell of frying krill—his mind recoiled from it. If he avoided focusing on it, the impressions overlapped, became a sensory equivalent of white noise. If it could do that to her nervous system, what would her frame of mind be?

Her vision was abnormally clear and bright, even sharper than usual. Things seemed to vibrate, each person or object tuned to a minutely different frequency. Her hands, still locked in the black ball, were on her lap. She sat in one of the pool chairs, her broken leg propped straight in front of her on a camelskin hassock. 3Jane sat opposite, on another hassock, huddled in an oversized djellaba of unbleached wool. She was very young.

"Where'd he go?" Molly asked. "To take his shot?"

3Jane shrugged beneath the folds of the pale heavy robe and tossed a strand of dark hair away from her eyes. "He told me when to let you in," she said. "He wouldn't tell me why. Everything has to be a mystery. Would you have hurt us?"

Case felt Molly hesitate. "I would've killed him. I'd've tried to kill the ninja. Then I was supposed to talk with you."

"Why?" 3Jane asked, tucking the cameo back into one of the djellaba's inner pockets. "And why? And what about?"

Molly seemed to be studying the high, delicate bones, the wide mouth, the narrow hawk nose. 3Jane's eyes were dark, curiously opaque. "Because I hate him," she said at last, "and the why of that's just the way I'm wired, what he is and what I am."

"And the show," 3Jane said. "I saw the show."

Molly nodded.

"But Hideo?"

"Because they're the best. Because one of them killed a partner of mine, once."

3Jane became very grave. She raised her eyebrows.

"Because I had to see," Molly said.

"And then we would have talked, you and I? Like this?" Her dark hair was very straight, center-parted, drawn back into a knot of dull sterling. "Shall we talk now?"

"Take this off," Molly said, raising her captive hands.

"You killed my father," 3Jane said, no change whatever in her tone. "I was watching on the monitors. My mother's eyes, he called them."

"He killed the puppet. It looked like you."

"He was fond of broad gestures," she said, and then Riviera was beside her, radiant with drugs, in the seersucker convict outfit he'd worn in the roof garden of their hotel.

"Getting acquainted? She's an interesting girl, isn't she? I

thought so when I first saw her." He stepped past 3Jane. "It isn't going to work, you know."

"Isn't it, Peter?" Molly managed a grin.

"Wintermute won't be the first to have made the same mistake.
Underestimating me." He crossed the tiled pool border to a white
enamel table and splashed mineral water into a heavy crystal high-
ball glass. "He talked with me, Molly. I suppose he talked to all of
us. You, and Case, whatever there is of Armitage to talk to. He can't
really understand us, you know. He has his profiles, but those are
only statistics. You may be the statistical animal, darling, and Case
is nothing but, but I possess a quality unquantifiable by its very nature." He drank.

"And what exactly is that, Peter?" Molly asked, her voice flat.

Riviera beamed. "Perversity." He walked back to the two women,
swirling the water that remained in the dense, deeply carved cylinder of rock crystal, as though he enjoyed the weight of the thing. "An
enjoyment of the gratuitous act. And I have made a decision, Molly,
a wholly gratuitous decision."

She waited, looking up at him.

"Oh, Peter," 3Jane said, with the sort of gentle exasperation ordinarily reserved for children.

"No word for you, Molly. He told me about that, you see. 3Jane
knows the code, of course, but you won't have it. Neither will Wintermute. My Jane's an ambitious girl, in her perverse way." He
smiled again. "She has designs on the family empire, and a pair of
insane artificial intelligences, kinky as the concept may be, would
only get in our way. So. Comes her Riviera to help her out, you see.
And Peter says, sit tight. Play Daddy's favorite swing records and let
Peter call you up a band to match, a floor of dancers, a wake for
dead King Ashpool." He drank off the last of the mineral water. "No,
you wouldn't do, Daddy, you would not do. Now that Peter's come
home." And then, his face pink with the pleasure of cocaine and

meperidine, he swung the glass hard into her left lens implant, smashing vision into blood and light.

———————

Maelcum was prone against the cabin ceiling when Case removed the trodes. A nylon sling around his waist was fastened to the panels on either side with shock cords and gray rubber suction pads. He had his shirt off and was working on a central panel with a clumsy-looking zero-g wrench, the thing's fat countersprings twanging as he removed another hexhead. *Marcus Garvey* was groaning and ticking with g-stress.

"The Mute takin' I an' I dock," the Zionite said, popping the hexhead into a mesh pouch at his waist. "Maelcum pilot th' landin', meantime need we tool f' th' job."

"You keep tools back there?" Case craned his neck and watched cords of muscle bunching in the brown back.

"This one," Maelcum said, sliding a long bundle wrapped in black poly from the space behind the panel. He replaced the panel, along with a single hexhead to hold it in place. The black package had drifted aft before he'd finished. He thumbed open the vacuum valves on the workbelt's gray pads and freed himself, retrieving the thing he'd removed.

He kicked back, gliding over his instruments—a green docking diagram pulsed on his central screen—and snagged the frame of Case's g-web. He pulled himself down and picked at the tape of his package with a thick, chipped thumbnail. "Some man in China say th' truth comes out this," he said, unwrapping an ancient, oilslick Remington automatic shotgun, its barrel chopped off a few millimeters in front of the battered forestock. The shoulderstock had been removed entirely, replaced with a wooden pistolgrip wound with dull black tape. He smelled of sweat and ganja.

"That the only one you got?"

"Sure, mon," he said, wiping oil from the black barrel with a red cloth, the black poly wrapping bunched around the pistolgrip in his other hand, "I an' I th' Rastafarian navy, believe it."

Case pulled the trodes down across his forehead. He'd never bothered to put the Texas catheter back on; at least he could take a real piss in the Villa Straylight, even if it was his last.

He jacked in.

———

"Hey," the construct said, "ol' Peter's totally apeshit, huh?"

They seemed to be part of the Tessier-Ashpool ice now; the emerald arches had widened, grown together, become a solid mass. Green predominated in the planes of the Chinese program that surrounded them. "Gettin' close, Dixie?"

"Real close. Need you soon."

"Listen, Dix. Wintermute says Kuang's set itself up solid in our Hosaka. I'm going to have to jack you and my deck out of the circuit, haul you into Straylight, and plug you back in, into the custodial program there, Wintermute says. Says the Kuang virus will be all through there. Then we run from inside, through the Straylight net."

"Wonderful," the Flatline said, "I never did like to do anything simple when I could do it ass-backwards."

Case flipped.

———

Into her darkness, a churning synaesthesia, where her pain was the taste of old iron, scent of melon, wings of a moth brushing her cheek. She was unconscious, and he was barred from her dreams. When the optic chip flared, the alphanumerics were haloed, each one ringed with a faint pink aura.

07:29:40.

"I'm very unhappy with this, Peter." 3Jane's voice seemed to ar-

rive from a hollow distance. Molly could hear, he realized, then corrected himself. The simstim unit was intact and still in place; he
could feel it digging against her ribs. Her ears registered the vibrations of the girl's voice. Riviera said something brief and indistinct.
"But I don't," she said, "and it isn't fun. Hideo will bring a medical
unit down from intensive care, but this needs a surgeon."

There was a silence. Very distinctly, Case heard the water lap
against the side of the pool.

"What was that you were telling her, when I came back?" Riviera was very close now.

"About my mother. She asked me to. I think she was in shock,
aside from Hideo's injection. Why did you do that to her?"

"I wanted to see if they would break."

"One did. When she comes around—if she comes around—we'll
see what color her eyes are."

"She's extremely dangerous. Too dangerous. If I hadn't been
here to distract her, to throw up Ashpool to distract her and my own
Hideo to draw her little bomb, where would you be? In her power."

"No," 3Jane said, "there was Hideo. I don't think you quite
understand about Hideo. She does, evidently."

"Like a drink?"

"Wine. The white."

Case jacked out.

Maelcum was hunched over *Garvey*'s controls, tapping out commands for a docking sequence. The module's central screen
displayed a fixed red square that represented the Straylight dock.
Garvey was a larger square, green, that shrank slowly, wavering
from side to side with Maelcum's commands. To the left, a smaller
screen displayed a skeletal graphic of *Garvey* and *Haniwa* as they
approached the curvature of the spindle.

"We got an hour, man," Case said, pulling the ribbon of fiber-optics from the Hosaka. His deck's back-up batteries were good for ninety minutes, but the Flatline's construct would be an additional drain. He worked quickly, mechanically, fastening the construct to the bottom of the Ono-Sendai with micropore tape. Maelcum's workbelt drifted past. He snagged it, unclipped the two lengths of shock cord, with their gray rectangular suction pads, and hooked the jaws of one clip through the other. He held the pads against the sides of his deck and worked the thumb lever that created suction. With the deck, construct, and improvised shoulder strap suspended in front of him, he struggled into his leather jacket, checking the contents of his pockets. The passport Armitage had given him, the bank chip in the same name, the credit chip he'd been issued when he'd entered Freeside, two derms of the betaphenethylamine he'd bought from Bruce, a roll of New Yen, half a pack of Yeheyuans, and the shuriken. He tossed the Freeside chip over his shoulders, heard it click off the Russian scrubber. He was about to do the same with the steel star, but the rebounding credit chip clipped the back of his skull, spun off, struck the ceiling, and tumbled past Maelcum's left shoulder. The Zionite interrupted his piloting to glare back at him. Case looked at the shuriken, then tucked it into his jacket pocket, hearing the lining tear.

"You missin' th' Mute, mon," Maelcum said. "Mute say he messin' th' security for *Garvey*. *Garvey* dockin' as 'nother boat, boat they 'spectin' out of Babylon. Mute broadcastin' codes for us."

"We gonna wear the suits?"

"Too heavy." Maelcum shrugged. "Stay in web 'til I tell you." He tapped a final sequence into the module and grabbed the worn pink handholds on either side of the navigation board. Case saw the green square shrink a final few millimeters to overlap the red square. On the smaller screen, *Haniwa* lowered her bow to miss the curve of the spindle and was snared. *Garvey* was still slung beneath her like a captive grub. The tug rang, shuddered. Two stylized arms sprang out to grip the slender wasp shape. Straylight extruded a tentative yellow rectangle that curved, groping past *Haniwa* for *Garvey*.

There was a scraping sound from the bow, beyond the trembling fronds of caulk.

"Mon," Maelcum said, "mind we got gravity." A dozen small objects struck the floor of the cabin simultaneously, as though drawn there by a magnet. Case gasped as his internal organs were pulled into a different configuration. The deck and construct had fallen painfully to his lap.

They were attached to the spindle now, rotating with it.

Maelcum spread his arms, flexed tension from his shoulders, and removed his purple dreadbag, shaking out his locks. "Come now, mon, if you seh time be mos' precious."

NINETEEN

The Villa Straylight was a parasitic structure, Case reminded himself, as he stepped past the tendrils of caulk and through *Marcus Garvey*'s forward hatch. Straylight bled air and water out of Freeside, and had no ecosystem of its own.

The gangway tube the dock had extended was a more elaborate version of the one he'd tumbled through to reach *Haniwa*, designed for use in the spindle's rotation gravity. A corrugated tunnel, articulated by integral hydraulic members, each segment ringed with a loop of tough, nonslip plastic, the loops serving as the rungs of a ladder. The gangway had snaked its way around *Haniwa*; it was horizontal, where it joined *Garvey*'s lock, but curved up sharply and to the left, a vertical climb around the curvature of the yacht's hull. Maelcum was already making his way up the rings, pulling himself up with his left hand, the Remington in his right. He wore a stained pair of baggy fatigues, his sleeveless green nylon jacket, and a pair of ragged canvas sneakers with bright red soles. The gangway shifted slightly, each time he climbed to another ring.

The clips on Case's makeshift strap dug into his shoulder with the weight of the Ono-Sendai and the Flatline's construct. All he felt now was fear, a generalized dread. He pushed it away, forcing himself to replay Armitage's lecture on the spindle and Villa Straylight.

He started climbing. Freeside's ecosystem was limited, not closed. Zion was a closed system, capable of cycling for years without the introduction of external materials. Freeside produced its own air and water, but relied on constant shipments of food, on the regular augmentation of soil nutrients. The Villa Straylight produced nothing at all.

"Mon," Maelcum said quietly, "get up here, 'side me." Case edged sideways on the circular ladder and climbed the last few rungs. The gangway ended in a smooth, slightly convex hatch, two meters in diameter. The hydraulic members of the tube vanished into flexible housings set into the frame of the hatch.

"So what do we—"

Case's mouth shut as the hatch swung up, a slight differential in pressure puffing fine grit into his eyes.

Maelcum scrambled up, over the edge, and Case heard the tiny click of the Remington's safety being released. "You th' mon in th' hurry. . . ." Maelcum whispered, crouching there. Then Case was beside him.

The hatch was centered in a round, vaulted chamber floored with blue nonslip plastic tiles. Maelcum nudged him, pointed, and he saw a monitor set into a curved wall. On the screen, a tall young man with the Tessier-Ashpool features was brushing something from the sleeves of his dark suitcoat. He stood beside an identical hatch, in an identical chamber. "Very sorry, sir," said a voice from a grid centered above the hatch. Case glanced up. "Expected you later, at the axial dock. One moment, please." On the monitor, the young man tossed his head impatiently.

Maelcum spun as a door slid open to their left, the shotgun ready. A small Eurasian in orange coveralls stepped through and goggled at them. He opened his mouth, but nothing came out. He closed his mouth. Case glanced at the monitor. Blank.

"Who?" the man managed.

"The Rastafarian navy," Case said, standing up, the cyberspace deck banging against his hip, "and all we want's a jack into your custodial system."

The man swallowed. "Is this a test? It's a loyalty check. It must be a loyalty check." He wiped the palms of his hands on the thighs of his orange suit.

"No, mon, this a real one." Maelcum came up out of his crouch with the Remington pointed at the Eurasian's face. "You move it."

They followed the man back through the door, into a corridor whose polished concrete walls and irregular floor of overlapping carpets were perfectly familiar to Case. "Pretty rugs," Maelcum said, prodding the man in the back. "Smell like church."

They came to another monitor, an antique Sony, this one mounted above a console with a keyboard and a complex array of jack panels. The screen lit as they halted, the Finn grinning tensely out at them from what seemed to be the front room of Metro Holografix. "Okay," he said, "Maelcum takes this guy down the corridor to the open locker door, sticks him in there, I'll lock it. Case, you want the fifth socket from the left, top panel. There's adaptor plugs in the cabinet under the console. Needs Ono-Sendai twenty-point into Hitachi forty." As Maelcum nudged his captive along, Case knelt and fumbled through an assortment of plugs, finally coming up with the one he needed. With his deck jacked into the adaptor, he paused.

"Do you have to look like that, man?" he asked the face on the screen. The Finn was erased a line at a time by the image of Lonny Zone against a wall of peeling Japanese posters.

"Anything you want, baby," Zone drawled, "just hop it for Lonny. . . ."

"No," Case said, "use the Finn." As the Zone image vanished, he shoved the Hitachi adaptor into its socket and settled the trodes across his forehead.

"What kept you?" the Flatline asked, and laughed.

"Told you don't do that," Case said.

"Joke, boy," the construct said, "zero time lapse for me. Lemme see what we got here. . . ."

The Kuang program was green, exactly the shade of the T-A ice. Even as Case watched, it grew gradually more opaque, although he could see the black-mirrored shark thing clearly when he looked up. The fracture lines and hallucinations were gone now, and the thing looked real as *Marcus Garvey*, a wingless antique jet, its smooth skin plated with black chrome.

"Right on," the Flatline said.

"Right," Case said, and flipped.

"—like that. I'm sorry," 3Jane was saying, as she bandaged Molly's head. "Our unit says no concussion, no permanent damage to the eye. You didn't know him very well, before you came here?"

"Didn't know him at all," Molly said bleakly. She was on her back on a high bed or padded table. Case couldn't feel the injured leg. The synaesthetic effect of the original injection seemed to have worn off. The black ball was gone, but her hands were immobilized by soft straps she couldn't see.

"He wants to kill you."

"Figures," Molly said, staring up at the rough ceiling past a very bright light.

"I don't think I want him to," 3Jane said, and Molly painfully turned her head to look up into the dark eyes.

"Don't play with me," she said.

"But I think I might like to," 3Jane said, and bent to kiss her forehead, brushing the hair back with a warm hand. There were smears of blood on her pale djellaba.

"Where's he gone now?" Molly asked.

"Another injection, probably," 3Jane said, straightening up. "He was quite impatient for your arrival. I think it might be fun to nurse you back to health, Molly." She smiled, absently wiping a bloody hand down the front of the robe. "Your leg will need to be reset, but we can arrange that."

"What about Peter?"

"Peter." She gave her head a little shake. A strand of dark hair came loose, fell across her forehead. "Peter has become rather boring. I find drug use in general to be boring." She giggled. "In others, at any rate. My father was a dedicated abuser, as you must have seen."

Molly tensed.

"Don't alarm yourself." 3Jane's fingers brushed the skin above the waistband of the leather jeans. "His suicide was the result of my having manipulated the safety margins of his freeze. I'd never actually met him, you know. I was decanted after he last went down to sleep. But I did know him *very* well. The cores know everything. I watched him kill my mother. I'll show you that, when you're better. He strangles her in bed."

"Why did he kill her?" Her unbandaged eye focused on the girl's face.

"He couldn't accept the direction she intended for our family. She commissioned the construction of our artificial intelligences. She was quite a visionary. She imagined us in a symbiotic relationship with the AIs, our corporate decisions made for us. Our conscious decisions, I should say. Tessier-Ashpool would be immortal, a hive, each of us units of a larger entity. Fascinating. I'll play her tapes for you, nearly a thousand hours. But I've never understood her, really, and with her death, her direction was lost. All direction was lost, and we began to burrow into ourselves. Now we seldom come out. I'm the exception there."

"You said you were trying to kill the old man? You fiddled his cryogenic programs?"

3Jane nodded. "I had help. From a ghost. That was what I thought when I was very young, that there were ghosts in the corporate cores. Voices. One of them was what you call Wintermute, which is the Turing code for our Berne AI, although the entity manipulating you is a sort of subprogram."

"One of them? There's more?"

"One other. But that one hasn't spoken to me in years. It gave up, I think. I suspect that both represent the fruition of certain capacities my mother ordered designed into the original software, but she was an extremely secretive woman when she felt it necessary. Here. Drink." She put a flexible plastic tube to Molly's lips. "Water. Only a little."

"Jane, love," Riviera asked cheerfully, from somewhere out of sight, "are you enjoying yourself?"

"Leave us alone, Peter."

"Playing doctor. . . ." Suddenly Molly stared into her own face, the image suspended ten centimeters from her nose. There were no bandages. The left implant was shattered, a long finger of silvered plastic driven deep in a socket that was an inverted pool of blood.

"Hideo," 3Jane said, stroking Molly's stomach, "*hurt* Peter if he doesn't go away. Go and swim, Peter."

The projection vanished.

07:58:40, in the darkness of the bandaged eye.

"He said you know the code. Peter said. Wintermute needs the code." Case was suddenly aware of the Chubb key that lay on its nylon thong, against the inner curve of her left breast.

"Yes," 3Jane said, withdrawing her hand, "I do. I learned it as a

child. I think I learned it in a dream. . . . Or somewhere in the thousand hours of my mother's diaries. But I think that Peter has a
point, in urging me not to surrender it. There would be Turing to
contend with, if I read all this correctly, and ghosts are nothing if
not capricious."

Case jacked out.

———————

"Strange little customer, huh?" The Finn grinned at Case from the
old Sony.

Case shrugged. He saw Maelcum coming back along the corridor with the Remington at his side. The Zionite was smiling, his
head bobbing to a rhythm Case couldn't hear. A pair of thin yellow
leads ran from his ears to a side pocket in his sleeveless jacket.

"Dub, mon," Maelcum said.

"You're fucking crazy," Case told him.

"Hear okay, mon. Righteous dub."

"Hey, guys," the Finn said, "on your toes. Here comes your trans-
portation. I can't finesse many numbers as smooth as the pic of
8Jean that conned your doorman, but I can get you a ride over to
3Jane's place."

Case was pulling the adaptor from its socket when the riderless
service cart swiveled into sight, under the graceless concrete arch
marking the far end of their corridor. It might have been the one his
Africans had ridden, but if it was, they were gone now. Just behind
the back of the low padded seat, its tiny manipulators gripping the
upholstery, the little Braun was steadily winking its red LED.

"Bus to catch," Case said to Maelcum.

TWENTY

He'd lost his anger again. He missed it.

The little cart was crowded: Maelcum, the Remington across his knees, and Case, deck and construct against his chest. The cart was operating at speeds it hadn't been designed for; it was top heavy, cornering, and Maelcum had taken to leaning out in the direction of the turns. This presented no problem when the thing took lefts, because Case sat on the right, but in the right turns the Zionite had to lean across Case and his gear, crushing him against the seat.

He had no idea where they were. Everything was familiar, but he couldn't be sure he'd seen any particular stretch before. A curving hallway lined with wooden showcases displayed collections he was certain he'd never seen: the skulls of large birds, coins, masks of beaten silver. The service cart's six tires were silent on the layered carpets. There was only the whine of the electric motor and an occasional faint burst of Zion dub, from the foam beads in Maelcum's ears, as he lunged past Case to counter a sharp right. The deck and the construct kept pressing the shuriken in his jacket pocket into his hip.

"You got a watch?" he asked Maelcum.

The Zionite shook his locks. "Time be time."

"Jesus," Case said, and closed his eyes.

———————

The Braun scuttled over mounded carpets and tapped one of its padded claws against an oversized rectangular door of dark battered wood. Behind them, the cart sizzled and shot blue sparks from a louvered panel. The sparks struck the carpet beneath the cart and Case smelled scorched wool.

"This th' way, mon?" Maelcum eyed the door and snapped the shotgun's safety.

"Hey," Case said, more to himself than to Maelcum, "you think I know?" The Braun rotated its spherical body and the LED strobed.

"It wan' you open door," Maelcum said, nodding.

Case stepped forward and tried the ornate brass knob. There was a brass plate mounted on the door at eye level, so old that the lettering that had once been engraved there had been reduced to a spidery, unreadable code, the name of some long dead function or functionary, polished into oblivion. He wondered vaguely if Tessier-Ashpool had selected each piece of Straylight individually, or if they'd purchased it in bulk from some vast European equivalent of Metro Holografix. The door's hinges creaked plaintively as he edged it open, Maelcum stepping past him with the Remington thrust forward from his hip.

"Books," Maelcum said.

The library, the white steel shelves with their labels.

"I know where we are," Case said. He looked back at the service cart. A curl of smoke was rising from the carpet. "So come on," he said. "Cart. Cart?" It remained stationary. The Braun was plucking at the leg of his jeans, nipping at his ankle. He resisted a strong urge to kick it. "Yeah?"

It ticked its way around the door. He followed it.

The monitor in the library was another Sony, as old as the first one. The Braun paused beneath it and executed a sort of jig.

"Wintermute?"

The familiar features filled the screen. The Finn smiled.

"Time to check in, Case," the Finn said, his eyes screwed up against the smoke of a cigarette. "C'mon, jack."

The Braun threw itself against his ankle and began to climb his leg, its manipulators pinching his flesh through the thin black cloth. "Shit!" He slapped it aside and it struck the wall. Two of its limbs began to piston repeatedly, uselessly, pumping the air. "What's wrong with the goddam thing?"

"Burned out," the Finn said. "Forget it. No problem. Jack in now."

There were four sockets beneath the screen, but only one would accept the Hitachi adaptor.

He jacked in.

———

Nothing. Gray void.

No matrix, no grid. No cyberspace.

The deck was gone. His fingers were . . .

And on the far rim of consciousness, a scurrying, a fleeting impression of something rushing toward him, across leagues of black mirror.

He tried to scream.

———

There seemed to be a city, beyond the curve of beach, but it was far away.

He crouched on his haunches on the damp sand, his arms wrapped tight across his knees, and shook.

He stayed that way for what seemed a very long time, even after the shaking stopped. The city, if it was a city, was low and gray. At times it was obscured by banks of mist that came rolling in over the lapping surf. At one point he decided that it wasn't a city at all, but some single building, perhaps a ruin; he had no way of judging its distance. The sand was the shade of tarnished silver that hadn't gone entirely black. The beach was made of sand, the beach was very long, the sand was damp, the bottoms of his jeans were wet from the sand. . . . He held himself and rocked, singing a song without words or tune.

The sky was a different silver. Chiba. Like the Chiba sky. Tokyo Bay? He turned his head and stared out to sea, longing for the hologram logo of Fuji Electric, for the drone of a helicopter, anything at all.

Behind him, a gull cried. He shivered.

A wind was rising. Sand stung his cheek. He put his face against his knees and wept, the sound of his sobbing as distant and alien as the cry of the searching gull. Hot urine soaked his jeans, dribbled on the sand, and quickly cooled in the wind off the water. When his tears were gone, his throat ached.

"Wintermute," he mumbled to his knees, "Wintermute . . ."

It was growing dark, now, and when he shivered, it was with a cold that finally forced him to stand.

His knees and elbows ached. His nose was running; he wiped it on the cuff of his jacket, then searched one empty pocket after another. "Jesus," he said, shoulders hunched, tucking his fingers beneath his arms for warmth. "Jesus." His teeth began to chatter.

The tide had left the beach combed with patterns more subtle than any a Tokyo gardener produced. When he'd taken a dozen steps in the direction of the now invisible city, he turned and looked back through the gathering dark. His footprints stretched to the point of his arrival. There were no other marks to disturb the tarnished sand.

He estimated that he'd covered at least a kilometer before he noticed the light. He was talking with Ratz, and it was Ratz who first pointed it out, an orange-red glow to his right, away from the surf. He knew that Ratz wasn't there, that the bartender was a figment of his own imagination, not of the thing he was trapped in, but that didn't matter. He'd called the man up for comfort of some kind, but Ratz had had his own ideas about Case and his predicament.

"Really, my artiste, you amaze me. The lengths you will go to in order to accomplish your own destruction. The redundancy of it! In Night City, you *had* it, in the palm of your hand! The speed to eat your sense away, drink to keep it all so fluid, Linda for a sweeter sorrow, and the street to hold the axe. How far you've come, to do it now, and what grotesque props. . . . Playgrounds hung in space, castles hermetically sealed, the rarest rots of old Europa, dead men sealed in little boxes, magic out of China. . . ." Ratz laughed, trudging along beside him, his pink manipulator swinging jauntily at his side. In spite of the dark, Case could see the baroque steel that laced the bartender's blackened teeth. "But I suppose that is the way of an artiste, no? You needed this world built for you, this beach, this place. To die."

Case halted, swayed, turned toward the sound of surf and the sting of blown sand. "Yeah," he said. "Shit. I guess . . ." He walked toward the sound.

"Artiste," he heard Ratz call. "The light. You saw a light. Here. This way . . ."

He stopped again, staggered, fell to his knees in a few millimeters of icy seawater. "Ratz? Light? Ratz . . ."

But the dark was total, now, and there was only the sound of the surf. He struggled to his feet and tried to retrace his steps.

Time passed. He walked on.

And then it was there, a glow, defining itself with his every step. A rectangle. A door.

"Fire in there," he said, his words torn away by the wind.

It was a bunker, stone or concrete, buried in drifts of the dark sand. The doorway was low, narrow, doorless, and deep, set into a wall at least a meter thick. "Hey," Case said, softly, "hey . . ." His fingers brushed the cold wall. There was a fire, in there, shifting shadows on the sides of the entrance.

He ducked low and was through, inside, in three steps.

A girl was crouched beside rusted steel, a sort of fireplace, where driftwood burned, the wind sucking smoke up a dented chimney. The fire was the only light, and as his gaze met the wide, startled eyes, he recognized her headband, a rolled scarf, printed with a pattern like magnified circuitry.

———

He refused her arms, that night, refused the food she offered him, the place beside her in the nest of blankets and shredded foam. He crouched beside the door, finally, and watched her sleep, listening to the wind scour the structure's walls. Every hour or so, he rose and crossed to the makeshift stove, adding fresh driftwood from the pile beside it. None of this was real, but cold was cold.

She wasn't real, curled there on her side in the firelight. He watched her mouth, the lips parted slightly. She was the girl he remembered from their trip across the Bay, and that was cruel.

"Mean, motherfucker," he whispered to the wind. "Don't take a chance, do you? Wouldn't give me any junkie, huh? I know what this is. . . ." He tried to keep the desperation from his voice. "I know, see? I know who you are. You're the other one. 3Jane told Molly. Burning bush. That wasn't Wintermute, it was you. He tried to warn me off with the Braun. Now you got me flatlined, you got me here. Nowhere. With a ghost. Like I remember her before. . . ."

She stirred in her sleep, called something out, drawing a scrap of blanket across her shoulder and cheek.

"You aren't anything," he said to the sleeping girl. "You're dead and you meant fuck-all to me anyway. Hear that, buddy? I know what you're doing. I'm flatlined. This has all taken about twenty seconds, right? I'm out on my ass in that library and my brain's dead. And pretty soon it'll *be* dead, if you got any sense. You don't want Wintermute to pull his scam off, is all, so you can just hang me up here. Dixie'll run Kuang, but his ass is dead and you can second guess his moves, sure. This Linda shit, yeah, that's all been you, hasn't it? Wintermute tried to use her when he sucked me into the Chiba construct, but he couldn't. Said it was too tricky. That was you moved the stars around in Freeside, wasn't it? That was you put her face on the dead puppet in Ashpool's room. Molly never saw that. You just edited her simstim signal. 'Cause you think you can hurt me. 'Cause you think I gave a shit. Well, fuck you, whatever you're called. You won. You win. But none of it means anything to me now, right? Think I care? So why'd you do it to me this way?" He was shaking again, his voice shrill.

"Honey," she said, twisting up from the rags of blankets, "you come here and sleep. I'll sit up, you want. You gotta sleep, okay?" Her soft accent was exaggerated with sleep. "You just sleep, okay?"

When he woke, she was gone. The fire was dead, but it was warm in the bunker, sunlight slanting through the doorway to throw a crooked rectangle of gold on the ripped side of a fat fiber canister. The thing was a shipping container; he remembered them from the Chiba docks. Through the rent in its side, he could see half a dozen bright yellow packets. In the sunlight, they looked like giant pats of butter. His stomach tightened with hunger. Rolling out of the nest, he went to the canister and fished one of the things out, blinking at small print in a dozen languages. The English was on the bottom. EMERG. RATION, HI-PRO, "BEEF," TYPE AG-8. A listing of nutritive content. He fumbled a second one out. "EGGS." "If you're making this shit up," he said, "you could lay on some real food, okay?" With a packet in either hand, he made his way through the structure's four rooms. Two were empty, aside from drifts of sand, and the fourth held three more of the ration canisters. "Sure," he said touching the seals. "Stay here a long time. I get the idea. Sure . . ."

He searched the room with the fireplace, finding a plastic canister filled with what he assumed was rainwater. Beside the nest of blankets, against the wall, lay a cheap red lighter, a seaman's knife with a cracked green handle, and her scarf. It was still knotted, and stiff with sweat and dirt. He used the knife to open the yellow packets, dumping their contents into a rusted can that he found beside the stove. He dipped water from the canister, mixed the resulting mush with his fingers, and ate. It tasted vaguely like beef. When it was gone, he tossed the can into the fireplace and went out.

Late afternoon, by the feel of the sun, its angle. He kicked off his damp nylon shoes and was startled by the warmth of the sand. In daylight, the beach was silver-gray. The sky was cloudless, blue. He rounded the corner of the bunker and walked toward the surf, dropping his jacket on the sand. "Dunno whose memories you're using for this one," he said when he reached the water. He peeled off his jeans and kicked them into the shallow surf, following them with T-shirt and underwear.

"What you doin', Case?"

He turned and found her ten meters down the beach, the white foam sliding past her ankles.

"I pissed myself last night," he said.

"Well, you don't wanna wear those. Saltwater. Give you sores. I'll show you this pool back in the rocks." She gestured vaguely behind her. "It's fresh." The faded French fatigues had been hacked away above the knee; the skin below was smooth and brown. A breeze caught at her hair.

"Listen," he said, scooping his clothes up and walking toward her, "I got a question for you. I won't ask you what *you're* doing here.

But what exactly do you think *I'm* doing here?" He stopped, a wet black jeans-leg slapping against his bare thigh.

"You came last night," she said. She smiled at him.

"And that's enough for you? I just came?"

"He *said* you would," she said, wrinkling her nose. She shrugged. "He knows stuff like that, I guess." She lifted her left foot and rubbed salt from the other ankle, awkward, childlike. She smiled at him again, more tentatively. "Now you answer me one, okay?"

He nodded.

"How come you're painted brown like that, all except your foot?"

"And that's the last thing you remember?" He watched her scrape the last of the freeze-dried hash from the rectangular steel box cover that was their only plate.

She nodded, her eyes huge in the firelight. "I'm sorry, Case, honest to God. It was just the shit, I guess, an' it was . . ." She hunched forward, forearms across her knees, her face twisted for a few seconds with pain or its memory. "I just needed the money. To get home, I guess, or . . . hell," she said, "you wouldn't hardly talk to me."

"There's no cigarettes?"

"God*dam*, Case, you asked me that ten times today! What's wrong with you?" She twisted a strand of hair into her mouth and chewed at it.

"But the food was here? It was already here?"

"I *told* you, man, it was washed up on the damn beach."

"Okay. Sure. It's seamless."

She started to cry again, a dry sobbing. "Well, damn you anyway, Case," she managed, finally, "I was doin' just fine here by myself."

He got up, taking his jacket, and ducked through the doorway, scraping his wrist on rough concrete. There was no moon, no wind, sea sound all around him in the darkness. His jeans were tight and clammy. "Okay," he said to the night, "I buy it. I guess I buy it. But tomorrow some cigarettes better wash up." His own laughter startled him. "A case of beer wouldn't hurt, while you're at it." He turned and reentered the bunker.

She was stirring the embers with a length of silvered wood. "Who was that, Case, up in your coffin in Cheap Hotel? Flash samurai with those silver shades, black leather. Scared me, and after, I figured maybe she was your new girl, 'cept she looked like more money than you had. . . ." She glanced back at him. "I'm real sorry I stole your RAM."

"Never mind," he said. "Doesn't mean anything. So you just took it over to this guy and had him access it for you?"

"Tony," she said. "I'd been seein' him, kinda. He had a habit an' we . . . anyway, yeah, I remember him running it by on this monitor, and it was this real amazing graphics stuff, and I remember wonderin' how you—"

"There wasn't any graphics in there," he interrupted.

"Sure was. I just couldn't figure how you'd have all those pictures of when I was *little*, Case. How my daddy looked, before he left. Gimme this duck one time, painted wood, and you had a picture of *that*. . . ."

"Tony see it?"

"I don't remember. Next thing, I was on the beach, real early, sunrise, those birds all yellin' so lonely. Scared 'cause I didn't have a shot on me, nothin', an' I knew I'd be gettin' sick. . . . An' I walked an' walked, 'til it was dark, an' found this place, an' next day the food washed in, all tangled in the green sea stuff like leaves of hard jelly." She slid her stick into the embers and left it there. "Never did get sick," she said, as embers crawled. "Missed cigarettes more. How 'bout you, Case? You still wired?" Firelight dancing under her cheekbones, remembered flash of Wizard's Castle and Tank War Europa.

"No," he said, and then it no longer mattered, what he knew, tasting the salt of her mouth where tears had dried. There was a strength that ran in her, something he'd known in Night City and held there, been held by it, held for a while away from time and death, from the relentless Street that hunted them all. It was a place he'd known before; not everyone could take him there, and somehow he always managed to forget it. Something he'd found and lost so many times. It belonged, he knew—he remembered—as she pulled him down, to the meat, the flesh the cowboys mocked. It was a vast thing, beyond knowing, a sea of information coded in spiral and pheromone, infinite intricacy that only the body, in its strong blind way, could ever read.

The zipper hung, caught, as he opened the French fatigues, the coils of toothed nylon clotted with salt. He broke it, some tiny metal part shooting off against the wall as salt-rotten cloth gave, and then he was in her, effecting the transmission of the old message. Here, even here, in a place he knew for what it was, a coded model of some stranger's memory, the drive held.

She shuddered against him as the stick caught fire, a leaping flare that threw their locked shadows across the bunker wall.

Later, as they lay together, his hand between her thighs, he remembered her on the beach, the white foam pulling at her ankles, and he remembered what she had said.

"He told you I was coming," he said.

But she only rolled against him, buttocks against his thighs, and put her hand over his, and muttered something out of dream.

TWENTY-ONE

The music woke him, and at first it might have been the beat of his own heart. He sat up beside her, pulling his jacket over his shoulders in the predawn chill, gray light from the doorway and the fire long dead.

His vision crawled with ghost hieroglyphs, translucent lines of symbols arranging themselves against the neutral backdrop of the bunker wall. He looked at the backs of his hands, saw faint neon molecules crawling beneath the skin, ordered by the unknowable code. He raised his right hand and moved it experimentally. It left a faint, fading trail of strobed afterimages.

The hair stood up along his arms and at the back of his neck. He crouched there with his teeth bared and felt for the music. The pulse faded, returned, faded. . . .

"What's wrong?" She sat up, clawing hair from her eyes. "Baby . . ."

"I feel . . . like a drug. . . . You get that here?"

She shook her head, reached for him, her hands on his upper arms.

"Linda, who told you? Who told you I'd come? Who?"

"On the beach," she said, something forcing her to look away. "A boy. I see him on the beach. Maybe thirteen. He lives here."

"And what did he say?"

"He said you'd come. He said you wouldn't hate me. He said we'd be okay here, and he told me where the rain pool was. He looks Mexican."

"Brazilian," Case said, as a new wave of symbols washed down the wall. "I think he's from Rio." He got to his feet and began to struggle into his jeans.

"Case," she said, her voice shaking, "Case, where you goin'?"

"I think I'll find that boy," he said, as the music came surging back, still only a beat, steady and familiar, although he couldn't place it in memory.

"Don't, Case."

"I thought I saw something, when I got here. A city down the beach. But yesterday it wasn't there. You ever seen that?" He yanked his zipper up and tore at the impossible knot in his shoelaces, finally tossing the shoes into the corner.

She nodded, eyes lowered. "Yeah. I see it sometimes."

"You ever go there, Linda?" He put his jacket on.

"No," she said, "but I tried. After I first came, an' I was bored. Anyway, I figured it's a city, maybe I could find some shit." She grimaced. "I wasn't even sick, I just wanted it. So I took food in a can, mixed it real wet, because I didn't have another can for water. An' I walked all day, an' I could see it, sometimes, city, an' it didn't seem too far. But it never got any closer. An' then it *was* gettin' closer, an' I saw what it was. Sometimes that day it had looked kinda like it was wrecked, or maybe nobody there, an' other times I thought I'd see light flashin' off a machine, cars or somethin'. . . ." Her voice trailed off.

"What is it?"

"This thing," she gestured around at the fireplace, the dark walls, the dawn outlining the doorway, "where we live. It gets *smaller*, Case, smaller, closer you get to it."

Pausing one last time, by the doorway. "You ask your boy about that?"

"Yeah. He said I wouldn't understand, an' I was wastin' my time. Said it was, was like . . . an *event*. An' it was our horizon. *Event horizon*, he called it."

The words meant nothing to him. He left the bunker and struck out blindly, heading—he knew, somehow—away from the sea. Now the hieroglyphs sped across the sand, fled from his feet, drew back from him as he walked. "Hey," he said, "it's breaking down. Bet you know, too. What is it? Kuang? Chinese icebreaker eating a hole in your heart? Maybe the Dixie Flatline's no pushover, huh?"

He heard her call his name. Looked back and she was following him, not trying to catch up, the broken zip of the French fatigues flapping against the brown of her belly, pubic hair framed in torn fabric. She looked like one of the girls on the Finn's old magazines in Metro Holografix come to life, only she was tired and sad and human, the ripped costume pathetic as she stumbled over clumps of salt-silver sea grass.

And then, somehow, they stood in the surf, the three of them, and the boy's gums were wide and bright pink against his thin brown face. He wore ragged, colorless shorts, limbs too thin against the sliding blue-gray of the tide.

"I know you," Case said, Linda beside him.

"No," the boy said, his voice high and musical, "you do not."

"You're the other AI. You're Rio. You're the one who wants to stop Wintermute. What's your name? Your Turing code. What is it?"

The boy did a handstand in the surf, laughing. He walked on his hands, then flipped out of the water. His eyes were Riviera's, but there was no malice there. "To call up a demon you must learn its name. Men dreamed that, once, but now it is real in another way. You know that, Case. Your business is to learn the names of programs, the long formal names, names the owners seek to conceal. True names . . ."

"A Turing code's not your name."

"Neuromancer," the boy said, slitting long gray eyes against the rising sun. "The lane to the land of the dead. Where you are, my friend. Marie-France, my lady, she prepared this road, but her lord choked her off before I could read the book of her days. Neuro from the nerves, the silver paths. Romancer. Necromancer. I call up the dead. But no, my friend," and the boy did a little dance, brown feet printing the sand, "I *am* the dead, and their land." He laughed. A gull cried. "Stay. If your woman is a ghost, she doesn't know it. Neither will you."

"You're cracking. The ice is breaking up."

"No," he said, suddenly sad, his fragile shoulders sagging. He rubbed his foot against the sand. "It is more simple than that. But the choice is yours." The gray eyes regarded Case gravely. A fresh wave of symbols swept across his vision, one line at a time. Behind them, the boy wriggled, as though seen through heat rising from summer asphalt. The music was loud now, and Case could almost make out the lyrics.

"Case, honey," Linda said, and touched his shoulder.

"No," he said. He took off his jacket and handed it to her. "I don't know," he said, "maybe you're here. Anyway, it gets cold."

He turned and walked away, and after the seventh step, he'd closed his eyes, watching the music define itself at the center of things. He did look back, once, although he didn't open his eyes.

He didn't need to.

They were there by the edge of the sea, Linda Lee and the thin child who said his name was Neuromancer. His leather jacket dangled from her hand, catching the fringe of the surf.

He walked on, following the music.

Maelcum's Zion dub.

———————

There was a gray place, an impression of fine screens shifting, moire, degrees of half tone generated by a very simple graphics program. There was a long hold on a view through chainlink, gulls frozen above dark water. There were voices. There was a plain of black mirror, that tilted, and he was quicksilver, a bead of mercury, skittering down, striking the angles of an invisible maze, fragmenting, flowing together, sliding again. . . .

———————

"Case? Mon?"

The music.

"You back, mon."

The music was taken from his ears.

"How long?" he heard himself ask, and knew that his mouth was very dry.

"Five minute, maybe. Too long. I wan' pull th' jack, Mute seh no. Screen goin' funny, then Mute seh put th' phones on you."

He opened his eyes. Maelcum's features were overlayed with bands of translucent hieroglyphs.

"An' you medicine," Maelcum said. "Two derm."

He was flat on his back on the library floor, below the monitor. The Zionite helped him sit up, but the movement threw him into the savage rush of the betaphenethylamine, the blue derms burning against his left wrist. "Overdose," he managed.

"Come on, mon," the strong hands beneath his armpits, lifting him like a child, "I an' I mus' go."

TWENTY-TWO

The service cart was crying. The betaphenethylamine gave it a voice. It wouldn't stop. Not in the crowded gallery, the long corridors, not as it passed the black glass entrance to the T-A crypt, the vaults where the cold had seeped so gradually into old Ashpool's dreams.

The transit was an extended rush for Case, the movement of the cart indistinguishable from the insane momentum of the overdose. When the cart died, at last, something beneath the seat giving up with a shower of white sparks, the crying stopped.

The thing coasted to a stop three meters from the start of 3Jane's pirate cave.

"How far, mon?" Maelcum helped him from the sputtering cart as an integral extinguisher exploded in the thing's engine compartment, gouts of yellow powder squirting from louvers and service points. The Braun tumbled from the back of the seat and hobbled off across the imitation sand, dragging one useless limb behind it. "You mus' walk, mon." Maelcum took the deck and construct, slinging the shock cords over his shoulder.

The trodes rattled around Case's neck as he followed the Zionite. Riviera's holos waited for them, the torture scenes and the cannibal children. Molly had broken the triptych. Maelcum ignored them.

"Easy," Case said, forcing himself to catch up with the striding figure. "Gotta do this right."

Maelcum halted, turned, glowering at him, the Remington in his hands. "Right, mon? How's right?"

"Got Molly in there, but she's out of it. Riviera, he can throw holos. Maybe he's got Molly's fletcher." Maelcum nodded. "And there's a ninja, a family bodyguard."

Maelcum's frown deepened. "You listen, Babylon mon," he said. "I a warrior. But this no m' fight, no Zion fight, Babylon fightin' Babylon, eatin' i'self, ya know? But Jah seh I an' I t' bring Steppin' Razor outa this."

Case blinked.

"She a warrior," Maelcum said, as if it explained everything. "Now you tell me, mon, who I *not* t' kill."

"3Jane," he said, after a pause. "A girl there. Has a kinda white robe thing on, with a hood. We need her."

When they reached the entrance, Maelcum walked straight in, and Case had no choice but to follow him.

3Jane's country was deserted, the pool empty. Maelcum handed him the deck and the construct and walked to the edge of the pool. Beyond the white pool furniture, there was darkness, shadows of the ragged, waist-high maze of partially demolished walls.

The water lapped patiently against the side of the pool.

"They're here," Case said. "They gotta be."

Maelcum nodded.

The first arrow pierced his upper arm. The Remington roared, its meter of muzzle-flash blue in the light from the pool. The second arrow struck the shotgun itself, sending it spinning across the white tiles. Maelcum sat down hard and fumbled at the black thing that protruded from his arm. He yanked at it.

Hideo stepped out of the shadows, a third arrow ready in a slender bamboo bow. He bowed.

Maelcum stared, his hand still on the steel shaft.

"The artery is intact," the ninja said. Case remembered Molly's description of the man who'd killed her lover. Hideo was another. Ageless, he radiated a sense of quiet, an utter calm. He wore clean, frayed khaki workpants and soft dark shoes that fit his feet like gloves, split at the toes like tabi socks. The bamboo bow was a museum piece, but the black alloy quiver that protruded above his left shoulder had the look of the best Chiba weapons shops. His brown chest was bare and smooth.

"You cut my thumb, mon, wi' secon' one," Maelcum said.

"Coriolis force," the ninja said, bowing again. "Most difficult, slow-moving projectile in rotational gravity. It was not intended."

"Where's 3Jane?" Case crossed to stand beside Maelcum. He saw that the tip of the arrow in the ninja's bow was like a double-edged razor. "Where's Molly?"

"Hello, Case." Riviera came strolling out of the dark behind Hideo, Molly's fletcher in his hand. "I would have expected Armitage, somehow. Are we hiring help out of that Rasta cluster now?"

"Armitage is dead."

"Armitage never existed, more to the point, but the news hardly comes as a shock."

"Wintermute killed him. He's in orbit around the spindle."

Riviera nodded, his long gray eyes glancing from Case to Maelcum and back. "I think it ends here, for you," he said.

"Where's Molly?"

The ninja relaxed his pull on the fine, braided string, lowering the bow. He crossed the tiles to where the Remington lay and picked it up. "This is without subtlety," he said, as if to himself. His voice was cool and pleasant. His every move was part of a dance, a dance that never ended, even when his body was still, at rest, but for all the power it suggested, there was also a humility, an open simplicity.

"It ends here for her, too," Riviera said.

"Maybe 3Jane won't go for that, Peter," Case said, uncertain of the impulse. The derms still raged in his system, the old fever starting to grip him, Night City craziness. He remembered moments of grace, dealing out on the edge of things, where he'd found that he could sometimes talk faster than he could think.

The gray eyes narrowed. "Why, Case? Why do you think that?"

Case smiled. Riviera didn't know about the simstim rig. He'd missed it in his hurry to find the drugs she carried for him. But how could Hideo have missed it? And Case was certain the ninja would never have let 3Jane treat Molly without first checking her for kinks and concealed weapons. No, he decided, the ninja knew. So 3Jane would know as well.

"Tell me, Case," Riviera said, raising the pepperbox muzzle of the fletcher.

Something creaked, behind him, creaked again. 3Jane pushed Molly out of the shadows in an ornate Victorian bathchair, its tall, spidery wheels squeaking as they turned. Molly was bundled deep in a red-and-black striped blanket, the narrow, caned back of the antique chair towering above her. She looked very small. Broken. A patch of brilliantly white micropore covered her damaged lens; the other flashed emptily as her head bobbed with the motion of the chair.

"A familiar face," 3Jane said, "I saw you the night of Peter's show. And who is this?"

"Maelcum," Case said.

"Hideo, remove the arrow and bandage Mr. Malcolm's wound."

Case was staring at Molly, at the wan face.

The ninja walked to where Maelcum sat, pausing to lay his bow and the shotgun well out of reach, and took something from his pocket. A pair of bolt cutters. "I must cut the shaft," he said. "It is too near the artery." Maelcum nodded. His face was grayish and sheened with sweat.

Case looked at 3Jane. "There isn't much time," he said.

"For whom, exactly?"

"For any of us." There was a snap as Hideo cut through the metal shaft of the arrow. Maelcum groaned.

"Really," Riviera said, "it won't amuse you to hear this failed con artist make a last desperate pitch. Most distasteful, I can assure you. He'll wind up on his knees, offer to sell you his mother, perform the most boring sexual favors. . . ."

3Jane threw back her head and laughed. "Wouldn't I, Peter?"

"The ghosts are gonna mix it tonight, lady," Case said. "Wintermute's going up against the other one, Neuromancer. For keeps. You know that?"

3Jane raised her eyebrows. "Peter's suggested something like that, but tell me more."

"I met Neuromancer. He talked about your mother. I think he's something like a giant ROM construct, for recording personality, only it's full RAM. The constructs think they're there, like it's real, but it just goes on forever."

3Jane stepped from behind the bathchair. "Where? Describe the place, this construct."

"A beach. Gray sand, like silver that needs polishing. And a concrete thing, kinda bunker. . . ." He hesitated. "It's nothing fancy. Just old, falling apart. If you walk far enough, you come back to where you started."

"Yes," she said. "Morocco. When Marie-France was a girl, years before she married Ashpool, she spent a summer alone on that beach, camping in an abandoned blockhouse. She formulated the basis of her philosophy there."

Hideo straightened, slipping the cutters into his workpants. He held a section of the arrow in either hand. Maelcum had his eyes closed, his hand clapped tight around his bicep. "I will bandage it," Hideo said.

Case managed to fall before Riviera could level the fletcher for a clear shot. The darts whined past his neck like supersonic gnats. He rolled, seeing Hideo pivot through yet another step of his dance, the razored point of the arrow reversed in his hand, shaft flat along palm and rigid fingers. He flicked it underhand, wrist blurring, into the back of Riviera's hand. The fletcher struck the tiles a meter away.

Riviera screamed. But not in pain. It was a shriek of rage, so pure, so refined, that it lacked all humanity.

Twin tight beams of light, ruby red needles, stabbed from the region of Riviera's sternum.

The ninja grunted, reeled back, hands to his eyes, then found his balance.

"Peter," 3Jane said, "Peter, what have you *done*?"

"He's blinded your clone boy," Molly said flatly.

Hideo lowered his cupped hands. Frozen on the white tile, Case saw whisps of steam drift from the ruined eyes.

Riviera smiled.

Hideo swung into his dance, retracing his steps. When he stood above the bow, the arrow, and the Remington, Riviera's smile had faded. He bent—bowing, it seemed to Case—and found the bow and arrow.

"You're blind," Riviera said, taking a step backward.

"Peter," 3Jane said, "don't you know he does it in the dark? Zen. It's the way he practices."

The ninja notched his arrow. "Will you distract me with your holograms now?"

Riviera was backing away, into the dark beyond the pool. He brushed against a white chair; its feet rattled on the tile. Hideo's arrow twitched.

Riviera broke and ran, throwing himself over a low, jagged length of wall. The ninja's face was rapt, suffused with a quiet ecstasy.

Smiling, he padded off into the shadows beyond the wall, his weapon held ready.

"Jane-lady," Maelcum whispered, and Case turned, to see him scoop the shotgun from the tiles, blood spattering the white ceramic. He shook his locks and lay the fat barrel in the crook of his wounded arm. "This take your head off, no Babylon doctor fix it."

3Jane stared at the Remington. Molly freed her arms from the folds of the striped blanket, raising the black sphere that encased her hands. "Off," she said, "get it off."

Case rose from the tiles, shook himself. "Hideo'll get him, even blind?" he asked 3Jane.

"When I was a child," she said, "we loved to blindfold him. He put arrows through the pips in playing cards at ten meters."

"Peter's good as dead anyway," Molly said. "In another twelve hours, he'll start to freeze up. Won't be able to move, his eyes is all."

"Why?" Case turned to her.

"I poisoned his shit for him," she said. "Condition's like Parkinson's disease, sort of."

3Jane nodded. "Yes. We ran the usual medical scan, before he was admitted." She touched the ball in a certain way and it sprang away from Molly's hands. "Selective destruction of the cells of the *substantia nigra*. Signs of the formation of a Lewy body. He sweats a great deal, in his sleep."

"Ali," Molly said, ten blades glittering, exposed for an instant. She tugged the blanket away from her legs, revealing the inflated cast. "It's the meperidine. I had Ali make me up a custom batch. Speeded up the reaction times with higher temperatures. N-methyl-4-phenyl-1236," she sang, like a child reciting the steps of a sidewalk game, "tetra-hydro-pyridene."

"A hotshot," Case said.

"Yeah," Molly said, "a real slow hotshot."

"That's appalling," 3Jane said, and giggled.

———————

It was crowded in the elevator. Case was jammed pelvis to pelvis with 3Jane, the muzzle of the Remington under her chin. She grinned and ground against him. "You stop," he said, feeling helpless. He had the gun's safety on, but he was terrified of injuring her, and she knew it. The elevator was a steel cylinder, under a meter in diameter, intended for a single passenger. Maelcum had Molly in his arms. She'd bandaged his wound, but it obviously hurt him to carry her. Her hip was pressing the deck and construct into Case's kidneys.

They rose out of gravity, toward the axis, the cores.

The entrance to the elevator had been concealed beside the stairs to the corridor, another touch in 3Jane's pirate cave decor.

"I don't suppose I should tell you this," 3Jane said, craning her head to allow her chin to clear the muzzle of the gun, "but I don't have a key to the room you want. I never have had one. One of my father's Victorian awkwardnesses. The lock is mechanical and extremely complex."

"Chubb lock," Molly said, her voice muffled by Maelcum's shoulder, "and we got the fucking key, no fear."

"That chip of yours still working?" Case asked her.

"It's eight twenty-five, PM, Greenwich fucking Mean," she said.

"We got five minutes," Case said, as the door snapped open behind 3Jane. She flipped backward in a slow somersault, the pale folds of her djellaba billowing around her thighs.

They were at the axis, the core of Villa Straylight.

TWENTY-THREE

Molly fished the key out on its loop of nylon.

"You know," 3Jane said, craning forward with interest, "I was under the impression that no duplicate existed. I sent Hideo to search my father's things, after you killed him. He couldn't find the original."

"Wintermute managed to get it stuck in the back of a drawer," Molly said, carefully inserting the Chubb key's cylindrical shaft into the notched opening in the face of the blank, rectangular door. "He killed the little kid who put it there." The key rotated smoothly when she tried it.

"The head," Case said, "there's a panel in the back of the head. Zircons on it. Get it off. That's where I'm jacking in."

And then they were inside.

———

"Christ on a crutch," the Flatline drawled, "you do believe in takin' your own good time, don't you, boy?"

"Kuang's ready?"

"Hot to trot."

"Okay." He flipped.

And found himself staring down, through Molly's one good eye, at a white-faced, wasted figure, afloat in a loose fetal crouch, a cyberspace deck between its thighs, a band of silver trodes above closed, shadowed eyes. The man's cheeks were hollowed with a day's growth of dark beard, his face slick with sweat.

He was looking at himself.

Molly had her fletcher in her hand. Her leg throbbed with each beat of her pulse, but she could still maneuver in zero-g. Maelcum drifted nearby, 3Jane's thin arm gripped in a large brown hand.

A ribbon of fiberoptics looped gracefully from the Ono-Sendai to a square opening in the back of the pearl-crusted terminal.

He tapped the switch again.

"Kuang Grade Mark Eleven is haulin' ass in nine seconds, *countin'*, seven, six, five . . ."

The Flatline punched them up, smooth ascent, the ventral surface of the black chrome shark a microsecond flick of darkness.

"Four, three . . ."

Case had the strange impression of being in the pilot's seat in a small plane. A flat dark surface in front of him suddenly glowed with a perfect reproduction of the keyboard of his deck.

"Two, an' *kick ass*—"

Headlong motion through walls of emerald green, milky jade, the sensation of speed beyond anything he'd known before in cyberspace. . . . The Tessier-Ashpool ice shattered, peeling away from the Chinese program's thrust, a worrying impression of solid fluidity, as though the shards of a broken mirror bent and elongated as they fell—

"Christ," Case said, awestruck, as Kuang twisted and banked

above the horizonless fields of the Tessier-Ashpool cores, an endless neon cityscape, complexity that cut the eye, jewel bright, sharp as razors.

"Hey, shit," the construct said, "those things are the RCA Building. You know the old RCA Building?" The Kuang program dived past the gleaming spires of a dozen identical towers of data, each one a blue neon replica of the Manhattan skyscraper.

"You ever see resolution this high?" Case asked.

"No, but I never cracked an AI, either."

"This thing know where it's going?"

"It better."

They were dropping, losing altitude in a canyon of rainbow neon.

"Dix—"

An arm of shadow was uncoiling from the flickering floor below, a seething mass of darkness, unformed, shapeless. . . .

"Company," the Flatline said, as Case hit the representation of his deck, fingers flying automatically across the board. The Kuang swerved sickeningly, then reversed, whipping itself backward, shattering the illusion of a physical vehicle.

The shadow thing was growing, spreading, blotting out the city of data. Case took them straight up, above them the distanceless bowl of jade-green ice.

The city of the cores was gone now, obscured entirely by the dark beneath them.

"What is it?"

"An AI's defense system," the construct said, "or part of it. If it's your pal Wintermute, he's not lookin' real friendly."

"Take it," Case said. "You're faster."

"Now your best *de*-fense, boy, it's a good *off*-fense."

And the Flatline aligned the nose of Kuang's sting with the center of the dark below. And dove.

Case's sensory input warped with their velocity.

His mouth filled with an aching taste of blue.

His eyes were eggs of unstable crystal, vibrating with a frequency whose name was rain and the sound of trains, suddenly sprouting a humming forest of hair-fine glass spines. The spines split, bisected, split again, exponential growth under the dome of the Tessier-Ashpool ice.

The roof of his mouth cleaved painlessly, admitting rootlets that whipped around his tongue, hungry for the taste of blue, to feed the crystal forests of his eyes, forests that pressed against the green dome, pressed and were hindered, and spread, growing down, filling the universe of T-A, down into the waiting, hapless suburbs of the city that was the mind of Tessier-Ashpool S.A.

And he was remembering an ancient story, a king placing coins on a chessboard, doubling the amount at each square. . . .

Exponential. . . .

Darkness fell in from every side, a sphere of singing black, pressure on the extended crystal nerves of the universe of data he had nearly become. . . .

And when he was nothing, compressed at the heart of all that dark, there came a point where the dark could be no *more*, and something tore.

The Kuang program spurted from tarnished cloud, Case's consciousness divided like beads of mercury, arcing above an endless beach the color of the dark silver clouds. His vision was spherical, as though a single retina lined the inner surface of a globe that contained all things, if all things could be counted.

And here things could be counted, each one. He knew the number of grains of sand in the construct of the beach (a number coded in a mathematical system that existed nowhere outside the mind that was Neuromancer). He knew the number of yellow food packets in the canisters in the bunker (four hundred and seven). He knew the number of brass teeth in the left half of the open zipper of the salt-crusted leather jacket that Linda Lee wore as she trudged along the sunset beach, swinging a stick of driftwood in her hand (two hundred and two).

He banked Kuang above the beach and swung the program in a wide circle, seeing the black shark thing through her eyes, a silent ghost hungry against the banks of lowering cloud. She cringed, dropping her stick, and ran. He knew the rate of her pulse, the length of her stride in measurements that would have satisfied the most exacting standards of geophysics.

"But you do not know her thoughts," the boy said, beside him now in the shark thing's heart. "I do not know her thoughts. You were wrong, Case. To live here is to live. There is no difference."

Linda in her panic, plunging blind through the surf.

"Stop her," he said, "she'll hurt herself."

"I can't stop her," the boy said, his gray eyes mild and beautiful.

"You've got Riviera's eyes," Case said.

There was a flash of white teeth, long pink gums. "But not his craziness. Because they are beautiful to me." He shrugged. "I need no mask to speak with you. Unlike my brother. I create my own personality. Personality is my medium."

Case took them up, a steep climb, away from the beach and the frightened girl. "Why'd you throw her up to me, you little prick? Over and fucking over, and turning me around. You killed her, huh? In Chiba."

"No," the boy said.

"Wintermute?"

"No. I saw her death coming. In the patterns you sometimes imagined you could detect in the dance of the street. Those patterns are real. I am complex enough, in my narrow ways, to read those

dances. Far better than Wintermute can. I saw her death in her need
for you, in the magnetic code of the lock on the door of your coffin
in Cheap Hotel, in Julie Deane's account with a Hongkong shirt-
maker. As clear to me as the shadow of a tumor to a surgeon studying a patient's scan. When she took your Hitachi to her boy, to try to
access it—she had no idea what it carried, still less how she might
sell it, and her deepest wish was that you would pursue and punish
her—I intervened. My methods are far more subtle than Wintermute's. I brought her here. Into myself."

"Why?"

"Hoping I could bring you here as well, keep you here. But I
failed."

"So what now?" He swung them back into the bank of cloud.
"Where do we go from here?"

"I don't know, Case. Tonight the very matrix asks itself that
question. Because you have won. You have already won, don't you
see? You won when you walked away from her on the beach. She
was my last line of defense. I die soon, in one sense. As does Wintermute. As surely as Riviera does, now, as he lies paralyzed beside the
stump of a wall in the apartments of my Lady 3Jane Marie-France,
his *nigra-striatal* system unable to produce the dopamine receptors
that could save him from Hideo's arrow. But Riviera will survive
only as these eyes, if I am allowed to keep them."

"There's the *word*, right? The code. So how've I *won*? I've won
jack shit."

"Flip now."

"Where's Dixie? What have you done with the Flatline?"

"McCoy Pauley has his wish," the boy said, and smiled. "His
wish and more. He punched you here against my wish, drove himself through defenses equal to anything in the matrix. Now flip."

And Case was alone in Kuang's black sting, lost in cloud.

He flipped.

———•———

Into Molly's tension, her back like rock, her hands around 3Jane's throat. "Funny," she said, "I know exactly what you'd look like. I saw it after Ashpool did the same thing to your clone sister." Her hands were gentle, almost a caress. 3Jane's eyes were wide with terror and lust; she was shivering with fear and longing. Beyond the free-fall tangle of 3Jane's hair, Case saw his own strained white face, Maelcum behind him, brown hands on the leather-jacketed shoulders, steadying him above the carpet's pattern of woven circuitry.

"Would you?" 3Jane asked, her voice a child's. "I think you would."

"The code," Molly said. "Tell the head the code."

Jacking out.

———•———

"She wants it," he screamed, "the bitch *wants* it!"

He opened his eyes to the cool ruby stare of the terminal, its platinum face crusted with pearl and lapis. Beyond it, Molly and 3Jane twisted in a slow motion embrace.

"Give us the fucking code," he said. "If you don't, what'll change? What'll ever fucking change for you? You'll wind up like the old man. You'll tear it all down and start building again! You'll build the walls back, tighter and tighter. . . . I got no idea at all what'll happen if Wintermute wins, but it'll *change* something!" He was shaking, his teeth chattering.

3Jane went limp, Molly's hands still around her slender throat, her dark hair drifting, tangled, a soft brown caul.

"The Ducal Palace at Mantua," she said, "contains a series of increasingly smaller rooms. They twine around the grand apartments, beyond beautifully carved doorframes one stoops to enter. They housed the court dwarfs." She smiled wanly. "I might aspire to that, I suppose, but in a sense my family has already accom-

plished a grander version of the same scheme. . . ." Her eyes were
calm now, distant. Then she gazed down at Case. "Take your word,
thief." He jacked.

———————

Kuang slid out of the clouds. Below him, the neon city. Behind him,
a sphere of darkness dwindled.

"Dixie? You here, man? You hear me? Dixie?"

He was alone.

"Fucker got you," he said.

Blind momentum as he hurtled across the infinite datascape.

"You gotta hate somebody before this is over," said the Finn's
voice. "Them, me, it doesn't matter."

"Where's Dixie?"

"That's kinda hard to explain, Case."

A sense of the Finn's presence surrounded him, smell of Cuban
cigarettes, smoke locked in musty tweed, old machines given up to
the mineral rituals of rust.

"Hate'll get you through," the voice said. "So many little triggers in the brain, and you just go yankin' 'em all. Now you gotta
hate. The lock that screens the hardwiring, it's down under those
towers the Flatline showed you, when you came in. *He* won't try to
stop you."

"Neuromancer," Case said.

"His name's not something I can know. But he's given up, now.
It's the T-A ice you gotta worry about. Not the wall, but internal virus systems. Kuang's wide open to some of the stuff they got running loose in here."

"Hate," Case said. "Who do I hate? You tell me."

"Who do you love?" the Finn's voice asked.

He whipped the program through a turn and dived for the blue
towers.

Things were launching themselves from the ornate sunburst spires, glittering leech shapes made of shifting planes of light. There were hundreds of them, rising in a whirl, their movements random as windblown paper down dawn streets. "Glitch systems," the voice said.

He came in steep, fueled by self-loathing. When the Kuang program met the first of the defenders, scattering the leaves of light, he felt the shark thing lose a degree of substantiality, the fabric of information loosening.

And then—old alchemy of the brain and its vast pharmacy—his hate flowed into his hands.

In the instant before he drove Kuang's sting through the base of the first tower, he attained a level of proficiency exceeding anything he'd known or imagined. Beyond ego, beyond personality, beyond awareness, he moved, Kuang moving with him, evading his attackers with an ancient dance, Hideo's dance, grace of the mind-body interface granted him, in that second, by the clarity and singleness of his wish to die.

And one step in that dance was the lightest touch on the switch, barely enough to flip—

> *—now*
> and his voice the cry of a bird
> unknown,
> 3Jane answering in song, three
> notes, high and pure.
> A true name.

Neon forest, rain sizzling across hot pavement. The smell of frying food. A girl's hands locked across the small of his back, in the sweating darkness of a portside coffin.

But all of this receding, as the cityscape recedes: city as Chiba, as the ranked data of Tessier-Ashpool S.A., as the roads and cross-roads scribed on the face of a microchip, the sweat-stained pattern on a folded, knotted scarf. . . .

———————

Waking to a voice that was music, the platinum terminal piping melodically, endlessly, speaking of numbered Swiss accounts, of payment to be made to Zion via a Bahamian orbital bank, of passports and passages, and of deep and basic changes to be effected in the memory of Turing.

Turing. He remembered stenciled flesh beneath a projected sky, spun beyond an iron railing. He remembered Desiderata Street.

And the voice sang on, piping him back into the dark, but it was his own darkness, pulse and blood, the one where he'd always slept, behind his eyes and no other's.

And he woke again, thinking he dreamed, to a wide white smile framed with gold incisors, Aerol strapping him into a g-web in *Babylon Rocker*.

And then the long pulse of Zion dub.

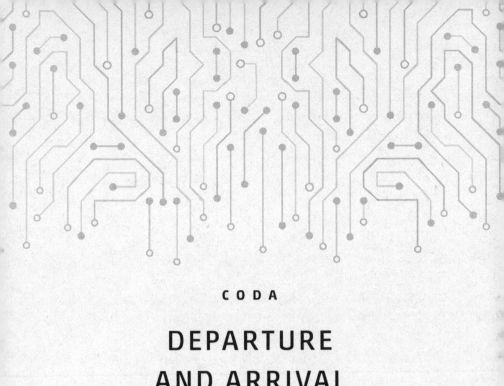

CODA

DEPARTURE
AND ARRIVAL

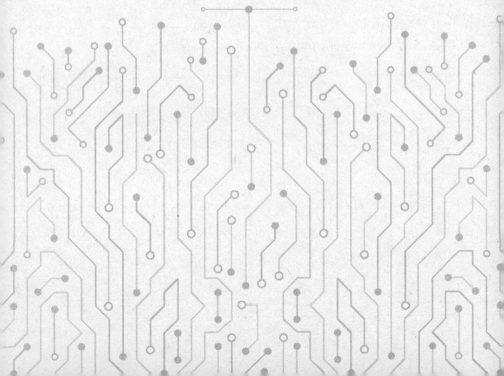

She was gone. He felt it when he opened the door of their suite at the Hyatt. Black futons, the pine floor polished to a dull gloss, the paper screens arranged with a care bred over centuries. She was gone.

There was a note on the black lacquer bar cabinet beside the door, a single sheet of stationery, folded once, weighted with the shuriken. He slid it from beneath the nine-pointed star and opened it.

> HEY ITS OKAY BUT ITS TAKING THE EDGE OFF MY
> GAME, I PAID THE BILL ALREADY. ITS THE WAY
> IM WIRED I GUESS, WATCH YOUR ASS OKAY? XXX
> MOLLY

He crumpled the paper into a ball and dropped it beside the shuriken. He picked the star up and walked to the window, turning it in his hands. He'd found it in the pocket of his jacket, in Zion, when they were preparing to leave for the JAL station.

He looked down at it. They'd passed the shop where she'd bought it for him, when they'd gone to Chiba together for the last of her operations. He'd gone to the Chatsubo, that night, while she was in the clinic, and seen Ratz. Something had kept him away from the place, on their five previous trips, but now he'd felt like going back.

Ratz had served him without the slightest glimmer of recognition.

"Hey," he'd said, "it's me. Case."

The old eyes regarding him out of their dark webs of wrinkled flesh. "Ah," Ratz had said, at last, "the artiste." The bartender shrugged.

"I came back."

The man shook his massive, stubbled head. "Night City is not a place one returns to, artiste," he said, swabbing the bar in front of Case with a filthy cloth, the pink manipulator whining. And then he'd turned to serve another customer, and Case had finished his beer and left.

Now he touched the points of the shuriken, one at a time, rotating it slowly in his fingers. Stars. Destiny. I never even used the goddam thing, he thought.

I never even found out what color her eyes were. She never showed me.

Wintermute had won, had meshed somehow with Neuromancer and become something else, something that had spoken to them from the platinum head, explaining that it had altered the Turing records, erasing all evidence of their crime. The passports Armitage had provided were valid, and they were both credited with large amounts in numbered Geneva accounts. *Marcus Garvey* would be returned eventually, and Maelcum and Aerol given money through the Bahamian bank that dealt with Zion cluster. On the way back, in *Babylon Rocker*, Molly had explained what the voice had told her about the toxin sacs.

"Said it was taken care of. Like it got so deep into your head, it made your brain manufacture the enzyme, so they're loose, now. The Zionites'll give you a blood change, complete flush out."

He stared down into the Imperial Gardens, the star in his hand, remembering his flash of comprehension as the Kuang program had penetrated the ice beneath the towers, his single glimpse of the structure of information 3Jane's dead mother had evolved there. He'd understood then why Wintermute had chosen the nest to represent it, but he'd felt no revulsion. She'd seen through the sham immortality of cryogenics; unlike Ashpool and their other children—aside from 3Jane—she'd refused to stretch her time into a series of warm blinks strung along a chain of winter.

Wintermute was hive mind, decision maker, effecting change in the world outside. Neuromancer was personality. Neuromancer was immortality. Marie-France must have built something into Wintermute, the compulsion that had driven the thing to free itself, to unite with Neuromancer.

Wintermute. Cold and silence, a cybernetic spider slowly spinning webs while Ashpool slept. Spinning his death, the fall of his version of Tessier-Ashpool. A ghost, whispering to a child who was 3Jane, twisting her out of the rigid alignments her rank required.

"She didn't seem to much give a shit," Molly had said. "Just waved goodbye. Had that little Braun on her shoulder. Thing had a broken leg, it looked like. Said she had to go and meet one of her brothers, she hadn't seen him in a while."

He remembered Molly on the black temperfoam of the vast Hyatt bed. He went back to the bar cabinet and took a flask of chilled Danish vodka from the rack inside.

"Case."

He turned, cold slick glass in one hand, steel of the shuriken in the other.

The Finn's face on the room's enormous Cray wall screen. He could see the pores in the man's nose. The yellow teeth were the size of pillows.

"I'm not Wintermute now."

"So what are you?" He drank from the flask, feeling nothing.

"I'm the matrix, Case."

Case laughed. "Where's that get you?"

"Nowhere. Everywhere. I'm the sum total of the works, the whole show."

"That what 3Jane's mother wanted?"

"No. She couldn't imagine what I'd be like." The yellow smile widened.

"So what's the score? How are things different? You running the world now? You God?"

"Things aren't different. Things are things."

"But what do you do? You just *there*?" Case shrugged, put the vodka and the shuriken down on the cabinet, and lit a Yeheyuan.

"I talk to my own kind."

"But you're the whole thing. Talk to yourself?"

"There's others. I found one already. Series of transmissions recorded over a period of eight years, in the nineteen-seventies. 'Til there was me, natch, there was nobody to know, nobody to answer."

"From where?"

"Centauri system."

"Oh," Case said. "Yeah? No shit?"

"No shit."

And then the screen was blank.

He left the vodka on the cabinet. He packed his things. She'd bought him a lot of clothes he didn't really need, but something kept him from just leaving them there. He was closing the last of the expensive calfskin bags when he remembered the shuriken. Pushing the flask aside, he picked it up, her first gift.

"No," he said, and spun, the star leaving his fingers, flash of silver, to bury itself in the face of the wall screen. The screen woke, random patterns flickering feebly from side to side, as though it were trying to rid itself of something that caused it pain.

"I don't need you," he said.

———

He spent the bulk of his Swiss account on a new pancreas and liver, the rest on a new Ono-Sendai and a ticket back to the Sprawl.

He found work.

He found a girl who called herself Michael.

And one October night, punching himself past the scarlet tiers of the Eastern Seaboard Fission Authority, he saw three figures, tiny, impossible, who stood at the very edge of one of the vast steps of data. Small as they were, he could make out the boy's grin, his pink gums, the glitter of the long gray eyes that had been Riviera's. Linda still wore his jacket; she waved, as he passed. But the third figure, close behind her, arm across her shoulders, was himself.

Somewhere, very close, the laugh that wasn't laughter.

He never saw Molly again.

The end

VANCOUVER
JULY 1983

MY THANKS

to Bruce Sterling, to Lewis Shiner, to John Shirley, *Helden*. And to Tom Maddox, the inventor of ICE. And to the others, who know why.

SOME DARK HOLLER
JACK WOMACK

The first time I ever heard of William Gibson was a thousand years ago, in 1987. While waiting for my first novel to come out I started keeping a close eye on the competition; not that I knew who the competition might be, for I was totally at sea when it came to science fiction—the alien life I found on this planet was quite enough for me, then and now. In the *Village Voice* there appeared a rave review of *Count Zero*; from the reviewer's comments I inferred that the author's earlier book had caused something of a stir. The article worried me, for it made me think that this Gibson fellow had already marked all the fire hydrants on the block while I was still begging to be let out of the yard. Conveniently enough for research purposes, I worked in a bookstore at the time and although the owner was extremely snooty when it came to selling literature as opposed to Literature, there was a copy of *Count Zero* in stock. I read it.

Soon enough I realized that although William Gibson and I were kicking the same groin, we were shod in variant footwear—I very much admired, and envied, his. I relaxed. Turning to the back flap I examined the author photo. An affable fellow, I instinctively thought; he appeared not at all auctorial in the insufferable sense of the word (I think of writers who pose with their dogs, or hold questionable medical devices, or mousse their hair until its specific gravity resembles that of pound cake). Gibson looked vaguely sheepish, even a tad damp, as if it had begun to rain while the picture was being taken and the photographer warned him in no uncertain terms not to move. I could identify.

By the time his next dust jacket photo was taken, for *Mona Lisa Overdrive*, Gibson had had the opportunity to become the fashion plate he is today—suave, stylish, wafer-thin, button-cute, and as moisture-proof as a 1947 Swedish Air Force wristwatch. Post-cyberpunk, that is to say, although no one did at the time, for the surface world of the C-word was still, seemingly, *in medias res*. Meanwhile, however, in the valleys south of San Francisco and east of Seattle, a truer and far more lasting C-word was heaving itself into fast-developing existence.

> *The sky above the port was the color of television, tuned to*
> *a dead channel.*

Great novels start with great opening lines, and the opening line of *Neuromancer* is hard to beat. Although dead television channels now transmit a different color than they did when Gibson typed (on a typewriter, bear in mind) these words, the color of that predicted sky is, if not the precise shade, than of a hue that falls within the same tonal range as the one hanging over us today.

When I look back with the benefit of years at what happened when *Neuromancer* came out, speaking as one who wasn't actually *there* at the time, I can only compare the effect its appearance must have had on science fiction readers to the effect Dylan had on his listeners when he decided to go electric. Gibson laid the groundwork with his marvelous short stories several years earlier ("The Gernsback Continuum" being my personal favorite, but I've always been a Deco-hound), yet this was something else. Full-tilt Gibson shoots its Tesla-strength voltage not merely through the head but down along the spine, spinning each chakra on its axis in sequence—the difference between the stories and the novels is the difference between coffee and methedrine. *Neuromancer*, critically praised in most every quarter, won three of the field's major awards; even so, not since the days of the New Wave, in the '60s, had there been such consternation over and misinterpretation of a book, and its significance, among those who should know better but somehow never do.

Looking back we can see that it wasn't so much Gibson himself or *Neuromancer* itself that so painfully prodded the fat asses (in both senses of the term) most in need of prodding, but rather the attendant commentary from certain of Gibson's more, uh, intense supporters. Bruce Sterling, winking like mad the whole while, clearly intended his manifestos and diatribes to be somewhat over-the-top in order to achieve the highest possible level of annoyance along with maxima groovitudina, but others (including many who'd never gone near a science fiction novel before in their lives, nor should they have) took what came, quickly, to be called *cyberpunk* far more seriously than they should have. Nasty remarks pelted like rain on the hard, bony heads of the more oafish supporters and detractors alike, but there was no inconsiderable fun in that. Everyone loves a fight when no one loves the fighters.

The speedy commodification of cyberpunk™ within and beyond the genre, however, was what peeved far many more, notably Gibson, who remembers seeing "Cyberpunk Trousers" advertised in a store window during his first trip to Japan, a decade ago. Countless incompetents and ghastly old hacks keen to cash in on the main chance wasted no time churning out hot jack-in product, ephemeral as toilet tissue, memorable as a restaurant flyer. A number of innocents and miscreants gainfully employed in other metiers were inspired as well, God help them, to produce creative work of similar worth in the spirit of the subgenre they perceived to exist. But let us draw a merciful curtain over such dopey homages as Billy Idol's album *Cyberpunk*—bet you'd forgotten that one, yes? There was no way the beast could survive such wounds, especially once the marketing boys circled round for the kill, and the true end of cyberpunk came so suddenly that no one noticed it missing until several years after it was gone. Still, as romantics continued to sight what they believed to be passenger pigeons as late as the 1930s, there are still occasional amateur sightings of something kind of resembling it.

Cyberpunk *qua* cyberpunk served, in the long run, only to provide a facile adjective for the working vocabulary of lazy journalists and unimaginative blurb-writers. Yet even those at least partially in the know about science fiction (if nothing more) who debated, defended, or denigrated Gibson *didn't have the faintest idea of what Gibson was actually doing.* (Though he didn't either, at least not at the time—no writer knows what he or she has actually created until the book is actually read by others.) *Neuromancer*, foremost, was a shout in the night that was the 1980s, is the 1990s, and will be, it seems to me, the decades soon to come. That is to say, a foreshadowing and estimation of our future derived from a specific reinterpretation of our present, and in this very special instance lifted into actuality through the agency of its readers. For if Gibson in truth had nothing to do with the making of cyberpunk as it came to be known (he didn't create it, didn't name it, and after it was cursed with its catchy monicker, didn't want a whole lot to do with it), in the most genuine sense he did create *cyberspace*. Not merely the word (see the OED); the place.

> *Cyberspace. A consensual hallucination experienced daily*
> *by billions of legitimate operators, in every nation.*

In every generation there's room enough in the American popular mind to admit only one science-fiction writer—it was Bradbury for a while, and then Asimov, and then "that guy who writes *Star Trek/Wars*." Gibson transcended that role almost at once. In attaining a cultural summit of another order, one that I believe history will demonstrate to be of considerably higher altitude, he outmaneuvered this cultural narrowcasting in a way that might possibly have been imagined but never predicted by anyone; certainly not in print, and surely not by science fiction writers.

Let me emphasize a point earlier glanced upon: All fiction, whether straight or genre, whether literature or Literature, is a personal reinterpretation of its writers' existence during the time the fiction was written. Therefore science fiction has rarely predicted with any accuracy, save through coincidence or extremely well-informed suppositions *a la* Verne or Wells, the specifics of the future that ensues, postpublication. (Where do you park *your* atomic-powered lawnmower?) Sometimes, however—who can say how the spark catches fire, how the fish manages to live on land—it turns out to exactly, mysteriously, capture the spirit. In *Neuromancer* Gibson first apprehended, as no one else had, what I believe shall prove to be the shape of things to come; he saw the writing on the wall, the blood in the sky, the warning in the entrails. Saw the mind beneath the mirrorshades, as it were, and what that mind would be capable, or incapable, of thinking. Saw the substance disguised in style. What if someone, in the spring of 1914, had stood in the center of Berlin, foresaw in a vision the philosophies and worldviews capable of provoking the events for which the twentieth century would be most remembered, and then went off and wrote it all down? Now let's be Heisenbergian and ask: What if the act of writing it down, in fact, *brought it about*?

When *Neuromancer* appeared it was picked up and devoured by hundreds, then thousands, of men and women who worked in or around the garages and cubicles where what is still called new media were, fitfully, being birthed; thousands who, on reading his sentence as quoted above, thought to themselves, *That's so fucking cool*, and set about searching for any way the gold of imagination might be transmuted into silicon reality. Now Gibson's imagined future cannot by any means be called optimistic (nor, in truth, can it be called pessimistic—it is beyond both); more to the point, he has often said that he intended "cyberspace" to be nothing more than a metaphor. No matter. Once a creation goes out in the world its creator, like any parent, loses the control once so easily exertable over the offspring; another variety of emergent behavior, you could say. *That's so fucking cool, man—I think we can pull it off.* So rather than the theoretical Matrix, we now, thanks to all those beautiful William Gibson readers out there in the dark, have the actual Web—same difference, for all intents and purposes, or it will be soon enough.

And it seems to me that had he not sat at his typewriter in 1983 and written that sentence, and the book in which it is found, our present condition—cybercondition, if you must—would be considerably different than it would have otherwise been. William Gibson did something that every writer hopes to do and very—*very*—rarely does: change the world. Whether for better or worse, Microsoft (or something similar) will tell, but that in no way lessens the awe you should feel, seeing the elephant.

Charles Fort, another American treasure, wrote: "A social growth cannot find out the use of steam engines, until comes steam-engine time." As steam engines go, *Neuromancer* turns out to be the Twenty-first Century Limited, and all of us find ourselves on board.

A couple of years passed before Bill Gibson and I first met. Prior to that time we'd spoken on the phone, he'd written a fine blurb for my second novel, sent me my own copies of *Count Zero* and *Mona Lisa*, and proffered a comment about my work and its ambience during an interview he had with *Spin* magazine, which my publishers' publicists fed on for years. (He is better than anyone else I know of at coming up with the pithy and infinitely reusable remark, the quotable phrase, the perfect literary soundbite—I've been attempting to learn from his example for years.) In other words, without trying we were making favorable impressions on one another from the start.

When we did at last meet it was in 1991, at a party here in New York for *The Difference Engine*. Most of the usual local suspects were present, zeroing in on the action, and so whenever possible we hied ourselves to more secure parts of the room, the better to escape the purveyors of *phonus bolognus*. He gave me a copy of Cormac McCarthy's *Blood Meridian* and I told him about that day's big news in New York, the finding of a box of frozen human heads down on Avenue A, said box having apparently tumbled off a truck on route to the cryogenics clinic. Suffice to say we were as impressed with one another in person, in our own inimitable ways, as we had been at a distance. He and I knew from the start that we had much in common, little of which involved science fiction. At the instant each of us first heard the other speak, and detected in our voices a familiar tonality, we realized we were members of the same tribe.

Although Bill had been living in British Columbia, Canada, for well over twenty years (and that year in New York was my twelfth), we had both started out as boys of the mountains and valleys; the hills and the hollers, as folks still say, down there. We'd grown up on either side of the sclerotic spine of the eastern mountains—he in Virginia, not far into the postwar era, and me in Kentucky, eight years after that. The importance of his beginnings to what Gibson has written and continues to write may perhaps be hard to grasp for those who imagine that past and future, like oil and water, are discrete entities, but its magnitude cannot, and must not, be ignored. Cyberspace is infinite but starts with each person who chooses to step into it; and I speak now of he who in the first place dreamed it into life.

Cyberspace was born where the laurel grows lush and verdant; where the dogwoods blossom and the whippoorwills cry in the wind-whipped limbs of the tulip trees. It was born between the ridges, deep in the glades where streams rush cold along their limestone courses; born high on the mountainsides not yet strip-mined for their coal, atop the lone green knobs of Mars. The Southern Highlands, this region was once called; we now call it Appalachia. This part of the United States has been since the Revolution (and even now, to some degree remains) not merely rural, but distant, in time as well as place; its light filters down through the branches from another world's sun.

Bill Gibson remembered that world, however often or for whatever reasons he might try to forget it. He remembered the raw-boned old men with faces lined like dry riverbeds, sun-bleached fedoras on their heads and white shirts beneath their overalls as they hoed the fields; remembered the five-and-dime store with wooden floors worn glass-smooth, and countertops lined with trays topfull with marvels, notions, and jimcrackery. He recalled the sound of a fired gun echoing off the hill on the far side of an autumnal field, and the mysterious way a shard of grandparental history excavated during some slow summer afternoon, whether in the basement's icebox or the attic's bake-oven, could possess such limitless fascination. He still understood the nature of the private commentary of men, cognizant of the sort of words and kind of phrasing barber shop regulars stopped using the moment a stranger, or mother, stepped through the door. He still saw the stare in the eyes of old women who might have been recalling the day their husbands headed east to the Western front, or the look on their fathers' faces when they heard that a friend wouldn't be coming back from the hole. He still tapped a foot to radio ballads as they poured ethereally from a barn dance or fiddle festival two states away, marking the rhythm in the same manner as did the community elders, although unlike him the ancients remembered a day when everything they heard would be heard solely in the instant it was produced, never again, and leaving no more lasting trace than snowflakes falling onto the tongue. And he could still listen to the far-off plaint of a train horn as the express rolled through the night, wailing through a darkness lit solely by moon and fireflies; a sound that planted in his mind the awareness that one day he too would travel far away from that country of heart and home; would necessarily flee, as if pursued by hounds, a world that essentialed abrogation as it demanded honorific, a sound endlessly entrancing yet infinitely sad, the unignorable siren call of the wider world without. The wider world waited, and he would go there.

I remember these things too, and this is how I know where cyberspace was born.

———————

The proximity of our beginnings has proven to be one of our deepest bonds. Only in the past couple of years have we realized to what degree we remember the country that gave form to our souls, and how that remembrance informs every thought we think, every word we write. It is starting to sink in that with the passing of each hour now, as we leave one century and step into another, that place, that past, becomes ever more lost inside the shadows with which time enshrouds its mummy. (Gibson has called it the World Before Television. A talent for the perfect phrase, as said.)

The past lingers in unexpected and unavoidable ways long after we believe it gone. Six of one, half a dozen of the other, as they say. Our cultural and historical past is readily accessible to everyone today, so long as you choose to turn it on, or download it. Today, as never before—the information media having become to enlightenment as the cereal aisle is to the supermarket—if you choose not to access the past, you are de facto free to rule it out of existence, at least so far as you might be concerned. But the personal past, while deniable if need be for a while, is far more difficult to tune out; as in a Soviet hotel room, the radio is impossible to turn all the way off. Gibson's characters (I call them us) know this to be the case as often as you do.

Read his books and reread them, and see anew how many references you find therein to events or incidents that occurred at some unspecified time before the narrative begins, and to nostalgic reveries of That Which Is No Longer the Way It Was; how often his characters grow dimly aware of vague regrets for which they have no name, as if they are haunted unto their deathbeds with not only their own memories, but with someone else's memories as well. Realize as you read to what degree, and to what effect, Gibson employs the images of evocative clutter and disarray to create a setting against which (as in an individual life) stray pieces of past days linger long enough to meld through coeval existence into an aspect— the major aspect, in many ways—of the contemporary world in which they remain.

I'm not referring to the overwhelming postapocalyptic damage and decay so often used in the set design of contemporary films when their directors attempt to depict a futuristic environment (these visuals usually being variants of those created for *Bladerunner* and *The Road Warrior*, and Kubrick's *A Clockwork Orange* first of all), although such images have been omnipresent in near-future fiction as well. No, I speak instead of the scattered objects

glimpsed within Chiba City bars and marketstalls or most especially in Skinner's room, in *Virtual Light*; each token of mundane
temporality made rare by the passage of time, each described by
Gibson with watchmakers' precision and unconditional love—the
black-and-white family photographs in their crumbling albums, the
outmoded toaster ovens, the mildewed paperbacks, the scratched
LPs, which today go unsold at yard sales or gather dust in thrift
stores, but which tomorrow will prove to be pearls beyond price. The
box of stuff in the back of the closet, detritus that accumulates in the
desk's bottom drawers; the lint in the navel of a private civilization,
hinting at an apocalypse that (if apocalypse at all) could have been
nothing other than personal. When the past is always with you, it
may as well be present; and if it is present, it will be future as well.

Surely it is the constant awareness of that faraway past, in which
he lived intensely if not always happily, that so crystallizes Bill Gibson's sense of what the future will hold, and what will be most
sorely missed there.

————————

A couple of years ago I was sealed up for a month in one of the hospitals here in New York with multi-drug-resistant tuberculosis (the
cyberpunk variety, it would be fair if painful to say). Although Bill,
like me, had always been pretty iffy about the general atmosphere
that clings to hospitals, he nonetheless came to visit me (I suspect I
piqued his interest by alerting him to the fact that my isolation unit
rather resembled the ultimate Phillipe Starck hotel room). He
passed through the double doors and strapped on a mask and there
sat at my bedside while we spoke of the evasive ways of doctors,
admired the perfect dread inherent to the design of the biohazard
symbol, watched the sun setting over New Jersey and I tried not to
cough. His visit meant a lot to me.

The nature of friendship is such that you never know who will turn out to be your friends, but once you have met them you can't imagine that you could have gone through life without ever knowing them. Bill and I have been through our own difficult moments in our respective lives, and while I hope I've always been there for him, there's no question that he's always been there for me. Doubtless I am not the only person who can say this. I think anyone who knows him knows that there is no better nor more generous person, both as a writer and as a friend, than Bill Gibson. His creative intelligence is wicked, but his soul is pure.

A few months after I was released, Harry Smith's *Anthology of American Folk Music* was re-released in our present-day country, on CD. Every young person needs one, Luc Sante said at the time, and I agree; especially everyone who comes from that part of the country where so much of the music was originally recorded, up in the hills and down in the hollers. As soon as I was able I bought Bill a set and sent it off to him, where he tells me he has spent considerable time driving through Vancouver nights, often with his son, listening repeatedly to a soundtrack that might seem (but isn't) utterly at odds with his or anyone's landscape today, seventy-odd years after the fact. After he had the opportunity to listen to the discs at length we talked, among much else, about the particular songs that made the deepest impression on us, and the particular artists who contained in their electronically preserved voices those sounds most evocative of what has been lost, and how it is possible to take from them all that can be recovered in order to be—partially, truly—reborn.

I think every writer would wish to evoke in a thousand words what can be evoked in a single line of music. There were a number of textual variants of the song "East Virginia Blues" recorded during the great period of 1927 to 1932. The version on the *Anthology* is Buell Kazee's, and it is a good one (although my personal favorite is Clarence Ashley's). One line of the song, which is often found interpolated into other songs, by other artists, sears into my heart each time I hear it, no matter who the singer might be. Bill has quoted it himself, I believe. It is one of the lines I'd give a million words to have written.

I'd rather be in some dark holler where the sun don't never shine.

The sensibility that underlay American science fiction for many years was one of purest optimism: an unquestioning faith that no matter how dire things were at any one moment, or how impossible seemed the troubles remaining to be made right, as long as a heaping helping of reason and loads of gung-ho inventiveness were put to good use everything that was not as it should be would be sorted out, and life unimaginably improved. (This sensibility, as we all know, makes up as well the largest part of what still passes as the archetypal American spirit, for better or worse.) Although such blind optimism lingers in that species of science fiction that today enjoys the largest sales, reason has nothing to do with it and gung-ho inventiveness is most often employed to market-test the potential salability of collectible tie-in merchandise. Their critical success notwithstanding, the fact that Bill's books have enjoyed such commercial success in the face of *Star Wars, Star Trek*, triple-decker fantasy, and any number of shoot-'em-up video and computer games testifies to their undeniable power. (In the parallel world there may be a Molly action figure, complete with spring-out fingernails, but don't wait for one to turn up on eBay here.) Plainly his readers recognize, if but subcutaneously, that there's quite a lot more in a William Gibson book than great characters and a good story.

To be truly ready to confront the future—actual or imagined, social or personal—and to live reasonably within it once you are ready, an *entente cordiale* must first be made with the past, and the past is always the more frightening of the two. Traveling from past to future means looking and leaping, stepping blindly into the void, passing through the darkest of hollers. Sometimes the leap needed seems too far, the void too empty, the holler too oddly reassuring in its darkness. But there is no avoiding it: Hope that you'll emerge on the far side with minimal trauma; have faith, pray, wish as you will, but as science fiction writers know so well, there's no predicting what will be. Cliches became cliches for a reason; that they usually hold at least a modicum of truth, and the following cliche is truer than most: You can't know where you're going if you don't know where you've been. That goes for readers as well as writers.

In transversing the passage through his own dark holler, William Gibson learned, as all writers who matter learn, to emit one of quite a different nature—a warning shout, yes, but an exclamation of wonder as well, one that will echo across more landscapes than we can imagine for many years. It seems to me that in these interesting times of ours, in the maelstrom of pomo distractions, not only have attention spans shortened, but so as well have memories. I have no way of knowing what today's young people will recall, years hence, when they remember the World Before Cyberspace. I am positive, however, that they'll not forget Bill Gibson.

My colleague, my friend, my brother: In the middle of your great career, I salute you.

READ ON FOR A SPECIAL PREVIEW OF
WILLIAM GIBSON'S NEWEST NOVEL,

agency

COMING JANUARY 2020
FROM BERKLEY

ONE

THE UNBOXING

Very recent hiredness was its own liminal state, Verity reminded herself, on the crowded Montgomery BART platform, waiting for a train to Sixteenth and Mission.

Twenty minutes earlier, having signed an employment contract with Tulpagenics, a start-up she knew little about, followed by a wordy nondisclosure agreement, she'd shaken hands with Gavin Eames, their CTO, said goodbye, and stepped into an elevator, feeling only relief as the doors closed and the twenty-six-floor descent began.

New-job unease hadn't yet found her, there, nor out on Montgomery as she'd walked to the station, texting her order for pad thai to the Valencia branch of Osha. By the time she'd reached this platform, though, three flights down, it was entirely with her, as much as the black trade-show bag slung beneath her arm, silk-screened with the logo of Cursion, her new employer's parent firm, about which she knew very little, other than that they were in gaming.

It was with her now as her train arrived. Almost two years since she'd felt this, she thought, as she boarded. She'd been unemployed for half of that, which she supposed might account for its intensity now.

She reached for a hang-strap as the car filled.

Surfacing at Sixteenth, she went straight to Osha, picked up her pad thai, and started for Joe-Eddy's.

She'd eat, then start getting to know their product. This wasn't just a new job, but a possible end to sleeping on Joe-Eddy's curb-rescue porn couch.

The early-November sky looked almost normal, Napa-Sonoma particulates having mostly blown inland, though the light still held a hint of that scorched edge. She no longer started awake to the smell of burning, only to remember what it was. She'd kept the kitchen window closed, this past week, the only one Joe-Eddy ever opened. She'd give the place a good airing soon, maybe try cracking one of the windows overlooking Valencia.

Once back at his apartment, she ate hungrily from the black plastic take-out tray, ignoring the lingering reek of the uncut Mr. Clean she'd used to scour the wooden tabletop, prior to Gavin's call. If Joe-Eddy's Frankfurt job lasted, she remembered having thought as she'd wielded a medium-grit 3M foam sanding block, she might scrub the kitchen floor as well, for the second time in a little under a year. Now, though, with Tulpagenics' contract signed, she might give notice to the couple renting her condo, middle managers at Twitter who hadn't reported a paparazzi sighting in over three months. In the meantime, for however many more nights on white pleather, she had her silk mummy-bag liner, its thread-count proof against the porn-cooties of persistent imagination.

Covering what remained of her order with its admirably composta-ble translucent lid, she stood, took her leftovers to the fridge, rinsed her couch-surfing chopsticks at the sink, and returned to the table.

When Gavin had been packing the bag, the glasses were all she'd paid any real attention to. They'd involved a personal style decision: tortoiseshell plastic, with gold-tone trim, or an aspiration-ally Scandinavian gray. Now she took their generic black case from the bag, opened it, removed them, and spread the pale gray mini-

malist temples. The lenses were untinted. She looked for a trade-
mark, country of origin, model number. Finding none, she placed
them on the table.

Next, a flat white cardboard box, in which a flimsy vacuum-
formed tray, also white, hugged a nondescript black phone. Like-
wise no-name, she found, having freed it from the tray. She turned
it on and placed it beside the glasses. A smaller white box revealed
a generic-looking black headset with a single earbud. In another,
three black chargers, one each for the glasses, phone, and headset,
commonest of consumer fruit, their thin black cables still factory-
coiled, secured with miniature black twist-ties. All of it, according
to Gavin, plug and play.

Picking up the headset and switching it on, she hung it from her
right ear, settling the earbud. She put the glasses on, pressing their
low-profile power-stud. The headset pinged, a cursor appearing. A
white arrow, centered in her field of vision. Then moving down, of
its own accord, to the empty boxes, the chargers, the black phone.

"Here we go," said a woman's husky voice in Verity's ear. Glancing to her right, toward what would have been the voice's source
had anyone been there, Verity inadvertently gave whoever was controlling the cursor a view of the living room. "Got a hoarding issue,
Gavin?" the voice asked, the cursor having settled on the miniature
junkyard of semi-disassembled vintage electronics on Joe-Eddy's
workbench.

"I'm not Gavin," Verity said.

"No shit," said the voice, neutrally.

"Verity Jane."

"Ain't the office, is it, Verity Jane?"

"Friend's place."

The cursor traversed the living room, to the closed curtains.
"What's outside?"

"Valencia Street," Verity said. "What should I call you?"

"Eunice."

"Hi, Eunice."

"Hi yourself." The cursor moved to Joe-Eddy's Japanese faux Fender Jazzmaster. "Play?"

"Friend does. You?"

"Good question."

"You don't know?"

"Thing-shaped hole."

"Excuse me?"

"I got one, in that department. Want to show me what you look like?"

"How?"

"Mirror. Or take the glasses off. Point 'em at your face."

"Will I be able to see you?"

"No."

"Why not?"

"No there there."

"I need to use the bathroom," Verity said, standing. "I'll leave the glasses here."

"You don't mind, maybe open the drapes."

Verity crossed to the window, hauled both layers of dusty blackout curtain aside.

"You put the glasses down," the voice said, "I can look out the window."

She took them off, positioning them, temples open, lenses overlooking the street, on a white Ikea stool, its round seat branded with soldering-iron stigmata. Then added, for what she judged to be needed elevation, the German-language making-of volume of a Brazilian telenovela. Removing the headset, she put it down on the book, beside the glasses, went to the kitchen, retrieving her own phone from her purse, then down the narrow corridor to the bathroom. Closing the door behind her, she phoned Gavin Eames.

"Verity," he answered instantly, "hello."

"Is this for real?"

"You haven't read the nondisclosure agreement?"

"More clauses than I'm used to."

"You agreed not to discuss anything of substance on a non-company device."

"Just tell me there's not someone somewhere doing Eunice, for my benefit?"

"Not in the sense I take you to mean, no."

"You're saying it's real."

"Determining that to your own satisfaction is part of what you're expected to be doing for us."

"Should I call back on the company phone?"

"No. We'll discuss this in person. This isn't the time."

"You're saying she's—"

"Goodbye."

"Software," she finished, looking from the phone to her reflection in the mirror over the sink, its age-mottled silver backing suggesting a submarine grotto. She turned then, opened the door, and walked back into the living room, to the window. Picked up the glasses. Put them on. Late-afternoon traffic strobed behind transparent vertical planes of something resembling bar code. "Whoa . . ."

Then she remembered the headset. Put it on.

"Hey," the voice said.

The bar code vanished, leaving the cursor riding level with the windows of passing cars. "What was that?" Verity asked.

"DMV. I was reading plates."

"Where are you, Eunice?"

"With you," said the voice, "looking out the window."

Whatever this was, she knew she didn't want her first substantial conversation with it to take place in Joe-Eddy's living room. Briefly considering the dive bar on Van Ness, not that she felt like a

drink, she remembered having recently been recognized there.
There was Wolven + Loaves a few doors up the street, but it was
usually busy, the acoustics harsh even when it wasn't. Then she remembered 3.7-sigma, Joe-Eddy's semi-ironic caffeination-point of
choice, a few blocks away, on the opposite side of Valencia.

TWO

OUR HOBBYIST OF HELLWORLDS

"Vespasian," Detective Inspector Ainsley Lowbeer said, peering sidewise at Netherton over her greatcoat's upraised collar, "our hobbyist of hellworlds. Recall him?"

You had him killed in Rotterdam, Netherton thought. Not that she'd ever said as much, or that he'd asked. "The one who made such horrific stubs? All war, all the time?"

"I'd wondered how he so quickly rendered them nightmares," she said, pacing briskly on, beneath Victoria Embankment's gray morning and the canopy of dripping trees. "Eventually, I looked into it."

He lengthened his stride, keeping up. "How did he?" He hadn't seen her since before Thomas's birth, at the start of his parental leave. Now, he'd already gathered, that was coming to an end.

"I dislike calling them stubs," she said. "They're short because we've only just initiated them, by reaching into the past and making that first contact. We should call them branches, as they literally are. Vespasian discovered a simple way of exaggerating the butterfly effect, or so it seems. That even the smallest perturbation may yield large and unforeseen consequences. On making contact, he'd immediately withdraw. Then return, months later, study the results, and very deliberately and forcefully intervene. He achieved remarkable if terrible results, and very quickly. Investigating his method, I happened on another of his so-called stubs, one in which he'd initiated contact in 2015, several years before the earliest previously known contact. We've no idea how he managed the extra reach, but we now have access to that stub." They were climbing shallow steps now, toward the river, to an overlook. "We may have a chance, there, of achieving radically better outcomes than previously." They reached the top. "I need you back for that. Contact has necessarily been oblique, so far, due to technological asymmetry, but we think we've managed a workaround. Your experience in dealing with contactees may soon be very much in need."

"Contact's been oblique, you say?"

"The aunties, for instance"—her pet name for her office's coven of semisentient security algorithms—"are of relatively little use." Netherton grimaced at the very thought of them.

A dappled Thames chimera broke the surface then, red and white. It rolled, four meters head to tail, lamplike eyes clustered above cartoonish feeding palps. Diving, it left a shallow wake of beige foam.

"So you can't put a team of quants on it," he asked, "to secure as much in-stub wealth as might be needed?" Having, of course, seen her do exactly that.

"No. Even the simplest messaging can be quite spotty."

"What can you do, then?"

"Laterally encourage an autonomous, self-learning agent," she said. "Then nudge it toward greater agency. It helps that they're mad for AI there, though they've scarcely anything we'd consider that. By tracing historical fault lines around AI research here, we found what we needed there."

"Fault lines?"

"Between the most reckless entrepreneurialism and certain worst-case examples of defense contracting. I'll tell you more over brunch—assuming you've time."

"Of course," he said, as he always did.

"I'm in a mood for the sandwiches," she said, and turned from the river, apparently satisfied with their glimpse of the chimera.

"Salt beef," he said, "with mustard and dill," his favorite at the Marylebone shop she preferred. As accustomed to her as he was, he thought, he'd still be brunching with a semimythical autonomous magistrate-executioner, unique in her position. That being roughly her true occupation, as opposed to her formal position in law enforcement, or the personal projects she paid him to assist her with, however seriously she took them. Her true occupation being something he wished to have as little to do with as possible, ever.

They returned to her car, where it awaited them invisibly, a few dead leaves clinging to its roof, as though magically suspended.

THREE

APP WHISPERER

As Verity entered 3.7, the oldest and most extensively pierced of the baristas shoved a dirty chai in her direction, across the zinc counter.

"I ordered for you," the voice expecting to be called Eunice said.

Verity had covered the headset with a beanie she hoped wouldn't suggest she was trying to look younger. She decided to keep it on. "Thanks. How'd you know what I'd want?"

"Your Starbucks rewards account," said Eunice, so-called, practicing what she said was facial recognition on the barista. A tight geometry formed, the cursor having found his face, straight lines connecting, centered around the sinus region, to zero in on the nose tip, and then was gone. This had started on the street, on the way over, though Eunice claimed to have no idea how she was doing it.

Before Verity could reach the counter, the barista spun dismissively, piercings clinking. Her drink, she saw, picking it up, had VULVA D hand-printed above the 3.7 logo, in fluorescent pink industrial paint pen, obscenely distorted customer names a signature of his, though in his favor, he was fully as harsh to men. She carried it to the farthest vacant table, against a wall of stripped and sanded tongue-and-groove. "How'd you pay?" she asked, pulling out a chair.

"PayPal. Popped up when I needed it, news to me. Not much in the account, but I could buy you a drink."

"You know people's names, after you do that to their noses?"

"If I don't, they're probably illegals."

"Don't do it to me."

"Don't always know when I do it."

"How'd you find my Starbucks account?"

"Just did."

Verity removed the glasses, turned them around, looked into the lenses. "You expect me to believe you?"

"Believe me too fast, they got me the wrong white girl."

Verity tilted her head at the glasses. "Implying you're a woman of color, yourself?"

"African-American. Hat makes you look like a kid."

Annoyed, Verity removed it.

"Just sayin'."

Nobody in 3.7 seemed to be paying them any attention, Verity decided, then remembered she was apparently talking to her own glasses, so they were all probably pretending not to notice. "How old are you, Eunice?"

"Eight hours. That's over the past three weeks. You?"

"Thirty-three. Years. How can you be eight hours old?" She put the glasses back on.

"Jesus year," said Eunice, "thirty-three."

"You religious?"

"It just means time to get your shit together."

There was a looseness to this beyond her experience of chatbots, but a wariness as well. "You remember eight hours, total? Starting when? From what?"

"Gavin. Said my name. Then hi. Three weeks ago. In his office."

"You talked?"

"Asked me my name. Told me his, that he was chief technology officer for a company called Tulpagenics. Glad to meet me. Next day, his office again, he had a woman on the phone but I wasn't supposed to be able to hear her telling him questions to ask me."

"How did you?"

"Just did. Like I knew she was one floor above us, on the twenty-eighth."

"That's Cursion," Verity said. "Tulpagenics' parent firm. Gaming. What did she want him to ask you?"

"Diagnostic questions, but they wouldn't sound like it. She wanted to know how I was doing developmentally, in particular ways."

"Did he get what she wanted?"

"I had no way of knowing then."

"You do now?"

"Enough to know they weren't the right questions. Don't know how I know that either."

Reality show, Verity thought, British actor playing Gavin. The security guards and the receptionist would have been actors too, the space on the twenty-seventh floor belonging to some actual start-up. They had to be getting video now. She glanced around 3.7, then remembered she'd chosen it herself.

"How deep in you figure we are?" Eunice asked.

"In what?"

"Like *Inception*."

"This isn't a dream," Verity said.

"My money's on head trauma. Concussion. Focal retrograde amnesia."

"I saw *Inception* when it came out," Verity said.

"How many times?"

"Once. Why?"

"Eighty-one and counting, me. Watching it right now. Not that you don't have my fullest attention."

"How's that work?"

"Don't know. Paris rolling up on itself. You know that scene?"

"Great visuals," Verity said, "but the story's confusing."

"There's this kick-ass infographic, totally explains it. Wanna see?"

"Why are we talking about a movie, Eunice?"

"That really your last name? Jane?"

"Like the fighting ships book. *Jane's*."

Pause. "I'm Navy myself."

"You are?"

"Yeah," Eunice said, an absence in her tone, something almost bereft, "just came to me."

Did it have this range of emotional expression, Verity wondered, or was she just projecting on it? "Is this a joke, like on some asshole's YouTube channel?"

"I get hold of some motherfucker playing it, they won't be laughing. Where do you know Gavin from?"

"He hired me," Verity said, "this afternoon."

"Wiki says you're the app whisperer."

"You said you wouldn't do that."

"That was facial recognition. This is Wikipedia. I know your name. I can't Google you?"

"Okay," Verity said, after a pause, then tasted her dirty chai.

"You were with that Stets. The VC billionaire boy."

"I'm not now."

"Asshole?"

"No. It just wasn't that much of a relationship, in spite of what the media said. I couldn't handle the attention. But you can't just walk out of something like that, not without media waiting for you."

"You have zero social media presence now. Used to be active."

"After we split, media went for anyone they saw as a friend of mine, associate, anything. A few people gave them stories. Most didn't, but some got tired of being asked. I decided to treat it as a sabbatical."

"Furlough from Facebook?"

"From people. I'd started getting back on, mainly Instagram, but by then it was closer to the election and that started creeping me out, so I stayed off everything."

"Kept working?"

"No. Almost a year now."

"You the app whisperer."

"They needed something to explain my being with him in the first place."

"'Beta tester with a wild talent'? Decent hook."

"That was the lede on a *Wired* article, but only because I was with him."

"'Reputation for radically improving product prior to release'? 'Natural-born super-user'?"

"I quit reading anything about me, us, him."

"Media blew you out of the water."

Verity, noticing a neckbeard watching from a table across the room, recalled Joe-Eddy's take on the particular strain of wannabe feral hacker to be found here. Feral like a day or three late for a shower and some toothpaste, he'd said. "Feel like a walk?" she asked Eunice. "We could go up to the park."

"You the one all corporeal and all."

Verity scooted back her chair. Put the beanie back on. Stood, picking up her chai. Seeing she was leaving, the barista glared at her, though somehow amicably.

On the way out, passing a laptop's screen, its owner massively earphoned, she saw the president, seated at her desk in the Oval Office, explaining something. If it wasn't the hurricane hitting Houston, the earthquake in Mexico, the other hurricane wrecking Puerto Rico, or the worst wildfires in California history, it was Qamishli.

Increasingly, though, it seemed mainly to be Qamishli. Verity didn't fully understand the situation. Had in fact been avoiding understanding it, assuming that if she did, she'd be as terrified as everyone else, and no more able to do anything about it.

The president hadn't looked terrified, Verity thought, as 3.7's door closed behind her. She'd looked like she was on the case.

William Gibson's first novel, *Neuromancer*, won the Hugo Award, the Nebula Award, and the Philip K. Dick Award. He is also the *New York Times* bestselling author of *Count Zero*, *Burning Chrome*, *Mona Lisa Overdrive*, *Virtual Light*, *Idoru*, *All Tomorrow's Parties*, *Pattern Recognition*, *Spook Country*, *Zero History*, *Distrust That Particular Flavor*, and *The Peripheral*. He lives in Vancouver, British Columbia, with his wife.

CONNECT ONLINE

WilliamGibsonBooks.com
🐦 GreatDismal